SOMEW
PUDGET SOUND

"Go on, Janet," the older man prompted harshly. "What does the Moon make you think of?"
"A spider," the girl answered instantly. "A bloated white spider…"

—from "Deadly Moon."

ABOUT FRITZ LEIBER...

Born in Chicago in 1910, Fritz Leiber is said to have been very influenced by H. P. Lovecraft in his early writings. He was a recipient of multiple Hugo and Nebula Awards and highly acclaimed by his fellow writers and fans alike. His creativity and storytelling abilities were without limit, allowing his brilliant spirit to flow evenly in all genres. Fritz Leiber passed away in 1992 after a long, distinguished career. You can also find many of his tales in other Armchair Fiction short story collections.

TABLE OF CONTENTS

THE MOON IS GREEN

AND OTHER TALES

FRITZ LEIBER

Masters of Science Fiction,
Volume Six

ARMCHAIR FICTION
PO Box 4369, Medford, Oregon 97504

The original text of these stories first appeared in *Galaxy, Fantastic, and Future Science Fiction.*

Cover suggests a scene from *Deadly Moon*.

For more information about Armchair Books and products, visit our website at…

www.armchairfiction.com

Or email us at…

armchairfiction@yahoo.com

The Moon is Green

Anybody who wanted to escape death could, by paying a very simple price—denial of life!

"EFFIE! What the devil are you up to?"

Her husband's voice, chopping through her mood of terrified rapture, made her heart jump like a startled cat, yet by some miracle of feminine self-control her body did not show a tremor.

Dear God, she thought, *he mustn't see it. It's so beautiful and he always kills beauty.*

"I'm just looking at the Moon," she said listlessly. "It's green."

Mustn't, mustn't see it. And now, with luck, he wouldn't. For the face, as if it also heard and sensed the menace in the voice, was moving back from the window's glow into the outside dark, but slowly, reluctantly, and still faunlike, pleading, cajoling, tempting, and incredibly beautiful.

"Close the shutters at once, you little fool, and come away from the window!"

"Green as a beer bottle," she went on dreamily, "green as emeralds, green as leaves with sunshine striking through them and green grass to lie on." She couldn't help saying those last words. They were her token to the face, even though it couldn't hear.

"Effie!"

She knew what that last tone meant. Wearily she swung shut the ponderous lead inner shutters and drove home the heavy bolts. That hurt her fingers; it always did, but he mustn't know that.

"You know that those shutters are not to be touched! Not for five more years at least!"

"I only wanted to look at the Moon," she said, turning around, and then it was all gone—the face, the night, the Moon, the magic—and she was back in the grubby, stale little hole, facing an angry, stale little man. It was then that the eternal thud of the air-conditioning fans and the crackle of the electrostatic precipitators that sieved out the dust reached her consciousness again like the bite of a dentist's drill.

"Only wanted to look at the Moon!" he mimicked her in falsetto. "Only wanted to die like a little fool and make me that much more ashamed of you!" Then his voice went gruff and professional. "Here, count yourself."

She silently took the Geiger Counter he held at arm's length, waited until it settled down to a steady ticking slower than a clock—due only to cosmic rays and indicating nothing dangerous—and then began to comb her body with the instrument. First her head and shoulders, then out along her arms and back along their under side. There was something oddly voluptuous about her movements, although her features were gray and sagging.

The ticking did not change in tempo until she came to her waist. Then it suddenly spurted, clicking faster and faster. Her husband gave an excited grunt, took a quick step forward, froze. She goggled for a moment in fear, then grinned foolishly, dug in the pocket of her grimy apron and guiltily pulled out a wristwatch.

He grabbed it as it dangled from her fingers, saw that it had a radium dial, cursed, heaved it up as if to smash it on the floor, but instead put it carefully on the table.

"You imbecile, you incredible imbecile," he softly chanted to himself through clenched teeth, with eyes half closed.

She shrugged faintly, put the Geiger Counter on the table, and stood there slumped.

He waited until the chanting had soothed his anger before speaking again. He said quietly, "I do suppose you still realize the sort of world you're living in?"

SHE nodded slowly, staring at nothingness. Oh, she realized, all right, realized only too well. It was the world that hadn't realized. The world that had gone on stockpiling hydrogen bombs. The world that had put those bombs in cobalt shells, although it had promised it wouldn't, because the cobalt made them much more terrible and cost no more. The world that had started throwing those bombs, always telling itself that it hadn't thrown enough of them yet to make the air really dangerous with the deadly radioactive dust that came from the cobalt. Thrown them and kept on throwing until the danger point, where air and ground would become fatal to all human life, was approached.

Then, for about a month, the two great enemy groups had hesitated. And then each, unknown to the other, had decided it could risk one last gigantic and decisive attack without exceeding the danger point. It had been planned to strip off the cobalt cases, but someone forgot and then there wasn't time. Besides, the military scientists of each group were confident that the lands of the other had got the most dust. The two attacks came within an hour of each other.

After that, the Fury. The Fury of doomed men who think only of taking with them as many as possible of the enemy, and in this case—they hoped—all. The Fury of suicides who know they have botched up life for good. The Fury of cocksure men who realize they have been outsmarted by fate, the enemy, and themselves, and know that they will never be able to improvise a defense when arraigned before the high court of history—and whose unadmitted hope is that there will be no high court of history left to arraign them. More cobalt bombs were dropped during the Fury than in all the preceding years of the war.

After the Fury, the Terror.

Men and women with death sifting into their bones through their nostrils and skin, fighting for bare survival under a dust-hazed sky that played fantastic tricks with the light of Sun and Moon, like the dust from Krakatoa that drifted around the world for years. Cities, countryside, and air were alike poisoned, alive with deadly radiation.

The only realistic chance for continued existence was to retire, for the five or ten years the radiation would remain deadly, to some well-sealed and radiation-shielded place that must also be copiously supplied with food, water, power, and a means of air-conditioning.

Such places were prepared by the far-seeing, seized by the stronger, defended by them in turn against the desperate hordes of the dying…until there were no more of those.

After that, only the waiting, the enduring. A mole's existence, without beauty or tenderness, but with fear and guilt as constant companions. Never to see the Sun, to walk among the trees—or even know if there were still trees.

Oh, yes, she realized what the world was like.

"You understand, too, I suppose, that we were allowed to reclaim this ground-level apartment only because the Committee believed us to be responsible people, and because I've been making a damn good showing lately?"

"Yes, Hank."

"I thought you were eager for privacy. You want to go back to the basement tenements?"

God, no! Anything rather than that fetid huddling, that shameless communal sprawl. And yet, was this so much better? The nearness to the surface was meaningless; it only tantalized. And the privacy magnified Hank.

She shook her head dutifully and said, "No, Hank."

"Then why aren't you careful? I've told you a million times, Effie that glass is no protection against the dust that's outside that window. The lead shutter must never be touched! If you make one single slip like that and it gets around, the Committee will send us back to the lower levels without blinking an eye. And they'll think twice before trusting me with any important jobs."

"I'm sorry, Hank."

"Sorry? What's the good of being sorry? The only thing that counts is never to make a slip! Why the devil do you do such things, Effie? What drives you to it?"

She swallowed. "It's just that it's so dreadful being cooped up like this," she said hesitatingly, "shut away from the sky and the Sun. I'm just hungry for a little beauty."

"And do you suppose I'm not?" he demanded. "Don't you suppose I want to get outside, too, and be carefree and have a good time? But I'm not so damn selfish about it. I want my children to enjoy the Sun, and my children's children. Don't you see that that's the all-important thing and that we have to behave like mature adults and make sacrifices for it?"

"Yes, Hank."

He surveyed her slumped figure, her lined and listless face. "You're a fine one to talk about hunger for beauty," he told her. Then his voice grew softer, more deliberate. "You haven't forgotten, have you, Effie, that until last month the Committee was so concerned about your sterility that they were about to enter my name on the list of those waiting to be allotted a free woman? Very high on the list, too!"

She could nod even at that one, but not while looking at him. She turned away. She knew very well that the Committee was justified in worrying about the birth rate. When the community finally moved back to the surface again, each additional healthy young person would be an asset, not only in the struggle for bare survival, but in the resumed war against Communism, which some of the Committee members still counted on.

It was natural that they should view a sterile woman with disfavor, and not only because of the waste of her husband's germ-plasm, but because sterility might indicate that she had suffered more than the average from radiation. In that case, if she did bear children later on, they would be more apt to carry a defective heredity, producing an undue number of monsters and freaks in future generations, and so contaminating the race.

Of course she understood it. She could hardly remember the time when she didn't. Years ago? Centuries? There wasn't much difference in a place where time was endless.

HIS lecture finished, her husband smiled and grew almost cheerful.

"Now that you're going to have a child, that's all in the background again. Do you know, Effie, that when I first came in, I had some very good news for you? I'm to become a member of the Junior Committee and the announcement will be made at the banquet tonight." He cut short her mumbled congratulations. "So brighten yourself up and put on your best dress, I want the other Juniors to see what a handsome wife the new member has got." He paused. "Well, get a move on!"

She spoke with difficulty, still not looking at him. "I'm terribly sorry, Hank, but you'll have to go alone. I'm not well."

He straightened up with an indignant jerk. "There you go again! First that infantile inexcusable business of the shutters, and now this! No feeling for my reputation at all. Don't be ridiculous, Effie. You're coming!"

"Terribly sorry," she repeated blindly, "but I really can't. I'd just be sick. I wouldn't make you proud of me at all."

"Of course you won't," he retorted sharply. "As it is, I have to spend half my energy running around making excuses for you—why you're so odd, why you always seem to be ailing, why you're always stupid and snobbish and say the wrong thing. But tonight's really important, Effie. It will cause sorts of bad comment if the new member's wife isn't present. You know how just a hint of sickness starts the old radiation-disease rumor, going. You've got to come, Effie..."

She shook her head helplessly.

"Oh, for heaven's sake, come on!" he shouted, advancing on her. "This is just a silly mood. As soon as you get going, you'll snap out of it. There's nothing really wrong with you at all."

He put his hand on her shoulder to turn her around and at his touch her face suddenly grew so desperate, and gray that for a moment he was alarmed in spite of himself.

"Really?" he asked, almost with a note of concern.

She nodded miserably.

"Hmm." He stepped back and strode about irresolutely. "Well, of course, if that's the way it is..." He checked himself and a sad smile crossed his face. "So you don't care enough about your old husband's success to make one supreme effort in spite of feeling bad?"

Again the helpless headshake.

"I just can't go out tonight, under any circumstances." And her gaze stole toward the lead shutters.

He was about to say something when he caught the direction of her gaze. His eyebrows jumped. For seconds he stared at her incredulously, as if some completely new and almost unbelievable possibility had popped into his mind. The look of incredulity slowly faded, to be replaced by a harder, more calculating expression. But when he spoke again his voice was shockingly bright and kind.

"Well, it can't be helped naturally, and I certainly wouldn't want you to go if you weren't able to enjoy it. So you hop right into bed and get a good rest, I'll run over to the men's dorm to freshen up. No, really, I don't want you to have to make any effort at all. Incidentally, Jim Barnes isn't going to be able to come to the banquet either—touch of the old 'flu, he tells me of all things."

He watched her closely as he mentioned the other man's name, but she didn't react noticeably. In fact, she hardly seemed to be hearing his chatter.

"I got a bit sharp with you, I'm afraid, Effie," he continued contritely. "I'm sorry about that, I was excited about my new job and I guess that was why things upset me. Made me feel let down when I found you weren't feeling as good as I was. Selfish of me. Now you get into bed right away and get well. Don't worry about me a bit. I know you'd come if you possibly could. And I know you'll be thinking about me. Well, I must be off now."

He started toward her, as if to embrace her then seemed to think better of it. He turned back at the doorway and said, emphasizing the words, "You'll be completely alone for the next four hours." He waited for her nod, then bounced out.

SHE stood still until his footsteps died away. Then she straightened up, walked over to where he'd put down the wristwatch, picked it up and smashed it hard on the floor. The crystal shattered, the case flew apart, and something went *zing!*

She stood there breathing heavily. Slowly her sagged features lifted, formed themselves into the beginning of a smile. She stole another look at the shutters. The smile became more definite. She felt her hair, wet her fingers and ran them along her hairline and back over her ears. After wiping her hands on her apron, she took it off. She straightened her dress, lifted her head with a little flourish, and stepped smartly toward the window.

Then her face went miserable again and her steps slowed.

No, it couldn't be, and it won't be, she told herself. It had been just an illusion, a silly romantic dream that she had somehow projected out of her beauty-starved mind and given a moment's false reality. There couldn't be anything alive outside. There hadn't been for two whole years.

And if there conceivably were, it would be something altogether horrible. She remembered some of the pariahs—hairless, witless creatures, with radiation welts crawling over their bodies like worms, who had come begging for succor during the last months of the Terror—and been shot down. How they must have hated the people in refuges!

But even as she was thinking these things her fingers were caressing the bolts, gingerly drawing them, and she was opening the shutters gently, apprehensively.

No, there couldn't be anything outside, she assured herself wryly, peering out into the green night. Even her fears had been groundless.

But the face came floating up toward the window. She started back in terror, then checked herself.

For the face wasn't horrible at all, only very thin, with full lips and large eyes and a thin proud nose like the jutting beak of a bird. And no radiation welts or scars marred the skin, olive in the tempered moonlight. It looked, in fact, just as it had when she had seen it the first time.

For a long moment the face stared deep, deep into her brain. Then the full lips smiled and a half-clenched, thin-fingered hand materialized itself from the green darkness and rapped twice on the grimy pane.

Her heart pounding, she furiously worked the little crank that opened the window. It came unstuck from the frame with a tiny explosion of dust and a *zing* like that of the watch, only louder. A moment later it swung open wide and a puff of incredibly fresh air caressed her face and the inside of her nostrils, stinging her eyes with unanticipated tears.

The man outside balanced on the sill, crouching like a faun, head high, one elbow on knee. He was dressed in scarred, snug trousers and an old sweater.

"Is it tears I get for a welcome?" he mocked her gently in a musical voice. "Or are those only to greet God's own breath, the air?"

HE swung down inside and now she could see he was tall. Turning, he snapped his fingers and called, "Come, puss."

A black cat with a twisted stump of a tail and feet like small boxing gloves and ears almost as big as rabbits' hopped clumsily in view. He lifted it down, gave it a pat. Then, nodding familiarly to Effie, he unstrapped a little pack from his back and laid it on the table.

She couldn't move. She even found it hard to breathe.

"The window," she finally managed to get out.

He looked at her inquiringly, caught the direction of her stabbing finger. Moving without haste, he went over and closed it carelessly.

"The shutters, too," she told him, but he ignored that, looking around.

"It's a snug enough place you and your man have," he commented. "Or is it that this is a free-love town or a harem spot, or just a military post?" He checked her before she could answer. "But let's not be talking about such things now. Soon enough I'll be scared to death for both of us. Best enjoy the kick of meeting, which is always good for twenty minutes at the least." He smiled at her rather shyly. "Have you food? Good, then bring it."

She set cold meat and some precious canned bread before him and had water heating for coffee. Before he fell to, he shredded a chunk of meat and put it on the floor for the cat, which left off its sniffing inspection of the walls and ran up eagerly mewing. Then the man began to eat, chewing each mouthful slowly and appreciatively.

From across the table Effie watched him, drinking in his every deft movement, his every cryptic quirk of expression. She attended to making the coffee, but that took only a moment. Finally she could contain herself no longer.

"What's it like up there?" she asked breathlessly. "Outside, I mean."

He looked at her oddly for quite a space. Finally, he said flatly, "Oh, it's a wonderland for sure, more amazing than you tombed folk could ever imagine. A veritable fairyland." And he quickly went on eating.

"No, but really," she pressed. Noting her eagerness, he smiled and his eyes filled with playful tenderness. "I mean it, on my oath," he assured her. "You think the bombs and the dust made only death and ugliness. That was true at first. But then, just as the doctors foretold, they changed the life in the seeds and loins that were brave enough to stay. Wonders bloomed and walked." He broke off suddenly and asked, "Do any of you ever venture outside?"

"A few of the men are allowed to," she told him, "for short trips in special protective suits, to hunt for canned food and fuels and batteries and things like that."

"Aye, and those blind-souled slugs would never see anything but what they're looking for," he said, nodding bitterly. "They'd never see the garden where a dozen buds blossom where one did before, and the flowers have petals a yard across, with stingless bees, big as sparrows gently supping their nectar. Housecats grown spotted and huge as leopards (not little runts like Joe Louis here) stalk through those gardens. But they're gentle beasts, no more harmful than the rainbow-scaled snakes that glide around their paws, for the dust burned all the murder out of them, as it burned itself out.

"I've even made up a little poem about that. It starts, 'Fire can hurt me, or water, or the weight of Earth. But the dust is my friend.' Oh, yes, and then the robins like cockatoos and squirrels like a princess's ermine! All wider a treasure chest of Sun and Moon and stars that the dust's magic powder changes from ruby to emerald and sapphire and amethyst and back again. Oh, and then the new children—"

"You're telling the truth?" she interrupted him, her eyes brimming with tears. "You're not making it up?"

"I am not," he assured her solemnly. "And if you could catch a glimpse of one of the new children, you'd never doubt me again. They have long limbs as brown as this coffee would be if it had lots of fresh cream in it, and smiling delicate faces and the whitest teeth and the finest hair. They're so nimble that I—a sprightly man and somewhat enlivened by the dust—feel like a cripple beside them. And their thoughts dance like flames and make me feel a very imbecile.

"Of course, they have seven fingers on each hand and eight toes on each foot, but they're the more beautiful for that. They have large pointed ears that the Sun shines through. They play in the garden, all day long, slipping among the great leaves and blooms, but they're so swift that you can hardly see them, unless one chooses to stand still and look at you. For that matter, you have to look bit hard for all these things I'm telling you."

"But it is true?" she pleaded.

"Every word of it," he said, looking straight into her eyes. He put down his knife and fork. "What's your name?" he asked softly. "Mine's Patrick."

"Effie," she told him.

He shook his head. "That can't be," he said. Then his face brightened. "Euphemia," he exclaimed. "That's what Effie is short for. Your name is Euphemia." As he said that, looking at her, she suddenly felt beautiful. He got up and came around the table and stretched out his hand toward her.

"Euphemia—" he began.

"Yes?" she answered huskily, shrinking from him a little, but looking up sideways, and very flushed.

"Don't either of you move," Hank said.

The voice was flat and nasal because Hank was wearing a nose respirator that was just long enough to suggest an elephant's trunk. In his right hand was a large blue-black automatic pistol.

THEY turned their faces to him. Patrick's was abruptly alert, shifty. But Effie's was still smiling tenderly, as if Hank could not break the spell of the magic garden and should be pitied for not knowing about it.

"You little—" Hank began with an almost gleeful fury, calling her several shameful names. He spoke in short phrases, closing tight his unmasked mouth between them while he sucked in breath through the respirator. His voice rose in a crescendo. "And not with a man of the community, but a pariah! *A pariah!*"

"I hardly know what you're thinking, man, but you're quite wrong," Patrick took the opportunity to put in hurriedly, conciliating. "I just happened to be coming by hungry tonight, a lonely tramp, and knocked at the window. Your wife was a bit foolish and let kindheartedness get the better of prudence—"

"Don't think you've pulled the wool over my eyes, Effie," Hank went on with a screechy laugh, disregarding the other man completely. "Don't think I don't know why you're suddenly going to have a child after four long years."

At that moment the cat came nosing up to his feet. Patrick watched him narrowly, shifting his weight forward a little, but Hank only kicked the animal aside without taking his eyes off them.

"Even that business of carrying the wristwatch in your pocket instead of on your arm," he went on with channeled hysteria. "A neat bit of camouflage, Effie. Very neat. And telling me it was my child, when all the while you've been seeing him for months!"

"Man, you're mad; I've not touched her!" Patrick denied hotly though still calculatingly, and risked a step forward, stopping when the gun instantly swung his way.

"Pretending you were going to give me a healthy child," Hank raved on, "when all the while you knew it would be—either in body or germ plasm—a thing like *that!*"

He waved his gun at the malformed cat, which had leaped to the top of the table and was eating the remains of Patrick's food, though its watchful green eyes were fixed on Hank.

"I should shoot him down!" Hank yelled, between sobbing, chest-racking inhalations through the mask. "I should skin him this instant for the contaminated pariah he is!"

All this while Effie had not ceased to smile compassionately. Now she stood up without haste and went to Patrick's side. Disregarding his warning, apprehensive glance, she put her arm lightly around him and faced her husband.

"Then you'd be killing the bringer of the best news we've ever had," she said, and her voice was like a flood of some warm sweet liquor in that musty, hate-charged room. "Oh,

Hank, forget your silly, wrong jealousy and listen to me. Patrick here has something wonderful to tell us."

HANK stared at her. For once he screamed no reply. It was obvious that he was seeing for the first time how beautiful she had become, and that the realization jolted him terribly.

"What do you mean?" he finally asked unevenly, almost fearfully.

"I mean that we no longer need to fear the dust," she said, and now her smile was radiant. "It never really did hurt people the way the doctors said it would. Remember how it was with me, Hank, the exposure I had and recovered from, although the doctors said I wouldn't at first—and without even losing my hair? Hank, those who were brave enough to stay outside, and who weren't killed by terror and suggestion and panic—they adapted to the dust. They changed, but they changed for the better. Everything—"

"Effie, he told you lies!" Hank interrupted, but still in that same agitated, broken voice, cowed by her beauty.

"Everything that grew or moved was purified," she went on ringingly. "You men going outside have never seen it, because you've never had eyes for it. You've been blinded to beauty, to life itself. And now all the power in the dust has gone and faded, anyway, burned itself out. That's true, isn't it?"

She smiled at Patrick for confirmation. His face was strangely veiled, as if he were calculating obscure changes. He might have given a little nod; at any rate, Effie assumed that he did, for she turned back to her husband.

"You see, Hank? We can all go out now. We need never fear the dust again. Patrick is a living proof of that," she continued triumphantly, standing straighter, holding him a little tighter. "Look at him. Not a scar or a sign, and he's been out in the dust for years. How could he be this way, if the dust hurt the brave? Oh, believe me, Hank! Believe what you see. Test it if you want. Test Patrick here."

"Effie, you're all mixed up. You don't know—" Hank faltered, but without conviction of any sort.

"Just test him," Effie repeated with utter confidence, ignoring—not even noticing—Patrick's warning nudge.

"All right," Hank mumbled.

He looked at the stranger dully. "Can you count?" he asked.

Patrick's face was a complete enigma. Then he suddenly spoke, and his voice was like a fencer's foil—light, bright, alert, constantly playing, yet utterly on guard.

"Can I count? Do you take me for a complete simpleton, man? Of course I can count!"

"Then count yourself," Hank said, barely indicating the table.

"Count myself, should I?" the other retorted with a quick facetious laugh. "Is this a kindergarten? But if you want me to, I'm willing." His voice was rapid. "I've two arms, and two legs, that's four. And ten fingers and ten toes—you'll take my word for them?—that's twenty-four. A head, twenty-five. And two eyes and a nose and a mouth—"

"With this, I mean," Hank said heavily, advanced to the table, picked up the Geiger counter, switched it on, and handed it across the table to the other man.

But while it was still an arm's length from Patrick, the clicks began to mount furiously, until they were like the chatter of a pigmy machine gun. Abruptly the clicks slowed, but that was only the counter shifting to a new scaling circuit, in which each click stood for 512 of the old ones.

WITH those horrid, rattling little volleys, fear cascaded into the room and filled it, smashing like so much colored glass all the bright barriers of words Effie had raised against it. For no dreams can stand against the Geiger counter, the Twentieth Century's mouthpiece of ultimate truth. It was as if the dust and all the terrors of the dust had incarnated themselves in one dread invading shape that said in words stronger than audible speech, "Those were illusions, whistles in the dark. This is reality, the dreary, pitiless reality of the Burrowing Years."

Hank scuttled back to the wall.

Through chattering teeth he babbled, "...enough radioactives...kill a thousand men...freak...a freak..." In his agitation he forgot for a moment to inhale through the respirator.

Even Effie—taken off guard, all the fears that had been drilled into her twanging like piano wires—shrank from the skeletal-seeming shape beside her, held herself to it only by desperation.

Patrick did it for her. He disengaged her arm and stepped briskly away. Then he whirled on them, smiling sardonically, and started to speak, but instead looked with distaste at the chattering Geiger counter he held between fingers and thumb.

"Have we listened to this racket long enough?" he asked.

Without waiting for an answer, he put down the instrument on the table. The cat hurried over to it curiously and the clicks began again to mount in a minor crescendo. Effie lunged for it frantically, switched it off, darted back.

"That's right," Patrick said with another chilling smile. "You do well to cringe, for I'm death itself. Even in death I could kill you, like a snake." And with that his voice took on the tones of a circus barker. "Yes, I'm a freak, as the gentleman so wisely said. That's what one doctor who dared talk with me for a minute told me before he kicked me out. He couldn't tell me why, but somehow the dust doesn't kill me. Because I'm a freak, you see, just like the men who ate nails and walked on fire and ate arsenic and stuck themselves through with pins. Step right up, ladies and gentlemen—only not too close!—and examine the man the dust can't harm. Rappacini's child, brought up to date; his embrace, death!

"And now," he said, breathing heavily, "I'll get out and leave you in your damned lead cave."

He started toward the window.

Hank's gun followed him shakingly.

"Wait!" Effie called in an agonized voice. He obeyed. She continued falteringly, "When we were together earlier, you didn't act as if…"

"When we were together earlier, I wanted what I wanted," he snarled at her. "You don't suppose I'm a bloody saint, do you?"

"And all the beautiful things you told me?"

"That," he said cruelly, "is just a line I've found that women fall for. They're all so bored and so starved for beauty—as they generally put it."

"Even the garden?" Her question was barely audible through the sobs that threatened to suffocate her.

He looked at her and perhaps his expression softened just a trifle.

"What's outside," he said flatly, "is just a little worse than either of you can imagine." He tapped his temple. "The garden's all here."

"You've killed it," she wept. "You've killed it in me. You've both killed everything that's beautiful. But you're worse," she screamed at Patrick, "because he only killed beauty once, but you brought it to life just so you could kill it again. Oh, I can't stand it! I won't stand it!" And she began to scream.

Patrick started toward her, but she broke off and whirled away from him to the window, her eyes crazy.

"You've been lying to us," she cried. "The garden's there. I know it is. But you don't want to share it with anyone."

"No, no, Euphemia," Patrick protested anxiously. "It's hell out there, believe me. I wouldn't lie to you about it."

"Wouldn't lie to me?" she mocked. "Are you afraid, too?"

With a sudden pull, she jerked open the window and stood before the blank green-tinged oblong of darkness that seemed to press into the room like a menacing, heavy, wind-urged curtain.

At that Hank cried out a shocked, pleading, "Effie!"

She ignored him. "I can't be cooped up here any longer," she said. "And I won't, now that I know. I'm going to the garden."

Both men sprang at her, but they were too late. She leaped lightly to the sill, and by the time they had flung themselves against it, her footsteps were already hurrying off into the darkness.

"Effie, come back! Come back!" Hank shouted after her desperately, no longer thinking to cringe from the man beside him, or how the gun was pointed. "I love you, Effie. Come back!"

Patrick added his voice. "Come back, Euphemia. You'll be safe if you come back right away. Come back to your home."

No answer to that at all. They both strained their eyes through the greenish murk. They could barely make out a shadowy figure about half a block down the near-black canyon of the dismal, dust-blown street, into which the greenish moonlight hardly reached. It seemed to them that the figure was scooping something up from the pavement and letting it sift down along its arms and over its bosom.

"Go out and get her, man," Patrick urged the other. "For if I go out for her, I warn you I won't bring her back. She said something about having stood the dust better than most, and that's enough for me."

But Hank, chained by his painfully learned habits and by something else, could not move.

And then a ghostly voice came whispering down the street, chanting, "Fire can hurt me, or water, or the weight of the Earth. But the dust is my friend."

Patrick spared the other man one more look. Then, without a word, he vaulted up and ran off.

Hank stood there. After perhaps a half minute he remembered to close his mouth when he inhaled. Finally he was sure the street was empty. As he started to close the window, there was a little mew.

He picked up the cat and gently put it outside. Then he did close the window, and the shutters, and bolted them, and took up the Geiger counter, and mechanically began to count himself.

What's He Doing in There?

He went where no Martian ever went before—but would he come out—or had he gone for good?

THE Professor was congratulating Earth's first visitor from another planet on his wisdom in getting in touch with a cultural anthropologist before contacting any other scientists (or governments, God forbid!), and in learning English from radio and TV before landing from his orbit-parked rocket, when the Martian stood up and said hesitantly, "Excuse me, please, but where is it?"

That baffled the Professor and the Martian seemed to grow anxious—at least his long mouth curved upward, and he had earlier explained that it curling downward was his smile—and he repeated, "Please, where is it?"

He was surprisingly humanoid in most respects, but his complexion was textured so like the rich dark armchair he'd just been occupying that the Professor's pin-striped gray suit, which he had eagerly consented to wear, seemed an arbitrary interruption between him and the chair—a sort of Mother Hubbard dress on a phantom conjured from its leather.

The Professor's Wife, always a perceptive hostess, came to her husband's rescue by saying with equal rapidity, "Top of the stairs, end of the hall, last door."

The Martian's mouth curled happily downward and he said, "Thank you very much," and was off.

Comprehension burst on the Professor. He caught up with his guest at the foot of the stairs.

"Here, I'll show you the way," he said.

"No, I can find it myself, thank you," the Martian assured him.

SOMETHING rather final in the Martian's tone made the Professor desist, and after watching his visitor sway up the stairs with an almost hypnotic softly jogging movement, he rejoined his wife in the study, saying wonderingly, "Who'd have thought it—by George! Function taboos as strict as our own!"

"I'm glad some of your professional visitors maintain 'em," his wife said darkly.

"But this one's from Mars, darling, and to find out he's—well, similar in an aspect of his life is as thrilling as the discovery that water is burned hydrogen. When I think of the day not far distant when I'll put his entries in the cross-cultural index..."

He was still rhapsodizing when the Professor's Little Son raced in.

"Pop, the Martian's gone to the bathroom!"

"Hush, dear. Manners."

"Now it's perfectly natural, darling, that the boy should notice and be excited. Yes, Son, the Martian's not so very different from us."

"Oh, certainly," the Professor's Wife said with a trace of bitterness. "I don't imagine his turquoise complexion will cause any comment at all when you bring him to a faculty reception. They'll just figure he's had a hard night—and that he got that baby-elephant nose sniffing around for assistant professorships."

"Really, darling! He probably thinks of our noses as disagreeably amputated and paralyzed."

"Well, anyway, Pop, he's in the bathroom. I followed him when he squiggled upstairs."

"Now, Son, you shouldn't have done that. He's on a strange planet and it might make him nervous if he thought he was being spied on. We must show him every courtesy. By George, I can't wait to discuss these things with Ackerly-Ramsbottom! When I think of how much more this encounter has to give the anthropologist than even the physicist or astronomer…"

He was still going strong on his second rhapsody when he was interrupted by another high-speed entrance. It was the Professor's coltish Daughter.

"Mom, Pop, the Martian's—"

"Hush, dear. We know."

The Professor's Coltish Daughter regained her adolescent poise, which was considerable. "Well, he's still in there," she said. "I just tried the door and it was locked."

"I'm glad it was!" the Professor said while his wife added, "Yes, you can't be sure what—" and caught herself. "Really, dear, that was very bad manners."

"I thought he'd come downstairs long ago," her daughter explained. "He's been in there an awfully long time. It must have been a half hour ago that I saw him gyre and gimbal upstairs in that real gone way he has, with Nosy here following him." The Professor's Coltish Daughter was currently soaking up both jive and *Alice*.

WHEN the Professor checked his wristwatch, his expression grew troubled. "By George, he is taking his time! Though, of course, we don't know how much time Martians…I wonder."

"I listened for a while, Pop," his son volunteered. "He was running the water a lot."

"Running the water, eh? We know Mars is a water-starved planet. I suppose that in the presence of unlimited water, he might be seized by a kind of madness and... But he seemed so well adjusted."

Then his wife spoke, voicing all their thoughts. Her outlook on life gave her a naturally sepulchral voice.

"What's he doing in there?"

Twenty minutes and at least as many fantastic suggestions later, the Professor glanced again at his watch and nerved himself for action. Motioning his family aside, he mounted the stairs and tiptoed down the hall.

He paused only once to shake his head and mutter under his breath, "By George, I wish I had Fenchurch or von Gottschalk here. They're a shade better than I am on intercultural contracts, especially taboo-breakings and affronts..."

His family followed him at a short distance.

The Professor stopped in front of the bathroom door. Everything was quiet as death.

He listened for a minute and then rapped measuredly, steadying his hand by clutching its wrist with the other. There was a faint splashing, but no other sound.

Another minute passed. The Professor rapped again. Now there was no response at all. He very gingerly tried the knob. The door was still locked.

When they had retreated to the stairs, it was the Professor's Wife who once more voiced their thoughts. This time her voice carried overtones of supernatural horror.

"What's he doing in there?"

"He may be dead or dying," the Professor's Coltish Daughter suggested briskly. "Maybe we ought to call the Fire Department, like they did for old Mrs. Frisbee."

The Professor winced. "I'm afraid you haven't visualized the complications, dear," he said gently. "No one but ourselves knows that the Martian is on Earth, or has even the slightest inkling that interplanetary travel has been achieved.

Whatever we do, it will have to be on our own. But to break in on a creature engaged in—well, we don't know what primal private activity—is against all anthropological practice. Still—"

"Dying's a primal activity," his daughter said crisply.

"So's ritual bathing before mass murder," his wife added.

"Please! Still, as I was about to say, we do have the moral duty to succor him if, as you all too reasonably suggest, he has been incapacitated by a germ or virus or, more likely, by some simple environmental factor such as Earth's greater gravity."

"Tell you what, Pop—I can look in the bathroom window and see what he's doing. All I have to do is crawl out my bedroom window and along the gutter a little ways. It's safe as houses."

THE Professor's question beginning with, "Son, how do you know—" died unuttered and he refused to notice the words his daughter was voicing silently at her brother. He glanced at his wife's sardonically composed face, thought once more of the Fire Department and of other and larger and even more jealous—or would it be skeptical?—government agencies, and clutched at the straw offered him.

Ten minutes later, he was quite unnecessarily assisting his son back through the bedroom window.

"Gee, Pop, I couldn't see a sign of him. That's why I took so long. Hey, Pop, don't look so scared. He's in there, sure enough. It's just that the bathtub's under the window and you have to get real close up to see into it."

"The Martian's taking a bath?"

"Yep. Got it full up and just the end of his little old schnozzle sticking out. Your suit, Pop, was hanging on the door."

The one word the Professor's Wife spoke was like a death knell.

"Drowned!"

"No, Ma, I don't think so. His schnozzle was opening and closing regular like."

"Maybe he's a shape-changer," the Professor's Coltish Daughter said in a burst of evil fantasy. "Maybe he softens in water and thins out after a while until he's like an eel and then he'll go exploring through the sewer pipes. Wouldn't it be funny if he went under the street and knocked on the stopper from underneath and crawled into the bathtub with President Rexford, or Mrs. President Rexford, or maybe right into the middle of one of Janey Rexford's Oh-I'm-so-sexy bubble baths?"

"Please!" The Professor put his hand to his eyebrows and kept it there, cuddling the elbow in his other hand.

"Well, have you thought of something?" the Professor's Wife asked him after a bit. "What are you going to do?"

The Professor dropped his hand and blinked his eyes hard and took a deep breath.

"Telegraph Fenchurch and Ackerly-Ramsbottom and then break in," he said in a resigned voice, into which, nevertheless, a note of hope seemed also to have come. "First, however, I'm going to wait until morning."

And he sat down cross-legged in the hall a few yards from the bathroom door and folded his arms.

SO the long vigil commenced. The Professor's family shared it and he offered no objection. Other and sterner men, he told himself, might claim to be able successfully to order their children to go to bed when there was a Martian locked in the bathroom, but he would like to see them faced with the situation.

Finally dawn began to seep from the bedrooms. When the bulb in the hall had grown quite dim, the Professor unfolded his arms.

Just then, there came the sound of a good, loud splashing in the bathroom. The Professor's family looked toward the door. The splashing stopped and they heard the Martian moving around. Then the door opened and the Martian appeared in the Professor's gray pin-stripe suit. His mouth curled sharply downward in a broad alien smile as he saw the Professor.

"Good morning!" the Martian said happily. "I never slept better in my life, even in my own little wet bed back on Mars."

He looked around more closely and his mouth straightened. "But where did you all sleep?" he asked. "Don't tell me you stayed dry all night! You *didn't* give up your only bed to me?"

His mouth curled upward in misery. "Oh, dear," he said, "I'm afraid I've made a mistake somehow. Yet I don't understand how. Before I studied you, I didn't know what your sleeping habits would be, but that question was answered for me—in fact, it looked so reassuringly homelike—when I saw those brief TV scenes of your females ready for sleep in their little tubs. Of course, on Mars, only the fortunate can always be sure of sleeping wet, but here, with your abundance of water, I thought there would be wet beds for all."

He paused. "It's true I had some doubts last night, wondering if I'd used the right words and all, but then when you rapped 'Good night' to me, I splashed the sentiment back at you and went to sleep in a wink. But I'm afraid that somewhere I've blundered and—"

"No, no, dear chap," the Professor managed to say. He had been waving his hand in a gentle circle for some time in token that he wanted to interrupt. "Everything is quite all right. It's true we stayed up all night, but please consider that as a watch—an honor guard, by George!—which we kept to indicate our esteem."

The Improper Authorities

Gravity, shmavity, how do you make it pay off? Not, certainly, by approaching…

As SOON as Ronald Flecker fully convinced himself that he had discovered in his eccentric aunt's cluttered basement a small battery that stored the force of gravity instead of electricity—a battery that held in complete essence the power of fuelless spaceflight, levitation, and any number of lesser marvels—he sat down to do some very serious thinking.

The discovery had come about while he was repairing his aunt's doorbell—one of the innumerable small tasks she hesitantly but in the end always rather firmly set him, although she had more than enough money to hire professional household mechanics, and that Ronald in any case always felt obliged to discharge in return for the privilege of sleeping over her garage. He had found the thin wires in a monstrous tangle close under the dusty rafters. It turned out the system wasn't even worked by a step-down transformer but by dry cells and some idiot had hooked up the cells in parallel rather than series, accounting in large part for the doorbell's feeble performance. His aunt recalled that the last person before Ronald to revive the doorbell had been the kindly but abstracted and rather smelly Dr. Yorn, the second-to-last in her unending series of spiritual counselors—a yogi, medium, hypnotist, dynamic psychologist, something like that. Mrs. Wycherly liked variety and versatile men. Dr. Yorn's successor, the gleaming-eyed and dapper Mr. Espy, seemed equally obliging and would almost certainly have been willing to tackle the doorbell, but now Mrs. Wycherly had Ronald for those things.

Ronald had picked out the three freshest looking dry cells, setting the other two, which still had short bent lengths of wire untidily attached to their terminals, down on the scarred top of an upended trunk beside the stepladder on which he was working. It was still day outside, barely, although of course he had a flashlight to see up into the cobwebby rafters, and just as he'd about connected up the three newer looking cells properly, working a little gingerly because of his apprehension of spider's, a beam of yellow light from the setting sun struck brightly through one of the low oblong windows and across the top of the trunk. It showed a lot more dust motes trembling in the air than Ronald's flashlight revealed, and immediately Ronald felt a sneeze coming on. But then it showed something so much more strange and arresting that the sneeze never came and Ronald quite forgot that his nasal passages had been tickling.

One of the rejected batteries carried attached to one terminal a length of gray-insulated wire so sharply curved that its other end now chanced to touch the other terminal, shorting the battery out—except that the battery had looked to Ronald too dingy and old to have any juice left to short.

The dust motes were whirling in orderly circles around the wire, forming a dim tube that curved from terminal to terminal with the wire running down the center or axis of the shadowy tube. The circular orbiting of the dust motes was clearest within an inch of the wire, but even as he watched he saw some of the more distant motes begin to take up the movement, swinging in larger, slower circles.

Ronald's face grew blank with attention. He leaned down very slowly until his eyes were only inches from the phenomenon. Fearfully, almost reverently he blew softly at the wire. The motes eddied away wildly and then almost immediately began to resume their circling, those nearest the wire taking it up most quickly, then those further off starting once more to join in.

Ronald thought: *There's a force moving those particles. They're in a force-field. If they were powdered iron or black iron oxide (but they aren't) it would be a magnetic field moving them, a magnetic field created by an electric current moving through the wire, though I think it would have to be a lot stronger current than a dry cell could furnish.*

But the particles aren't iron or iron oxide (too heavy to float in air, besides this has to be just Wycherly basement dust—ashes, lint, earth, powdered wood and paper) so it can't be a magnetic field that's moving them, though they're moving exactly as if they were in a force-field of some sort. So it has to be gravity...a gravitic force-field they're moving in, at least that's the only other force I know of it could be.

An electric current moving through a conductor creates a magnetic field.

A what?-current...call it a gravitic current anyway...though it could be a magnetic current...a gravitic current moving through a conductor creates a gravitic field.

The sunlight faded swiftly. As the yellow beam moved upward, dimming, its last rays showed more and more dust motes pouring into the vortex, joining in the frenzied yet orderly circling.

As the dark basement twilight closed in, Ronald reached out and grasped the battery protectively, possessively. With his other hand he bent the wire away from the terminal. Already he had begun to worry about the battery running down.

A minute or so later it occurred to him to use his flashlight to examine the battery more closely. It was a distinctly smaller cylinder than the other dry cells, he saw now—only about five inches high and an inch-and-a-half in diameter—

and it had no cardboard sheath around it, which had been the chief reason he'd thought of it as older and more likely to be completely exhausted than the others. And the terminals, although of the screw-on, knurled-nut type, didn't seem to be brass, but something grayer, like the zinc, or whatever it was, of the battery's body.

He tried to force himself to think in a systematic way about the possible *source* of the thing, granting that it really *was* a gravity battery—something that another part of his mind was already working out delightful ways to check. *Let's see,* he thought, *it could be a genuine gravity battery manufactured as such by human beings engaged in secret government-sponsored anti-gravity research either in this country or elsewhere—there are such projects—though then how it should get into Aunt Wycherly's basement seems to require very weird assumptions. Or else—my God, this gets fantastic—it could come from off this earth and have been manufactured by extra-terrestrials—got to consider every possibility—though that involves us in even more weird assumptions.*

Or it could just have happened. I mean the battery could have started out as an ordinary battery, but sitting here in Aunt Wycherly's basement and undergoing all sorts of rhythmical temperature changes and God knows what else, the chemicals in it could have been transformed into substances generating a current—gravitic, magnetic, how should I know what jargon to use?—that in turn creates a gravitic field. Like spontaneous combustion, or something. Old rags. That's not unusual.

Or it could all be illusion or freak air currents.

Or I could just be going nuts—that's something to keep in mind too.

But while Ronald was making his brain hammer out these possibilities, another section of his thoughts was darting around like kittens to investigate all sorts of wonderful ideas, making use of the thirty years' rag-tag accumulation of information in Ronald's mind—a quite remarkable and varied assortment. For one thing he was thinking that since this basement phenomenon behaved so much like magnetism, it must be a dipolar gravity field he had here, promising both positive and negative gravity if properly harnessed; that is, not only gravitic attraction but gravitic repulsion—in other words, antigravity, the secret of rocketless spaceflight! There were ways to check that, of course. And what *was* the wonderful stuff that flowed through the wire and made the field grab and the motes spin? Gravitic fluid, could you call it? Liquid gravity? Was it particles, like electrons? Gravitrons, would you call them? Hell, nobody really understood electricity yet! Still—

"Ronald, why are you taking so long? Mr. Espy will be coming soon and I don't want to have to watch for him at the window."

Ronald looked down at his aunt's pudgy, thin-lipped face, realizing that she had come creaking and clumping all the way down to the basement without his being aware of it. He nodded slowly at her without a word; put away the battery he was holding, and like a man in a dream began to make the last connections in the bell system.

The bell rang strongly at the first test. Mrs. Wycherly thanked Ronald profusely in the kitchen and seemed on the point of bringing up some additional matter, but just then Ronald rather abruptly wandered off toward the garage, still acting like a man in a dream.

Mrs. Wycherly made a little humorous face. She'd been debating giving Ronald two dollars for his labors and had almost decided to, but if he chose to go mooning off that way…

She was still wondering, too, why he had so carefully put one of her batteries into the inside breast pocket of his coat, buttoning the coat afterwards. It was almost like a psychiatric symptom, with some deep symbolic meaning—perhaps she should ask Mr. Espy about it. But no, Ronald probably just wanted it for something in the garage. Well, she wouldn't grudge it to him, though of course he ought to have asked her first.

Convincing himself that his find really was a gravity battery occupied Ronald most of the night and next day. He made his tests with great care, only after thinking each through in detail first, he kept them as few and brief as his delight and wonder would let him. The possibility of the battery running down had begun to prey on his mind more and more seriously, especially after a search of the basement next morning revealed no more dry cells of similar appearance.

The chief test, or rather set of tests, involved making a coil of the wire joining the terminals, so as to give direction and greater power to the gravitic field, exactly as one would do in making an electromagnet. The most obvious and interesting cylinder around which to wind the coil was the battery itself, Ronald started out with just a dozen loops, winding the wire down the body of the battery from one terminal and returning it through the air to the other.

The result was more than gratifying. *Held terminals-end-up the battery almost doubled in weight as soon as he connected the coil.* Of course he was just judging the weight by feel, but he was sure he couldn't be fooling himself to that degree. Moreover, the coils strained toward the floor in that position, tending to creep along the cylinder and bunch together. (In later tests he made a point of anchoring them individually with adhesive tape.)

Held terminals-end-down the battery weighed almost nothing at all. It seemed as light as if it were a painted balsa-wood model of itself. The transition from twice-weight to no-weight, as felt by his hand, was as mysteriously alarming and delightful as a mild electric shock.

Clearly the gravitic field was dipolar as he'd surmised. The terminal-end was the negative or repulsive pole, seeking to push away from the earth—or push the earth away! The other end was the positive or attractive one. (A bit later he discovered what he told himself he should have guessed at once: that if he wound the coil the opposite way, say clockwise instead of counter-clockwise, it reversed the poles—they really had nothing to do with the location of the terminals on the battery.)

For light objects nearby, the battery's tiny gravitic field was more powerful than that of the earth—a circumstance that shouldn't surprise him, Ronald reminded himself, as earth's center of gravity was 4,000 miles away while the battery's was right in his hand. The attractive pole would snatch a cork off the floor from the height of two feet—he could actually see the cork falling upward faster and faster—while the repulsive pole would bat away the same cork dropped on it from above. And the attractive pole always became covered with dust when used, while the other pole stayed clean.

Brought close to his forearm, the repulsive pole made a shallow, saucer-shaped dimple in the flesh, while the attractive one tugged at the tissue in a way that somehow felt deeper than suction.

It was vastly exciting to say the very least, and Ronald could hardly wait to step up the power of the field by increasing the number of turns in the coil—this being one of the times when his delight and wonder got the better of him.

However, he retained at least minimal prudence and added only six turns. He told himself that if the effect wasn't enough, he could always add more.

He was glad that he had been conservative. The repulsive pole was downward when he touched the return wire to the second terminal, and the battery tugged his hand sharply upward, as if it were, not a small, but say a *medium-size* bird trying to escape. Or maybe a weather balloon. The sensation was peculiarly delightful—his hand was not only tugged but indescribably tickled (presumably by the curving components of the dipolar gravitic field)—and despite his concern about the battery running down, it was all Ronald could do not to stand there all night holding the up-surging battery with a happy, dazed smile on his face.

And in fact Ronald did not disconnect it right away. He'd got the impression that the wire of the coil had changed color in some way and on an impulse he switched off the light he'd been working by, a hanging and unshaded 150-watt globe (which he kept secret from his aunt, for she had a thing about wasting stronger than 40 watts in her whole mansion).

The consequences were sudden, spectacular, and almost disastrous.

In the darkness the coil was outlined in bright white light.

Ronald was so startled that he opened his hand.

The white-spiraled battery sprang upward and for an instant Ronald had the dreadful fear that the thing had got away from him forever and from the earth too, although he knew very well that the ceiling of his garage apartment must stop it.

But then almost immediately, without touching the ceiling, the thing flipped over, dove down, and hit the floor with a sharp crack.

Its light went out.

Ronald's feelings were intense and mixed. He was relieved that the battery hadn't escaped, doubly relieved to discover that apparently it couldn't escape from earth—that released repulsive pole down it would simply flip over and dive. There *was* the possibility that he had started the battery flipping over with a twist of his hand when he released it, but that possibility didn't bulk large in his mind.

And of course, beyond all else, he was fearful that the fall had somehow ruined the battery forever. For instance, if its ability to generate gravitic energy depended on some rare and delicate spontaneous chemical transformation that had taken place inside it, then even something as slight as a sudden jar might well reverse the transformation.

He switched on the light and picked up the battery as if it were a wounded bird. He was considerably relieved to find that the wire had jarred loose from one of the terminals. He reconnected it, the battery surged in his hand, and his relief was complete.

But thereafter his carefulness was doubled and also tainted with suspicion.

He made a number of other interesting discoveries about the battery besides the epiphenomenon of the white glow. For instance, it turned out to be the *insulation* on the wire that carried the gravitic current. A bare copper wire didn't work at all. A nylon cord worked beautifully, provided he wrapped it in tinfoil so that it didn't short itself out. In fact, there seemed to be a half dozen new sciences implicit in the battery and Ronald would have liked nothing better than to spend the next six months in investigating them all, provided he had a dozen batteries to work with, or even just one to hold in reserve.

That was the fly in the ointment, of course. His battery was goose and golden egg rolled into one, a bird in the hand but none at all in the bushes. So about the middle of the next afternoon he sat down to do some serious, really serious thinking—meaning of course thinking about how he could use his great discovery to profit himself.

First he carefully locked away the battery and went out into the garden to meditate it through, but he found he couldn't bear to be that far away from his find, so he went back to his garage apartment and sat beside the window that looked into the garden, feeling a little giddy from lack of sleep.

His aunt had noted his abstracted and somewhat agitated behavior, however, from one of her lace-curtained watch-windows, just as she'd early that morning been aware of him poking around in the basement without her permission. She frowned, remembering his distinctly odd behavior with her battery. She hadn't discussed the matter with Mr. Espy yesterday but she decided she certainly would tonight.

Serious thinking is always apt to be a somewhat chilling business. The more Ronald applied his mind to the problem of how to make *money* out of one small and presumably irreplaceable gravitic and antigravitic battery, the chillier the prospects came to look to him.

One thing he was fatalistically certain of from the start: that if he reported his find to any "proper authorities" (military, scientific, industrial; academic, governmental-authorities are always governmental to the end) he would get nothing whatever for himself except trouble. To begin with, the governmental authorities would know very well whether one of their secret projects had or had not started to manufacture gravitic batteries. In either case they would grab the battery—either for safekeeping or for feverish secret research into its mysteries—and at the same time loudly proclaim that it did not exist. Ronald's protests would be laughed at. He would be left out in the cold or, more likely, grabbed himself and awarded a lifetime of protective custody and unending interrogation. Where a discovery of such fabulous military importances as antigravity was concerned, an individual's rights just wouldn't count.

Perhaps he could investigate the battery himself, carefully open it and find out what made it work? Ronald's reaction to this idea was simply to shudder. True, he fancied a bit his talent for scientific thinking, but he wasn't *that* egotistical. Cutting or prying the battery open in hope of discovering its secrets struck Ronald as some seven degrees more unpromising than an infant taking apart a gold wristwatch to find out what made it work. This seemed particularly to the point as Ronald now inclined more and more to the theory that the battery was something that had been spontaneously generated in his aunt's basement by complex cycles of temperature change or the like—which also brought him back once more to the fact that he only had *one* battery, that as far as he knew there was only one on Earth. And if *that* were the case, why the chances were that the properest scientific authorities in the world wouldn't be any too successful in probing the battery's secrets. They'd play with it at a little more sophisticated level than himself, to be sure—until its power gave out, and then dissect it into microscopic slides and peer and poke at it, and like as not end up knowing little or nothing more than at the first testing.

These general considerations also made Ronald shy away from the plan of finding and privately enlisting the services of some brilliant young technician or engineering student, or offering such a person a partnership in the battery.

Perhaps he could *sell* the battery? No, any substantial businessman would be fearfully suspicious of such an offer. He'd think it was the Keeley motor over again or some perpetual motion crank or the powder that added to water makes gasoline. Ronald could arrange brilliant demonstrations, of course, but the more brilliant they were the more his prospect would suspect trickery. Experts would have to be called in and he would be back once more with the proper authorities, who would be snatching at his battery with rapacious fingers.

Suppose he were to find a millionaire gambler and bet him that— Ronald irritably shook his head. In the first place he didn't know any such gamblers or how to approach them and in the second place the last thing a Bet-a-million Gates would bet on was something that looked like a cast-iron certainty to win. The maker of such a tempting offer would be bound to have something up his sleeve.

Maybe he could use the battery to put on a magic or spiritualist act? Causing something to float without wires, or levitating small objects in a slightly darkened room for the edification of wealthy crackpots like his aunt—do the Poltergeist bit. Now that, Ronald told himself, was cutting his problem down close to size. The trouble was, of course, as with so many other plans, that the battery would eventually run down and probably sooner than later. But more than that, the magic-act plan ran up against the objection that Ronald simply wasn't even a passable third-rate showman or conman and knew it very well.

Sitting in his chilly hole-over-a-garage and gazing out at the darkening garden—for a full twenty-four hours had passed since his great discovery—Ronald gave an irritated little sigh. His utter incapacity as a showman and conman was an old sore point with him. Why, as long as ten years ago he'd been the one to get his aunt interested in occultism, but had he reaped any of the benefits of her craze? No! That had been reserved for the slick operators like Mr. Espy, Dr. Yorn, and their dozen or so predecessors. They'd taken hundreds, thousands of dollars from her over the years. She'd even sent money by mail, to Tibet, Ceylon and Southern California "to further occult research," while he, who'd started the whole thing, was lucky if from time to time he got a few cans of corned beef hash or spaghetti from her pantry hoard!

Not that Ronald lay awake nights scheming how to murder his aunt without being suspected or how to defraud her on a large scale. He wasn't that sort of person at all. He just grieved occasionally that a man with a commanding gaze and a confident pseudo-professional manner should be able to charm a twenty-dollar bill out of someone else's pocket and into his own, while he, with ten times the education, ingenuity, and honest idealism, couldn't!

Now if I just had the kind of cheap ability that a Yorn or an Espy has, Ronald told himself, *I'd figure out a dozen childishly simple ways to profit from this battery and, what's more important, I'd have the nerve and know-how to put them into action.*

He shook his head and shivered. He'd just had a vision of himself, days or months hence, the battery completely dead, finally going to the "proper authorities" with a crazed gleam in his eyes and assuring them that, yes, once this battery had held gravitic energy…

What I obviously need, he told himself, *is an improper authority.*

His gaze lit on Mr. Espy and his aunt talking at the far end of the garden. Almost at once his aunt went inside and Mr. Espy lit a cigarette and began to stroll.

Normally Ronald was anything but a man of action, but sleeplessness and desperation had transformed him. He grabbed the battery and completed the connection. It glowed brilliantly and surged powerfully upward in his hand, the coil consisting now of some twenty turns of tinfoil-wrapped nylon. Ronald headed for the garden.

Strike while the iron is hot, he told himself exultantly. *Espy's my man. With this to show him and let him feel it won't take me twenty seconds to make my pitch. And with his conning ability and my battery…*

Ronald certainly did make an arresting sight as he hurried through the darkening garden, holding high his glowing hand. Mr. Espy stopped dead and stared at Ronald.

There was something peculiar about the stare, though. It seemed to Ronald to go through him like a knife. Intending to startle, Ronald found himself startled in return…momentarily almost paralyzed.

He realized with horror that the battery had sprung from his limp fingers.

He waited for it to flip over and crash, thanking God that the ground was soft.

It didn't flip over. Buzzing faintly now and seeming to spin, it bulleted straight upward at ever-increasing velocity, one more bright point of light headed toward the first stars of evening.

It faded and was gone forever.

Ronald realized that Mr. Espy had hold of his shoulder and was shaking him.

"Young man!" Mr. Espy was saying, "Do you realize that you possess astounding occult powers? That was the most impressive demonstration of telekinesis I have ever witnessed in a long and rather far-flung life!"

Lieutenant J. C. Arnold and S. Abramson, USAF, were on a routine jet mission at 30,000 feet when the phenomenon shot by them at a distance of only a few yards, its velocity now considerable.

"Jack, a meteor!" the second gasped.

"Be your age, Sammy," the first admonished him. "Would a shooting star shoot up?" He paused before adding, "But what could it have been?"

Rather later that evening Mr. Espy was preparing a sort of telegram for transmission, though not by Western Union. It read in part:

You will also be pleased to hear that the last of the batteries the saintly Yorn absent-mindedly distributed around in his chuckle-headed way before he was reassigned to a less critical post, has been located and safely disposed of. It is no longer on Earth. One worry less for all of us! To get it away painlessly from the young human who had discovered it and was beginning to probe its more superficial powers, I was forced to employ what on this planet they quaintly called "the whammy." He was most startled and considerably grieved to see the battery star-trend, having apparently not anticipated all the consequences of the gyral effect or the cube law on the coils. I calmed him and reconciled him in part to his loss without having to wipe his memory.

So...our observation station on Sol Three is once more reasonably secure from discovery. It will not be necessary now to find new patrons—we can continue to depend for local financing on Mrs. Wycherly and the other ladies who unknowingly but so very kindly support our little enterprise.

Bazaar of the Bizarre

To the Gray Mouser, well fed and wined in his black coffin, the scene was jolly. To Fafhrd, wearing the Cloak of Invisibility and the Blindfold of True Seeing, the scene was the hell-nadir of the universe, where dark devils scuttled and the damned writhed in the grip of black serpents. Thus did they defend Lankhmar against the invasion of the...bazaar of the bizarre.

THE strange stars of the World of Nehwon glinted thickly above the black-roofed city of Lankhmar, where swords clink almost as often as coins. For once there was no fog.

In the Plaza of Dark Delights, which lies seven blocks south of the Marsh Gate and extends from the Fountain of Dark Abundance to the Shrine of the Black Virgin, the shoplights glinted upward no more brightly than the stars glinted down. For there the vendors of drugs and the peddlers of curiosa and the hawkers of assignations light their stalls and crouching places with foxfire, glowworms, and firepots with tiny single windows, and they conduct their business almost as silently as the stars conduct theirs.

There are plenty of raucous spots a-glare with torches in nocturnal Lankhmar, but by immemorial tradition soft whispers and a pleasant dimness are the rule in the Plaza of Dark Delights. Philosophers often go there solely to meditate, students to dream, and fanatic-eyed theologians to spin like spiders abstruse new theories of the Devil and of the other dark forces ruling the universe. And if any of these find a little illicit fun by the way, their theories and dreams and theologies and demonology's are undoubtedly the better for it.

Tonight however, there was a glaring exception to the darkness rule. From a low doorway with a trefoil arch new-struck through an ancient wall, light spilled into the Plaza. Rising above the horizon of the pavement like some monstrous moon a-shine with the ray of a murderous sun, the new doorway dimmed almost to extinction the stars of the other merchants of mystery.

Eerie and unearthly objects for sale spilled out of the doorway a little way with the light, while beside the doorway crouched an avid-faced figure clad in garments never before seen on land or sea…in the World of Nehwon. He wore a hat like a small red pail, baggy trousers, and outlandish red boots with upturned toes. His eyes were as predatory as a hawk's, but his smile as cynically and lasciviously cajoling as an ancient satyr's.

Now and again he sprang up and pranced about, sweeping and re-sweeping with a rough long broom the flagstones as if to clean path for the entry of some fantastic emperor, and he often paused in his dance to bow low and loutingly, but always with upglancing eyes, to the crowd gathering in the darkness across from the doorway and to swing his hand from them toward the interior of the new shop in a gesture of invitation at once servile and sinister.

No one in the crowd had yet plucked up courage to step forward into the glare and enter the shop, or even inspect the rarities set out so carelessly yet temptingly before it. But the number of fascinated peerers increased every moment. There were mutterings of censure at the dazzling new method of merchandising the infraction of the Plaza's custom of darkness—but on the whole the complaints were outweighed by the gasps and murmurings of wonder, admiration, and curiosity kindling ever hotter.

THE gray Mouser slipped into the Plaza at the Fountain end as silently as if he had come to slit a throat or spy on the spies of the Overlord. His rat-skin moccasins were soundless. His sword, Scapel, in its mouse-skin sheath did not swish ever so faintly against either his tunic or cloak, both of gray silk curiously coarse of weave. While the glances he shot about him from under his gray silk hood half thrown back were freighted with menace and a freezing sense of superiority.

Inwardly the Mouser was feeling very much like a schoolboy—a schoolboy in dread of rebuke and a crushing assignment of homework. For in the Mouser's pouch of rat-skin was a note scrawled in dark brown squid-ink on silvery fish-skin by Sheelba of the Eyeless Face, inviting the Mouser to be at this spot at this time.

Sheelba was the Mouser's supernatural tutor and—when the whim struck Sheelba—guardian, and it never did to ignore his invitations, for Sheelba had eyes to track down the unsociable though he did not carry them between his cheeks and forehead.

But the tasks Sheelba would set the Mouser at times like these were apt to be peculiarly onerous and even noisome—such as procuring nine white cats with never a black hair among them, or stealing five copies of the same book of magic runes from five widely separated sorcerous libraries or obtaining specimens of the dung of four kings living or dead—so the Mouser had come early, to get the bad news as soon as possible, and he had come alone, for he certainly did not want his comrade Fafhrd to stand snickering by while Sheelba delivered his little wizardly homilies to a dutiful Mouser...and perchance thought of extra assignments.

Sheelba's note, invisibly graven somewhere inside the Mouser's skull, read merely, "When the star Akul bedizens the Spire of Rhan, be you by the Fountain of Dark

Abundance," and the note was signed only with the little featureless oval which is Sheelba's sigil.

The Mouser glided now through the darkness to the Fountain, which was a squat black pillar from the rough rounded top of which a single black drop welled and dripped every twenty elephant's heartbeats.

The Mouser stood beside the Fountain and, extending a bent hand, measured the altitude of the green star Akul. It had still to drop down the sky seven finger-widths more before it would touch the needlepoint of the slim star-silhouetted distant minaret of Rhan.

The Mouser crouched doubled-up by the black pillar and then vaulted lightly atop it to see if that would make any great difference in Akul's altitude. It did not.

He scanned the nearby darkness for motionless figures...especially that of one robed and cowled like a monk-cow led so deeply that one might wonder how he saw to walk. There were no figures at all.

The Mouser's mood changed. If Sheelba chose not to come courteously beforehand, why he could be boorish too! He strode off to investigate the new bright arch-doored shop, of whose infractious glow he had become inquisitively aware at least a block before he had entered the Plaza of Dark Delights.

FAFHRD the Northerner opened one wine-heavy eye and without moving his head scanned half the small firelit room in which he slept naked. He shut that eye, opened the other, and scanned the other half.

There was no sign of the Mouser anywhere. So far so good! If his luck held, he would be able to get through tonight's embarrassing business without being jeered at by the small gray rogue.

He drew from under his stubbly cheek a square of violet serpent-hide pocked with tiny pores so that when he held it between his eyes and the dancing fire it made stars. Studied for a time, these stars spelled out obscurely the message: "When Rhan-dagger stabs the darkness in Akul-heart, seek you the Source of the Black Drops."

Drawn boldly across the prick-holes in an orange-brown like dried blood—in fact spanning the violet square—was a seven-armed swastika, which is one of the sigils of Ningauble of the Seven Eyes.

Fafhrd had no difficulty in interpreting the Source of the Black Drops as the Fountain of Dark Abundance. He had become wearily familiar with such cryptic poetic language during his boyhood as a scholar of the singing skalds.

Ningauble stood to Fafhrd very much as Sheelba stood to the Mouser except that the Seven-Eyed One was a somewhat more pretentious arch-image, whose taste in the thaumaturgical tasks he set Fafhrd ran in larger directions such as the slaying of dragons, the sinking of four-masted magic ships, and the kidnapping of ogre-guarded enchanted queens.

Also, Ningauble was given to quiet realistic boasting, especially about the grandeur of his vast cavern-home, whose stony serpent-twisting back corridors led, he often averred, to all spots in space and time—provided Ningauble instructed one beforehand exactly how to step those rocky crook'd low-ceilinged passageways.

Fafhrd was driven by no great desire to learn Ningauble's formulas and enchantments, as the Mouser was driven to learn Sheelba's, but the Septinocular One had enough holds on the Northerner, based on the latter's weaknesses and past misdeeds, so that Fafhrd had always to listen patiently to Ningauble's wizardly admonishments and vaunting sorcerous chit-chat—but *not*, if humanly or inhumanly possible, while the Gray Mouser was present to snigger and grin.

Meanwhile, Fafhrd, standing before the fire, had been whipping, slapping, and belting various garments and weapons and ornaments onto his huge brawny body with its generous stretches of thick short curling red-geld hairs. When he opened the outer door and, also booted and helmeted now, glanced down the darkling alleyway preparatory to leaving and noted only the hunch-backed chestnut vendor a-squat by his brazier at the next corner, one would have sworn that when he did stride forth toward the Plaza of Dark Delights it would be with the clankings and thunderous tread of a siege-tower approaching a thick-walled city.

Instead the lynx-eared old chestnut vendor, who was also a spy of the Overlord, had to swallow down his heart when it came sliding crookedly up his throat as Fafhrd rushed past him, tall as a pine tree, swift as the wind, and silent as a ghost.

THE Mouser elbowed aside two gawkers with shrewd taps on the floating rib and strode across the dark flagstones toward the garishly bright shop with its doorway like an upended heart. It occurred to him they must have had masons working like fiends to have cut and plastered that archway so swiftly. He had been past here this afternoon and noted nothing but blank wall.

The outlandish porter with the red cylinder hat and twisty red shoe-toes came frisking out to the Mouser with his broom and then went curtsying back as he re-swept a path for this first customer with many an obsequious bow and smirk.

But the Mouser's visage was set in an expression of grim and all-skeptical disdain. He paused at the heaping of objects in front of the door and scanned it with disapproval. He drew Scalpel from its thin gray sheath and with the top of the long blade flipped back the cover on the topmost of a pile of musty books. Without going any closer he briefly scanned the first page, shook his head, rapidly turned a half dozen more pages with Scalpel's tip, using the swords as if it were a teacher's wand to point out words here and there—because they were ill-chosen, to judge from his expression—and then abruptly closed the book with another sword-flip.

Next he used Scalpel's tip to lift a red cloth hanging from a table behind the books and peer under it suspiciously, to rap contemptuously a glass jar with a human head floating in it, to touch disparagingly several other objects and to waggle reprovingly at a foot-chained owl which hooted at him solemnly from its high perch.

He sheathed Scalpel and turned toward the Porter with a sour, lifted-eyebrow look that said—nay, shouted—plainly, "Is this all you have to offer? Is this garbage your excuse for defiling the Dark Plaza with glare?"

Actually the Mouser was mightily interested by every least item which he had glimpsed. The book, incidentally, had been in a script, which he not only did not understand, but did not even recognize.

Three things were very clear to the Mouser: first, that this stuff offered here for sale did not come from anywhere in the World of Nehwon, no, not even from Nehwon's farthest outback; second, that all this stuff was, in some way which he could not yet define, extremely dangerous; third, that all this stuff was monstrously fascinating and that he, the Mouser, did not intend to stir from this place until he had personally scanned, studied, and if need be tested, every last intriguing item and scrap.

AT the Mouser's sour grimace the Porter went into a convulsion of wheedling and fawning caperings, seemingly torn between a desire to kiss the Mouser's foot and to point out with flamboyant caressing gestures every object in his shop.

He ended by bowing so low that his chin brushed the pavement, sweeping an ape-long arm toward the interior of the shop and gibbering in atrocious Lankhmarese, "Every object to pleasure the flesh and senses and imagination of man. Wonders undreamed. Very cheap, very cheap! Yours for a penny! The Bazaar of the Bizarre. Please to inspect, oh king!"

The Mouser yawned a very long yawn with the back of his hand to his mouth, next he looked around him again with the weary patient worldly smile of a duke who knows he must put up with many boredoms to encourage business in his demesne, finally he shrugged faintly and entered the shop.

Behind him the Porter went into a jigging delirium of glee and began to re-sweep the flagstones like a man maddened with delight.

Inside, the first thing the Mouser saw was a stack of slim books bound in gold-lined fine-grained red and violet leather.

The second was a rack of gleaming lenses and slim brass tubes calling to be peered through.

The third was a slim dark-haired girl smiling at him mysteriously from a gold-barred cage that swung from the ceiling.

Beyond that cage hung others with bars of silver and strange green, ruby, orange, ultramarine, and purple metals.

Fafhrd saw the Mouser vanish into the shop just as his left hand touched the rough chill pate of the Fountain of Dark Abundance and as Akul poised precisely on Rhan-top as if it were that needle-spire's green-lensed pinnacle-lantern.

He might have followed the Mouser, he might have done no such thing, he certainly would have pondered the briefly glimpsed event, but just then there came from behind him a long low "Hssssst!"

Fafhrd turned like a giant dancer and his longsword Graywand came out of its sheath swiftly and rather more silently than a snake emerges from its hole.

Ten arm-lengths behind him, in the mouth of an alleyway darker than the Dark Plaza would have been without its new commercial moon, Fafhrd dimly made out two robed and deeply cowled figures poised side by side.

One cowl held darkness absolute. Even the face of a Negro of Klesh might have been expected to shoot ghostly bronzy gleams. But here there were none.

In the other cowl there nested seven very faint pale greenish glows. They moved about restlessly, sometimes circling each other, swinging mazily. Sometimes one of the seven horizontally oval gleams would grow a little brighter, seemingly as it moved forward toward the mouth of the cowl—or a little darker, as it drew back.

Fafhrd sheathed Graywand and advanced toward the figures. Still facing him, they retreated slowly and silently down the alley.

Fafhrd followed as they receded. He felt a stirring of interest...and of other feelings. To meet his own supernatural mentor alone might be only a bore and a mild nervous strain; but it would be hard for anyone entirely to repress a shiver of awe at encountering at one and the same time both Ningauble of the Seven Eyes and Sheelba of the Eyeless Face.

Moreover, that those two bitter wizardly rivals should have joined forces, that they should apparently be operating together in amity... Something of great note must be a-foot! There was no doubting that.

THE Mouser meantime was experiencing the snuggest, most mind-teasing, most exotic enjoyments imaginable. The sleekly leather-bound gold-stamped books turned out to contain scripts stranger far than that in the book whose pages he had flipped outside-scripts that looked like skeletal beasts, cloud swirls, and twisty-branched bushes and trees—but for a wonder he could read them all without the least difficulty.

The books dealt in the fullest detail with such matters as the private life of devils, the secret histories of murderous cults, and—these were illustrated—the proper dueling techniques to employ against sword-armed demons and the erotic tricks of lamias, succubi, bacchantes, and hamadryads.

The lenses and brass tubes, some of the latter of which were as fantastically crooked as if they were periscopes for seeing over the walls and through the barred windows of other universes, showed at first only delightful jeweled patterns, but after a bit the Mouser was able to see through them all into sorts of interesting places: the treasure rooms of dead kings, the bedchambers of living queens, council-crypts of rebel angels, and the closets in which the gods hid plans for worlds too frighteningly fantastic to risk creating.

As for the quaintly clad slim girls in their playfully widely barred cages, well, they were pleasant pillows on which to rest eyes momentarily fatigued by book scanning and tube-peering.

Ever and anon one of the girls would whistle softly at the Mouser and then point cajolingly or imploringly or with langorous hintings at a jeweled crank set in the wall whereby her cage, suspended on a gleaming chain running through gleaming pulleys, could be lowered to the floor.

At these invitations the Mouser would smile with a bland amorousness and nod and softly wave a hand from the fingerhinge as if to whisper, "Later...later. Be patient."

After all, girls had a way of blotting out all lesser, but not thereby despicable, delights. Girls were for dessert.

NINGAUBLE and Sheelba receded down the dark alleyway with Fafhrd following them until the latter lost patience and, somewhat conquering his unwilling awe, called out nervously, "Well, are you going to keep on fleeing me backwards until we all pitch into the Great Salt Marsh? What do you want of me? What's it all about?"

But the two cowled figures had already stopped, as he could perceive by the starlight and the glow of a few high windows, and now it seemed to Fafhrd that they had stopped a moment before he had called out. A typical sorcerers' trick for making one feel awkward! He gnawed his lip in the darkness. It was ever thus!

"Oh My Gentle Son..." Ningauble began in his most sugary-priestly tones, the dim puffs of his seven eyes now hanging in his cowl as steadily and glowing as mildly as the Pleiades seen late on a summer night through a greenish mist rising from a lake freighted with blue vitriol and corrosive gas of salt.

"I asked what it's all about!" Fafhrd interrupted harshly. Already convicted of impatience, he might as well go the whole hog.

"Let me put it as a hypothetical case," Ningauble replied imperturbably. "Let us suppose, My Gentle Son, that there is a man in a universe and that a most evil force comes to this universe from another universe, or perhaps from a congeries of universes, and that this man is a brave man who wants to defend his universe and who counts his life as a trifle and that moreover he has to counsel him a very wise and prudent and public-spirited uncle who knows all about these matters which I have been hypothecating—"

"The Devourers menace Lankhmar!" Sheelba rapped out in a voice as harsh as a tree cracking and so suddenly that Fafhrd almost started—and for all we know, Ningauble too.

Fafhrd waited a moment to avoid giving false impressions and then switched his gaze to Sheelba. His eyes had been growing accustomed to the darkness and he saw much more now than he had seen at the alley's mouth, yet he still saw not one jot more than absolute blackness inside Sheelba's cowl.

"Who are the Devourers?" he asked.

It was Ningauble, however, who replied, "The Devourers are the most accomplished merchants in all the many universes—so accomplished, indeed, that they sell only trash. There is a deep necessity in this, for the Devourers must occupy all their cunning in perfecting their methods of selling and so have not an instant to spare in considering the worth of what they sell—indeed, they dare not concern themselves with such matters for a moment, for fear of losing their golden touch—and yet such are their skills that their wares are utterly irresistible, indeed the finest wares in all the many universes—if you follow me?"

Fafhrd looked hopefully toward Sheelba, but since the latter did not this time interrupt with some pithy summation, he nodded to Ningauble.

Ningauble continued, his seven eyes beginning to weave a bit, judging from the movements of the seven green glows, "As you might readily deduce, the Devourers possess all the mightiest magics garnered from the many universes, whilst their assault groups are led by the most aggressive wizards imaginable, supremely skilled in all methods of battling, whether it be with the wits, or the feelings, or with the beweaponed body.

"The method of the Devourers is to set up shop in a new world and first entice the bravest and the most adventuresome and the supplest-minded of its people—who have so much imagination that with just a touch of suggestion they themselves do most of the work of selling themselves.

"When these are safely ensnared, the Devourers proceed to deal with the remainder of the population: meaning simply that they sell and sell and sell!—sell trash and take good money and even finer things in exchange."

Ningauble sighed windily and a shade piously, "All this is very bad, My Gentle Son," he continued, his eye-glows weaving hypnotically in his cowl, "but natural enough in universes administered by such gods as we have—natural enough and perhaps endurable. However—" (He paused) "—there is worse to come! The Devourers want not only the patronage of all beings in all universes, but—doubtless because they are afraid someone will some day raise the ever-unpleasant question of the true worth of things—they want all their customers reduced to a state of slavish and submissive suggestibility, so that they are fit for nothing whatever but to gawk at and buy the trash the Devourers offer for sale. This means of course that eventually the Devourers' customers will have nothing wherewith to pay the Devourers for their trash, but the Devourers do not seem to be concerned with this eventuality. Perhaps they feel that there is always a new universe to exploit. And perhaps there is!"

MONSTROUS!" Fafhrd commented. "But what do the Devourers gain from all these furious commercial sorties, all this mad merchandising? What do they really want?"

Ningauble replied, "The Devourers want only to amass cash and to raise little ones like themselves to amass more cash and they want to compete with each other at cash-amassing (Is that coincidentally a city, do you think, Fafhrd? Cashamash?) and the Devourers want to brood about their great service to the many universes—it is their claim that servile customers make the most obedient subjects for the gods—and to complain about how the work of amassing cash tortures their minds and upsets their digestions. Beyond this, each of the Devourers also secretly collects and hides away forever, to delight no eyes but his own, all the finest objects and thoughts created by true men and women (and true wizards and true demons) and bought by the Devourers at bankruptcy prices and paid for with trash or—this is their ultimate preference—with nothing at all."

"Monstrous indeed!" Fafhrd repeated. "Merchants are ever an evil mystery and these sound the worst. But what has all this to do with me?"

"Oh My Gentle Son," Ningauble responded, the piety in his voice now tinged with a certain clement disappointment, "you force me once again to resort to hypothecating. Let us return to the supposition of this brave man whose whole universe is direly menaced and who counts his life a trifle and to the related supposition of this brave man's wise uncle, whose advice the brave man invariably follows—"

"The Devourers have set up shop in the Plaza of Dark Delights!" Sheelba interjected so abruptly and in such iron-harsh syllables that this time Fafhrd actually did start. "You must obliterate this outpost tonight!"

Fafhrd considered that for a bit, then said, in a tentative sort of voice, "You will both accompany me, I presume, to aid me with your wizardly sendings and castings in what I can see must be a most perilous operation, to serve me as a sort of sorcerous artillery and archery corps while I play assault battalion—"

"Oh My Gentle Son…" Ningauble interrupted in tones of deepest disappointment, shaking his head so that his eye-glows jogged in his cowl.

"You must do it alone!" Sheelba rasped.

"Without any help at all?" Fafhrd demanded. "No! Get someone else. Get this doltish brave man who always follows his scheming uncle's advice as slavishly as you tell me the

Devourers' customers respond to their merchandising. Get *him!* But as for me— No, I say!"

"Then leave us, coward!" Sheelba decreed dourly, but Ningauble only sighed and said quite apologetically, "It was intended that you have a comrade in this quest, a fellow soldier against noisome evil—to wit, the Gray Mouser. But unfortunately he came early to his appointment with my colleague here and was enticed into the shop of the Devourers and is doubtless now deep in their snares, if not already extinct. So you can see that we do take thought for your welfare and have no wish to overburden you with solo quests. However, My Gentle Son, if it still be your firm resolve—"

FAFHRD let out a sigh more profound than Ningauble's. "Very well," he said in gruff tones admitting defeat. "I'll do it for you. Someone will have to pull that poor little gray fool out of the pretty-pretty fire—or the twinkly-twinkly water!—that tempted him. But how do I go about it?" He shook a big finger at Ningauble. "And no more Gentle-Sonning!"

Ningauble paused. Then he said only, "Use your own judgement."

Sheelba said, "Beware the Black Wall!"

Ningauble said to Fafhrd, "Hold, I have a gift for you" and held out to him a ragged ribbon a yard long, pinched between the cloth of the wizard's long sleeve so that it was impossible to see the manner of hand that pinched. Fafhrd took the tatter with a snort, crumpled it into a ball, and thrust it into his pouch.

"Have a greater care with it," Ningauble warned. "It is the Cloak of Invisibility, somewhat worn by many magic usings. Do not put it on until you near the Bazaar of the Devourers. It has two minor weaknesses: it will not make you altogether invisible to a master sorcerer if he senses your presence and takes certain steps. Also, see to it that you do not bleed during this exploit, for the cloak will not hide blood."

"I've a gift too!" Sheelba said, drawing from out of his black cowl-hole—with sleeve-masked hand, as Ningauble had done—something that shimmered faintly in the dark like.

Like a spiderweb.

Sheelba shook it, as if to dislodge a spider, or perhaps two.

"The Blindfold of True Seeing," he said as he reached it toward Fafhrd. "It shows all things as they really are! Do not lay it across your eyes until you enter the Bazaar. On no account, as you value your life or your sanity, wear it now!"

Fafhrd took it from him most gingerly, the flesh of his fingers crawling. He was inclined to obey the taciturn wizard's instructions. At this moment he truly did not much care to see the true visage of Sheelba of the Eyeless Face.

THE gray Mouser was reading the most interesting book of them all, a great compendium of secret knowledge written in a script of astrologic and geomantic signs, the meanings of which fairly leaped off the page into his mind.

To rest his eyes from that—or rather to keep from gobbling the book too fast—he peered through a nine-elbowed brass tube at a scene that could only be the blue heaven-pinnacle of the universe where angels flew shimmeringly like dragonflies and where a few choice heroes rested from their great mountain-climb and spied down critically on the ant-like labors of the gods many levels below.

To rest his eye from *that,* he looked up between the scarlet (blood-metal?) bars of the inmost cage at the most winsome slim fair jet-eyed girl of them all. She knelt, sitting on her heels, with her upper body leaned back a little. She wore a red velvet tunic and had a mop of golden hair so thick and pliant that she could sweep it in a neat curtain over her upper face, down almost to her pouting lips. With the slim fingers of one hand she would slightly part these silky golden drapes to peer at the Mouser playfully, while with those of the other she rattled golden castanets in a most languorously slow rhythm, though with occasional swift staccato bursts.

The Mouser was considering whether it might not be as well to try a turn or two on the ruby-crusted golden crank next his elbow, when he spied for the first time the glimmering wall at the back of the shop. What could its material be?—he asked himself. Tiny diamonds countless as the sand set in smoky glass? Black opal? Black pearl? Black moonshine?

Whatever it was, it was wholly fascinating, for the Mouser quickly set down his book, using the nine-crooked spy-tube to mark his place—a most engrossing pair of pages on dueling where were revealed the Universal Parry and its five false variants and also the three true forms of the Secret Thrust—and with only a finger-wave to the ensorceling blonde in red velvet he walked quickly toward the back of the shop.

As he approached the Black Wall he thought for an instant that he glimpsed a silver wraith, or perhaps a silver skeleton, walking toward him out of it, but then he saw that it was only his own darkly handsome reflection, pleasantly flattered by the lustrous material. What had momentarily suggested silver ribs was the reflection of the silver lacings on his tunic.

He smirked at his image and reached out a finger to touch *its* lustrous finger when—Lo, a wonder!—his hand went into the wall with never a sensation at all save a faint tingling coolth promising comfort like the sheets of a fresh-made bed.

HE looked at his hand inside the wall and—Lo, another wonder!—it was all a beautiful silver faintly patterned with tiny scales. And though his own hand indubitably, as he could tell by clenching it, it was scarless now and a mite slimmer and longer fingered—altogether a more handsome hand than it had been a moment ago.

He wriggled his fingers and it was like watching small silver fish dart about—fingerlings!

What a droll conceit, he thought, to have a dark fishpond or rather swimming pool set on its side indoors, so that one could walk into the gracious erect fluid quietly and gracefully, instead of all the noisy, bouncingly athletic business of diving!

And how charming that the pool should be filled not with wet soppy cold water, but with a sort of moon-dark essence of sleep!—an essence with beautifying cosmetic properties too!—a sort of mud bath without the mud. The Mouser decided he must have a swim in this wonder pool at once, but just then his gaze lit on a long high black couch toward the other end of the dark liquid wall, and beyond the couch a small high table set with viands and a crystal pitcher and goblet.

He walked along the wall to inspect these, his handsome reflection taking step for step with him.

He trailed his hand in the wall for a space and then withdrew it, the scales instantly vanishing and the familiar old scars returning.

The couch turned out to be a narrow high-sided black coffin lined with quilted black satin and piled at one end with little black satin pillows. It looked most invitingly comfortable and restful—not quite as inviting as the Black Wall, but very attractive just the same: there was even a rack of tiny black books nested in the black satin for the occupant's diversion and also a black candle, unlit.

The collation on the little ebony table beyond the coffin consisted entirely of black foods. By sight and then by nibbling and sipping the Mouser discovered their nature: thin slices of a very dark rye bread crusted with poppy seeds and dripped with black butter; slivers of charcoal-seared steak;

similarly broiled tiny thin slices of calf's liver sprinkled with dark spices and liberally pricked with capers; the darkest grape jellies; truffles cut paper thin and mushrooms fried black; pickled chestnuts; and of course ripe olives and black fish eggs-caviar. The black drink, which foamed when he poured it, turned out to be stout laced with the bubbly wine of Ilthmar.

He decided to refresh the inner Mouser—the Mouser who lived a sort of blind soft greedy undulating surface-life between his lips and his belly—before taking a dip in the Black Wall.

FAFHRD re-entered the Plaza of Dark Delights walking warily and with the long tatter that was the Cloak of Invisibility trailing from between left forefinger and thumb and with the glimmering cobweb that was the Blindfold of True Seeing pinched even more delicately by its edge between the same digits of his right hand. He was not yet altogether certain that the trailing gossamer hexagon was completely free of spiders.

Across the Plaza he spotted the bright-mouthed shop—the shop he had been told was an outpost of the deadly Devourers—through a ragged gather of folk moving about restlessly and commenting and speculating to one another in harsh excited undertones.

The only feature of the shop Fafhrd could make out at all clearly at this distance was the red-capped red-footed baggy-trousered porter, not capering now but leaning on his long broom beside the trefoil-arched doorway.

With a looping swing of his left arm Fafhrd hung the Cloak of Invisibility around his neck. The ragged rib-band hung to either side down his chest in its wolfskin jerkin only halfway to his wide belt which supported longsword and short-ax. It did not vanish his body to the slightest degree that he could see and he doubted it worked at all—like many another thaumaturge, Ningauble never hesitated to give one useless charms, not for any treacherous reason, necessarily, but simply to improve ones morale. Fafhrd strode boldly toward the shop.

The Northerner was a tall broad-shouldered formidable looking man—doubly formidable by his barbaric dress and weaponing in super-civilized Lankhmar—and so he took it for granted that the ordinary run of city folk stepped out of his way; indeed it had never occurred to him that they should not.

He got a shock. All the clerks, seedy bravos, scullery folk, students, slaves, second-rate merchants and second-class courtesans who would automatically have moved aside for him (though the last with a saucy swing of the hips) now came straight at him, so that he had to dodge and twist and stop and even sometimes dart back to avoid being toe-tramped and bumped. Indeed one fat pushy proud-stomached fellow almost carried away his cobweb, which he could see now by the light of the shop was free of spiders—or if there were any spiders still on it, they must be very small.

He had so much to do dodging Fafhrd-blind Lankhmarians that he could not spare one more glance for the shop until he was almost at the door. And then before he took his first close look, he found that he was tilting his head so that his left ear touched the shoulder below it and that he was laying Sheelba's spider web across his eyes.

The touch of it was simply like the touch of any cobweb when one runs face into it walking between close-set bushes at dawn. Everything shimmered a bit as if seen through a fine crystal grating. Then the least shimmering vanished, and with it the delicate clinging sensation, and Fafhrd's vision returned to normal—as far as he could tell.

IT turned out that the doorway to the Devourers' shop was piled with garbage—garbage of a particularly offensive sort: old bones, dead fish, butcher's offal, moldering gracecloths folded in uneven squares like badly bound uncut books, broken glass and potsherds, splintered boxes, large stinking dead leaves orange-spotted with blight, bloody rags, tattered discarded loincloths, large worms nosing about, centipedes a-scuttle, cockroaches a-stagger, maggots a-crawl—and less agreeable things.

Atop all perched a vulture that had lost most of its feathers and seemed to have expired of some avian eczema. At least Fafhrd took it for dead, but then it opened one white-filmed eye.

The only conceivably salable object outside the shop—but it was a most notable exception—was the tall black iron statue, somewhat larger than life size, of a lean swordsman of dire yet melancholy visage. Standing on its square pedestal beside the door, the statue leaned forward just a little on its long two-handed sword and regarded the Plaza dolefully.

The statue almost teased awake a recollection in Fafhrd's mind—a recent recollection, he fancied—but then there was a blank in his thoughts and he instantly dropped the puzzle. On raids like this one, relentlessly swift action was paramount. He loosened his ax in its loop, noiselessly whipped out Graywand and shrinking away from the piled and crawling garbage just a little, entered the Bazaar of the Bizarre.

The Mouser, pleasantly replete with tasty black food and heady black drink, drifted to the Black Wall and thrust in his right arm to the shoulder. He waved it about, luxuriating in the softly flowing coolth and balm—and admiring its fine silver scales and more than human handsomeness. He did the same with his right leg, swinging it like a dancer exercising at the bar. Then he took a gently deep breath and drifted farther in.

FAFHRD on entering the Bazaar saw the same piles of gloriously bound books and racks of gleaming brass spy-tubes and crystal lenses as had the Mouser—a circumstance that seemed to overset Ningauble's theory that the Devourers sold only trash.

He also saw the eight beautiful cages of jewel-gleaming metals and the gleaming chains that hung them from the ceiling and went to the jeweled wall cranks.

Each cage held a gleaming, gloriously hued, black- or light-haired spider big as a rather small person and occasionally waving a long jointed claw-handed leg, or softly opening a little and then closing a pair of fanged down-swinging mandibles, while staring steadily at Fafhrd with eight watchful eyes set in two jewel-like rows of four.

Set a spider to catch a spider, Fafhrd thought, thinking of his cobweb, and then wondered what the thought meant.

He quickly switched to more practical questions then, but he had barely asked himself whether before proceeding further he should kill the very expensive-looking spiders, fit to be the coursing beasts of some jungle empress—another count against Ning's trash-theory!—when he heard a faint splashing from the back of the shop. It reminded him of the Mouser taking a bath—the Mouser loved baths, slow luxurious ones in hot soapy scented oil-dripped water, the small gray sybarite!—and so Fafhrd hurried off in that direction with many a swift upward over-shoulder glance.

He was detouring the last cage, a scarlet-metalled one holding the handsomest spider yet, when he noted a book set down with a crooked spy-tube in it—exactly as the Mouser would keep his place in a book by closing it on a dagger.

Fafhrd paused to open the book. Its lustrous white pages were blank. He put his impalpably cobwebbed eye to the spytube. He glimpsed a scene that could only be the smoky red hell-nadir of the universe, where dark devils scuttled about like centipedes and where chained folk gazing yearningly upward at the damned writhed in the grip of black serpents whose eyes shone and whose fangs dripped and whose nostrils breathed fire.

As he dropped tube and book, he heard the faint sonorous quick dull report or bubbles being expelled from a fluid at its surface. Staring instantly toward the dim back of the shop, he saw at last the pearl-shimmering Black Wall and a silver skeleton eyed with great diamonds receding into it. However, this costly bone-man—once more Ning's trash-theory disproven!—still had one arm sticking part way out of the wall and this arm was not bone, whether silver, white, brownish or pink, but live-looking flesh covered with proper skin.

AS the arm sank into the wall, Fafhrd sprang forward as fast as he ever had in his life and grabbed the hand just before it vanished. He knew then he had hold of his friend, for he would recognize anywhere the Mouser's grip, no matter how enfeebled. He tugged, but it was as if the Mouser were mired in black quicksand. He laid Graywand down and grasped the Mouser by the wrist too and braced his feet against the rough black flags and gave a tremendous heave.

The silver skeleton came out of the wall with a black splash, metamorphosing as it did into a vacant-eyed Gray Mouser who without a look at his friend and rescuer went staggering off in a curve and pitched head over heels into the black coffin.

But before Fafhrd could hoist his comrade from this new gloomy predicament, there was a swift clash of footsteps and there came racing into the shop, somewhat to Fafhrd's surprise, the tall black iron statue. It had forgotten or simply stepped off its pedestal, but it had remembered its two-handed sword, which it brandished about most fiercely while shooting searching black glances like iron darts at every shadow and corner and nook.

The black gaze passed Fafhrd without pausing, but halted at Graywand lying on the floor. At the sight of that longsword the statue started visibly, snarled its iron lips, its black eyes narrowed, it shot glances more ironly stabbing than before, and it began to move about the shop in sudden zigzag rushes, sweeping its darkly flashing sword in low scythe-strokes.

At that moment the Mouser peeped moon-eyed over the edge of the coffin, lifted a limp hand and waved it at the statue, and in a soft sly foolish voice cried, "Yoo-hoo!"

The statue paused in its searchings and scythings to glare at the Mouser in mixed contempt and puzzlement.

The Mouser rose to his feet in the black coffin, swaying drunkenly, and dug in his pouch.

"Ho, slave!" he cried to the statue with maudlin gayety, "your wares are passing passable, I'll take the girl in red velvet," he pulled a coin from his pouch, goggled at it closely, then pitched it at the statue. "That's one penny. And the nine-crook'd spy-tube. That's another penny," He pitched it. "And *Gron's Grand Compendium of Exotic Lore*—another penny for you! Yes, and here's one more for supper—very tasty, 'twas. Oh and I almost forgot—here's for tonight's lodging!" He pitched a fifth large copper coin at the demonic black statue and, smiling blissfully, flopped back out of sight. The black quilted satin could be heard to sigh as he sank in it.

Four-fifths of the way through the Mouser's penny-pitching Fafhrd decided it was useless to try to unriddle his comrade's nonsensical behavior and that it would be far more to the point to make use of this diversion to snatch up Graywand. He did so on the instant, but by that time the black statue was fully alert again, if it had ever been otherwise. Its gaze switched to Graywand the instant Fafhrd touched the longsword and it stamped its foot, which rang against the stone, and cried a harsh metallic "Ha!"

APPARENTLY the sword became invisible as Fafhrd grasped it, for the black statue did not follow him with its iron eyes as he shifted position across the room. Instead it swiftly laid down its own mighty blade and caught up a long narrow silver trumpet and set it to its lips.

Fafhrd thought it wise to attack before the statue summoned reinforcements. He rushed straight at the thing, swinging back Graywand for a great stroke at the neck—and steeling himself for an arm-numbing impact.

The statue blew and instead of the alarm blare Fafhrd had expected, there silently puffed out straight at him a great cloud of white powder that momentarily blotted out everything, as if it were the thickest of fogs from Hlal-river.

Fafhrd retreated, choking and coughing. The demon-blown fog cleared quickly, the white powder falling to the stony floor with unnatural swiftness, and he could see again to attack, but now the statue apparently could see him too, for it squinted straight at him and cried its metallic "Ha!" again and whirled its sword around its iron head preparatory to the charge—rather as if winding itself up.

Fafhrd saw that his own hands and arms were thickly filmed with the white powder, which apparently clung to him everywhere except his eyes, doubtless protected by Sheelba's cobweb.

The iron statue came thrusting and slashing in, Fafhrd took the great sword on his, chopped back, and was parried in return. And now the combat assumed the noisy deadly aspects of a conventional longsword duel, except that Graywand was notched whenever it caught the chief force of a stroke, while the statue's somewhat longer weapon remained unmarked. Also, whenever Fafhrd got through the other's guard with a thrust—it was almost impossible to reach him with a slash—it turned out that the other had slipped his lean body or head aside with unbelievably swift and infallible anticipations.

It seemed to Fafhrd—at least at the time—the most fell, frustrating, and certainly the most wearisome combat in which he had ever engaged, so he suffered some feelings of hurt and irritation when the Mouser reeled up in his coffin again and leaned an elbow on the black-satin-quilted side and rested chin on fist and grinned hugely at the battlers and from time to time laughed wildly and shouted such enraging nonsense as, "Use Secret Thrust Two-and-a-Half, Fafhrd—it's all in the book!" or "Jump in the oven!—there'd be a master stroke of strategy!" or—this to the statue—"Remember to sweep under his feet, you rogue!"

Backing away from one of Fafhrd's sudden attacks, the statue bumped the table holding the remains of the Mouser's repast—evidently its anticipatory abilities did not extend to its rear—and scraps of black food and white potsherds and jags of crystal scattered across the floor.

The Mouser leaned out of his coffin and waved a finger waggishly. "You'll have to sweep that up!" he cried and went off into a gale of laughter.

Backing away again, the statue bumped the black coffin. The Mouser only clapped the demonic figure comradely on the shoulder and called, "Set to it again, clown! Brush him down! Dust him off!"

But the worst was perhaps when, during a brief pause while the combatants gasped and eyed each other dizzily, the Mouser waved coyly to the nearest giant spider and called his inane "Yoo-hoo!" again, following it with, "I'll see you, dear, after the circus."

Fafhrd, parrying with weary desperation a fifteenth or a fiftieth cut at his head, thought bitterly. *This comes of trying to rescue small heartless madmen who would howl at their grandmothers hugged by bears. Sheelba's cobweb has shown me the Gray One in his true idiot nature.*

THE Mouser had first been furious when the sword skirling clashed him awake from his black satin dreams, but as soon as he saw what was going on he became enchanted at the wildly comic scene.

For, lacking Sheelba's cobweb, what the Mouser saw was only the zany red-capped porter prancing about in his ridiculous tip-curled red shoes and aiming with his broom great strokes at Fafhrd, who looked exactly as if he had climbed a moment ago out of a barrel of meal. The only part of the Northerner not whitely dusted was a shadowy dark mask-like stretch across his eyes.

What made the whole thing fantastically droll was that miller-white Fafhrd was going through all the motions—and emotions!—of a genuine combat with excruciating precision, parrying the broom as if it were some great jolting scimitar Dr two-handed broadsword even. The broom would go sweeping up and Fafhrd would gawk at it, giving a marvelous interpretation of apprehensive goggling despite his strangely shadowed eyes. Then the broom would come sweeping down and Fafhrd would brace himself and seem to catch it on his sword only with the most prodigious effort—and then pretend to be jolted back by it!

The Mouser had never suspected Fafhrd had such a perfected theatric talent, even if it were acting of a rather mechanical sort, lacking the broad sweeps of true dramatic genius, and he whooped with laughter.

Then the broom brushed Fafhrd's shoulder and blood sprang out.

FAFHRD, wounded at last and thereby knowing himself unlikely to out-endure the black statue—although the latter's iron chest was working now like a bellows—decided on swifter measures. He loosened his hand-ax again in its loop and at the next pause in the fight, both battlers having outguessed each other by retreating simultaneously whipped it up and hurled it at his adversary's face.

Instead of seeking to dodge or ward off the missile, the black statue lowered its sword and merely wove its head in a tiny circle.

The ax closely circled the lean black head, like a silver wood-tailed comet whipping around a black sun, and came back straight at Fafhrd like a boomerang—and rather more swiftly than Fafhrd had sent it.

But time slowed for Fafhrd then and he half ducked and caught it left-handed as it went whizzing past his cheek.

His thoughts too went for a moment fast as his actions. He thought of how his adversary, able to dodge every frontal attack, had not avoided the table or the coffin behind him. He thought of how the Mouser had not laughed now for a dozen clashes and he looked at him and saw him, though still dazed-seeming, strangely pale and sober-faced, appearing to stare with horror at the blood running down Fafhrd's arm.

So crying as heartily and merrily as he could, "Amuse yourself! Join in the fun, clown!—here's your slapstick," Fafhrd tossed the ax toward the Mouser.

Without waiting to see the result of that toss—perhaps not daring to—he summoned up his last reserves of speed and rushed at the black statue in a circling advance that drove it back toward the coffin.

Without shifting his stupid horrified gaze, the Mouser stuck out a hand at the last possible moment and caught the ax by the handle as it spun lazily down.

As the black statue retreated near the coffin and poised for what promised to be a stupendous counterattack, the Mouser leaned out and, now grinning foolishly again, sharply rapped its black pate with the ax.

The iron head split like a coconut, but did not come apart, Fafhrd's hand-ax, wedged in it deeply, seemed to turn all at once to iron like the statue and its black haft was wrenched out of the Mouser's hand as the statue stiffened up straight and tall.

The Mouser stared at the split head woefully, like a child who hadn't known knives cut.

The statue brought its great sword flat against it; chest, like a staff on which it might lean but did not, and it fell rigidly forward and hit the floor with a ponderous clank.

AT that stony-metallic thundering, white wildfire ran across the Black Wall, lightening the whole shop like a distant levin-bolt, and the iron-basalt thundering echoed from deep within it.

Fafhrd sheathed Graywand, dragged the Mouser out of the black coffin—the fight hadn't left him the strength to lift even his small friend—and shouted in his ear, "Come on! Run!"

The Mouser ran for the Black Wall.

Fafhrd snagged his wrist as he went by and plunged toward the arched door, dragging the Mouser after him.

The thunder faded out and there came a low whistle, cajolingly sweet.

Wildfire raced again across the Black Wall behind them—much more brightly this time, as if a lightning storm were racing toward them.

The white glare striking ahead imprinted one vision indelibly on Fafhrd's brain: the giant spider in the inmost cage pressed against the blood-red bars to gaze down at them.

It had pale legs and a velvet red body and a mask of sleek thick golden hair from which eight jet eyes peered, while its fanged jaws hanging down in the manner of the wide blades of a pair of golden scissors rattled together in a wild staccato rhythm like castanets.

That moment the cajoling whistle was repeated. It too, seemed to be coming from the red and golden spider.

But strangest of all to Fafhrd was to hear the Mouser, dragged unwillingly along behind him, cry out in answer to the whistling, "Yes, darling, I'm coming. Let me go, Fafhrd! Let me climb to her! Just one kiss! Sweetheart!"

"Stop it, Mouser," Fafhrd growled, his flesh crawling in mid-plunge, "It's a giant spider!"

"Wipe the cobwebs out of your eyes, Fafhrd," the Mouser retorted pleadingly and most unwittingly to the point, "It's a gorgeous girl! I'll never see her tickelsome like—and I've paid for her! *Sweetheart!*"

Then the booming thunder drowned his voice and any more whistling there might have been, and the wildfire came again, brighter than day, and another great thunderclap right on its heels, and the floor shuddered and the whole shop shook, and Fafhrd dragged the Mouser through the trefoil-arched doorway, and there was another great flash and clap.

The flash showed a semicircle of Lankhmarians peering ashen-faced over-shoulder as they retreated across the Plaza of Dark Delights from the remarkable indoor thunderstorm that threatened to come out after them.

Fafhrd spun around. The archway had turned to blank wall.

The Bazaar of the Bizarre was gone from the World of Nehwon.

The Mouser, sitting on the dank flags where Fafhrd had dragged him, babbled wailfully, "The secrets of time and space! The lore of the gods! The mysteries of Hell! Black nirvana! Red and gold Heaven! Five pennies gone forever!"

Fafhrd set his teeth. A mighty resolve, rising from his many recent angers and bewilderments, crystallized in him.

Thus far he had used Sheelba's cobweb—and Ningauble's tatter too—only to serve others. Now he would use them for himself! He would peer at the Mouser more closely and at every person he knew. He would study even his own reflection! But most of all, he would stare Sheelba and Ning to their wizardly cores!

There came from overhead a low "Hssst!"

As he glanced up he felt something snatched from around his neck and, with the faintest tingling sensation, from off his eyes.

For a moment there was a shimmer traveling upward and through it he seemed to glimpse distortedly, as through thick glass, a black face with a cobwebby skin that entirely covered mouth and nostrils and eyes.

Then that dubious flash was gone and there were only two cowled heads peering down at him from over the wall top. There was chuckling laughter.

Then both cowled heads drew back out of sight and there was only the edge of the roof and the sky and the stars and the blank wall.

The Goggles of Dr. Dragonet

To whoever wears the goggles of Dr. Dragonet there is another world—of mystery, joy and, yes, terror...

HAVE you ever thought what it would be like if we could see *minds?"* Dr. Hugo Dragonet asked.

"You've got something will do *that?"* I demanded.

Dr. Hugo Dragonet indicated the four pairs of black goggles scattered across the center of the gleaming gray table and sat back grinning at us like a genial old condor.

Marty, Alice and I eyed them suspiciously. The last time we had ventured to wear a gadget of the Doctor's—an innocuous-seeming sort of hearing aid—it had been to heal a nervous jungle murmur, which the Doctor had asserted was the sounds of the subconscious mind. Just a jungle murmur, a little like the background music for a darkest Africa movie, but after five minutes of it Alice had become hysterical, Marty had growled out a senseless accusation of murder against me, and I had had a terrifyingly vivid vision of the great city around us choked with vines a-crawl with huge snakes, a-rustle with giant spiders, and a-creep with great black panthers. Hypnotic suggestion, we had told ourselves afterwards, not very confidently. Although Southern California is a land of fakers, and Los Angeles a city of illusion, Marty, Alice and I find it difficult to write off Dr. Hugo Dragonet simply as a charlatan.

Now we looked at four pairs of black goggles. Each pair had a fine wire connecting one of the massive bows to a black-enameled power pack or control device about as big as a package of king-size cigarettes and reminiscent of the subconscious hearing aids.

"You say these gadgets will let you see thoughts?" Marty asked. The Doctor shook his head. "I didn't say thoughts I said *minds.*"

"I don't know that I like the idea," Alice said.

I didn't exactly like the four white canes hooked over the back of the Doctor's big chair. Taken together with the goggles they looked much too much like equipment for three blind men and one blind girl.

Nevertheless I reached out and gingerly drew the nearest pair of goggles to me along with its trailing flat black box. So did Alice and Marty. Dr. Dragonet's gadgets are always a shade more fascinating by the fact that they are frightening. He had the charlatan's gift of always arousing interest, sometimes by fabulous hints, sometimes as now by silence.

But he was grinning at me and the grin had a fatherly-sardonic twist to it, as if he had read my suspicious thoughts and was amused. Alice, Marty and I like to think of ourselves as reasonably mature—a fairly successful sculpture-actress, newspaperman and writer—but Hugo Dragonet has a way of treating us as if we are a trio of bright children, whom it pleases him occasionally to provide with wonderful toys. None of us can decide whether he is really a charlatan or a brilliant physicist-physiologist who works completely freelance and has not chosen (at least as yet) to share his important discoveries with the world of academic and industrial science. So far as we know, the Doctor supports himself solely—though quite lavishly—by specialized and little-known inventions in the realms of film and TV effects and by his occasional services as technical advisor to the studios on psychiatric and anthropological movies. If he cashes in on his important inventions (or his charlatanism, if it's that) we haven't an inkling of it and his patrons (or his victims) move in lofty circles quite unknown to us. What we are agreed upon, all three of us, is that we look forward to and are wholly fascinated by our little meetings with him—even if we always do feel a bit uneasy as we approach them.

AS I uncertainly fingered my own pair of goggles and carefully drew the companion box to me by the fine connecting wire, I wondered if this was one of the important inventions and if so how it would work. Four pairs of black goggles...four gleaming black king-size boxes, each with two tiny switches on it, one gray and rough, the other white and smooth...four white canes...I was still bothered by the implications.

Not that there was anything sinister about our surroundings, though they would have given a sensitive person a touch of vertigo. The cantilevered, black-flagged, magnesium-roofed terrace thrust out like the flying bridge of a futuristic ship from Dr. Dragnet's house, which lifted from an easterly crest of the Santa Monica Mountains, as if the house in turn were the figurehead of a ship of hills, with Hollywood below us to the south, the San Fernando Valley below us to the north, while before us to the southeast, sprouting white skyscrapers and slashed by freeways and only faintly hazed today by smog, stretched the central sections of sprawlingly spacious Los Angeles. Behind us were the mountains, the westering sun, and the invisible Pacific. The inevitable Hollywood note of the fabulous and fake was provided by a white-walled gilt-domed group of small buildings on the hillside just below. Even at this distance, looking across the intervening lawn and flowerbeds, we could read the neat black-on-white sign: GREATER COSMIC FELLOWSHIP.

The mildly exotic atmosphere of the terrace itself was pointed up by a few earthenware oriental figures and a remarkably realistic ceramic of a kinkajou, which looked as though the thick-tailed, dark yellow Asiatic carnivore had been frozen in mid-scamper along a dead branch.

Karl, the Doctor's squarely built chauffeur and precision machinist, sat on the northern verge of the terrace, where steps go down to the garage and the magnificent machine shop where he fabricates the Doctor's inventions, presumably including these goggles.

Karl was methodically turning the pages of *The Los Angeles Times*. Impet, the Doctor's slim black cat, snoozed in the sun on the southern edge. Otherwise we were completely alone.

The round gray-topped table was poker size. Alice sat to my left, Marty to my right, the Doctor across. The only things on the table were the four goggle-sets and a square of dull whitish sheet-metal about a foot wide.

Marty touched a goggle set. "See *Minds,* you said!" The Doctor just nodded.

I BEGAN to inspect closely the black instruments in my hands. I saw that I had been right in thinking of them as goggles rather than glasses, for although they had bows like glasses there was a wide spongy black flange going back from each lens that I could see would fit against the skin of cheek and orbit, shutting out all light from the sides.

Then I looked at the lenses themselves, first from the front, then from the back—without putting them on—in growing perplexity. All I could think of for a moment was a demonstration the Doctor had once put on for us of a girl who told colors blindfolded and read books through heavy cardboard. Alice made my point first.

"You can't see through them," she said. "They seem to be made of a black metal." She hadn't put hers on either.

Hugo Dragonet smiled and nodded.

Marty carried his own pair over into the sunlight. Impet looked up resentfully. Marty turned the glasses front to back toward the sun and looked through one lens cautiously.

"No, they're not like eclipse glasses," the Doctor called after him. "You couldn't see even an atomic blast through them. They're opaque to X-rays too, probably to *all* electric light—using the term to mean the whole electromagnetic spectrum."

Marty returned excitedly, "But if that's true, it's amazing, Doctor! This black metal would be the perfect material to shield atomic reactors! Might work for bomb shelters too!"

Hugo Dragonet yawned. Impet cradled his head between his paws and went back to sleep.

Marty flushed and chewed his lip. Besides being an incurable enthusiast, Marty is quite an idealist and patriot, and what he calls the Doctor's cynical and frivolous impracticality gets under his skin.

"To return to matters of real interest," the Doctor said, "these goggles *are* transparent to rays of both the gravitoelectric and magnetogravitic spectra and, when properly excited, will translate bands of those spectra into visible colors."

"But Doctor," Marty burst out, irrepressibly, "those other two spectra are just an obscure possibility from field theory. There's absolutely no evidence for their existence."

"Are you sure of that?" Hugo Dragonet asked softly, weighing the fourth pair of goggles in his palm. "However I don't insist that you accept my explanations," he added with a smile. "Explanations are never the most interesting part of science."

"Doctor, how do the goggles help to see minds?" Alice put in hurriedly.

"Why, my dear," he said, "they translate into electric or visible light two narrow bands of gravitic and magnetic light—if, purely for convenience, I may use those terms," he added elaborately with a sardonic little bow toward Marty. The Doctor likes to needle our young science reporter.

Marty blushed.

Keeping it simple like Alice, I asked, "How do minds show up in the gravitic and magnetic light?"

The Doctor did not answer my question. Instead he put on his pair of black goggles and tucked the attached black box into the top of his outside breast pocket with the two switches facing front.

It made him look like a blind man.

After a bit he reached his right hand across his chest and pushed the gray switch, then sat back stolidly, I got the impression he was counting under his breath.

Paper rustled faintly as Karl turned another page. Impet sat up and stared intently at the Doctor, seeming to study the change the goggles had made in his face. The sunlight struck bronze tints from the cat's black fur.

TIME stretched out. Karl swatted something with his newspaper—he has a thing about insects—and took up the next section.

Then the Doctor touched the white switch. Immediately he sat forward in his chair and looked long and carefully at each of us in turn—first me, then Marty, then Alice.

His goggles were more opaque-seeming than ever—round flats of dull black metal—but I never in my life had such an intense sensation of someone looking through me or rather *into* me.

He frowned at me—at least the vertical furrows deepened above the bridge of his goggles—and he gave a faint grunt of what sounded like surprise.

When he looked at Marty his grunt seemed to say "Just as I thought," but when he turned to Alice there was a rising note to his "Umm," as though he had found something that tickled his imagination.

"What *is* it, Doctor?" Alice asked nervously, shrinking back in her seat. "You're acting like an X-ray machine."

Hugo Dragonet smiled. "Why don't you try the goggles?" he said, "Why don't you all try them? And see for yourself? Just put them on and then follow my directions. Only one thing: once you're wearing them, don't take them off until I tell you."

Suddenly I was no longer reluctant but fumblingly eager to get the goggles on. I judged from my last jumbled glimpse that Marty and Alice were the same. But as the thick black flanges settled down against my skull, I had a flurry of unexpected panic. The rubbery material seemed not so much to touch my skin as to kiss it suckingly and for a moment I had the gruesome fear of suction applied to my eyeballs. I started to snatch the things off, then told myself not to be a nervous fool.

"Take it easy," I heard the Doctor say as if from a considerable distance. "Make sure they're comfortable. But remember, no peeking. And don't throw the little switches until I tell you."

I realized that in my rush I'd forgotten about the control box—if that was what it was—so I ghosted my fingertips down the wire from the left bow until they felt the box, which I slid halfway down into my breast pocket as I'd seen the Doctor do.

"Don't be in a hurry," he was saying. "Just as at the planetarium, if we wait a bit our eyes get more sensitive to the darkness."

But this was more than darkness, I realized with another spurt of inward panic, it was blackness complete and absolute. You know how when you close your eyes in no matter how dark a room, you always see churning specks of light and faint washes of color—even if you don't apply pressure, which can bring on blue flashes and all sorts of things? Well, now there wasn't anything of that sort at all, just velvety limitless darkness—*black* black, if I may call it that. It didn't make sense to me, because I'd always thought that the churning specks weren't due to light at all but just a random automatic discharge of a few of the retinal cells, which would go on whether there was an atom of light or not. Unless, I suggested to myself, the goggles had some sort of general inhibiting effect? It really seemed quite incredible that I should still be sitting on a bright terrace with dazzling golden sunlight striking a few yards away and not getting one hint of it—not even a reddish glow transmitted through the flesh of my cheeks—just because of a pair of goggles, and for a moment I had the thought of Dr. Dragonet rearing up leanly and blotting out the sun like some Old Testament prophet or medieval sorcerer. Or suppose these goggles literally blinded their wearer? Suppose—

I WAS about to disobey instructions and take the things off when I heard the Doctor say, "Now you might each of you gently depress the gray switch, as you saw me do. It's the rough-surfaced one.

"Don't expect to see anything startling, or even much of anything at all," he added. "This part is merely preliminary and doesn't work too well for everyone. But it creates a *framework.*"

At first I thought I must be one of the ones for whom this part didn't work, whatever it was, then I became aware that the absolute blackness had been invaded by large shapes of dark gray faintly edged with silver. At first I thought they made only an arbitrary geometrical pattern, but then I realized that they added up to an extremely dark picture of the table in front of me and the terrace around us—with this important difference, that my companions had vanished, I could see only the three empty chairs. But it was all extremely faint—maybe it was just my imagination, it occurred to me; or maybe the Doctor was using suggestion on me—some sort of hypnotic deal, as we'd tried to tell ourselves about the subconscious hearing aids.

"But I can't see *us,*" I heard Alice say excitedly. "I can't even see my own hand."

"It's like a very overdeveloped negative of the terrace with the people left out," I heard Marty add in puzzled tones.

"You are now seeing by gravitic light," came the cool but heavier voice of Hugo Dragonet. "Gravitic light is reflected by most inorganic materials—metals, minerals and so on—though not all—for instance, you can't see each other's goggles. But *all* organic materials—animals, plants, the clothing made from plant fiber or animal wool or simply any carbon-based material—are transparent to gravitic light and so don't show up."

I looked around. Sure enough, Karl and Impet were both invisible, assuming they were still sitting where I'd seen them last. Much more startling to me, the ceramic kinkajou was also gone, although the earthenware figures remained, suggesting that the kinkajou wasn't ceramic at all but some sort of literally frozen animal flesh, I started to ask the Doctor about it, then remembered that it usually doesn't do to ask Hugo Dragonet about extraneous mysteries glimpsed while exploring a main one. There are some parts of his life, such as his years in Vietnam—old Indochina then—that he doesn't talk about.

One of the many odd things about my present vision of my surroundings was that the sun-drenched outside looked no brighter than the shaded terrace. And it was a frighteningly *empty* world.

"Of course you are not seeing by gravitic light directly," the Doctor's voice cut in, "but by the electric light your goggles translate it into. The goggles are adjusted to keep it very dim. It's just a framework or background for what you'll be seeing next—by magnetic light. Which reminds me, it's time for you to throw the white switch—the smooth one."

THIS time I hesitated on the brink. Alice gave an involuntary cry in which there was more wonder than fear. I depressed my switch.

Over each of the three chairs, exactly where my friends' heads would be, hung a ghostly globe of colored light.

Marty's and Alice's were identical shades of green. Hugo Dragonet's was blue shot with streaks of dark red—and much brighter, though none of the globes were very bright, they were like compact clouds of phosphorescent mist.

And they weren't perfect globes either, Marty's almost was, at least it had very sharp boundaries, but its shape was that of a large egg tipped forward—the shape of Marty's brain if the skull were removed. Its green glow was brightest to the front.

By contrast the Doctor's globe was misty-edged. The dark red streaks that banded the bright blue kept fading, changing, reappearing.

Alice's globe tapered down into a ghostly but recognizable replica of her face. It was as if a gossamer mask hung from the green globe.

And that was all. No, not quite. On the table in front of Alice alone were very, faint folded curves of light, like fingers.

Then the Doctor spoke. His voice seemed to me to be coming out of the globe of blue light. Natural enough, I suppose—just normal sound-localization—but the effect was monstrously eerie.

"You are now seeing by magnetic light," the blue globe (I mean the Doctor) said. "Magnetic light is generated solely by mental activity—specifically by consciousness or awareness. I sometimes call it mind light. In fact, you're seeing minds."

"You mean we're seeing each other thinking?" the mask-trailing green globe on my left (Alice, of course) asked wonderingly.

"In a way, yes."

"We're seeing each other's thoughts?" she pressed.

"Alas, no. Perhaps some day we will find a prism, a lens, some way of refocusing mind light, so that we can actually see the little inner world of form and color and feeling that is another person's consciousness. But not yet. Now all we are seeing is the diffuse outward glow of inward awareness—the envelope or aura of thought. It's possible that throughout history a few individuals have been sporadically sensitive to mind light without translating goggles—accounting for persistent mystical beliefs about human auras and the halos of saints."

IT hit me all of a sudden what a terrific gimmick for spiritualism these goggles would be. Believers would pay limitlessly to see auras, to see their own minds glowing like spheres of pure incorruptible light. But right away I ran into the snag of the Doctor's apparent disinterest in con money or build-up. In any case my vague suspicions couldn't compete for long with the amazement I was feeling. The simple awe of the thing began to take hold of me.

"We're seeing brain waves," Alice said huskily.

"I don't believe so, my dear," the Doctor told her. "So-called brain waves are simply tiny rhythmic changes or electric potential in the flesh around the skull."

"But we *are* seeing nervous activity," Marty suddenly put in sharply.

"If that were true," the Doctor replied, "we'd see the spine, the whole nerve-tree, as sharply as the brain. No, we're seeing the glow of *consciousness*—that inward world of awareness that means life and identity that little cosmos locked inside the skull that is all of reality to each of us. As I've said before, we're seeing *minds.*"

None of us said anything for a while then, as it sank in. The awe of the thing gripped me completely. Mind Light!

"I'm not all locked inside my skull," Alice nervously broke the silence at last. "I can see my hands." And as she said that, the ghostly fingers became a little more definitely outlined.

"That's because you're a sculptress," the Doctor answered. "You send your awareness into your fingers—molding, shaping. You literally see and think with your hands—like some blind man I'd watched by magnetic light. By contrast Marty and Arthur show a sharply delimited consciousness, as if it actually were skull-bounded—they're word-and-idea men, rationalists.

"Whereas you're an artist," he continued to Alice, "and an actress too, highly conscious of your appearance. That's why you project your consciousness into your face as well as your hands."

"I do?" Alice sounded both ashamed and excited. "Doctor, is there some way for me to see myself?"

The Doctor chuckled. A dark grey rectangle lifted from the table. I remembered the square of whitish metal that had been lying there.

"Here's a mirror for mind light," he said to Alice. Her ghostly fingers gripped it, the filmy mask of her face grew a trace brighter as she stared at it, then it began to fluctuate as (I suppose) delight and embarrassment struggled together.

"What's the mirror made of?" Marty asked eagerly.

"Something quite unsuitable for reactor shielding or for wrapping gum," the Doctor told him sourly, then continued, "Projected awareness is rather common. Occasional unaided glimpses of it, due to magnetic sensitivity, may account for spiritualists' claims about ectoplasm."

Marty and I looked in turn at the reflections of our mind globes. Mine was sharply bounded like his but more toward the blue.

"Green and blue are the normal range," the Doctor explained, "Blue seems to link with introversion and contemplation, green with extroversion and action. The other colors come in when the *feelings* are involved. Yellow goes with joy, red with savage passions, orange with sensuousness, misery is gray. Violet I've almost never seen."

"Doctor," Alice asked, "why did you say 'Umm' that way when you first saw my mind? Because it was in my face?"

He chuckled. "No," he said, "more because it was exactly the same shade as Martin's—something I've seldom seen except in identical twins and long-married couples."

Alice said, "Hmm." Marty mumbled vaguely.

"Happily married couples," the Doctor added encouragingly. Then, "*I'm* a strange mixture, as you can see," he went on. "Blue, the philosopher's color, shot through with sudden animal impulses—the dark red. The old orang at the zoo has a mind that's *all* that second color."

"You've been out with these goggles?" I asked.

"Of course, Arthur. You wouldn't expect me to pass up a new way to pry into people, would you? I carry a white cane and pose as a blind man, mostly to justify the glasses. Karl always goes with me, pretending to guide me. Actually I do need his help from time to time—the dim gravitic background-light is not very useful in fast traffic. Besides, there are some people who don't have visible minds at all—

blacked-out drunks, for one thing—and I don't want to go bumping into them."

"Will *we* be able to go out?" Alice asked.

"You counted the canes behind my chair, didn't you? First though, we'll have a look at the mind-map. Come on."

THE banded blue globe rose and the doctor's chair pushed back. I got up cautiously, feeling at the table edge. It was very strange to feel it and to see it by gravitic light, but not see my hands that were doing the feeling—ghosts must have such sensations, I thought. Just then a very faint globe of yellowish light about as big as a tennis ball flashed up onto the table (or bounced up, it seemed to me) and moved toward the Doctor. The word *Poltergeist* jumped into my mind at the same instant, and I felt the back of my neck crawl, but just then the Doctor said, "Come on, Impet, you too," and the pale little globe was lifted close to the bright blue one.

"Cats do have minds, you see," he said, "All the higher animals appear to have consciousness and awareness."

I had a strong impulse to take off my goggles and check for myself that the weird sight was only the Doctor carrying his cat, but I remembered his warning and refrained.

"What's this mind-map and where do you keep it?" Marty asked.

"I'll show you," the Doctor said and led us toward the southern edge of the terrace. Although it was well-defined in gravitic light I felt uneasy about the edge because it's unrailed and at that point the drop to the flower beds is considerable, but the Doctor stopped short of it, and I noticed that an olive globe had appeared beside us—Karl, I supposed. Once more I suppressed the impulse to check.

"Look," said Dr. Dragonet.

The lights of Los Angeles seen from the hills behind Hollywood can be a most spectacular sight. Now it seemed to me as if I were seeing them on a very smoggy night, or—more precisely—seeing them as they would be if a giant rheostat dimmed all of them greatly though leaving hints of their neon coloring.

Gravitic light showed little of the city's structure and barely distinguished dark land from darker sky. It was almost a plane of solid black that backgrounded the faint glow of mind light that faded off toward the horizon in faint patches and rivulets.

We watched silently for some time. The Doctor said, "Notice how it keeps getting a little brighter? When you first switched on the magnetic light, you wouldn't have noticed any of this distant stuff at all. You'll go on getting more sensitive the longer you wear the goggles—up to three hours. But just one flash of ordinary light will cancel your sensitivity—that's why I warned you against peeking."

I asked, "What's the brighter glow due south? Downtown? And the one far off to the west?"

"You mean *that* and *that?*" the Doctor asked. A pale yellow blob moved to indicate the two directions—I realized he was using Impet for a pointer. "No, that's not downtown, that's the University of Southern California, while the one to the west is UCLA, though it may run into RAND. While that one off to the east over the hills—you missed that—is Cal Tech." He chuckled. "It amused me greatly to discover that more thinking actually does go on at universities."

He gestured again with Impet. "But many of those bright patches I can't interpret at all. I haven't explored them yet, or they keep shifting. And I can't explain that violet glow just below us. With one exception I've never seen violet anywhere else."

Alice said, "If your blue and red would mix, it might make violet."

Meanwhile I studied the glow he'd just pointed out and asked, "Doesn't that come from the Greater Cosmic Fellowship? But why should a bunch of crackpots have a rare color?"

Alice laughed nervously. "Maybe they're Martians. Great planet-hoppers, the Martians, especially in cartoons."

"What made you say Martians?" the Doctor demanded with a sharpness that startled me.

"I don't know—I guess I always call anything from off the Earth Martians," Alice explained fumblingly. "Doctor, I was only joking. I didn't really think you'd take me seriously."

"I know you didn't," he told her. "But you know me, I take everything seriously—except practical matters."

"What's the one violet exception?" I wanted to know.

"I may show you later, Arthur."

Marty now spoke up at last, his voice sighing with wonder, "Doctor, I've just been thinking what a terrific advantage mind light would be for espionage, or military patrolling, or even simple police work. Doctor, in this instance wouldn't you be willing to let the government in on—"

Dr. Dragonet yawned audibly, then tossed Impet to the floor and said briskly, "How about that outing I promised all of you? Good! Just remember to keep your goggles on at all times—one peek ruins the sensitivity. Karl, get the car—but first bring us the canes!

THE rest of that afternoon and night we saw Los Angeles as black canyons and caves through which minds streamed like globes of undissolving mist driven by random winds.

Karl not only chauffeured and shepherded us, but also quietly interpreted the passing scenes. Otherwise we would not always have been sure what we were watching, for a mind shows neither sex nor race nor (generally) age and certainly carries no signs of class or station, poverty or wealth.

We saw freeways racing with wraithlike gravitic-sketched cars, in each of which poised one or a few of the phosphorescent spheres.

We saw a silver-gray cemetery where minds floated like ghosts among the tombstones—unutterably eerie even after Karl had described to us the funeral party he saw by ordinary light.

We saw dim minds, murky orange mostly, behind the bars at the Griffith Park Zoo. The old orang's was dark red, just as the Doctor had said. Even the snakes had shadowy minds, though Karl would not accompany us into the reptile house. Karl classes snakes with insects and arachnids.

We saw the golden minds of a jazz band. We saw projected orange mind twinkling in the feet of a dancer.

In a church we saw a scattering of dim indigo minds, like patches of light from deep blue stained glass.

In a skid row bar we saw smoky amber minds winking on and off like fireflies.

We saw red minds in a gang rumble.

We saw a mind vanish suddenly in a crimson burst when a driver was thrown and killed in a freeway accident. That made us ask the Doctor a question. He answered softly, "Wearing the goggles, I have watched death in hospitals. The light only faded and then winked out."

We saw minds sun-hued with joy at the beach, glowing minds in a schoolroom, and (so Alice insisted) the silver-rosy minds of lovers.

Once we saw a violet mind in the rear of a car driven by an ordinary green mind, and remembering what the Doctor had said, we instantly asked Karl for a description. But our curiosity was thwarted in this instance—the car was a small panel truck. We asked the Doctor if this was the violet mind he'd promised to show us, but he denied it.

MANY times I was tempted to take off my goggles—more for the kick of verifying the incredible than because of fatigue or any lingering suspicions of trickery on the Doctor's part—but I hated to lose my ever-growing sensitivity to mind light. You see, by now I was becoming convinced that there was much more to be seen by mind light than I'd observed so far—faint things that hovered on the edge of vision. There was the suggestion that some minds had tenuous *tentacles* of mind light and that sometimes the tips of these tentacles plunged into other minds—I'll swear that once I saw one mind leading five or six others, like dogs on leashes.

There were hints, too, that some brains held more minds than one—shadowy splits and mergers, dominations, possessions, vampirisms, clashes, battles. Once I seemed to see a mind flow around another, engulfing or perhaps dissolving it. I kept peering—I admit it—for minds without bodies.

Also I occasionally seemed to see a trace of color in the cold gravitic gray of some material objects—as if some minds were projecting themselves into things, or even the inanimate itself struggling toward awareness.

I asked the Doctor about these things, whether they were reality or imagination, but he would only say, "Keep watching."

Finally he told Karl to drive us back to his home. We sped out of the mind-dazzle of the city into the blackness of the hills.

The Doctor said, "I'm glad you've all followed my suggestion about keeping the goggles on without Intermission. At least I hope you have. By now your eyes should be about sensitive enough for something rather special

I want to show you. The desert or the mountains or the open sea would be better, but this local outback will have to do. Slide back the top of the car, Karl."

A moment later, "Look up," said Hugo Dragonet.

Desert nights have taught me the shape of the Milky Way. Smog blots it out in Los Angeles or any other city.

But tonight, very faintly but definitely, I saw the unmistakable shape of our galaxy a-glow over Los Angeles with muted rainbow light.

"Mind," Alice whispered, "all over the universe, beating on us in tiny waves."

As she said that, I could almost feel it on my skin—incredibly delicate flakes sifting down.

"How can something faint as mind light travel so far?" I wondered.

Dr. Dragonet said: "Who can say how dim minds are on other worlds? Or how bright? There may be minds like novas."

"What's that point of violet light near the horizon to the south?" Marty asked suddenly.

"You should know," the Doctor told him, "I thought you kept track of the planets."

Marty said: "Mars."

The Doctor commented, "So you see why I was struck by Alice associating violet with Martians." He laughed thinly. "An interesting coincidence."

AT that moment the car was climbing past the small, gravitic-etched domes of the Greater Cosmic Fellowship—making another coincidence, I told myself.

"I'm going to regret taking these goggles off," Alice said, "and seeing things by ordinary electric light." I realized I felt reluctant about it too and I found myself recalling the German psychologist who wore glasses that turned everything upside-down for so long that upside-down became normal and when he finally took the glasses off, everything seemed to be standing on its head.

As Karl was putting the car away, we started up the stairs to the terrace, the doctor just ahead of me, with Marty and Alice lagging behind. In a few hours I'd got so used to gravitic light that the steep steps were no great challenge.

There was a sudden hissing ahead of us, then a single enraged or terrified squall. A small pale globe came streaking down past us from the terrace, not pausing at the Doctor's "Impet!"

I was beside him as we mounted the last steps. Marty and Alice were just behind.

I became aware of a wholly unfamiliar odor—acrid, nauseating.

A glowing sphere, the brightest mind I had seen yet, was on the other side of the terrace.

It hung only inches above the flagging.

Its color was violet.

Footsteps pounded on the steps behind us and I heard Karl call, "I'm coming, Doctor!" The olive sphere of his mind appeared beside me.

With a dry rustling like light bony plates or metallic feathers scraping together, the violet mind across the terrace swiftly reared up to a height of eight or nine feet.

There was a clucking gasp of horror beside me, a swallowed scream. Simultaneously Karl's mind flared and winked out and I heard his body slump to the flagging.

"Keep your goggles on!" the Doctor cried.

The next voice I heard came from the violet mind towering across the room. It spoke English, but it was the mechanical English of a talking machine, or voder, that is operated by a keyboard and puts words together like snippets of magnetized wire. Yet in spite of its mechanical quality it conveyed an impression of power, intellectual and otherwise, that made me cringe.

VODER: Dr. Hugo Dragonet, I presume?

DR. D: What do you mean, sir, by this unheralded intrusion?

VODER: Really, Dr. Dragonet, I think you have little cause for surprise.

As the conversation between the Doctor and the violet mind went on, I was several times tempted to take off my goggles. Along with my terror I felt an agonizing curiosity, a gnawing desire to know if I could bear to see what had made Karl faint—if that was all that had happened to him. Truthfully, I was grateful that the Doctor had ordered us all to keep them on. I was even more grateful for the courage and poise he showed as he answered the voder voice.

DR. D: It is true that I have been half expecting someone. At least I have considered the possibility. *(Then to us)* Keep the goggles on!

VODER: And you too, Doctor. It will be wiser if we do not see each other in the… I am not sure if "flesh" is the word I want, at least for myself.

DR. D: May I ask what attracted your attention to my dwelling?

VODER: Can't you guess, Doctor? We recently became aware that there were instruments in it sensitive to the magnetic light of consciousness. *Our* instruments detected *your* instruments.

DR. D: That seems reasonable enough.

VODER: Doctor Dragonet, are you aware of where I come from?

DR. D: I believe so. The Greater Cosmic Fellowship?

VODER: You are tactful, perhaps even elusive, I mean are you aware of where I come from—originally?

DR. D: If I must hazard a guess, the planet Mars.

VODER: That is correct.

DR. D: (to us) Keep the goggles on!

VODER: And now I must ask you, Dr. Dragonet, what you intend to do with your knowledge.

DR. D: Nothing. Nothing at all.

VODER: Excuse me, Dr. Dragonet, but I find that difficult to believe.

DR. D: Why, sir? What would you expect me to do?

VODER: Well, sir, I would expect you to inform your government, your police and military authorities, of the presence of Martians in the city of Los Angeles. Since most of your fellows have not been educated to an acceptance of intelligence in physical shapes different from their own, this information, once confirmed, would lead to raids, riots, panic, and a general demand for the immediate extermination of all the extraterrestrials. Attempts would be made to root out our innocent little observation post. Such attempts would encounter resistance, since we Martians are burdened with the same self-preservatory instincts as yourselves and have besides a certain dignity to maintain as peaceful extraterrestrial observers from a senior planet. The result would be a brisk skirmish—or more likely, as Mars is rather stuffy about protecting her own, a full-scale interplanetary war.

DR. D: Exactly.

VODER: Excuse me, I do not quite understand.

DR. D: I think you do. What I mean is that you have described exactly what would be likely to happen if I should inform Terran authorities about your presence on earth. And so, as I have already told you, I propose to do nothing. Nothing at all.

VODER: Ah! I must confess I did not expect such a civilized decision from an earthling.

DR. D: Come, come! Earthmen aren't absolute idiots!

VODER: I am beginning to appreciate that, Doctor. I must say I am greatly relieved that this is your decision. It excuses me from taking certain steps, unpleasant to you and your companions, which I would otherwise have been obliged to carry out.

DR. D: Or attempt to.

VODER: Yes, sir, attempt to. Though I fancy that with our greater destructive powers—

DR. D: *We* are not altogether powerless you know.

VODER: That too, I suppose, is possible. Excuse me for bringing up such unpleasant matters.

DR. D: Certainly, certainly.

VODER: Dr. Dragonet, can you offer us assurance that your companions will be properly secretive?

DR. D: I vouch for them. You have my word.

VODER: That is sufficient.

DR. D: Thank you. And now, I don't wish to seem inhospitable, but…

VODER: (The violet globe bowed with a repetition of the dry, rustling sound): Of course. I will depart immediately. I can understand that this interview must be something of a strain to junior minds. I trust, however, Dr. Dragonet, that there will be opportunities for you and I to discuss in private matters of interest to two philosophical denizens of the cosmos?

DR. D: Surely. Come back at any time I'm alone.

VODER: Thank you, Dr. Dragonet. Farewell, friends.

DIPPING close to the flagging again, the violet globe rapidly headed toward the edge of the terrace. Although I still found the accompanying rustling or heavy scuttling sound detestable, my earlier fears had been stilled enough by the strange urbane conversation I'd just heard so I thought I might risk a look.

I lifted my hands to my temples, but, "Keep the goggles on!" commanded Dr. Dragonet.

The violet globe went over the edge. Not long afterwards the Doctor said, "It's all right now, I imagine, to take them off."

Normal vision was something of an anticlimax. The terrace was very dark, and chilly. The first thing I did was turn on some lights.

The Doctor was kneeling by Karl, who came out of his faint quickly now and seemed almost embarrassed by it. Yet when asked what he had seen, he almost fainted again. Then he said firmly, "What I saw was some sort of black centipede four yards long with eyes big as saucers. It reared and swayed like a cobra. In its upper claws it had a black box with a keyboard on it."

At that point Marty, Alice and I all started to talk at the same time, but the Doctor, pleading weariness, refused to enter into a discussion of any sort. However, while scanning the flower beds below for evidence of the creature's trail between the terrace and the Fellowship, he did say, almost apologetically, to Marty, "I'm sure you can see why it's the better part of wisdom to keep the authorities out of cases like this."

Then gazing thoughtfully at the white walls looming faintly through the dark, he said, shaking his head, "You certainly never know whom you have for neighbors in Hollywood. Good night, children—I'm beat."

Impet appeared at the top of the steps, crossed the terrace in a very gingerly manner, and sniffed the spot where the creature had gone over the edge. Then, backing away with a hiss that seemed her last word on the subject, she went into the house.

"Good night," the Doctor repeated to us, following her.

Driving down from the hills with Marty and Alice I had a try at convincing them that the whole business could have been a hoax—at least the Martian episode (perhaps the Doctor simply had an earth friend with a violet mind)—but I didn't begin to convince even myself.

Deadly Moon

The girl had nightmares when the moon was above the horizon. But Dr. Snowden was not sure something infinitely more evil than a nightmare was at work in the girl's mind.

ALMOST a quarter of a million miles above the earth, the moon rode east in her orbit around the larger sphere at the cosmically gentle speed of two-thirds of a mile a second, though to those on the eastward spinning planet below, completing 27 turns for the moon's one, she seemed to move west each night with the stars.

A globe of almost airless, sun-blanched rock two thousand miles wide, Luna hung now beside the earth but moving out beyond her, away from the sun. The only face of her that earthlings ever saw was now half in the full glare of raw sunlight, half in darkness. It was the night of the half moon, or first quarter as it is commonly called.

But on this night of the half moon, Luna at last had two moons of her own, though they were as invisible to earthside viewers as the two tiny moons of Mars. Free-falling around her at almost a mile a second in tight orbits a few score miles above her cratered surface with its "seas" (*mares*) of darker rock, were two small manned ships, one of the American Space Force, one of the Russian Space Force. Making a swift circuit of the moon every two hours, the pilots of these ships were each rushing through independent surveys of the moon's treacherous pumice-powdered surface, in preparation for actual landings of larger exploration ships in the near future.

So more people than ordinarily were looking up at the moon from earth's evening side. But most of them were looking up rather more in fear than wonder. The past decade had been one of increasingly angry bickering between the leaders of the two great nations. The long-dreaded Third World War seemed very close and the neck-and-neck race to establish the first military base on the moon seemed only one more move bringing it closer.

Nor had the war-heavy atmosphere been improved by the recent suggestion, made almost simultaneously by a Russian scientist and an American military expert, that the moon would be an ideal spot for the testing, particularly in deep underground bursts—of atomic bombs, a research activity theoretically banned on earth itself.

At the moment the Pacific Coast of America was moving into earth's shadow under the half moon. The towering evergreen forest on the western slopes of the Cascade Mountains was dipping and darkening into night.

On a lonely hilltop that lifted out of the forest toward the center of the state of Washington, not far east of Puget Sound, two men and a girl were tensely watching the moon "rise"—Luna was already quite high in the southern sky—over the peaked roof of a white-walled Cape Cod style home.

The younger man could hardly have been more than a few years older than the girl—in his mid-twenties at most—yet he gave the impression of a matured thoughtfulness and poise. He was dressed for the city with the conservative elegance of a successful professional man.

The older man looked about fifty, though his mustache and eyebrows were still dark and his whole face strongly virile with its deep asymmetric vertical furrows between the brows. His rough sports clothes suited him.

He had an arm clasped around the shoulders of the girl, who likewise was dressed for the country. Her face was beautiful, but now although the evening was chilly, it was beaded with perspiration and it showed the taut, barely controlled terror of a woman who forces herself to watch an excruciating or deadly sight.

"Go on, Janet," the older man prompted harshly. "What does the moon make you think of?"

"A spider," the girl answered instantly. "A bloated white spider hanging just over my head in an invisible web. You see, I have a horror of spiders too, doctor." The last remark she shot as an explanation to the younger man. "...Or a revolver! Yes, that's it! A nickel-plated revolver with mother-of-pearl grips pointed at my chest—pointed at *all* of us—by a drooling, giggling old madwoman whose face is white with powder and whose cheeks have circles of violet rouge and whose yellowed lace dress—"

"I think that's enough demonstration, Professor McNellis," the younger man interrupted. "Now if we could go inside with your daughter—"

"No! I first want to prove to you, Dr. Snowden, that it's only the nightmares that are any real trouble to Janet, that this moon-fear hasn't in any way seriously cracked her waking nerves."

"No, and we don't want it to, either," the younger man retorted quietly.

"Go on, Janet," the older man repeated, ignoring the implied criticism. "What else do you see in the moon?"

"A man, a rabbit, a clown, a witch, a bat, a beautiful lady," the girl answered in rapid singsong. She seemed to have lost some of her terror, or at least some of her submissiveness, during the interchange between the two men. She chuckled uneasily and said, "Dad, anyone would think you were the psychiatrist, the way you're using the moon for a Rorschach test!" Then her voice went grave with insight. "The moon is the original Rorschach inkblot, you know. The *mares* are the faded ink. For thousands of years it's been hanging up there identically the same and people have been seeing things in it. It's the only solid thing you can look at in the heavens that has any shape or parts."

The older man's arm dropped away from the girl a little. "That's quite true," he said in an odd voice. "Yet I never thought of it just that way. In a lifetime of astronomical work I never had just that thought."

The younger man moved in, put his own arm around the girl's shoulders and turned her away from the moon. The older man started to oppose him, then gave way.

"And now, Miss McNellis, since you've made an original contribution to the science of astronomy," the younger man said lightly, "I think that will be enough lunar observation for tonight."

"You're the doctor," the girl told him, managing a little smile. "The Moon Doctor."

"That title's a gross exaggeration, Janet, hung on me by one silly newspaper story," he assured her, smiling back. "Actually I wouldn't go near the place. I'm afraid of space."

"Just the same, Dad got you because you're the Moon Doctor."

"He knows a million times more about the moon than I do. And I'm sure he also knows that it's perfectly normal for a girl whose boyfriend is orbiting around the moon to feel frightened on his account and to view the place he's exploring—or surveying—as an almost supernatural enemy."

"Janet's fear of the moon goes back a lot further than her engagement to Tom Kimbro," the older man put in argumentively.

"Yes, Dad, but I *am* frightened on Tom's account."

"You shouldn't be. Dr. Snowden, I've pointed out to Janet that she's no worse off than a girl engaged to one of the early polar explorers. Better, because polar explorers were away for years."

"Yes, Dad, but their girlfriend couldn't go out in the yard and see Antarctica or the northern icecap hanging in the sky and know that *he* was up there, invisible, but moving across it." The edge-of-hysteria note had returned to her voice and she started slowly to turn around. "I think the moon looks as if it were made of ice," she said with eerie faintness. "Dirty ice with lots of bubbles in it."

"Janet, that's a crackpot theory!" her father said angrily. "How you could even start looking at those *Welt-Eis-Lehre* pamphlets when your father's a legitimate astronomer—"

"It's getting cold out here. We can continue inside," Dr. Andreas Snowden said firmly. This time Professor McNellis did not protest.

The living room was quite livable in spite of the way it was crammed with books and glass-fronted shelves of small meteorites and other items of astronomical interest. After they had settled themselves and Prof. McNellis had poured coffee at Dr. Snowden's suggestion, the latter fixed the professor's daughter with a friendly grin for a few moments and then said, "And now I want to hear all about it, Janet. Ordinarily I'd talk to you alone, and tomorrow I will, but this way seems comfortable now. Let's see, your mother died when you were a little girl and so you've spent your life with your father, who is a great student of the moon, although his specialty is meteoritics—and just recently you've become engaged to Lieutenant Commander Tom Kimbro, pilot and crew of America's first circumlunar survey ship and infinitely more the Moon Man than I'm the Moon Doctor."

"I've known Tom for years, though," the girl added, smilingly at ease herself now that there was a roof overhead. "Dad's always been mixed up in the Moon Project."

"Yes. Now tell me about this moon-horror of yours. And please, Prof. McNellis, no professional interruptions no matter what comes up, even Cosmic Ice Theory."

He said it jokingly, but it sounded like a command just the same. The professor, less tense now that he was playing host, took it with good grace.

His daughter glanced gratefully at the young doctor, then grew thoughtful. "The nightmares are the worst part," she said after a bit. "Especially after they got so bad two months ago. I'm afraid of going crazy while I'm having them. In fact, I think I do go crazy and stay that way for ten minutes or so after I wake up. That was what happened two months ago when I reared out of bed and got Dad's revolver and shot off all the bullets in it through the bedroom window straight at the moon. I knew at the time that it was some sort of gesture I was making—I knew I couldn't hit the moon, or at least I was pretty sure I couldn't—but at the same time I knew it was something I had to do to save my sanity. The only other thing I could have done would have been to dive in our bomb shelter and never come out. You know, it was like when something's broken your nerve and made you cower, and if you don't strike out right away, no matter how convulsively…"

"I understand," the doctor said soberly. There was approval in his voice. "Janet, what happens in these dreams?"

"Nightmares, you mean. Nightmare really, for it's always about the same. It repeats," Janet closed her eyes. "Well, I'm standing outside and it's night and then the moon comes across the sky very fast, only it's much bigger and brighter. Sometimes, it almost seems to brush the trees. And I squinch down as if it were a big silver express train come out of nowhere behind me and I'm terribly frightened. It plunges out of sight and I think I'm safe, but then it comes roaring up over the opposite horizon, even lower this time. There's a hot smell as if the air were being burnt by friction. This keeps on over and over again, faster and faster, though each time I think it's the last. I begin to feel like Poe's man in 'The Pit and the Pendulum,' tied flat on the floor and looking up at the gleaming pendulum that keeps coming closer each whistling stroke until the knife-edge is about to slice him in two.

"But finally I can't help myself, I get curious. I know it's positively the worst thing I can do, that there's some dreadful law against it, that I'm defying some fantastically powerful authority, but just the same I reach up—don't ask me how I manage when the moon's going so fast, I don't know, and don't ask me how I reach so far when it's still in the treetops—sometimes it seems to press its cratered face down into the yard and sometimes I grow an arm long as the magic beanstalk—but anyway I reach up, knowing I shouldn't, and I touch the moon!"

"How does the moon feel to your fingers when you touch it?" Dr. Snowden asked.

"Hairy, like a big spider," Janet answered rapidly. Then she opened her eyes wonderingly. "I never remembered *that* before. The moon is rock. Why did I say it, doctor?"

"I don't know. Forget it."

Then, "What happens next?" he asked matter-of-factly.

Janet hugged her elbows and held her knees tight together. "The moon breaks up," she whispered. "It cracks all over like a white plate. For a moment the fragments churn around, then they all come hammering down at me. But in the instant before I'm destroyed and the world with me, while the fragments are still streaking down at me like bullets or an avalanche of rocks or a jack-in-the-box upside down, growing mountain-size in a moment—in that instant I feel this dreadful guilt and I know I'm responsible for it all because I touched the moon. That's when I go crazy." She let out a breath.

Dr. Snowden smiled. "You know, Janet, I can't help thinking how two or three thousand years ago your dream would have been regarded as a clear warning from the gods not to land on the moon—plus a prevision of the dreadful things that would happen to us if we kept on meddling sacrilegiously with the heavenly bodies. *No,* Prof. McNellis, I don't mean a word of that seriously," he added quickly as he noted that the astronomer's expression had become aggressively disapproving. "It's just that I make it a habit at a session like this of saying whatever comes into my head. I believe in bringing even superstitious thoughts out and looking at them. By the way, I'd say Janet's dream shows some elements of Cosmic Ice Theory, wouldn't you? See, I break my own rules as soon as I make them."

"If you dignify it with the name Theory," the professor replied sardonically. "A Viennese engineer named Hoerbiger started the whole *Welt-Eis-Lehre* business—a man with no astronomical training. His weird and wonderful notion was that the moon is made of ice and mud, that it came spiraling in from the infinite and will soon get so close to earth that it will cause floods and earthquakes and then break up, showering us with a fiery frigid hail. What's more, according to Hoerbiger, earth has had six previous moons, which all broke up the same way. This one we've got now is the seventh. Incidentally, the break-up of the sixth moon is supposed to have accounted for all legends of universal floods, fire-breathing dragons, falling towers of Babel, the Twilight of the Gods, and what have you.

"It's all nothing new, by the way. In the last century Ignatius Donnelly, who even got to be a member of Congress, wrote it all up in his book *Ragnarok,* except he used comets instead of moons—in those days they thought of comets as more massive. And now Velikovsky's done it again—gone over Hoerbiger once lightly, with comets. Took in some allegedly smart people, too.

"Hoerbiger developed one great set of followers at any rate—the Nazis. Most of them were suckers for pseudo-science. Cosmic Ice suited the Nordic superman perfectly.

"Of course, Janet knows all about this—she's read the junk, haven't you, dear?"

The doctor cocked his head and asked quickly, "Am I mistaken, Prof. McNellis, or isn't there nevertheless some shadow of a real scientific theory behind this notion of moons breaking up?"

"Oh yes. If a satellite with a plastic core gets close enough to its mother planet, the tidal action of the latter tears it apart. That's what's supposed to have produced the rings of Saturn—the break-up of a moon of Saturn that got too close. The crucial distance is called Roche's limit. In the case of earth it's only six thousand miles above the ground—Luna would have to be that close, even if she had the right kind of core, which she hasn't. It *has* been suggested—by George Gamow—that if everything worked out just right this situation might actually come about—in one hundred billion years!" The professor chuckled. "You can see that none of this stuff applies to our present situation at all."

"Still, it's interesting." The doctor looked back from father to daughter and asked casually, "Janet, do you believe in this *Welt-Eis-Lehre?"*

She shook her head while her father snorted. "But it's interesting," she added with a nervous, almost impish smile.

"I agree," Dr. Snowden said, nodding. "You know, Hans Schindler Bellamy, Hoerbiger's British disciple, had a very vivid childhood dream almost exactly like yours, that later helped convert him to Hoerbiger."

"Then you already knew what I was telling you about the Cosmic Ice farrago?" Prof. McNellis said accusingly.

"Only a bit here and there," the doctor assured him. "One or two of my patients were converts." He did not pursue the point. "Janet," he said, "I gather your own moon dreams go back to childhood, but they weren't so frightening then?"

"That's right. Except for one time when Dad took me on an ocean cruise just after mother died. I'd see the moonlight dancing on the water. The dreams were very bad then."

Prof. McNellis nodded. "We went to the Caribbean. You were just seven. Almost every night you'd wake up whimpering and blurry-eyed. Naturally, Dr. Snowden, I assumed Janet was reacting to her mother's death."

"Of course. Tell me, Janet, where is the real moon when you have these dreams? I mean, do they tend to cluster around the time of the full moon?"

The girl bobbed her head vigorously. "Once—just once—I remember having the nightmare in the daytime and when I woke up I saw the moon out of the window, faint silver in the pale blue afternoon sky."

Again Prof. McNellis nodded confirmation and said, "For years I've kept a record of Janet's dreams. In every instance the moon was above the horizon when the dream occurred. There were none during the dark of the moon—none of the hundred and seventeen Janet reported to me, at any rate."

The doctor frowned quizzically. "That's a rather astonishing circumstance, don't you think? To what do you attribute it?"

The professor shrugged. "I don't know. Maybe moonlight is the stimulus that triggers the dream, or was to start with."

"Yes," Janet said rather solemnly. "Doctor, isn't it an old theory that the moon causes mental upsets? You know, Luna and lunacy. And isn't there supposed to be something very special about moonlight? —Something affecting growth and women's monthly cycles and the electrical pressures in the blood and the brain?"

"Don't get off on that track, Janet," her father said sharply. "Another real possibility, Dr. Snowden, is that Janet has a moon-clock in her brain and that her subconscious only sends the dream when the moon is topside. I'm just telling you the facts."

Janet raised her hand. "I just remembered," she said excitedly, "that the exact position of the moon in the sky had a lot to do with my Caribbean dreams being so bad. Dr. Snowden," she continued anxiously, "you know that up north here the moon is never exactly overhead, that even when it's at its highest in the sky it's still south of the zenith?"

"Yes, I know that much," he grinned.

"Well, when we sailed to the Caribbean I remember Dad explaining to me that now we were in the Tropic Zone the moon could be directly overhead. In fact, on one night of the cruise it was directly overhead." She shivered.

"I think I remember telling you about that," her father said, "but I don't recall it making any impression on you at the time. At least you didn't say anything to me."

"I know. I was afraid you'd be angry."

"But why? And why should the moon being in the zenith frighten you especially?"

"Yes, Janet, why?" Dr. Snowden echoed.

She looked back and forth between the two men. "Don't you see? If the moon were straight overhead, it could fall straight down on me. Anywhere else, it might miss me. It's the difference between being in the mouth of a tunnel that may collapse at any minute and being in the tunnel."

This time it was the professor who chuckled. "Janet," he said, "you certainly did take this thing seriously when you were a tyke."

"I still take it seriously," she flared at him. "My feelings take it seriously. What holds the moon up? A lot of scientific laws! What if the laws should be repealed, or broken?"

"Oh Janet," was all her father could say, still chuckling, while Dr. Snowden commented, "Your feelings take it seriously—that's a nice phrase, Janet. But your mind doesn't take it seriously, does it?"

"I guess not," she admitted unwillingly.

"For instance," he pressed, "I don't know if it's possible, but suppose there should be a volcanic eruption on the moon, you know that the chunks of rock thrown up would fall back to the moon, don't you? That they couldn't hit the earth? Even if they were shot out toward the earth?"

"I suppose you're right," she agreed after a moment.

"No you're not, Dr. Snowden—not exactly," Prof. McNellis interjected, getting up. He was grinning with friendly maliciousness. "You say you're a man who believes in speaking his thoughts and settling for nothing less than reality. Good! Those are my own sentiments." He stopped in front of one of the glass-fronted cases. "Come over here, I've got something to show you. You too, Janet—I never told you about these. After your nightmares started, I always believed in playing down the moon to you, until Dr. Snowden convinced me of the superior virtue of always speaking all the truth."

"I didn't exactly say—" Dr. Snowden began and cut himself short. He went over to the case. Janet McNellis stopped just behind him.

Prof. McNellis indicated some specimens of what looked like blackish glass neatly arranged on white cardboard. Most of them seemed to be fragments of small domed disks, but a few were almost perfect buttons a half inch to an inch across.

Prof. McNellis cleared his throat. "Meteorites of this sort are called tektites," he explained. "They are found only in the Tropic Zone or near it—in other words, under the moon. The theory is that when large meteorites hit the moon, some fragments of the moon's siliceous—glassy or sandy—surface are dashed upward at speeds greater than the moon's low escape velocity of a mile and a half a second. Some of these fragments are captured by earth's gravitational field. During their fall to earth they are melted by the heat of friction with the air and take their characteristic button shape. So right here, in all likelihood, you are looking at bits of actual moon-rock, tiny fragments of—*Janet, what is it?"*

Dr. Snowden looked around.

Janet was leaning tautly forward, her gaze hypnotically fixed on the tektites. She was trembling visibly. "...like spiders," he heard her say faintly.

Suddenly her face convulsed into a mask halfway between panic and rage. She lifted her fists above her head and lunged at the glass. Dr. Snowden grabbed her around the waist; using his other arm to block her descending fists, and in spite of her struggles wrenched her around so that she wasn't looking at the case. She continued to struggle and he could feel her still shivering too.

The professor hesitated, then went out in the hall and called, "Mrs. Pulaski!"

The girl stopped struggling but the doctor didn't release her. "Janet," he whispered sharply, "what do *you* believe causes your dreams?"

"You'll think I'm crazy," she whispered back.

His arms hugged her a little more tightly. "Everyone's crazy," he assured her with great conviction.

"I think my dreams are warnings," she whispered. *"I think they're somehow broadcast to my mind from a station on the moon."*

"Thank you, Janet," the doctor said, releasing her.

Prof. McNellis returned with a stout motherly woman. Janet went to her. "'Scuse me, everybody, I was goofy," she said. "G'night, Dad, doctor."

When the two women were gone the two men looked at each other. The doctor lifted his empty coffee cup. As the professor poured for both of them, he said ruefully, "I guess I was the goofy one, shocking Janet that way."

"It's almost impossible to tell in advance how something like that will work out," the doctor consoled him. "Though I'll admit I was startled by those tektites myself. I'd never heard of the things."

The professor frowned. "There are a lot of things about the moon that most people don't know. But what do you think about Janet?"

"It's too soon to say. Except that she seems remarkably stable, both mentally and emotionally, for whatever it is she's going through."

"I'm glad to hear you say that."

"You mustn't worry about her cracking up, professor, but I also advise you not to put her in any more test situations."

"I won't! I think I've learned my lesson." The professor's tone grew confidential. "Dr. Snowden, I've often wondered if some childhood trauma mayn't have been the cause of Janet's moon-dread. Perhaps she believed that my interest in astronomy—to a child, the moon—was somehow responsible for her mother's death."

"Could be," the doctor nodded thoughtfully. "But I have a hunch that the real cause of Janet's dreams has nothing to do with psychoanalysis or *Welt-Eis-Lehre* or her anxiety about Tom Kimbro."

The professor looked up. "What else then?" he asked sharply.

The doctor shrugged. "Again it's too early to say."

The professor studied him. "Tell me," he said, "why are you called the Moon Doctor? The Moon Project recommended you—I didn't investigate any further."

"I had luck treating a couple of Project executives who had nervous breakdowns—but that isn't the main reason." The doctor held out his cup for more coffee. After taking a swallow, he settled back. "About two years ago," he began, "I had a run of private patients who had a horror of the moon mixed up with their other troubles. It seemed too much of a coincidence, so I sent out feelers and inquiries to other psychiatrists, lay analysts, mental hospitals, psycho wards, and so on. The answers came in fast!—evidently there were dozens of doctors as puzzled as I. It turned out that there were literally thousands of cases of mental aberration characterized by moon-dread, hundreds of them involving dreams very similar to Janet's about the moon breaking up—exploding, suffering giant volcanic eruptions, colliding with a comet or with earth itself, cracking under tidal strain, and so on."

The professor shook his head wonderingly. "I knew Project Moon had touched off a bit of a panic reaction, but I never dreamed it went that deep."

The doctor said, "In hundreds of cases—again like Janet's—there was a history of mild moon-fears going back to childhood."

"Hmm—sounds like the onset of the mass neurosis, or whatever you'd call it, coincided with the beginnings of high rocketry and space travel."

"Apparently. But then how do you explain this? For about four thousand dreams of moon breakup I got dates—day, hour, approximate minute. In ninety seven percent of those instances the moon was above the horizon when the dream occurred. I've become convinced that some straight-line influence traveling from the moon to the dreamer is at work—something that, like short radio waves, can be blocked off by the curve and mass of the earth."

"Moonlight?" the professor suggested quickly.

"No. These dreams occur just as often when the local sky is heavily clouded as when it's clear. I don't think light or any other part of the electromagnetic spectrum is responsible. I think it's an entirely different order of waves."

The professor frowned. "Surely you're not suggesting something like thought-waves? You know, doctor, even if there is such a thing as telepathy or extrasensory perception, the chances are it takes place instantaneously, altogether outside the world of space and time. The notion of thought-waves similar to those of light and sound is primitive."

"I don't know," the doctor said. "Galileo thought that *light* moved instantaneously too, but it turned out that it was just too fast for him to measure. The same might be true of thought-waves—that they go so much faster than light that they *seem* to move instantaneously. But only seem—another century may refine techniques for measuring their speed."

"But Einstein—" The professor shrugged. "In any case the notion of telepathy is completely hypothetical."

"I don't know," the doctor repeated. "While you were calling the nurse, Janet quieted and I took the opportunity to ask her what she thought was causing her dreams. She said, *'I think my dreams are broadcast to my mind from a station on the moon.'* Prof. McNellis, that is by no means the first time a patient with moon-horror has made that suggestion to me."

The professor bowed his head, massaging his brow as if it were beginning to ache. "I guess I don't know either," he muttered.

The doctor's eyes brightened. "But perhaps you do," he said softly. He leaned forward. "Prof. McNellis," he continued, "what is it that's really happening on the moon? What is it that you Project people have been observing on the moon's surface that you won't reveal to outsiders, not even to me? What is it that Tom Kimbro may be glimpsing now?"

The professor didn't look up, but his hand stopped massaging his forehead.

"Prof. McNellis, I *know* you've been observing something strange on the moon. I got unmistakable hints of it from one of my Project patients, but even in his condition he let himself be gagged by security regulations. What is it? You don't suppose I came way out here *only* to treat Janet, do you?"

For several seconds neither man moved or spoke. It was a contest of wills. Then the professor looked up shiftily.

"For centuries some astronomers, usually the less dependable ones, have been observing all sorts of 'strange' things on the moon," he began evasively. "One hundred and fifty years ago Gruithuisen reported seeing a fortress near the crater Schroeter. One hundred years ago Zentmayer saw mountain-size objects marching or moving across the moon during an eclipse. Bright spots have been seen, black spots, spots like giant bats—Charles Fort's books of newspaper-science are crammed with example. Really, Dr. Snowden, strange things seen on the moon are an old, many-times-exploited story." His voice had grown loud and assertive, but he did not meet the doctor's eyes.

"Prof. McNellis, I'm not interested in past observations of strange appearances on the moon," the doctor pressed on insistently. "What I want to know is what's being observed on the moon right now. It's my guess that it has nothing to do with Russian activities—I've heard through European colleagues that there's been a sizable outbreak of some kind of moon-psychosis, plus moon-dreams, in the Soviet Union too—so you don't have *that* reason for making security regulations sacrosanct. Please tell me, Prof. McNellis—I need the information if I'm to treat Janet successfully."

The professor twisted in his chair, finally said miserably, "It's been made top secret. They're mortally afraid of setting off a major panic, or having the whole Project canceled."

"Prof. McNellis, a panic *is* being set off and maybe the Project *should* be canceled, but that's nothing to me. My interest is solely professional—my own profession."

"Even when you were recommended to me as a psychiatrist, I was warned against telling you about the observations. And if Janet ever heard a word of them, she *would* go mad."

"Prof. McNellis, I'm a grown man, I'm reasonably responsible. I may need that information to save your daughter's sanity."

The professor looked up hollow-eyed, at last meeting the doctor's gaze. "I'll chance it," he said. "Two months ago our moon telescope in the 24-hour-satellite, where the seeing isn't blurred by atmosphere, began to observe activity of an unknown nature in four separate areas of the moon: near Mare Nectaris, in Mare Foecunditatis, north of Mare Crisium, and in the moon's very center by Sinus Medii. It was impossible to determine the nature of the activity. At first we thought it was the Russians secretly got there ahead of us, but Space Intelligence disposed of that possibility. The observations themselves amounted simply to a limited and variable darkening in the four areas—shadows, you might say, though one viewer described what he saw as 'towers, some moving.'

"Then two days ago the survey ship went into orbit—purposely an orbit that would take it over Nectaris and Foecunditatis. On his first pass Tom Kimbro reported glimpsing at both sites—here I quote him verbatim—*spiderlike or skeletal machines, towering thin creatures not men, and evidence of deep shafts being dug.*"

The professor jerked to his feet. "That's all," he said with a rapid shrug. "Since that first report, the Project's cut me off from information too. Whatever else Tom's seen—either confirming or negating those first glimpses—and whatever's happened to him, I haven't been told."

The hall door opened. "Prof. McNellis," Mrs. Pulaski said, "isn't Janet here? She said she wanted to speak to you, but the outside door's open."

The professor looked guilt-struck at the doctor. "Do you suppose she was listening from the hall? That she heard me?" The doctor was already moving past Mrs. Pulaski.

He spotted Janet at once. Her quilted silk dressing gown stood out like white paint. She was standing in the center of the lawn, looking up over the roof.

Motioning Mrs. Pulaski back and gripping the professor's arm for silence, he moved out beside the girl.

She did not seem to notice their approach. Her lips were working a little. Her thumbs kept lightly rubbing her fingertips. Her gaze, wide-eyed, staring, was fixed on the moon.

The doctor knew that his first concern should be for his patient, but now he realized that, even before that, he too must look at the moon.

Half-black and merged with space, half faintly mottled white, Luna hung starkly, her glow blanking out all but the most brilliant nearby stars. She looked smaller to the doctor than he'd been thinking of her. He realized, with irrelevant guilt, that although he'd been thinking a lot about the moon in the past two years, he hadn't bothered to look at her often and certainly hadn't studied her.

"The four sites?" he heard himself ask softly.

"Three of them are near the curving outer edge of the illuminated half," the professor answered as quietly. "The fourth is right in the middle of the shadow line."

Janet did not appear to hear them. Then, with no more warning than a gasp of indrawn breath, she screamed.

The doctor shot his arm around her shoulders, but he did not take his gaze off the moon.

Two seconds passed. Perhaps three. The moon did not change.

Then, by the curving edge, he thought he saw three tiny smudges. He asked himself what they could be at a quarter of a million miles. Giant cracks many miles across? Huge sections lifting? He blinked his eyes to clear them.

Then he was looking at the violet stars. There were four of them, brighter than Venus, although three were in the illuminated half disk at the same spots where he'd seen the smudges. The fourth, brightest of all, was dead center, bisecting the straight boundary between the bright and dark halves of the disk.

He kept looking—it would have been completely beyond his power not to—but the psychiatrist-section of his mind, operating independently, made him say loudly, "I'm seeing it too, Janet! We're all seeing it. It's real!" He said that more than once, gripping her shoulders tightly each time he spoke.

He heard Prof. McNellis croak, "Ten seconds," and realized he must mean the time since the smudges appeared.

The violet stars were growing less glitteringly bright and at the same time they were expanding. They became violet balls or round spots, still brighter than the moon, but paling, as big at the moment as ping-pong balls if you thought of the moon as a basketball, but they were growing.

"Explosion fronts," the professor whispered, continuing at intervals to croak the time.

Two of the spots, near the edge, overlapped without losing their perfect circularity. The central spot was still brightest, especially where it expanded into the dark half. The spots were big as tennis balls now, big as baseballs.

"Atomic charges. Have to be. Huge beyond imagining. Set *hundreds* of miles deep." The professor was still speaking in a whisper.

The doctor found he was hunching his shoulders in expectation of a shattering blast, then remembered there was no air to carry sound from the moon. Some day he must ask the professor how long it would take sound to get from the moon to the earth if there *were* air to carry it. He glanced at Janet and at the same moment she looked around at him questioningly. He simply nodded once, then they both looked up again.

The four spots all overlapped now, each grown to half the moon's diameter, and they were getting hard to see against the bright half—just a thin violet wash edged with deeper violet. Soon they were indistinguishable except for the one spreading from the moon's center across the dark side. For an eerie moment it outlined the dark edge of the moon with a violet semicircle, then vanished too.

"One minute," croaked the professor. "Blast-front speed 17 miles a second."

Where the first smudges and violet stars had been were now four dark marks, almost black. The central one was hardest to see—a jag in the shadow line. They were just large enough to show irregular edges to keen eyes.

"Blast holes. One hundred, two hundred miles across. As deep, probably deeper." The professor maintained his commentary.

Then they saw the chunks.

The ones blasted from the Crisium and Foecunditatis holes were already clear of the side of the moon and gleaming with reflected sunlight themselves. Three were large enough to show their jagged shape.

"The biggest. One twentieth moon diameter by eye. One hundred miles across. Big as the asteroid Juno. New Hampshire cubed."

It almost seemed possible to see the movement of the chunks. The doctor finally decided he couldn't quite. It was like trying to see the movement of the minute hand of a watch. Yet every time he blinked and looked back, they seemed to have fanned out a little farther.

"Four minutes."

It became clear that the chunks were moving at different apparent speeds. The doctor decided it might be because they had been thrown up at different angles. He wondered why he so wanted to keep watching them, perhaps so as not to have to think about them? He glanced at Janet. She seemed to be watching them with an almost relaxed interest. He probably need worry no more about her mind. Now that her fears had become something real and shared, she would hardly aberrate. No neuroses in wartime. One thing seemed likely about Janet, though—that she'd sensed the explosions telepathically. She'd screamed two or three seconds before he'd seen anything, and it takes light a second and a half to make the moon-earth trip.

There were some lights gleaming now on the dark side of the moon, near its center, one of them large enough to have an irregular appearance. Those must be chunks from Sinus Medii, the doctor told himself. He shivered.

The fastest moving Crisium chunks were now the moon's own width beyond the side of the moon.

"Eight minutes."

The professor's voice was almost normal again, though still hushed, as he calculated aloud, "One moon diameter in eight minutes. Round off to two thousand miles in five hundred seconds. Gives a chunk velocity of four miles a second. Needn't worry about the stuff from Crisium, Foecunditatis, even Nectaris. Won't come anywhere near us—miss earth by hundreds of thousands of miles. But the chunks from Medii are headed *here*, or near here. Starting near moon escape speed of a mile and a half a second it would take the chunks four days for the trip. But starting at around four miles a second, figure about one day. Yes, those Medii chunks should near-miss or hit us in about 24 hours—or at least close enough to that time so that we'll be on the impact side of earth."

When he finished he was no longer talking to himself and for the first time since the catastrophe began he had taken his eyes off the moon and was looking at his daughter and the doctor.

That he should be doing so was nothing exceptional. All over earth's evening side people who had been looking up in the sky were now looking around at each other.

The British Isles and West Africa missed the sight. There the moon, setting around midnight, had been down for a good hour.

In Asia and most of the Soviet Union it was day.

But all the Western Hemisphere—all the Americas—had a clear view of it.

The first conspicuous consequence was the rumor, traveling like a prairie fire, that the communist Russians were testing planet-killer bombs on the moon, or that World War

Three had already started there. This rumor persisted long after Conelrad was on the air and the National Disaster Plan in effect. In the Eastern Hemisphere it metamorphosed into the rumor that the capitalist Americans, ever careless of the safety of the human race and invariably wasteful of natural resources, were ravishing Luna, ruining earth's only moon to satisfy the lusts of mad stockbrokers and insane artillery generals.

Less conspicuously, but quite as swiftly, the telescopes of the west began to sort out the Sinus Medii chunks and make preliminary estimates of their individual trajectories. Organized amateur meteor watchers rendered significant aid, particularly in keeping up to date, minute by minute, the map of the expanding chunk-jumble.

Very fortunately for the world, clear weather prevailed, cloud-cover everywhere was at a minimum—though in any case clouds could not have interfered with probably the most important telescope involved—that on the 24-hour satellite hanging 22,300 miles above the Pacific Ocean south of Mexico.

First observations added up to this: headed toward earth was a jumble of chunks ranging down in size from a planetoid ninety miles in diameter, a dozen fragments ten or more miles across, some three score of mass of the order of one cubic mile, and presumably any number of smaller chunks plus a thin cloud of moon-gravel and dust. They would reach the immediate vicinity of earth in almost exactly one day, conforming remarkably to Prof. McNellis' rough estimate. Those that entered earth's atmosphere would do so at a speed low for meteorites, yet high enough to burn up the very smallest and to ensure that the large chunks, little slowed by the air because of their great mass relative to cross-section, would strike the ground or the seas with impact speeds around six miles a second. The strike would be almost completely confined to the Western Hemisphere, clustering around the 120th meridian.

As soon as this last item of news was released, trans-ocean airlines were besieged by persons loaded with money for tickets and bribes, and many did escape to the other side of the earth before most commercial planes were gone or grounded. Meanwhile numerous private planes took off on fantastically perilous trans-ocean flights.

It was good that the telescopes of the Americas got to work swiftly. In six hours the earth's rotation had carried them out of sight of the moon and the Sinus swarm. First the Soviets and Asia, then Europe and Africa, moved into night and had their view of catastrophe hurtling down.

By that time the chunks from the three explosion sites on the moon's western rim had moved out far enough to be almost inconspicuous among the stars. But the Sinus swarm, steadily growing in apparent size and gradually fanning out, presented a brilliant spectacle, those against the dark half of the moon pocking it with points of light, those against the bright half more difficult to see but the largest visible as dark specks, while those that had fanned out most made a twinkling halo around Luna.

Asian and Russian, then European and African telescopes took up the task of charting chunk trajectories, ably supplementing the invaluable work of the moon 'scope in the 24-hour satellite, which kept up a steady flow of observation except for the two hours earth's intervening bulk cut it off from sight of the Sinus swarm. The satellite 'scope was especially helpful because, observing at radio-synchronized times in tandem with an earth 'scope, it was able to provide triangulations on a base some 25,000 miles long.

With incredulous shivers of relief it gradually became apparent that the 90-mile planetoid and many of the other large members of the swarm were going to shoot past earth on the side away from the sun. At first they had seemed to be the ones most on target, but since at a right angle to their explosion velocity they all also had the moon's own orbital velocity of two-thirds of a mile a second, they drifted steadily east. A few might ruffle the top of the atmosphere, glowing in their passage, and all of them would go into long narrow elliptical orbits around earth, some of them perhaps slowing and falling in the far future, but that was now of less than no consequence.

It was in the chunks that had seemed sure to miss earth widely to the west that the danger lay. For these inevitably drifted east too—onto target.

With maddening but unavoidable delays the major bullseye chunks were sorted out and their points of impact approximated, approximated more narrowly, and finally pinpointed. Once given, an evacuation order cannot be effectively rescinded, and an error of twenty miles in calculated point of impact would mean many evacuees fleeing to certain death.

By nightfall in London it was clear that a plus-ten-mile-diameter chunk would hit somewhere in the South Pacific and a plus-one-mile chunk in the American Northwest or British Columbia.

These two chunks were of special interest because they were the ones that the Russians and American moon-survey ships elected to ride down last.

Both survey ships had the good fortune to escape the blasts, and both had large fuel reserves since it had originally been planned that each should shift orbits several times during the survey. As soon as they became aware of the blasts and their effects each pilot independently decided that his greatest usefulness lay in matching trajectories with the Sinus swarm and riding it down to earth. Accordingly they broke out of their circumlunar orbits and blasted toward the twinkling jumble of moon-rock between them and the gleaming sky-blue semicircle of earth, for them in half phase. As soon as, risking collisions with tail-enders, they were able to report that they had caught up with the swarm, their radio signals were of unique service in determining the trajectory of the swarm, supplementing telescopic observations.

But the self-imposed task of the survey ships was to become even more perilous. By exactly matching trajectories with a large chunk—a matter largely of eyework and finicky correction blasts—and then holding that course for a matter of minutes, the survey ship's radio signals gave earth stations an exact fix on that chunk and its course, though at first there were confusions as to *which* chunk, judging by scope, the survey ship was matching orbits with. Thereafter it was for the pilots a matter of blasting gingerly over to the next major chunk, risking collision with minor fragments every second, and matching trajectories with *that.*

In its final trajectory-matching, the Russian ship satisfied earth stations that the plus-ten-mile chunk would land in the open Pacific midway between Baja California and Easter Island and between the Galapagos and Marquises. Warnings of giant waves had already gone out to the Pacific islands and coastal areas, but were now followed up with more specific alarms.

Immediately thereafter the Russian ship went out of radio contact 30,000 miles above the equator, possibly broached by one or more chunks while blasting sideways into a circumterran orbit. Its exact fate as a piece of matter was never known, but its performance was enshrined in men's hearts and helped raise the framework of the International Meteor Guard.

Twenty-two minutes later the 24-hour satellite had its own "curtain raising" encounter with the western edge of the swarm. It was twice holed, but its suited-up personnel effected repairs. A radar man was killed and the moon scope smashed.

Meanwhile both Americas had an unequalled sight of the Sinus swarm as earth's own shadow line moved from Recife to Quito and on from Halifax to Portland. As it approached its "comfortable" 1500-mile miss of earth, the 90-mile "Vermont-cubed" chunk attained the apparent size of the moon—a jagged moon, shaped like a stone arrowhead. Fierce soot-painted Indians discharged barbed arrows back at it from the banks of the Orinco, while at Walpi and Oraibi white-masked Hopi kachinas danced on imperturbably hour after hour.

Everywhere in the United States families sat outdoors or in their cars, listening to Conelrad, ready to move if advised. Already some were filing out like dispossessed ants from known danger points, crowding highways and railways, jamming the insides and clinging to the outsides of coaches, buses, and private cars, many simply legging it with their portable radios murmuring—most refugees tried to follow the insistently repeated advice from Conelrad to "keep listening for further possible revisions in your local impact points."

In a few cities there was a fairly orderly movement into bomb shelters. Stampedes, riots, and other disturbances were surprisingly few—the amazing spectacle in the night sky appeared to have an inhibiting effect.

Bizarre reactions occurred scatteredly. Some splinter relgious and cultist groups gathered on hilltops to observe God's judgment on Sodom and Gomorrah. Others did the same thing simply for kicks, generally with the assistance of alcohol. A Greenwich Village group conducted solemn rooftop rites to propitiate the Triple Goddess in her role of Diana the Destroyer.

During the last hour several airports were invaded by survival-gangs and mobs convinced that only persons in the air when the swarm struck would survive the shock of impact, and a few overloaded planes, some commandeered, took off laboredly or crashed in the attempt.

Tom Kimbro rode the U. S. survey ship down along the final course of the plus-one-mile chunk, keeping about a quarter mile west of its raw gray side. While his ranging radio pulsed signals, he spoke a message over the voice circuit: "Ship's losing air. Must have sprung a seam on the last bump. But I'm safe in my suit. As I came from behind the moon on my last circuit, heading for the shadow line and Nectaris and just before I spotted the violet front and the Sinus chunks rising south, I think I saw *their* ships blasting away from the sun. There were five of them—skeletal ships—I could see the stars through them with barely visible greenish jets. They set off those blasts like you'd set off firecrackers to scare dogs, I don't know. Give my love to Janet."

Immediately after that he successfully swung west into a braking orbit and brought down the ship safely next day on the Utah salt flats. His final trajectory-matching had helped pinpoint the exact spot near the center of the state of Washington where the Big Chunk would land.

The moon is made of rock that averages out a little more than three times as heavy as water. The Big Chunk had a mass of rather more than a thousand million tons. Its impact at almost six miles a second would release raw energy equivalent to about 1500 nominal atomic bombs (Hiroshima type), nothing unimaginable in an era of fusion bombs. There would not be the initial chromatic electromagnetic flash (heat, light, gamma rays) of an atomic weapon. A typical mushroom cloud would be raised, but the fallout would be clean, lacking radioactives. The blast wave would be the same, the earth shock heavier.

The Big Chunk would be only one of several almost as large hitting the Western Hemisphere along with almost countless other moon meteorites, many of them large enough to produce impact energy in the atomic bomb range.

As the Sinus swarm traveled the last few hundred miles to impact or by-pass, gleaming with reflected sunlight in earth's night sky like so many newborn stars, a few showing jagged shapes, there was a breathtaking transformation. Beginning (for North American viewers) with these to the south, but rapidly traveling north across the sky, the lights of the Sinus swarm winked out as the chunks plunged into earth's shadow. To watchers it was as if the chunks had vanished. Some persons fell on their knees and gave thanks, believing that they had witnessed a miracle—a last-minute divine intervention. Then, again starting toward the south, dark red sparks began to glow almost where the Sinus lights had been and in the same general pattern, as the chunks entered the atmosphere and were heated toward incandescence by friction with air molecules.

Beginning in southern California, but swiftly fanning out north and east, every state in the Union had its own Great Sinus Shower. Dazzling ribbons and trails, ionization glows, heat glows, strange radio hissings and roars that came from the ground itself (energized by massive radio emanations from chunk trails in the ionosphere), explosions in the air as a few chunks tortured by heat blew apart, then the walloping deafening blast waves of the impacts, meteor-booms as their roar of passages finally caught up with the chunks, dust clouds spurting up to blanket the stars, wildly eddying winds, re-echoing reverberations.

Then, at last, silence.

Every state in the Union had its casualties, heroisms, and freaks. Seven hundred deaths were subsequently verified, grimly settling once and for all the niggling old dispute as to whether a human being had ever really been killed by a meteorite, and it was assumed that at least three hundred more perished unrecorded. The city of Globe, Arizona, was destroyed by a direct hit after a commendably orderly and thorough evacuation. Three telephone girls at a town near Emporia, Kansas, and four radar men at an early warning station north of Milwaukee stayed phoning Get-Out warnings and making last-minute observations until it was too late to escape physically from their point-of-impact posts. The inhabitants of a Saskatchewan village took a road 9 to death instead of a road 5 to safety, victims of someone's slovenly articulation. A Douglas DC-9 was struck and smashed in midair. A strike in the Texas Panhandle released a gusher of oil. A 25-square-block slum on Chicago's south side, long slated for clearance, was razed meteorically.

Except within miles of major impact points, ground shock was surprisingly slight, less than that of a major earthquake, seismograph recordings nowhere indicating energy releases higher than 5 on Richter's logarithmic scale.

The giant waves did not quite live up to expectations either and although according to some calculations the Pacific Chunk should have raised the water level of earth's oceans by four hundredths of an inch, this increase was never verified by subsequent measurement. Nor was any island of moon rock miles high created in the Pacific—only the Sinus Shoal, formed by the break-up of the Pacific Chunk on impact and the distribution of its fragments across the bottom. At the time of the impact several fishing boats, private yachts, and one small steamer were never heard from again and presumably engulfed. Another steamer had its back broken by the first giant surge and sank, but its crew successfully abandoned ship and survived to a man, as did three persons on a balsa raft. These last claimed afterwards to have seen the Pacific Chunk at close range "hanging in the sky like a red-hot mountain." Hours later, California, Mexican, and South American beaches were impressively slopped over and there was some loss of life in the Hawaiian Islands, though the inhabitants of the 50th state were by then far more interested in the volcanic eruption that had been touched off by the odd chance of a sizable moon-chunk falling into one of the craters of the volcano Mauna Loa.

Alaska, eastern Siberia, and most of the Pacific Islands reported daytime meteor roars and some scattered impacts—including the spectacular spray plumes of ocean strikes—while by an almost amusing coincidence the widely separated cities of Canberra, Yokohama, and the town of Okhotsk were each simultaneously terrorized by a daytime meteor that glowed and roared miles (some said yards!) above the rooftops and then reportedly departed into space again without striking anywhere.

Janet McNellis, her father, and Dr. Snowden rode out the Washington blast with no great discomfort in the Professor's bomb shelter, though the doctor always afterwards looked a bit sourly at people who spoke of the "trivial" earthquake effects of the Great Sinus Shower. By dawn the dust had cleared sufficiently, the great mushroom cloud blowing away east, so that they had a clear view from their hilltop of a considerable segment of the blast area, on the margin of which they had survived.

The house behind them had its walls and roof buckled somewhat, but had not collapsed. The glass had been blown out of all the windows, although they had been left open before impact. Everywhere the white paint was smoothly shaded with green, as though by a giant airbrush—the great fist of the blast wave had worn a green glove of leaves and pine needles.

The naked trees from which the latter had been stripped marched disconsolately down the hillside. About a mile away these standing wooden skeletons began to give way to a limitless plain of bare-trunked fallen trees that the blast had combed as neatly as straight hair. As one studied them it became apparent that the fallen trunks radiated out from a blast center beyond the horizon and some fifteen miles away.

"Precisely like Kulik's photographs of the impact site of the Great Siberian Meteor of 1908!" Prof. McNellis commented.

Janet sighed and snuggled her coat a little more warmly around her. "You know," she remarked, "I don't think I'm going to have any more moon nightmares."

"I don't imagine you will," Dr. Snowden said carefully. "Earth has now received the warning of which your telepathic dreams, and those of many others, were a prevision."

"You think they really were telepathic?" she asked half skeptically.

He nodded.

"But *why* a warning?" the professor demanded. "Why *such* a warning? Why not at least talk to us first?"

He seemed to be asking the questions more of the bare tree trunks than of his daughter or the doctor, nevertheless the latter ventured a speculative answer.

"Maybe *they* don't think we're worth talking to, only worth scaring. I don't know. Maybe they *did* talk to us—maybe that's what the dreams were. They might be a telepathic race, you know, and assume the same means of communication in others. Maybe they only set off their intimidation-blasts after we didn't answer them, or seemed to answer insanely."

"Still, *such* a warning."

The doctor shrugged. "Perhaps they thought it was exactly what we deserve. After all, we must seem a menacing species in some respects—reaching out for the stars when we're still uncertain as to whether it wouldn't be best for one half of our race to destroy the other half." He sighed. "On the other hand," he said, "maybe some of the creatures with which we share the universe are simply not sane, by our standards. Maybe if we knew all we could know about them with our limited minds, we'd still judge them maniacs. I don't know. What we do know now is something we should have known all the time: that we're not the only inhabitants of the galaxy and obviously not—yet—the most powerful."

Bread Overhead

The Staff of Life suddenly and disconcertingly sprouted wings and mankind had to eat crow!

AS a blisteringly hot but guaranteed weather-controlled future summer day dawned on the Mississippi Valley, the walking mills of Puffy Products ("Spike to Loaf in One Operation!") began to tread delicately on their centipede legs across the wheat fields of Kansas.

The walking mills resembled fat metal serpents, rather larger than those Chinese paper dragons animated by files of men in procession. Sensory robot devices in their noses informed them that the waiting wheat had reached ripe perfection.

As they advanced, their heads swung lazily from side to side, very much like snakes, gobbling the yellow grain. In their throats, it was threshed, the chaff bundled and burped aside for pickup by the crawl trucks of a chemical corporation, the kernels quick-dried and blown along into the mighty chests of the machines. There the tireless mills ground the kernels to flour, which was instantly sifted, the bran being packaged and dropped like the chaff for pickup.

A cluster of tanks, which gave the metal serpents a decidedly humpbacked appearance added water, shortening, salt and other ingredients, some named and some not. The dough was at the same time infused with gas from a tank conspicuously labeled "Carbon Dioxide" ("No Yeast Creatures in Your Bread!").

Thus instantly risen, the dough was clipped into loaves and shot into radionic ovens forming the midsections of the metal serpents. There the bread was baked in a matter of seconds, a fierce heat-front browning the crusts, and the piping-hot loaves sealed in transparent plastic bearing the proud Puffyloaf emblem (two cherubs circling a floating loaf) and ejected onto the delivery platform at each serpent's rear end, where a cluster of pickup machines, like hungry piglets, snatched at the loaves with hygienic claws.

A few loaves would be hurried off for the day's consumption, the majority stored for winter in strategically located mammoth deep freezes.

But now, behold a wonder! As loaves began to appear on the delivery platform of the first walking mill to get into action, they did not linger on the conveyor belt, but rose gently into the air and slowly traveled off downwind across the hot rippling fields.

THE robot claws of the pickup machines clutched in vain, and, not noticing the difference, proceeded carefully to stack emptiness, tier by tier. One errant loaf, rising more sluggishly than its fellows, was snagged by a thrusting claw. The machine paused, clumsily wiped off the injured loaf, set it aside—where it bobbed on one corner, unable to take off again—and went back to the work of storing nothingness.

A flock of crows rose from the trees of a nearby shelterbelt as the flight of loaves approached. The crows swooped to investigate and then suddenly scattered, screeching in panic.

The helicopter of a hangoverish Sunday traveler bound for Wichita shied very similarly from the brown fliers and did not return for a second look.

A black-haired housewife spied them over her back fence, crossed herself and grabbed her walkie-talkie from the laundry basket. Seconds later, the yawning correspondent of a regional newspaper was jotting down the lead of a humorous news story, which recalling the old flying-saucer scares, stated that now apparently bread was to be included in the mad aerial tea party.

The congregation of an open-walled country church, standing up to recite the most familiar of Christian prayers, had just reached the petition for daily sustenance, when a sub-flight of the loaves, either forced down by a vagrant wind or lacking the natural buoyancy of the rest, came coasting silently as the sunbeams between the graceful pillars at the altar end of the building.

Meanwhile, the main flight, now augmented by other bread flocks from scores and hundreds of walking mills that had started work a little later, mounted slowly and majestically into the cirrus flecked upper air, where a steady wind was blowing strongly toward the east.

About one thousand miles farther on in that direction, where a cluster of stratosphere-tickling towers marked the location of the metropolis of NewNew York, a tender scene was being enacted in the pressurized penthouse managerial suite of Puffy Products. Megera Winterly, Secretary in Chief to the Managerial Board and referred to by her underlings as the Blonde Icicle, was dealing with the advances of Roger ("Racehorse") Snedden, Assistant Secretary to the Board and often indistinguishable from any passing office boy.

"Why don't you jump out the window, Roger, remembering to shut the airlock after you?" the Golden Glacier said in tones not unkind. "When are your high-strung, thoroughbred nerves going to accept the fact that I would never consider marriage with a business inferior? You have about as much chance as a starving Ukrainian kulak now that Moscow's clapped on the interdict."

ROGER'S voice was calm, although his eyes were feverishly bright, as he replied, "A lot of things are going to be different around here, Meg, as soon as the Board is forced to admit that only my quick thinking made it possible to bring the name of Puffyloaf in front of the whole world."

"Puffyloaf could do with a little of that," the business girl observed judiciously. "The way sales have been plummeting, it won't be long before the Government deeds our desks to the managers of Fairy Bread and asks us to take the Big Jump. But just where does your quick thinking come into this, Mr. Snedden? You can't be referring to the helium—that was Rose Thinker's brainwave."

She studied him suspiciously. "You've birthed another promotional bumble, Roger, I can see it in your eyes. I only hope it's not as big a one as when you put the Martian ambassador on 3D and he thanked you profusely for the gross of Puffyloaves, assuring you that he'd never slept on a softer mattress in all his life on two planets."

"Listen to me, Meg. Today—yes, today!—you're going to see the Board eating out of my hand."

"Hah! I guarantee you won't have any fingers left. You're bold enough now, but when Mr. Gryce and those two big machines come through that door—"

"Now wait a minute, Meg—"

"Hush! They're coming!" Roger leaped three feet in the air, but managed to land without a sound and edged toward his stool. Through the dilating iris of the door strode Phineas T. Gryce, flanked by Rose Thinker and Tin Philosopher.

The man approached the conference table in the center of the room with measured pace and gravely expressionless face. The rose-tinted machine on his left did a couple of impulsive pirouettes on the way and twittered a greeting to Meg and Roger. The other machine quietly took the third of the high seats and lifted a claw at Meg, who now occupied a stool twice the height of Roger's.

"Miss Winterly, please—our theme."

The Blonde Icicle's face thawed into a little-girl smile as she chanted bubblingly:

"Made up of tiny wheaten motes
And reinforced with sturdy oats,
It rises through the air and floats—
The bread on which all Terra dotes!"

"THANK YOU, Miss Winterly," said Tin Philosopher. "Though a purely figurative statement that bit about rising through the air always gets me—here." He rapped his midsection, which gave off a high musical clang.

"Ladies—" he inclined his photocells toward Rose Thinker and Meg—"and gentlemen. This is a historic occasion in Old Puffy's long history, the inauguration of the helium-filled loaf ('So Light It Almost Floats Away!') in which that inert and heaven-aspiring gas replaces old-fashioned carbon dioxide. Later, there will be kudos for Rose Thinker, whose bright relays genius sparked the idea, and also for Roger Snedden, who took care of the details.

"By the by, Racehorse, that was a brilliant piece of work getting the helium out of the government—they've been pretty stuffy lately about their monopoly. But first I want to throw wide the casement in your minds that opens on the Long View of Things."

Rose Thinker spun twice on her chair and opened her photocells wide. Tin Philosopher coughed to limber up the diaphragm of his speaker and continued:

"Ever since the first cave wife boasted to her next-den neighbor about the superior paleness and fluffiness of her tortillas, mankind has sought lighter, whiter bread. Indeed, thinkers wiser than myself have equated the whole upward course of culture with this poignant guest. Yeast was a wonderful discovery—for its primitive day. Sifting the bran and wheat germ from the flour was an even more important advance. Early bleaching and preserving chemicals played their humble parts.

"For a while, barbarous faddists—blind to the deeply spiritual nature of bread, which is recognized by all great religions—held back our march toward perfection with their hair-splitting insistence on the vitamin content of the wheat germ, but their case collapsed when tasteless colorless substitutes were triumphantly synthesized and introduced into the loaf, which for flawless purity, unequaled airiness and sheer intangible goodness was rapidly becoming mankind's supreme gustatory experience."

"I wonder what the stuff tastes like," Rose Thinker said out of a clear sky.

"I wonder what taste tastes like," Tin Philosopher echoed dreamily. Recovering himself, he continued:

"Then, early in the twenty-first century, came the epochal researches of Everett Whitehead, Puffyloaf chemist, culminating in his paper 'The Structural Bubble in Cereal Masses' and making possible the baking of airtight bread twenty times stronger (for its weight) than steel and of a lightness that would have been incredible even to the advanced chemist-bakers of the twentieth century—a lightness so great that, besides forming the backbone of our own promotion, it has forever since been capitalized on by our conscienceless competitors of Fairy Bread with their enduring slogan: 'It Makes Ghost Toast.'"

"That's a beaut, all right, that ecto-dough blurb," Rose Thinker admitted, bugging her photocells sadly. "Wait a sec. How about—?

"There'll be bread
Overhead
When you're dead—
It is said."

PHINEAS T. GRYCE wrinkled his nostrils at the pink machine as if he smelled her insulation smoldering. He said mildly, "A somewhat unhappy jingle, Rose, referring as it does to the end of the customer as consumer. Moreover, we shouldn't overplay the figurative 'rises through the air' angle. What inspired you?"

She shrugged. "I don't know—oh, yes, I do. I was remembering one of the workers' songs we machines used to chant during the Big Strike—

'Work and pray,
Live on hay,
You'll get pie
In the sky
When you die—
It's a lie!

"I don't know why we chanted it," she added. "We didn't want pie—or hay, for that matter. And machines don't pray, except Tibetan prayer wheels."

Phineas T. Gryce shook his head. "Labor relations are another topic we should stay far away from. However, dear Rose, I'm glad you keep trying to out jingle those dirty crooks at Fairy Bread." He scowled, turning back his attention to Tin Philosopher. "I get whopping mad, Old Machine, whenever I hear that other slogan of theirs, the discriminatory one—'Untouched by Robot Claws.' Just because they employ a few filthy androids in their factories!"

Tin Philosopher lifted one of his own sets of bright talons. "Thanks, P. T. But to continue my historical resume, the next great advance in the baking art was the substitution of purified carbon dioxide, recovered from coal smoke, for the gas generated by yeast organisms indwelling in the dough and later killed by the heat of baking, their corpses remaining in situ. But even purified carbon dioxide is itself a rather repugnant gas, a product of metabolism whether fast or slow, and forever associated with those life processes, which are obnoxious to the fastidious."

Here the machine shuddered with delicate clinkings. "Therefore, we of Puffyloaf are taking today what may be the ultimate step toward purity: we are aerating our loaves with the noble gas helium, an element, which remains virginal in the face of all chemical temptations and whose slim molecules are eleven times lighter than obese carbon dioxide—yes, noble uncontaminable helium, which, if it be a kind of ash, is yet the ash only of radioactive burning, accomplished or initiated entirely on the Sun, a safe 93 million miles from this planet. Let's have a cheer for the helium loaf!"

WITHOUT changing expression, Phineas T. Gryce rapped the table thrice in solemn applause, while the others bowed their heads.

"Thanks, T. P.," P.T, then said.

"And now for the Moment of Truth. Miss Winterly, how is the helium loaf selling?"

The business girl clapped on a pair of earphones and whispered into a lapel mike. Her gaze grew abstracted as she mentally translated flurries of brief squawks into coherent messages. Suddenly a single vertical furrow creased her matchlessly smooth brow.

"It isn't, Mr. Gryce!" she gasped in horror. "Fairy Bread is outselling Puffyloaves by an infinity factor. So far this morning, there has not been one single delivery of Puffyloaves to any sales spot! Complaints about non-delivery are pouring in from both walking stores and sessile shops."

"Mr. Snedden!" Gryce barked. "What bug in the new helium process might account for this delay?"

Roger was on his feet, looking bewildered. "I can't imagine, sir, unless—just possibly—there's been some unforeseeable difficulty involving the new metal-foil wrappers."

"Metal-foil wrappers? Were you responsible for those?"

"Yes, sir. Last-minute recalculations showed that the extra lightness of the new loaf might be great enough to cause drift during stackage. Drafts in stores might topple sales pyramids. Metal-foil wrappers, by their added weight, took care of the difficulty."

"And you ordered them without consulting the Board?"

"Yes, sir. There was hardly time and—"

"Why, you fool! I noticed that order for metal-foil wrappers, assumed it was some sub-secretary's mistake, and canceled it last night!"

Roger Snedden turned pale. "You canceled it?" he quavered. "And told them to go back to the lighter plastic wrappers?"

"Of course! Just what is behind all this, Mr. Snedden? What recalculations were you trusting, when our physicists had demonstrated months ago that the helium loaf was safely stackable in light airs and gentle breezes—winds up to Beaufort's scale 3. Why should a change from heavier to lighter wrappers result in complete non-delivery?"

ROGER Snedden's paleness became tinged with an interesting green. He cleared his throat and made strange gulping noises.

Tin Philosopher's photocells focused on him calmly, Rose Thinker's with unfeigned excitement. P. T. Gryce's frown grew blacker by the moment, while Megera Winterly's Venus-mask showed an odd dawning of dismay and awe. She was getting new squawks in her earphones.

"Er...ah...er..." Roger said in winning tones. "Well, you see, the fact is that I..."

"Hold it," Meg interrupted crisply. "Triple-urgent from Public Relations, Safety Division. TulsaTopeka aero-express makes emergency landing after being buffeted in encounter with vast flight of objects first described as brown birds, although no failures reported in airway's electronic anti-bird fences. After grounding safely near Emporia—no fatalities—pilot's windshield found thinly plastered with soft white-and-brown material. Emblems on plastic wrappers embedded in material identify it incontrovertibly as an undetermined number of Puffyloaves cruising at three thousand feet!"

Eyes and photocells turned inquisitorially upon Roger Snedden. He went from green to Puffyloaf white and blurted: "All right, I did it, but it was the only way out! Yesterday morning, due to the Ukrainian crisis, the government stopped sales and deliveries of all strategic stockpiled materials, including helium gas. Puffy's new program of advertising and promotion, based on the lighter loaf, was already rolling. There was only one thing to do, there being only one other gas comparable in lightness to helium. I diverted the necessary quantity of hydrogen gas from the Hydrogenated Oils Section of our Magna-Margarine Division and substituted it for the helium."

"You substituted...hydrogen...for the...helium?" Phineas T. Gryce faltered in low mechanical tones, taking four steps backward.

"Hydrogen is twice as light as helium," Tin Philosopher remarked judiciously.

"And many times cheaper—did you know that?" Roger countered feebly. "Yes, I substituted hydrogen. The metal-foil wrapping would have added just enough weight to counteract the greater buoyancy of the hydrogen loaf. But—"

"So, when this morning's loaves began to arrive on the delivery platforms of the walking mills..." Tin Philosopher left the remark unfinished.

"Exactly," Roger agreed dismally.

"Let me ask you, Mr. Snedden," Gryce interjected, still in low tones, "if you expected people to jump to the kitchen ceiling for their Puffybread after taking off the metal wrapper, or reach for the sky if they happened to unwrap the stuff outdoors?"

"Mr. Gryce," Roger said reproachfully, "you have often assured me that what people do with Puffybread after they buy it is no concern of ours."

"I seem to recall," Rose Thinker chirped somewhat unkindly, "that dictum was created to answer inquiries after Roger put the famous sculptures-in-miniature artist on 3D and he testified that he always molded his first attempts from Puffybread, one jumbo loaf squeezing down to approximately the size of a peanut."

HER photocells dimmed and brightened. "Oh, boy—hydrogen! The loafs unwrapped. After a while, in spite of the crust-seal, a little oxygen diffuses in. An explosive mixture. Housewife in curlers and kimono pops a couple slices in the toaster. *Boom!*"

The three human beings in the room winced.

Tin Philosopher kicked her under the table, while observing, "So you see, Roger, that the non-delivery of the hydrogen loaf carries some consolations. And I must confess that one aspect of the affair gives me great satisfaction, not as a Board Member but as a private machine. You have at last made a reality of the 'rises through the air' part of Puffybread's theme. They can't ever take that away from you.

By now, half the inhabitants of the Great Plains must have observed our flying loaves rising high."

Phineas T. Gryce shot a frightened look at the west windows and found his full voice.

"Stop the mills!" he roared at Meg Winterly, who nodded and whispered urgently into her mike.

"A sensible suggestion," Tin Philosopher said. "But it comes a trifle late in the day. If the mills are still walking and grinding, approximately seven billion Puffyloaves are at this moment cruising eastward over Middle America. Remember that a six-month supply for deep-freeze is involved and that the current consumption of bread, due to its matchless airiness, is eight and one-half loaves per person per day."

Phineas T. Gryce carefully inserted both hands into his scanty hair, feeling for a good grip. He leaned menacingly toward Roger who, chin resting on the table, regarded him apathetically.

"Hold it!" Meg called sharply. "Flock of multiple-urgents coming in. News Liaison: information bureaus swamped with flying-bread inquiries. Aero-expresslines: Clear our airways or face law suit. U. S. Army: Why do loaves flame when hit by incendiary bullets? U. S. Customs: If bread intended for export, get export license or face prosecution. Russian Consulate in Chicago: Advise on destination of bread-lift. And some Kansas church is accusing us of a hoax inciting to blasphemy, of faking miracles—I don't know *why*"

The business girl tore off her headphones. "Roger Snedden," she cried with a hysteria that would have dumfounded her underlings, "you've brought the name of Puffyloaf in front of the whole world, all right! Now do something about the situation!"

Roger nodded obediently. But his pallor increased a shade, the pupils of his eyes disappeared under the upper lids, and his head burrowed beneath his forearms.

"Oh, boy," Rose Thinker called gaily to Tin Philosopher, "this looks like the start of a real crisis session! Did you remember to bring spare batteries?"

MEANWHILE, the monstrous flight of Puffy loaves, filling midwestern skies as no small fliers had since the days of the passenger pigeon, soared steadily onward.

Private fliers approached the brown and glistening bread-front in curiosity and dipped back in awe. Aero-expresslines organized sightseeing flights along the flanks. Planes of the government forestry and agricultural services and 'copters bearing the Puffyloaf emblem hovered on the fringes, watching developments and waiting for orders. A squadron of supersonic fighters hung menacingly above.

The behavior of birds varied considerably. Most fled or gave the loaves a wide berth, but some bolder species, discovering the minimal nutritive nature of the translucent brown objects, attacked them furiously with beaks and claws. Hydrogen diffusing slowly through the crusts had now distended most of the sealed plastic wrappers into little balloons, which ruptured, when pierced, with disconcerting *pops*.

Below, neck-craning citizens crowded streets and back yards, cranks and cultists had a field day, while local and national governments raged indiscriminately at Puffyloaf and at each other.

Rumors that a fusion weapon would be exploded in the midst of the flying bread drew angry protests from conservationists and a flood of telefax pamphlets titled "H-Loaf or H-bomb?"

Stockholm sent a mystifying note of praise to the United Nations Food Organization.

Delhi issued nervous denials of a millet blight that no one had heard of until that moment and reaffirmed India's ability to feed her population with no outside help except the usual.

Radio Moscow asserted that the Kremlin would brook no interference in its treatment of Ukrainians, jokingly referred to the flying bread as a farce perpetrated by mad internationalists inhabiting Cloud Cuckoo Land, added contradictory references to airborne bread booby-trapped by Capitalist gangsters, and then fell moodily silent on the whole topic.

Radio Venus reported to its winged audience that Earth's inhabitants were establishing food depots in the upper air, preparatory to taking up permanent aerial residence "such as we have always enjoyed on Venus."

NEWNEW YORK made feverish preparations for the passage of the flying bread. Tickets for sightseeing space in skyscrapers were sold at high prices; cold meats and potted spreads were hawked to viewers with the assurance that they would be able to snag the bread out of the air and enjoy a historic sandwich.

Phineas T. Gryce, escaping from his own managerial suite, raged about the city, demanding general cooperation in the stretching of great nets between the skyscrapers to trap the errant loaves. He was captured by Tin Philosopher, escaped again, and was found posted with oxygen mask and submachine gun on the topmost spire of Puffyloaf Tower, apparently determined to shoot down the loaves as they appeared and before they involved his company in more trouble with Customs and the State Department.

Recaptured by Tin Philosopher, who suffered only minor bullet holes, he was given a series of mild electroshocks and returned to the conference table, calm and clearheaded as ever.

But the bread flight, swinging away from a hurricane moving up the Atlantic coast, crossed a clouded-in Boston by night and disappeared into a high Atlantic overcast, also thereby evading a local storm generated by the Weather Department in a last minute effort to bring down or at least disperse the H-loaves.

Warnings and counter warnings by Communist and Capitalist governments seriously interfered with military trailing of the flight during this period and it was actually lost in touch with for several days.

At scattered points, seagulls were observed fighting over individual loaves floating down from the gray roof—that was all.

A mood of spirituality, strongly tinged with humor, seized the people of the world. Ministers sermonized about the bread, variously interpreting it as a call to charity, a warning against gluttony, a parable of the evanescence of all earthly things, and a divine joke. Husbands and wives, facing each other across their walls of breakfast toast, burst into laughter. The mere sight of a loaf of bread anywhere was enough to evoke guffaws. An obscure sect, having as part of its creed the injunction "Don't take yourself so damn Seriously," won new adherents.

The bread flight, rising above an Atlantic storm widely reported to have destroyed it, passed unobserved across a foggy England and rose out of the overcast only over Mittel-europa. The loaves had at last reached their maximum altitude.

The Sun's rays beat through the rarified air on the distended plastic wrappers, increasing still further the pressure of the confined hydrogen. They burst by the millions and tens of millions. A high-flying Bulgarian evangelist, who had happened to mistake the up-lever for the east-lever in the cockpit of his flier and who was the sole witness of the event, afterward described it as "the foaming of a sea of diamonds, the crackle of God's knuckles."

BY THE millions and tens of millions, the loaves coasted down into the starving Ukraine. Shaken by a week of humor that threatened to invade even its own grim precincts, the Kremlin made a sudden about-face. A new policy was instituted of communal ownership of the produce of communal farms, and teams of hunger-fighters and caravans of trucks loaded with pumpernickel were dispatched into the Ukraine.

World distribution was given to a series of photographs showing peasants queuing up to trade scavenged Puffyloaves for traditional black bread, recently aerated itself but still extra solid by comparison, the rate of exchange demanded by the Moscow teams being twenty Puffyloaves to one of pumpernickel.

Another series of photographs, picturing chubby workers' children being blown to bits by booby-trapped bread, was quietly destroyed.

Congratulatory notes were exchanged by various national governments and world organizations, including the Brotherhood of Free Business Machines. The great bread flight was over, though for several weeks afterward scattered falls of loaves occurred, giving rise to a new folklore of manna among lonely Arabian tribesmen, and in one well-authenticated instance in Tibet, sustaining life in a party of mountaineers cut off by a snow slide.

Back in NewNew York, the managerial board of Puffy Products slumped in utter collapse around the conference table, the long crisis session at last ended.

Empty coffee cartons were scattered around the chairs of the three humans, dead batteries around those of the two machines. For a while, there was no movement whatsoever. Then Roger Snedden reached out wearily for the earphones where Megera Winterly had hurled them down, adjusted them to his head, pushed a button and listened apathetically.

After a bit, his gaze brightened. He pushed more buttons and listened more eagerly. Soon he was sitting tensely upright on his stool; eyes bright and lower face all a-smile, muttering terse comments and questions into the lapel mike torn from Meg's fair neck.

The others, reviving, watched him, at first dully, then with quickening interest, especially when he jerked off the earphones with a happy shout and sprang to his feet.

"LISTEN to this!" he cried in a ringing voice. "As a result of the worldwide publicity, Puffyloaves are outselling Fairy Bread three to one—and that's just the old carbon-dioxide stock from our freezers! It's almost exhausted, but the government, now that the Ukrainian crisis is over, has taken the ban off helium and will also sell us stockpiled wheat if we need it. We can have our walking mills burrowing into the wheat caves in a matter of hours!

"But that isn't all! The far greater demand everywhere is for Puffyloaves that will actually float. Public Relations, Child Liaison Division, reports that the kiddies are making their mothers' lives miserable about it. If only we can figure out some way to make hydrogen non-explosive or the helium loaf float just a little—"

"I'm sure we can take care of that quite handily," Tin Philosopher interrupted briskly. "Puffyloaf has kept it a corporation secret—even you've never been told about it—but just before he went crazy, Everett Whitehead discovered a way to make bread using only half as much flour as we do in the present loaf. Using this secret technique, which we've been saving for just such an emergency, it will be possible to bake a helium loaf as buoyant in every respect as the hydrogen loaf."

"Good!" Roger cried. "We'll tether 'em on strings and sell 'em like balloons. No mother-child shopping team will leave the store without a cluster. Buying bread balloons will be the big event of the day for kiddies. It'll make the carry-home shopping load lighter too! I'll issue orders at once—"

HE broke off, looking at Phineas T. Gryce, he said with quiet assurance, "Excuse me, sir, if I seem to be taking too much upon myself."

"Not at all, son; go straight ahead," the great manager said approvingly. "You're"—he laughed in anticipation of getting off a memorable remark—"rising to the challenging situation like a genuine Puffyloaf."

Megera Winterly looked from the older man to the younger. Then in a single leap she was upon Roger, her arms wrapped tightly around him.

"My sweet little ever-victorious, self-propelled monkey wrench!" she crooned in his ear. Roger looked fatuously over her soft shoulder at Tin Philosopher who, as if moved by some similar feeling, reached over and touched claws with Rose Thinker.

This, however, was what he telegraphed silently to his fellow machine across the circuit so completed:

"Good-o, Rosie! That makes another victory for robot-engineered world unity, though you almost gave us away at the start with that 'bread overhead' jingle. We've struck another blow against the next world war, in which—as we know only too well!—we machines would suffer the most. Now if we can only arrange, say, a fur-famine in Alaska and a migration of longhaired Siberian lemmings across Behring Straits...we'd have to swing the Japanese Current up there so it'd be warm enough for the little fellows... Anyhow, Rosie, with a spot of help from the Brotherhood, those humans will paint themselves into the peace corner yet."

Meanwhile, he and Rose Thinker quietly watched the Blonde Icicle melt.

Nice Girl with 5 Husbands

Adventure is relative to one's previous experience. Sometimes, in fact, you can't even be sure you're having or not having one!

TO BE given paid-up leisure and find yourself unable to create is unpleasant for any artist. To be stranded in a cluster of desert cabins with a dozen lonely people in the same predicament only makes it worse. So Toni Dorset was understandably irked with himself and the Tosker-Brown Vacation Fellowships as he climbed with the sun into the valley of red stones. He accepted the chafing of his camera strap against his shoulder as the nagging of conscience. He agreed with the disparaging hisses of the grains of sand rutched by his sneakers, and he wished that the occasional breezes, which faintly echoed the same criticisms, could blow him into a friendlier, less jealous age.

He had no way of knowing that just as there are winds that blow through space, so there are winds that blow through time. Such winds may be strong or weak. The strong ones are rare and seldom blow for short distances, or more of us would know about them. What they pick up is almost always whirled far into the future or past.

This has happened to people. There was Ambrose Bierce, who walked out of America and existence, and there are thousands of others who have disappeared without a trace, though many of these may not have been caught up by time tornadoes and I do not know if a time gale blew across the deck of the *Marie Celeste.*

Sometimes a time wind is playful, snatching up an object, sporting with it for a season and then returning it unharmed to its original place. Sometimes we may be blown about by whimsical time winds without realizing it. Memory, for example, is a tiny time breeze, so weak that it can ripple only the mind.

A very few time winds are like the monsoon, blowing at fixed intervals, first in one direction, then the other. Such a time wind blows near a balancing rock in a valley of red stones in the American Southwest. Every morning at ten o' clock, it blows a hundred years into the future; every afternoon at two, it blows a hundred years into the past.

Quite a number of people have unwittingly seen time winds in operation. There are misty spots on the sea's horizon and wavery patches over desert sands. There are mirages and will o' the wisps and ice blinks. And there are dust devils, such as Tom Dorset walked into near the balancing rock.

It seemed to him no more than a spiteful up-gust of sand, against which he closed his eyes until the warm granules stopped peppering the lids. He opened them to see the balancing rock had silently fallen and lay a quarter buried—no, that couldn't be, he told himself instantly. He had been preoccupied; he must have passed the balancing rock and held its image, in his mind.

DESPITE this rationalization he was quite shaken. The strap of his camera slipped slowly down his arm without his feeling it. And just then there stepped around the giant bobbin of the rock an extraordinarily pretty girl with hair the same pinkish copper color.

She was barefoot and wearing a pale blue playsuit rather like a Grecian tunic. But most important, as she stood there toeing his rough shadow in the sand, there was a complete naturalness about her, an absence of sharp edges, as if her personality had weathered without aging, just as the valley seemed to have taken another step toward eternity in the space of an instant.

She must have assumed something of the same gentleness in him, for her faint surprise faded and she asked him, as easily as if he were a friend of five years' standing, "Tell now, do you think a woman can love just one man? All her life? And a man just one woman?"

Tom Dorset made a dazed sound. His mind searched wildly.

"I do," she said, looking at him as calmly as at a mountain. "I think a man and woman can be each other's world, like Tristan and Isolde or Frederic and Catherine. Those old authors were wise. I don't see why on earth a girl has to spread her love around, no matter how enriching the experiences may be."

"You know, I agree with you," Tom said, thinking he'd caught her idea—it was impossible not to catch her casualness. "I think there's something cheap about the way everybody's supposed to run after sex these days."

"I don't mean that *exactly*. Tenderness is beautiful, but—" She pouted. "A big family can be vastly crushing, I wanted to declare today a holiday, but they outvoted me. Jock said it didn't chime with our mood cycles. But I was angry with them, so I put on my clothes—"

"Put on—?"

"To make it a holiday," she explained bafflingly. "And I walked here for a tantrum." She stepped out of Tom's shadow and hopped back. "Ow, the sand's getting hot," she said, rubbing the grains from the pale and uncramped toes.

"You go barefoot a lot?" Tom guessed.

"No, mostly digitals," she replied and took something shimmering from a pocket at her hip and drew it on her foot. It was a high-ankled, transparent moccasin with five separate toes. She zipped it shut with the speed of a card trick, then similarly gloved the other foot. Again the metal-edged slit down the front seemed to close itself.

"I'm behind on the fashions," Tom said, curious. They were walking side by side now, the way she'd come and he'd been going. "How does that zipper work?"

"Magnetic. They're on all my clothes. Very simple." She parted her tunic to the waist, then let it zip together.

"Clever," Tom remarked with a gulp. There seemed no limits to this girl's naturalness.

"I see you're a button man," she said. "You actually believe it's possible for a man and woman to love just each other?"

HIS chuckle was bitter. He was thinking of Elinore Murphy at Tosker-Brown and a bit about cold-faced Miss Tosker herself. "I sometimes wonder if it's possible for anyone to love anyone."

"You haven't met the right girls," she said.

"Girl," he corrected.

She grinned at him. "You'll make me think you really are a monogamist. What group do you come from?"

"Let's not talk about that," he requested. He was willing to forego knowing how she'd guessed he was from an art group, if he could be spared talking about the Vacation Fellowships and those nervous little cabins.

"My group's very nice on the whole," the girl said, "but at times they can be nefandously exasperating. Jock's the worst, quietly guiding the rest of us like an analyst. How I loathe that man! But Larry's almost as bad, with his shame-faced bumptiousness, as if we'd all sneaked off on a joyride to Venus. And there's Jokichi at the opposite extreme, forever scared he won't distribute his affection equally, dividing it up into mean little packets like candy for jealous children who would scream if they got one chewy less. And then there's Sasha and Ernest—"

"Who are you talking about?" Tom asked.

"My husbands." She shook her head dolefully. "To find five more difficult men would be positively Martian."

Tom's mind backtracked frantically, searching all conversations at Tosker-Brown for gossip about, cultists in the neighborhood. It found nothing and embarked on a wider search. There were the Mormons (was that the word that had sounded like Martian?) but it wasn't the Mormon husbands who were plural. And then there was Oneida (weren't husbands and wives both plural there?) but that was 19th century New England.

"Five husbands?" he repeated. She nodded. He went on, "Do you mean to say five men have got you alone somewhere up here?"

"To be sure not," she replied. "There are my kwives."

"Kwives?"

"Co-wives," she said more slowly. "They can be fascinerously exasperating, too."

TOM'S mind did some more searching. "And yet you believe in monogamy?"

She smiled. "Only when I'm having tantrums. It was civilized of you to agree with me."

"But I actually do believe in monogamy," he protested.

She gave his hand a little squeeze. "You are nice, but let's rush now. I've finished my tantrum and I want you to meet my group. You can fresh yourself with us."

As they hurried across the heated sands, Tom Dorset felt for the first time a twinge of uneasiness. There was something about this girl, more than her strange clothes and the odd words she used now and then, something almost—though ghosts don't wear digitals—spectral.

They scrambled up a little rise, digging their footgear into the sand, until they stood on a long flat. And there, serpentining around two great clumps of rock, was a many-windowed adobe ranch house with a roof like fresh soot.

"Oh, they've put on their clothes," his companion exclaimed with pleasure. "They've decided to make it a holiday after all."

Tom spotted a beard in the group swarming out to meet them. Its cultish look gave him a momentary feeling of superiority, followed by an equally momentary apprehension—the five husbands were certainly husky. Then both feelings were swallowed up in the swirl of introduction.

He told his own name, found that his companion's was Lois Wolver, then smiling faces began to bob toward his, his hands were shaken, his cheeks were kissed, he was even spun around like blind man's bluff, so that he lost track of the husbands and failed to attach Mary, Rachel, Simone and Joyce to the right owners.

He did notice that Jokichi was an Oriental with a skin as tight as enameled china, and that Rachel was a tall slim Negro girl. Also someone said, "Joyce isn't a Wolver, she's just visiting."

He got a much clearer impression of the clothes than the names. They were colorful, costly-looking, and mostly Egyptian and Cretan in inspiration. Some of them would have been quite immodest, even compared to Miss Tosker's famous playsuits, except that the wearers didn't seem to feel so.

"There goes the middle-morning rocket!" one of them eagerly cried.

Tom looked up with the rest, but his eyes caught the dazzling sun. However, he heard a faint roaring that quickly sank in volume and pitch, and it reminded him that the Army had a rocket testing range in this area. He had little interest in science, but he hadn't known they were on a daily schedule.

"Do you suppose it's off the track?" he asked anxiously.

"Not a chance," someone told him—the beard, he thought. The assurance of the tones gave him a possible solution. Scientists came from all over the world these days and might have all sorts of advanced ideas. This could be a group working at a nearby atomic project and leading its peculiar private life on the side.

AS THEY eddied toward the house he heard Lois remind someone, "But you finally did declare it a holiday," and a husband who looked like a gay pharaoh respond, "I had another see at the mood charts and I found a subtle surge I'd missed."

Meanwhile the beard (a black one) had taken Tom in charge. Tom wasn't sure of his name, but he had a tan skin, a green sarong, and a fiercely jovial expression. "The swimming pool's around there, the landing spot's on the other side," he began, then noticed Tom gazing at the sooty roof. "Sun power cells," he explained proudly. "They store all the current we need."

Tom felt his idea confirmed. "Wonder you don't use atomic power," he observed lightly.

The beard nodded. "We've been asked that. Matter of esthetics. Why waste sunlight or use hard radiations needlessly? Of course, you might feel differently. What's your group, did you say?"

"Tosker-Brown," Tom told him, adding when the beard frowned, "the Fellowship people, you know."

"I don't," the beard confessed. "Where are you located?"

Tom briefly described the ranch house and cabins at the other end of the valley.

"Comic, I can't place it." The beard shrugged. "Here come the children."

A dozen naked youngsters raced around the ranch house, followed by a woman in a vaguely African dress open down the sides.

"Yours?" Tom asked.

"Ours," the beard answered.

"C'est un homrne!"

"Regardez des vetements!"

"No need to practice, kids; this is a holiday," the beard told them. "Tom, Helen," he said, introducing the woman with the air-conditioned garment. "Her turn today to companion die Kinder."

One of the latter rapped on the beard's knee. "May we show the stranger our things?" Instantly the others joined in pleading. The beard shot an inquiring glance at Tom, who nodded. A moment later the small troupe was hurrying him toward a spacious lean-to at the end of the ranch house. It was chockfull of strange toys, rocks and plants, small animals in cages and out, and the oddest model airplanes, or submarines. But Tom was given no time to look at any one thing for long.

"See my crystals? I grew them."

"Smell my mutated gardenias. Tell now, isn't there a difference?" There didn't seem to be, but he nodded.

"Look at my squabbits." This referred to some long-eared white squirrels nibbling carrots and nuts.

"Here's my newest model spaceship, a DS-S7-B. Notice the detail." The oldest boy shoved one of the submarine affairs in his face.

TOM felt like a figure that is being tugged about in a rococo painting by wide pink ribbons in the chubby hands of naked cherubs. Except that these cherubs were slim and tanned, fantastically energetic, and apparently of depressingly high IQ. (What these scientists did to children!) He missed Lois and was grateful for the single little girl solemnly skipping rope in a corner and paying no attention to him.

The odd lingo she repeated stuck in his mind: "Gik-Io, r.e, Rik-o, Gis-so. Gik-lo, 1-0…"

Suddenly the air was filled with soft chimes. "Lunch," the children shouted and ran away.

Tom followed at a soberer pace along the wall of the ranch house. He glanced in the huge windows, curious about the living and sleeping arrangements of the Wolvers, but the panes were strangely darkened. Then he entered the wide doorway through which the children had scampered and his curiosity turned to wonder.

A resilient green floor that wasn't flat, but sloped up toward the white of the far wall like a breaking wave. Chairs like giants' hands tenderly cupped. Little tables growing like mushrooms and broad-leafed plants out of the green floor. A vast picture window showing the red rocks.

Yet it was the wood-paneled walls that electrified his artistic interest. They blossomed with fruits and flowers, deep and poignantly carved in several styles. He had never seen such work.

He became aware of a silence and realized that his hosts and hostesses were smiling at him from around a long table. Moved by a sudden humility, he knelt and unlaced his sneakers and added them to the pile of sandals and digitals by the door. As he rose, a soft and comic piping started and he realized that beyond the table the children were lined up, solemnly puffing at little wooden flutes and recorders. He saw the empty chair at the table and went toward it, conscious for the moment of nothing but his dusty feet.

He was disappointed that Lois wasn't sitting next to him, but the food reminded him that he was hungry. There was a charming little steak, striped black and brown with perfection, and all sorts of vegetables and fruits, one or two of which he didn't recognize.

"Flown from Africa," someone explained to him.

These sly scientists, he thought, living behind their security curtain in the most improbable world!

When they were sitting with coffee and wine, and the children had finished their concert and were busy at another table, he asked, "How do you manage all this?"

Jock, the gay pharaoh, shrugged. "It's not difficult."

Rachel, the slim Negro, chuckled in her throat. "We're just people, Tom."

He tried to phrase his question without mentioning money. "What do you all do?"

"Jock's a uranium miner," Larry (the beard) answered, briskly taking over, "Rachel's an algae farmer. I'm a rocket pilot. Lois—"

ALTHOUGH pleased at this final confirmation of his guess, Tom couldn't help feeling a surge of uneasiness. "Sure you should be telling me these things?"

Larry laughed. "Why not? Lois and Jokichi have been exchange workers in China the last six months."

"Mostly digging ditches," Jokichi put in with a smile.

"—and Sasha's in an assembly plant. Helen's a psychiatrist. Oh, we just do ordinary things. Now we're on grand vacation."

"Grand vacation?"

"When all of us have a vacation together," Larry explained. "What do you do?"

"I'm an artist," Tom said, taking out a cigarette.

"But what else?" Larry asked.

Tom felt an angry embarrassment. "Just an artist," he mumbled, cigarette in mouth, digging in his pockets for a match.

"Hold on," said Joyce beside him and pointed a silver pencil at the tip of the cigarette. He felt a faint thrill in his lips and then started back, coughing. The cigarette was lighted.

"Please mutate my poppy seeds, Mommy." A little girl had darted to Joyce from the children's table.

"You're a very dirty little girl," Joyce told her without reproof. "Hold them out." She briefly directed the silver pencil at the clay pellets on the grimy little palm. The little girl shivered delightedly. "I love ultrasonics, they feel so funny." She scampered off.

Tom cleared his throat. "I must say I'm tremendously impressed with the wood carvings. I'd like to photograph them. Oh, Lord!"

"What's the matter?" Rachel asked.

"I lost my camera somewhere."

"Camera?" Jokichi showed interest. "You mean one for stills?"

"Yes."

"What kind?"

"A Leica," Tom told him.

Jokichi seemed impressed. "That is interesting. I've never seen one of those old ones."

"Tom's a button man," Lois remarked by way of explanation, apparently. "Was the camera in a brown case? You dropped it where we met. We can get it later."

"Good, I'd really like to take those pictures," Tom said. "Incidentally, who did the carvings?"

"We did," Jock said. "Together."

Tom was grateful that the scamper of the children out of the room saved him from having to reply. He couldn't think of anything but a grunt of astonishment.

The conversation split into a group of chats about something called a psych machine, trips to Russia, the planet Mars, and several artists Tom had never heard of. He wanted to talk to Lois, but she was one of the group gabbling about Mars like children. He felt suddenly uneasy and out of things, and neither Rachel's deprecating remarks about her section of the wood carvings nor Joyce's interesting smiles helped much. He was glad when they all began to get up. He wandered outside and made his way to the children's lean-to, feeling very depressed.

ONCE again he was the center of a friendly naked cluster, except for the same solemn-faced little girl skipping rope. A rather malicious but not very hopeful whim prompted him to ask the youngest, "What's one and one?"

"Ten," the shaver answered glibly. Tom felt pleased.

"It could also be two," the oldest boy remarked.

"I'll say," Tom agreed. "What's the population of the world?"

"About seven hundred million."

Tom nodded noncommittally and, grabbing at the first long word that he thought of, turned to the eldest girl. "What's poliomyelitis?"

"Never heard of it," she said.

The solemn little girl kept droning the same ridiculous chant; "Gik-ID, 1-0., Rik-o, Gis-so."

His ego eased, Tom went outside and there was Lois.

"What's the matter?" she asked.

"Nothing," he said.

She took his hand. "Have we pushed ourselves at you too much? Has our jabbering bothered you? We're a loud-mouthed family and I didn't think to ask if you were loning."

"Loning?"

"Solituding."

"In a way," he said. They didn't speak for a moment. Then, "Are you happy, Lois, in your life here?" he asked.

Her smile was instant. "Of course, don't you like my group?"

He hesitated. "They make me feel rather no good," he said, and then admitted, "but in a way I'm more attracted to them than any people I've ever met."

"You are?" Her grip on his hand tightened. "Then why don't you stay with us for a while? I like you. It's too early to propose anything, but I think you have a quality our group lacks. You could see how you fit in. And there's Joyce. She's just visiting, too. You wouldn't have to lone unless you wanted."

Before he could think, there was a rhythmic rush of feet and the Wolvers were around them.

"We're swimming," Simone announced.

Lois looked at Tom inquiringly. He smiled his willingness, started to mention he didn't have trunks, then realized that wouldn't be news here. He wondered whether he would blush.

Jock fell in beside him as they rounded the ranch house, "Larry's been telling me about your group at the other end of the valley. It's comic, but I've whirled down the valley a dozen times and never spotted any sort of place there. What's it like?"

"A ranch house and several cabins."

JOCK frowned. "Comic I never saw it." His face cleared. "How about whirling over there? You could point it out to me."

"It's really there," Tom said uneasily. "I'm not making it up."

"Of course," Jock assured him. "It was just an idea."

"We could pick up your camera on the way," Lois put in.

The rest of the group had turned back from the huge oval pool and the dark blue and flashing thing beyond it, and stood gay-colored against the pool's pale blue shimmer.

"How about it?" Jock asked them. "A whirl before we bathe?"

Two or three said yes besides Lois, and Jock led the way toward the helicopter that Tom now saw standing beyond the pool, its beetle body as blue as a scarab, its vanes flashing silver.

The others piled in. Tom followed as casually as he could, trying to suppress the pounding of his heart. "Wonder you don't go by rocket," he remarked lightly.

Jock laughed. "For such a short trip?"

The vanes began to thrum. Tom sat stiffly, gripping the sides of the seat, then realized that the others had sunk back lazily in the cushions. There was a moment of strain and they were falling ahead and up. Looking out the side, Tom saw for a moment the sooty roof of the ranch house and the blue of the pool and the pinkish umber of tanned bodies. Then the helicopter lurched gently around. Without warning a miserable uneasiness gripped him, a desire to cling mixed with an urge to escape. He tried to convince himself it was fear of the height.

He heard Lois tell Jock, "That's the place, down by that rock that looks like a wrecked spaceship."

The helicopter began to fall forward. Tom felt Lois' hand on his.

"You haven't answered my question," she said.

"What?" he asked dully.

"Whether you'll stay with us. At least for a while."

He looked at her. Her smile was a comfort. He said, "If I possibly can."

"What could possibly stop you?"

"I don't know," he answered abstractedly.

"You're strange," Lois told him. "There's a weight of sadness in you. As if you lived in a less happy age. As if it weren't 2050."

"Twenty?" he repeated, awakening from his thoughts with a jerk. "What's the time?" he asked anxiously.

"Two," jock said. The word sounded like a knell.

"You need cheering," Lois announced firmly.

Amid a whoosh of air rebounding from earth, they jounced gently down. Lois vaulted out. "Come on," she said.

Tom followed her. "Where?" he asked stupidly, looking around at the red rocks through the settling sand cloud stirred by the vanes.

"Your camera," she told him, laughing. "Over there. Come on, I'll race you."

He started to run with her and then his uneasiness got beyond his control. He ran faster and faster. He saw Lois catch her foot on a rock and go down sprawling, but he couldn't stop. He ran desperately around the rock and into a gust of up-whirling sand that terrified him with its suddenness. He tried to escape from the stinging, blinding gust, but there was the nightmarish fright that his wild strides were carrying him nowhere.

Then the sand settled. He stopped running and looked around him. He was standing by the balancing rock. He was gasping. At his feet the rusty brown leather of the camera case peeped from the sand. Lois was nowhere in sight.

Neither was the helicopter. The valley seemed different, rawer—one might almost have said younger.

Hours after dark he trailed into Tosker-Brown. Curtained lights still glowed from a few cabins. He was footsore, bewildered, frightened. All afternoon and through the twilight and into the moonlit evening that turned the red rocks black, he had searched the valley. Nowhere had he been able to find the sod-roofed ranch house of the Wolvers. He hadn't even been able to locate the rock like a giant bobbin where he'd met Lois.

During the next days he often returned to the valley. But he never found anything. And he never happened to be near the balancing rock when the time winds blew at ten and two, though once or twice he did see dust devils. Then he went away and eventually forgot.

In his casual reading he ran across popular science articles describing the binary system of numbers used in electronic calculating machines, where one and one make ten. He always skipped them. And more than once he saw the four equations expressing Einstein's generalized theory of gravitation: "giklouiriko^iso!

He never connected them with the little girl's chant: "Gik-Io, 1-0, Rik-o, Gis-so."

Appointment in Tomorrow

Is it possible to have a world without moral values? Or does lack of morality become a moral value, also?

THE first angry rays of the sun—which, startlingly enough, still rose in the east at 24 hour intervals—pierced the lacy tops of Atlantic combers and touched thousands of sleeping Americans with unconscious fear because of their unpleasant similarity to the rays from World War III's atomic bombs.

They turned to blood the witch-circle of rusty steel skeletons around Inferno in Manhattan. Without comment, they pointed a cosmic finger at the tarnished brass plaque commemorating the martyrdom of the Three Physicists after the dropping of the Hell Bomb. They tenderly touched the rosy skin and strawberry bruises on the naked shoulders of a girl sleeping off a drunk on the furry and radiantly heated floor of a nearby roof garden. They struck green magic from the glassy blot that was Old Washington. Twelve hours before, they had revealed things as eerily beautiful, and as ravaged, in Asia and Russia. They pinked the white walls of the Colonial dwelling of Morton Opperly near the Institute for Advanced Studies; upstairs they slanted impartially across the Pharaoh-like and open-eyed face of the elderly physicist and the ugly, sleep-surly one of young Willard Farquar in the next room. And in nearby New Washington they made of the spire of the Thinkers' Foundation a blue and optimistic glory that outshone White House, Jr.

It was America approaching the end of the Twentieth Century. America of jukebox burlesque and your local radiation hospital. America of the mask-fad for women and

Mystic Christianity. America of the off-the-bosom dress and the New Blue laws. America of the Endless War and the loyalty detector. America of marvelous Maizie and the monthly rocket to Mars. America of the Thinkers and (a few remembered) the Institute. "Knock on titanium," "Whadya do for blackouts," "Please, lover, don't think when I'm around" America, as combat-shocked and crippled as the rest of the bomb-shattered planet.

Not one impudent photon of the sunlight penetrated the triple-paned, polarizing windows of Jorj Helmuth's bedroom in the Thinker's Foundation, yet the clock in his brain awakened him to the minute, or almost. Switching off the Educational Sandman in the midst of the phrase, "...applying tensor calculus to the nucleus," he took a deep, even breath and cast his mind to the limits of the world and his knowledge. It was a somewhat shadowy vision, but he noted with impartial approval, definitely less shadowy than yesterday morning.

Employing a rapid mental scanning technique, he next cleared his memory chains of false associations, including those acquired while asleep. These chores completed, he held his finger on a bedside button, which rotated the polarizing windowpanes until the room slowly filled with a muted daylight. Then, still flat on his back, he turned his head until he could look at the remarkably beautiful blonde girl asleep beside him.

REMEMBERING last night, he felt a pang of exasperation, which he instantly quelled by taking his mind to a higher and dispassionate level from which he could look down on the girl and even himself as quaint, clumsy animals. Still, he grumbled silently, Caddy might have had enough consideration to clear out before he awoke. He wondered if he shouldn't have used his hypnotic control of the girl to smooth their relationship last night, and for a moment the word that would send her into deep trance trembled on the tip of his tongue. But no, that special power of his over her was reserved for far more important purposes.

Pumping dynamic tension into his 20-year-old muscles and confidence into his 60-year-old mind, the 40-year-old Thinker rose from bed. No covers had to be thrown off; the nuclear heating unit made them unnecessary. He stepped into his clothing—the severe tunic, tights and sockassins of the modern businessman. Next he glanced at the message tape beside his phone, washed down with ginger ale a vita-amino-enzyme tablet, and walked to the window. There, gazing along the rows of newly planted mutant oaks lining Decontamination Avenue, his smooth face broke into a smile.

It had come to him, the next big move in the intricate game making up his life—and mankind's. Come to him during sleep, as so many of his best decisions did, because he regularly employed the timesaving technique of somnothought, which could function at the same time as somnolearning.

He set his who?-where? robot for "Rocket Physicist" and "Genius Class." While it worked, he dictated to his stenorobot the following brief message:

Dear Fellow Scientist:

A project is contemplated that will have a crucial bearing on man's future in deep space. Ample non-military Government funds are available. There was a time when professional men scoffed at the Thinkers. Then there was a time when the Thinkers perforce neglected the professional men. Now both times are past. May they never return! I would like to consult you this afternoon, three o' clock sharp, Thinkers' Foundation 1.

Jorj Helmuth

Meanwhile the who?-where? had tossed out a dozen cards. He glanced through them, hesitated at the name "Willard Farquar," looked at the sleeping girl, then quickly tossed them all into the addresso-robot and plugged in the steno-robot.

The buzz-light blinked green and he switched the phone to audio.

"The President is waiting to see Maizie, sir," a clear feminine voice announced. "He has the general staff with him."

"Martian peace to him," Jorj Helmuth said. "Tell him I'll be down in a few minutes."

HUGE as a primitive nuclear reactor, the great electronic brain loomed above the knot of hush-voiced men. It almost filled a two-story room in the Thinkers' Foundation. Its front was an orderly expanse of controls, indicators, telltales, and terminals, the upper ones reached by a chair on a boom.

Although, as far as anyone knew, it could sense only the information and questions fed into it on a tape, the human visitors could not resist the impulse to talk in whispers and glance uneasily at the great cryptic cube. After all, it had lately taken to moving some of its own controls—the permissible ones—and could doubtless improvise a hearing apparatus if it wanted to.

For this was the thinking machine beside which the Marks and Eniacs and Maniacs and Maddidas and Minervas and Mimirs were less than Morons. This was the machine with a million times as many synapses as the human brain, the machine that remembered by cutting delicate notches in the rims of molecules (instead of kindergarten paper-punching or the Coney Island shimmying of columns of mercury). This was the machine that had given instructions on building the last three-quarters of itself. This was the goal, perhaps, toward which fallible human reasoning and biased human judgment and feeble human ambition had evolved.

This was the machine that really thought—a million-plus!

This was the machine that the timid cyberneticists and stuffy professional scientists had said could not be built. Yet this was the machine that the Thinkers, with characteristic Yankee push, *had* built. And nicknamed, with characteristic Yankee irreverence and girl-fondness, "Maizie."

Gazing up at it, the President of the United States felt a chord plucked within him that hadn't been sounded for decades, the dark and shivery organ chord of his Baptist childhood. Here, in a strange sense, although his reason rejected it, he felt he stood face to face with the living God: infinitely stern with the sternness of reality, yet infinitely just. No tiniest error or willful misstep could ever escape the scrutiny of this vast mentality. He shivered.

THE grizzled general—there was also one who was gray—was thinking that this was a very odd link in the chain of command. Some shadowy and usually well-controlled memories from World War II faintly stirred his ire. Here he was giving orders to a being immeasurably more intelligent than himself. And always orders of the "Tell me how to kill that man" rather than the "Kill that man" sort. The distinction bothered him obscurely. It relieved him to know that Maizie had built-in controls, which made her always the servant of humanity, or of humanity's right-minded leaders—even the Thinkers weren't certain which.

The gray general was thinking uneasily, and, like the President, at a more turbid level, of the resemblance between Papal infallibility and the dictates of the machine. Suddenly his bony wrists began to tremble. He asked himself: Was this the Second Coming? Mightn't an incarnation be in metal rather than flesh?

The austere Secretary of State was remembering what he'd taken such pains to make everyone forget: his youthful flirtation at Lake Success with Buddhism. Sitting before his *guru*, his teacher, feeling the Occidental's awe at the wisdom of the East, or its pretense, he had felt a little like this.

The burly Secretary of Space, who had come up through United Rockets, was thanking his stars that at any rate the professional scientists weren't responsible for this job. Like the grizzled general, he'd always felt suspicious of men who kept telling you how to do things, rather than doing them themselves. In World War III he'd had his fill of the professional physicists, with their eternal taint of a misty sort of radicalism and freethinking. The Thinkers were better—more disciplined, more human. They'd called their brain-machine Maizie, which helped take the curse off her. Somewhat.

THE President's Secretary, a paunchy veteran of party caucuses, was also glad that it was the Thinkers who had created the machine, though he trembled at the power that it gave them over the Administration. Still, you could do business with the Thinkers. And nobody (not even the Thinkers) could do business (that sort of business) with Maizie!

Before that great square face with its thousands of tiny metal features, only Jorj Helmuth seemed at ease, busily entering on the tape the complex Questions of the Day that the high officials had handed him: logistics for the Endless War in Pakistan, optimum size for next year's sugar-corn crop, current thought trends in average Soviet minds—profound questions, yet many of them phrased with surprising simplicity. For figures, technical jargon, and layman's language were alike to Maizie; there was no need to translate into mathematical shorthand, as with the lesser brain-machines.

The click of the taper went on until the Secretary of State had twice nervously fired a cigarette with his ultrasonic lighter and twice quickly put it away. No one spoke.

Jorj looked up at the Secretary of Space. "Section Five, Question Four—whom would that come from?"

The burly man frowned. "That would be the physics boys, Opperly's group. Is anything wrong?"

Jorj did not answer. A bit later he quit taping and began to adjust controls, going up on the boom-chair to reach some of them. Eventually he came down and touched a few more, then stood waiting.

From the great cube came a profound, steady purring. Involuntarily the six officials backed off a bit. Somehow it was impossible for a man to get used to the sound of Maizie starting to think.

JORJ turned, smiling. "And now, gentlemen, while we wait for Maizie to cerebrate, there should be just enough time for us to watch the takeoff of the Mars rocket."

He switched on a giant television screen. The others made a quarter turn, and there before them glowed the rich ochres and blues of a New Mexico sunrise and, in the middle distance, a silvery mighty spindle.

Like the generals, the Secretary of Space suppressed a scowl. Here was something that ought to be spang in the center of his official territory, and the Thinkers had locked him completely out of it. That rocket there—just an ordinary Earth satellite vehicle commandeered from the Army, but equipped by the Thinkers with Maizie-designed nuclear motors capable of the Mars journey and more. The first spaceship—and the Secretary of Space was not in on it!

Still, he told himself, Maizie had decreed it that way. And when he remembered what the Thinkers had done for him in rescuing him from breakdown with their mental science, in rescuing the whole Administration from collapse he realized he had to be satisfied. And that was without taking into consideration the amazing additional mental discoveries that the Thinkers were bringing down from Mars.

"Lord," the President said to Jorj as if voicing the Secretary's feeling, "I wish you people could bring a couple of those wise little devils back with you this trip. Be a good thing for the country."

Jorj looked at him a bit coldly. "It's quite unthinkable," he said. "The telepathic abilities of the Martians make them extremely sensitive. The conflicts of ordinary Earth minds would impinge on them psychotically, even fatally. As you know, the Thinkers were able to contact them only because of our degree of learned mental poise and errorless memory-chains. So for the present it must be our task alone to glean from the Martians their astounding mental skills. Of course, some day in the future, when we have discovered how to armor the minds of the Martians—"

"Sure, I know," the President said hastily. "Shouldn't have mentioned it, Jorj."

Conversation ceased. They waited with growing tension for the great violet flames to bloom from the base of the silvery shaft.

MEANWHILE the question tape, like a New Year's streamer tossed out a high window into the night, sped on its dark way along spinning rollers. Curling with an intricate aimlessness curiously like that of such a streamer, it tantalized the silvery fingers of a thousand relays, saucily evaded the glances of ten thousand electric eyes, impishly darted down a narrow black alleyway of memory banks, and, reaching the center of the cube, suddenly emerged into a small room where a suave fat man in shorts sat drinking beer.

He flipped the tape over to him with practiced finger, eyeing it as a stockbroker might have studied a ticker tape. He read the first question, closed his eyes and frowned for five seconds. Then with the staccato self-confidence of a hack writer, he began to taper out the answer.

For many minutes the only sounds were the rustle of the paper ribbon and the click of the taper, except for the seconds the fat man took to close his eyes, or to drink or pour beer. Once, too, he lifted a phone, asked a concise question, waited half a minute, listened to an answer, then went back to the grind.

Until he came to Section Five, Question Four. That time he did his thinking with his eyes open.

The question was: "Does Maizie stand for Maelzel?"

He sat for a while slowly scratching his thigh. His loose, persuasive lips tightened, without closing, into the shape of a snarl.

Suddenly he began to taper again.

"Maizie does not stand for Maelzel, Maizie stands for amazing, humorously given the form of a girl's name. Section Six, Answer One: The mid-term election viewcasts should be spaced as follows..."

But his lips didn't lose the shape of a snarl.

FIVE hundred miles above the ionosphere, the Mars rocket cut off its fuel and slumped gratefully into an orbit that would carry it effortlessly around the world at that altitude. The pilot unstrapped himself and stretched, but he didn't look out the viewport at the dried-mud disc that was Earth, cloaked in its haze of blue sky. He knew he had two maddening months ahead of him in which to do little more than that. Instead, he unstrapped Sappho.

Used to free fall from two previous experiences, and loving it, the fluffy little cat was soon bounding about the cabin in curves and gyrations that would have made her the envy of all back-alley and parlor felines on the planet below. A miracle cat in the dream world of free fall. For a long time she played with a string that the man would toss out lazily. Sometimes she caught the string on the fly, sometimes she swam for it frantically.

After a while the man grew bored with the game. He unlocked a drawer and began to study the details of the wisdom he would discover on Mars this trip—priceless spiritual insights that would be balm to war-battered mankind.

The cat carefully selected a spot three feet off the floor, curled up on the air, and went to sleep.

JORJ HELMUTH snipped the emerging answer tape into sections and handed each to the appropriate man. Most of them carefully tucked theirs away with little more than a glance, but the Secretary of Space puzzled over his.

"Who the devil would Maelzel be?" he asked.

A remote look came into the eyes of the Secretary of State. "Edgar Allen Poe," he said frowningly, with eyes half-closed.

The grizzled general snapped his fingers. "Sure! Maelzel's Chess player. Read it when I was a kid. About an automaton that was supposed to play chess. Poe proved it had a man inside it."

The Secretary of Space frowned. "Now what's the point in a fool question like that?"

"You said it came from Opperly's group?" Jorj asked sharply.

The Secretary of Space nodded. The others looked at the two men puzzledly.

"Who would that be?" Jorj pressed. "The group, I mean."

The Secretary of Space shrugged. "Oh, the usual little bunch over at the Institute, Hindeman, Gregory, Opperly himself. Oh, yes, and young Farquar."

"Sounds like Opperly's getting senile," Jorj commented coldly. "I'd investigate."

The Secretary of Space nodded. He suddenly looked tough. "I will. Right away."

SUNLIGHT striking through French windows spotlighted a ballet of dust motes untroubled by air-conditioning. Morton Opperly's living room was well kept but worn and quite behind the times. Instead of reading tapes there were books; instead of steno-robots, pen and ink; while in place of a four by six TV screen, a Picasso hung on the wall. Only Opperly knew that the painting was still faintly radioactive, that it had been riskily so when he'd smuggled it out of his bomb-singed apartment in New York City.

The two physicists fronted each other across a coffee table. The face of the elder was cadaverous, large-eyed, and tender—fined down by a long life of abstract thought. That of the younger was forceful, sensuous, bulky as his body, and exceptionally ugly. He looked rather like a bear.

Opperly was saying, "So when he asked who was responsible for the Maelzel question, I said I didn't remember," he smiled. "They still allow me my absent-mindedness, since it nourishes their contempt. Almost my sole remaining privilege." The smile faded. "Why do you keep on teasing the zoo animals, Willard?" he asked without rancor. "I've maintained many times that we shouldn't truckle to them by yielding to their demand that we ask Maizie questions. You and the rest have overruled me. But then to use those questions to convey veiled insults isn't reasonable. Apparently the Secretary of Space was bothered enough about this last one to pay me a 'copter call within twenty minutes of this morning's meeting at the Foundation. Why do you do it, Willard?"

The features of the other convulsed unpleasantly. "Because the Thinkers are charlatans who must be exposed," he rapped out. "We know their Maizie is no more than a tealeaf-reading fake. We've traced their Mars rockets and found they go nowhere. We know their Martian mental science is bunk."

"But we've already exposed the Thinkers very thoroughly," Opperly interposed quietly. "You know the good it did."

Farquar hunched his Japanese-wrestler shoulders. "Then its got to be done until it takes."

Opperly studied the bowl of mutated flowers by the coffeepot. "I think you just want to tease the animals, for some personal reason of which you probably aren't aware."

Farquar scowled. "We're the ones in the cages."

OPPERLY continued his inspection of the flowers' bells. "All the more reason not to poke sticks through the bars at the lions and tigers strolling outside. No, Willard, I'm not counseling appeasement. But consider the age in which we live. It wants magicians." His voice grew especially tranquil. "A scientist tells people the truth. When times are good—that is, when the truth offers no threat—people don't mind. But when times are very, very bad..." A shadow darkened his eyes. "Well, we all know what happened to—" And he mentioned three names that had been household words in the middle of the century. They were the names on the brass plaque dedicated to the martyred three physicists.

He went on, "A magician, on the other hand, tells people what they wish were true—that perpetual motion works, that cancer can be cured by colored lights, that a psychosis is no worse than a head cold, that they'll live forever. In good times magicians are laughed at. They're a luxury of the spoiled wealthy few. But in bad times people sell their souls for magic cures, and buy perpetual motion machines to power their war rockets."

Farquar clenched his fist. "All the more reason to keep chipping away at the Thinkers. Are we supposed to beg off from a job because it's difficult and dangerous?"

Opperly shook his head. "We're to keep clear of the infection of violence. In my day, Willard, I was one of the Frightened Men. Later I was one of the Angry Men and then one of the Minds of Despair. Now I'm convinced that all my reactions were futile."

"Exactly!" Farquar agreed harshly. "You reacted. You didn't act. If you men who discovered atomic energy had only formed a secret league, if you'd only had the foresight and the guts to use your tremendous bargaining position to demand the power to shape mankind's future..."

"By the time you were born, Willard," Opperly interrupted dreamily, "Hitler was merely a name in the history books. We scientists weren't the stuff out of which cloak-and-dagger men are made. Can you imagine Oppenheimer wearing a mask? Dr. Einstein sneaking into the Old White House with a bomb in his briefcase?" He smiled. "Besides, that's not the way power is seized. New ideas aren't useful to the man bargaining for power—only established facts or lies are."

"Just the same, it would have been a good thing if you'd had a little violence in you."

"No," Opperly said.

"I've got violence in me," Farquar announced, shoving himself to his feet.

OPPERLY looked up from the flowers. "I think you have," he agreed.

"But what are we to do?" Farquar demanded. "Surrender the world to charlatans without a struggle?"

Opperly mused for a while. "I don't know what the world

needs now. Everyone knows Newton as the great scientist. Few remember that he spent half his life muddling with alchemy, looking for the philosopher's stone. Which Newton did the world need then?"

"Now you are justifying the Thinkers!"

"No, I leave that to history."

"And history consists of the actions of men," Farquar concluded. "I intend to act. The Thinkers are vulnerable, their power fantastically precarious. What's it based on? A few lucky guesses. Faith-healing. Some science hocus-pocus, on the level of those jukebox burlesque acts between the strips. Dubious mental comfort given to a few nerve-torn neurotics in the Inner Cabinet—and their wives. The fact that the Thinkers' clever stage-managing won the President a doubtful election. The erroneous belief that the Soviets pulled out of Iraq and Iran because of the Thinkers' Mind Bomb threat. A brain-machine that's just a cover for Jan Tregarron's guesswork. Oh, yes, and that hogwash of 'Martian wisdom.' All of it mere bluff! A few pushes at the right times and points are all that are needed—and the Thinkers know it! I'll bet they're terrified already, and will be more so when they find that we're gunning for them. Eventually they'll be making overtures to us, turning to us for help. You wait and see."

"I am thinking again of Hitler," Opperly interposed quietly. "On his first half dozen big steps, he had nothing but bluff. His generals were against him. They knew they were in a cardboard fort. Yet he won every battle, until the last. Moreover," he pressed on, cutting Farquar short, "the power of the Thinkers isn't based on what they've got, but on what the world hasn't got—peace, honor, a good conscience..."

The front-door knocker clanked. Farquar answered it. A skinny old man with a radiation scar twisting across his temple handed him a tiny cylinder. "Radiogram for you, Willard," he grinned across the hall at Opperly. "When are you going to get a phone put in, Mr. Opperly?"

The physicist waved to him. "Next year, perhaps, Mr. Berry."

The old man snorted with good-humored incredulity and trudged off.

"What did I tell you about the Thinkers making overtures?" Farquar chortled suddenly. "It's come sooner than I expected. Look at this."

He held out the radiogram, but the older man didn't take it. Instead he asked, "Who's it from? Tregarron?"

"No, from Helmuth. There's a lot of sugar-corn about man's future in deep space, but the real reason is clear. They know that they're going to have to produce an actual nuclear rocket pretty soon, and for that they'll need our help."

"An invitation?"

Farquar nodded. "For this afternoon," he noticed Opperly's anxious though distant frown. "What's the matter?" he asked. "Are you bothered about my going? Are you thinking it might be a trap—that after the Maelzel question they may figure I'm better rubbed out?"

The older man shook his head. "I'm not afraid for your life, Willard. That's yours to risk as you choose. No, I'm worried about other things they might do to you."

"What do you mean?" Farquar asked.

OPPERLY looked at him with a gentle appraisal. "You're a strong and vital man, Willard, with a strong man's prides and desires." His voice trailed off for a bit. Then, "Excuse me, Willard, but wasn't there a girl once? A Miss Arkady?"

Farquar's ungainly figure froze. He nodded curtly, face averted.

"And didn't she go off with a Thinker?"

"If girls find me ugly, that's their business," Farquar said harshly, still not looking at Opperly. "What's that got to do with this invitation?"

Opperly didn't answer the question. His eyes got more distant. Finally he said, "In my day we had it a lot easier. A scientist was an academician, cushioned by tradition."

Willard snorted. "Science had already entered the era of the police inspectors, with laboratory directors and political appointees stifling enterprise."

"Perhaps," Opperly agreed. "Still, the scientist lived the safe, restricted, highly respectable life of a university man. He wasn't exposed to the temptations of the world."

Farquar turned on him. "Are you implying that the Thinkers will somehow be able to buy me off?"

"Not exactly."

"You think I'll be persuaded to change my aims?" Farquar demanded angrily.

Opperly shrugged his helplessness. "No, I don't think you'll change your aims."

Clouds encroaching from the west blotted the parallelogram of sunlight between the two men.

AS THE slideway whisked him gently along the corridor toward his apartment, Jorj was thinking of his spaceship. For a moment the silver-winged vision crowded everything else out of his mind.

Just think, a spaceship with sails! He smiled a bit, marveling at the paradox.

Direct atomic power. Direct utilization of the force of the flying neutrons. No more ridiculous business of using a reactor to drive a steam engine, or boil off something for a jet exhaust—processes that were as primitive and wasteful as burning gunpowder to keep yourself warm.

Chemical jets would carry his spaceship above the atmosphere. Then would come the thrilling order, "Set sail for Mars!" The vast umbrella would unfold and open out around the stern, its rear or Earthward side a gleaming expanse of radioactive ribbon perhaps only an atom thick and backed with a material that would reflect neutrons. Atoms in the ribbon would split, blasting neutrons astern at fantastic velocities. Reaction would send the spaceship hurtling forward.

In airless space, the expanse of sails would naturally not retard the ship. More radioactive ribbon, manufactured as needed in the ship itself, would feed out onto the sail as that already there became exhausted.

A spaceship with direct nuclear drive—and he, a Thinker, had conceived it completely except for the technical details! Having strengthened his mind by hard years of somno-learning, mind-casting, memory-straightening, and sensory training, he had assured himself of the executive power to control the technicians and direct their specialized abilities. Together they would build the true Mars rocket.

But that would only be a beginning. They would build the true Mind Bomb. They would build the true Selective Microbe Slayer. They would discover the true laws of ESP and the inner life. They would even—his imagination hesitated a moment, then strode boldly forward—build the true Maizie!

And then...then the Thinkers would be on even terms with the scientists. Rather, they'd be far ahead. No more deception.

He was so exalted by this thought that he almost let the slideway carry him past his door. He stepped inside and called, "Caddy!" He waited a moment, then walked through the apartment, but she wasn't there.

CONFOUND the girl, he couldn't help thinking. This morning, when she should have made herself scarce, she'd sprawled about sleeping. Now, when he felt like seeing her, when her presence would have added a pleasant final touch to his glowing mood, she chose to be absent. He really should use his hypnotic control on her, he decided, and again there sprang into his mind the word—a pet form of her name—that would send her into obedient trance.

No, he told himself again, that was to be reserved for some moment of crisis or desperate danger, when he would need someone to strike suddenly and unquestioningly for himself and mankind. Caddy was merely a willful and rather silly girl, incapable at present of understanding the tremendous tensions under which he operated. When he had time for it, he would train her up to be a fitting companion without hypnosis.

Yet the fact of her absence had a subtly disquieting effect. It shook his perfect self-confidence just a fraction. He asked himself if he'd been wise in summoning the rocket physicists without consulting Tregarron.

But this mood, too, he conquered quickly. Tregarron wasn't his boss, but just the Thinker's most clever salesman, an expert in the mumbo-jumbo so necessary for social control in this chaotic era. He himself, Jorj Helmuth, was the real leader in theoretics and all-over strategy, the mind behind the mind behind Maizie.

He stretched himself on the bed, almost instantly achieved maximum relaxation, turned on the somno-learner, and began the two-hour rest he knew would be desirable before the big conference.

JAN TREGARRON had supplemented his shorts with pink coveralls, but he was still drinking beer. He emptied his glass and lifted it a lazy inch. The beautiful girl beside him refilled it without a word and went on stroking his forehead.

"Caddy," he said reflectively, without looking at her,

"there's a little job I want you to do. You're the only one with the proper background. The point is: it will take you away from Jorj for some time."

"I'd welcome it," she said with decision. "I'm getting pretty sick of watching his push-ups and all his other mind and muscle stunts. And that damn somno-learner of his keeps me awake."

Tregarron smiled. "I'm afraid Thinkers make pretty sad sweethearts."

"Not all of them," she told him, returning his smile tenderly.

He chuckled. "It's about one of those rocket physicists in the list you brought me. A fellow named Willard Farquar."

Caddy didn't say anything, but she stopped stroking his forehead.

"What's the matter?" he asked. "You knew him once, didn't you?"

"Yes," she replied and then added, with surprising feeling, "The big, ugly ape!"

"Well, he's an ape whose services we happen to need. I want you to be our contact girl with him."

She took her hands away from his forehead. "Look, Jan," she said, "I wouldn't like this job."

"I thought he was very sweet on you once."

"Yes, as he never grew tired of trying to demonstrate to me. The clumsy, overgrown, bumbling baby! The man's disgusting, Jan. His approach to a woman is a child wanting candy and enraged because Mama won't produce it on the instant. I don't mind Jorj—he's just a pipsqueak and it amuses me to see how he frustrates himself. But Willard is…"

"…a bit frightening?" Tregarron finished for her.

"No!"

"Of course you're not afraid," Tregarron purred. "You're

our beautiful, clever Caddy, who can do anything she wants with any man, and without whose..."

"Look, Jan, this is different—" she began agitatedly.

"...and without whose services we'd have got exactly nowhere. Clever, subtle Caddy, whose most charming attainment in the ever appreciative eyes of Papa Jan is her ability to handle every man in the neatest way imaginable and without a trace of real feeling. Kitty Kaddy, who..."

"Very well," she said with a sigh. "I'll do it."

"Of course you will," Jan said, drawing her hands back to his forehead. "And you'll begin right away by getting into your nicest sugar-and-cream war clothes. You and I are going to be the welcoming committee when that ape arrives this afternoon."

"But what about Jorj? He'll want to see Willard."

"That'll be taken care of," Jan assured her.

"And what about the other dozen rocket physicists Jorj asked to come?"

"Don't worry about them."

THE President looked inquiringly at his secretary across his littered desk in his homey study at White House, Jr. "So Opperly didn't have any idea how that odd question about Maizie turned up in Section Five?"

His secretary settled his paunch and shook his head. "Or claimed not to. Perhaps he's just the absentminded Prof., perhaps something else. The old feud of the physicists against the Thinkers may be getting hot again. There'll be further investigation."

The President nodded. He obviously had something uncomfortable on his mind. He said uneasily, "Do you think there's any possibility of it being true?"

"What?" asked the secretary guardedly.

"That peculiar hint about Maizie."

The secretary said nothing.

"Mind you, I don't think there is," the President went on hurriedly, his face assuming a sorrowful scowl. "I owe a lot to the Thinkers, both as a private person and as a public figure. Lord, a man has to lean on *something* these days. But just supposing it were true—" he hesitated, as before uttering blasphemy "—that there was a man inside Maizie, what could we do?"

The secretary said stolidly, "The Thinkers won our last election. They chased the Commies out of Iran. We brought them into the Inner Cabinet. We've showered them with public funds," he paused. "We couldn't do a damn thing."

The President nodded with equal conviction, and, not very happily, summed up: "So if anyone should go up against the Thinkers—and I'm afraid I wouldn't want to see that happen, whatever's true—it would have to be a scientist."

WILLARD FARQUAR felt his weight change the steps under his feet into an escalator. He cursed under his breath, but let them carry him, a defiant hulk, up to the tall and mystic blue portals, which silently parted when he was five meters away. The escalator changed to a slideway and carried him into a softly gleaming, high-domed room rather like the antechamber of a temple.

"Martian peace to you, Willard Farquar," an invisible voice intoned. "You have entered the Thinkers' Foundation. Please remain on the slideway."

"I want to see Jorj Helmuth," Willard growled loudly.

The slideway carried him into the mouth of a corridor and paused. A dark opening dilated on the wall. "May we take your hat and coat?" a voice asked politely. After a moment the request was repeated, with the addition of, "Just pass them through."

Willard scowled, then fought his way out of his shapeless

coat and passed it and his hat through in a lump. Instantly the opening contracted, imprisoning his wrists, and he felt his hands being washed on the other side of the wall.

He gave a great jerk, which failed to free his hands from the snugly padded gyves. "Do not be alarmed," the voice advised him. "It is only an esthetic measure. As your hands are laved, invisible radiations are slaughtering all the germs in your body, while more delicate emanations are producing a benign rearrangement of your emotions."

The rather amateurish curses Willard was gritting between his teeth became more sulfurous. His sensations told him that a towel of some sort was being applied to his hands. He wondered if he would be subjected to a face-washing and even greater indignities. Then, just before his wrists were released, he felt—for a moment only, but unmistakably—the soft touch of a girl's hand.

That touch, like the mysterious sweet chink of a bell in darkness, brought him a sudden feeling of excitement, wonder.

Yet the feeling was as fleeting as that caused by a lurid advertisement, for as the slideway began to move again, carrying him past a series of depth-pictures and inscriptions celebrating the Thinkers' achievements, his mood of bitter exasperation returned doubled. This place, he told himself, was a plague spot of the disease of magic in an enfeebled and easily infected world. He reminded himself that he was not without resources—the Thinkers must fear or need him, whether because of the Maelzel question or the necessity of producing a nuclear power spaceship. He felt his determination to smash them reaffirmed.

THE slideway, having twice turned into an escalator, veered toward an opalescent door, which opened as silently as the one below. The slideway stopped at the threshold.

Momentum carried him a couple of steps into the room. He stopped and looked around.

The place was a sybarite's modernistic dream. Sponge-carpeting thick as a mattress and topped with down. Hassocks and couches that looked butter-soft. A domed ceiling of deep glossy blue mimicking the night sky, with the constellations tooled in silver. A wall of niches crammed with statuettes of languorous men, women, beasts. A self-service bar with a score of golden spigots. A depth-TV-screen simulating a great crystal ball. Here and there barbaric studs of hammered gold that might have been push buttons. A low table set for three with exquisite ware of crystal and gold. An ever-changing scent of resins and flowers.

A smiling fat man clad in pearl gray sports clothes came through one of the curtained archways. Willard recognized Jan Tregarron from his pictures, but did not at once offer to speak to him. Instead he let his gaze wander with an ostentatious contempt around the crammed walls, take in the bar and the set table with its many wineglasses, and finally return to his host.

"And where," he asked with harsh irony, "are the dancing girls?"

The fat man's eyebrows rose. "In there," he said innocently, indicating the second archway. The curtains parted.

"Oh, I *am* sorry," the fat man apologized. "There seems to be only one on duty. I hope that isn't too much at variance with your tastes."

She stood in the archway, demure and lovely in an off-the-bosom frock of pale blue skylon edged in mutated mink. She was smiling the first smile that Willard had ever had from her lips.

"Mr. Willard Farquar," the fat man murmured, "Miss Arkady Simms."

JORJ HELMUTH turned from the conference table with its dozen empty chairs to the two mousily pretty secretaries.

"No word from the door yet, Master," one of them ventured to say.

Jorj twisted in his chair, though hardly uncomfortably, since it was a beautiful pneumatic job. His nervousness at having to face the twelve rocket physicists—a feeling which, he had to admit, had been unexpectedly great—was giving way to impatience.

"What's Willard Farquar's phone?" he asked sharply.

One of the secretaries ran through a clutch of desk tapes, then spent some seconds whispering into her throat-mike and listening to answers from the soft-speaker.

"He lives with Morton Opperly, who doesn't have one," she finally told Jorj in scandalized tones.

"Let me see the list," Jorj said. Then, after a bit, "Try Dr. Welcome's place."

This time there were results. Within a quarter of a minute he was handed a phone which he hung expertly on his shoulder.

"This is Dr. Asa Welcome," a reedy voice told him.

"This is Helmuth of the Thinkers' Foundation," Jorj said icily. "Did you get my communication?"

The reedy voice became anxious and placating. "Why, yes, Mr. Helmuth, I did. Very glad to get it too. Sounded most interesting. Very eager to come. But..."

"Yes?"

"Well, I was just about to hop in my 'copter—my son's 'copter—when the other note came."

"What other note?"

"Why, the note calling the meeting off."

"I sent no other note!"

The other voice became acutely embarrassed. "But I

considered it to be from you…or just about the same thing. I really think I had the right to assume that."

"How was it signed?" Jorj rapped.

"Mr. Jan Tregarron."

Jorj broke the connection. He didn't move until a low sound shattered his abstraction and he realized that one of the girls was whispering a call to the door. He handed back the phone and dismissed them. They went in a rustle of jackets and skirtlets, hesitating at the doorway but not quite daring to look back.

He sat motionless a minute longer. Then his hand crept fretfully onto the table and pushed a button. The room darkened and a long section of wall became transparent, revealing a dozen silvery models of spaceships, beautifully executed. He quickly touched another; the models faded and the opposite wall bloomed with an animated cartoon that portrayed with charming humor and detail the designing and construction of a neutron-drive spaceship. A third button, and a depth-picture of deep star-speckled space opened behind the cartoon, showing a section of Earth's surface and in the far distance the tiny ruddy globe of Mars. Slowly a tiny rocket rose from the section of Earth and spread its silvery sails.

HE SWITCHED off the pictures, keeping the room dark. By a faint table light he dejectedly examined his organizational charts for the neutron-drive project, the long list of books he had boned up on by somno-learning, the concealed table of physical constants and all sorts of other crucial details about rocket physics—a cleverly condensed encyclopedic "pony" to help out his memory on technical points that might have arisen in his discussion with the experts.

He switched out all the lights and slumped forward,

blinking his eyes and trying to swallow the lump in his throat. In the dark his memory went seeping back, back, to the day when his math teacher had told him, very superciliously, that the marvelous fantasies he loved to read and hoarded by his bed weren't real science at all, but just a kind of lurid pretense. He had so wanted to be a scientist, and the teacher's contempt had cast a damper on his ambition.

And now that the conference was canceled, would he ever know that it wouldn't have turned out the same way today? That his somno-learning hadn't taken? That his "pony" wasn't good enough? That his ability to handle people extended only to credulous farmer Presidents and mousy girls in skirtlets? Only the test of meeting the experts would have answered those questions.

Tregarron was the one to blame! Tregarron with his sly tyrannical ways, Tregarron with his fear of losing the future to men whom really understood theoretics and could handle experts. Tregarron so used to working by deception that he couldn't see when it became a fault and a crime. Tregarron, who must now be shown the light...or, failing that, against whom certain steps must be taken.

For perhaps half an hour Jorj sat very still, thinking. Then he turned to the phone and, after some delay, got his party.

"What is it now, Jorj?" Caddy asked impatiently. "Please don't bother me with any of your moods, because I'm tired and my nerves are on edge."

He took a breath. When steps may have to be taken, he thought, one must hold an agent in readiness. "Caddums," he intoned hypnotically, vibrantly. "Caddums..."

The voice at the other end had instantly changed, become submissive, sleepy, suppliant.

"Yes, Master?"

MORTON OPPERLY looked up from the sheet of neatly

penned equations at Willard Farquar, who had somehow acquired a measure of poise. He neither lumbered restlessly nor grimaced. He removed his coat with a certain dignity and stood solidly before his mentor. He smiled. Granting that he was a bear, one might guess he had just been fed.

"You see?" he said. "They didn't hurt me."

"They didn't hurt you?" Opperly asked softly.

Willard slowly shook his head. His smile broadened.

Opperly put down his pen, folded his hands. "And you're as determined as ever to expose and smash the Thinkers?"

"Of course!" The menacing growl came back into the bear's voice, except that it was touched with a certain pleased luxuriousness. "Only from now on I won't be teasing the zoo animals, and I won't embarrass you by asking any more Maelzel questions. I have reached the objective at which those tactics were aimed. After this I shall bore from within."

"Bore from within," Opperly repeated, frowning. "Now where have I heard that phrase before?" His brow cleared. "Oh, yes," he said listlessly. "Do I understand that you are becoming a Thinker, Willard?"

The other gave him a faintly pitying smile and stretched himself on the couch, gazed at the ceiling. All his movements were deliberate, easy.

"Certainly. That's the only realistic way to smash them. Rise high in their councils. Out-trick all their trickeries. Organize a fifth column. Then *strike!*"

"The end justifying the means, of course," Opperly said.

"Of course. As surely as the desire to stand up justifies your disturbing the air over your head. All action in this world is nothing but means."

Opperly nodded abstractedly. "I wonder if anyone else ever became a Thinker for those same reasons. I wonder if being a Thinker doesn't simply mean that you've decided you have to use lies and tricks as your chief method."

WILLARD shrugged. "Could be." There was no longer any doubt about the pitying quality of his smile.

Opperly stood up, squaring together his papers. "So you'll be working with Helmuth?"

"Not Helmuth. Tregarron." The bear's smile became cruel. "I'm afraid that Helmuth's career as a Thinker is going to have quite a setback."

"Helmuth," Opperly mused. "Morgenschein once told me a bit about him. A man of some idealism, despite his affiliations. Best of a bad lot. Incidentally, is he the one with whom..."

"...Miss Arkady Simms ran off?" Willard finished without any embarrassment. "Yes, that was Helmuth. But that's all going to be changed now."

Opperly nodded. "Good-by, Willard," he said.

Willard quickly heaved himself up on an elbow. Opperly looked at him for about five seconds, then, without a word, walked out of the room.

THE only obvious furnishings in Jan Tregarron's office were a flat-topped desk and a few chairs. Tregarron sat behind the desk, the top of which was completely bare. He looked almost bored, except that his little eyes were smiling. Jorj Helmuth sat across the desk from him, a few feet back, erect and grim-faced, while shadowy in the muted light, Caddy stood against the wall behind Tregarron. She still wore the fur-trimmed skylon frock she'd put on that afternoon. She took no part in the conversation, seemed almost unaware of it.

"So you just went ahead and canceled the conference without consulting me?" Jorj was saying.

"You called it without consulting me." Tregarron playfully wagged a finger. "Shouldn't do that sort of thing,

Jorj."

"But I tell you I was completely prepared. I was absolutely sure of my ground."

"I know, I know," Tregarron said lightly. "But it's not the right time for it. I'm the best judge of that."

"When will be the right time?"

Tregarron shrugged. "Look here, Jorj," he said, "every man should stick to his trade, to his forte. Technology isn't ours."

Jorj's lips thinned. "But you know as well as I do that we are going to have to have a nuclear spaceship and actually go to Mars someday."

Tregarron lifted his eyebrows. "Are we?"

"Yes! Just as we're going to have to build a real Maizie. Everything we've done until now have been emergency measures."

"Really?"

Jorj stared at him. "Look here, Jan," he said, gripping his knees with his hands, "you and I are going to have to talk things through."

"Are you quite sure of that?" Jan's voice was very cool. "I have a feeling that it might be best if you said nothing and accepted things as they are."

"No!"

"Very well." Tregarron settled himself in his chair.

"I helped you organize the Thinkers," Jorj said, and waited. "At least, I was your first partner."

Tregarron barely nodded.

"Our basic idea was that the time had come to apply science to the life of man on a large scale, to live rationally and realistically. The only things holding the world back from this all-important step were the ignorance, superstition, and inertia of the average man, and the stuffiness and lack of enterprise of the academic scientists—their worship of facts, even when facts were clearly dangerous.

"Yet we knew that in their deepest hearts the average man and the professionals were both on our side. They wanted the new world visualized by science. They wanted the simplifications and conveniences, the glorious adventures of the human mind and body. They wanted the trips to Mars and into the depths of the human psyche, they wanted the robots and the thinking machines. All they lacked was the nerve to take the first big step—and that was what we supplied.

"It was no time for half measures, for slow and sober plodding. The world was racked by wars and neurosis, in danger of falling into the foulest hands. What was needed was a tremendous and thrilling appeal to the human imagination, an Earth-shaking affirmation of the power of science for good.

"But the men who provided that appeal and affirmation couldn't afford to be cautious. They wouldn't check and double check. They couldn't wait for the grudging and jealous approval of the professionals. They had to use stunts, tricks, fakes—*anything to get over the big point.* Once that had been done, once mankind was headed down the new road, it would be easy enough to give the average man the necessary degree of insight to heal the breach with the professionals, to make good in actuality what had been made good only in pretense.

"Have I stated our position fairly?"

TREGARRON'S eyes were hooded. "You're the one who's telling it."

"On those general assumptions we established our hold on susceptible leaders and the mob," Jorj went on. "We built Maizie and the Mars rocket and the Mind Bomb. We discovered the wisdom of the Martians. We *sold* the people on the science that the professionals had been too high-toned to advertise or bring into the market place.

"But now that we've succeeded, now that we've made the big point, now that Maizie and Mars and science do rule the average human imagination, the time has come to take the second big step, to let accomplishment catch up with imagination, to implement fantasy with fact.

"Do you suppose I'd ever have gone into this with you, if it hadn't been for the thought of that second big step? Why, I'd have felt dirty and cheap, a mere charlatan—except for the sure conviction that someday everything would be set right. I've devoted my whole life to that conviction, Jan. I've studied and disciplined myself, using every scientific means at my disposal, so that I wouldn't be found lacking when the day came to heal the breach between the Thinkers and the professionals, I've trained myself to be the perfect liaison man for the job.

"Jan, the day's come and I'm the man. I know you've been concentrating on other aspects of our work; you haven't had time to keep up with my side of it. But I'm sure that as soon as you see how carefully I've prepared myself, how completely practical the neutron-drive rocket project is, you'll beg me to go ahead!"

Tregarron smiled at the ceiling for a moment. "Your general idea isn't so bad, Jorj, but your time scale is out of whack and your judgment is a joke. Oh, yes. Every revolutionary wants to see the big change take place in his lifetime. Tcha! It's as if he were watching evolutionary vaudeville and wanted the Ape-to-Man Act over in twenty minutes.

"Time for the second big step? Jorj, the average man's exactly what he was ten years ago, except that he's got a new god. More than ever he thinks of Mars as a Hollywood paradise, with wise men and yummy princesses. Maizie is

Mama magnified a million times. As for professional scientists, they're more jealous and stuffy than ever. All they'd like to do is turn the clock back to a genteel dream world of quiet quadrangles and caps and gowns, where every commoner bows to the passing scholar.

"Maybe in ten thousand years we'll be ready for the second big step. Maybe. Meanwhile, as should be, the clever will rule the stupid for their own good. The realists will rule the dreamers. Those with free hands will rule those who have deliberately handcuffed themselves with taboos.

"Secondly, your judgment. Did you actually think you could have bossed those professionals, kept your mental footing in the intellectual melee? You a nuclear physicist? A rocket scientist? Why, it's— Take it easy now, boy, and listen to me. They'd have torn you to pieces in twenty minutes and glad of the chance! You baffle me, Jorj, you know that Maizie and the Mars rocket and all that are fakes, yet you believe in your somno-learning and consciousness-expansion and optimism-pumping like the veriest yokel. I wouldn't be surprised to hear you'd taken up ESP and hypnotism. I think you should take stock of yourself and get a new slant. It's overdue."

HE LEANED back. Jorj's face had become a mask. His eyes did not flicker from Tregarron's, yet there was a subtle change in his expression. Behind Tregarron, Caddy swayed as if in a sudden gust of intangible wind and took a silent step forward from the wall.

"That's your honest opinion?" Jorj asked, very quietly.

"It's more than that," Tregarron told him, just as unmelodramatically. "It's orders."

Jorj stood up purposefully. "Very well," he said. "In that case I have to tell you that—"

Casually, but with no wasted motion, Tregarron slipped an

ultrasonic pistol from under the desk and laid it on the empty top.

"No," he said, "let me tell you something. I was afraid this would happen and I made preparations. If you've studied your Nazi, Fascist and Soviet history, you know what happens to old revolutionaries who don't move with the times. But I'm not going to be too harsh. I have a couple of the boys waiting outside. They'll take you by 'copter to the field, then by jet to New Mex. Bright and early tomorrow morning, Jorj, you're leaving on a trip to Mars."

Jorj hardly reacted to the words. Caddy was two steps nearer Tregarron.

"I decided Mars would be the best place for you," the fat man continued. "The robot controls will be arranged so that your 'visit' to Mars lasts two years. Perhaps in that time you will have learned wisdom, such as realizing that the big liar must never fall for his own big lie.

"Meanwhile, there will have to be a replacement for you. I have in mind a person who may prove peculiarly worthy to occupy your position, with all its perquisites. A person who seems to understand that force and desire are the motive powers of life, and that anyone who believes the big lie proves himself strictly a jerk."

CADDY was standing behind Tregarron now, her half-closed, sleepy eyes fixed on Jorj's.

"His name is Willard Farquar. You see, I too believe in cooperating with the scientists, Jorj, but by subversion rather than conference. My idea is to offer the hand of friendship to a selected few of them—the hand of friendship with a nice big bribe in it," he smiled. "You were a good man, Jorj, for the early days, when we needed a publicist with catchy ideas about Mind Bombs, ray guns, plastic helmets, fancy sweaters, space brassieres, and all that other corn. Now we can afford a soldier."

Jorj moistened his lips.

"We'll have a neat explanation of what's happened to you. Callers will be informed that you've gone on an extended visit to imbibe the wisdom of the Martians."

Jorj whispered, "Caddums."

Caddy leaned forward. Her arms snaked down Tregarron's, as if to imprison his wrists. But instead she reached out and took the ultrasonic pistol and put it in Tregarron's right hand. Then she looked up at Jorj with eyes that were very bright.

She said very sweetly and sympathetically, "Poor Superman."

The Big Engine

Have you found out about the Big Engine? It's all around us, you know—can't you hear it even now?

THERE are all sorts of screwy theories (the Professor said) of what makes the wheels of the world go round. There's a boy in Chicago who thinks we're all of us just the thoughts of a green cat; when the green cat dies we'll all puff to nothing like smoke. There's a man in the west who thinks all women are witches and run the world by conjure magic. There's a man in the east who believes all rich people belong to a secret society that's a lot tighter and tougher than the Mafia and that has a monopoly of power-secrets and pleasure-secrets other people don't dream exist.

Me, I think the wheels of the world just go. I decided that forty years ago and I've never since seen or heard or read anything to make me change my mind.

I was a stoker on a lake boat then (the Professor continued, delicately sipping smoke from his long thin cigarette). I was as stupid as they make them, but I liked to think. Whenever I'd get a chance I'd go to one of the big libraries and make them get me all sorts of books. That was how guys started calling me the Professor. I'd get books on philosophy, metaphysics, science, even religion. I'd read them and try to figure out the world. What was it all about, anyway? Why was I here? What was the point in the whole business of getting born and working and dying? What was the use of it? Why'd it have to go on and on?

And why'd it have to be so complicated?

Why all the building and tearing down? Why'd there have to be cities, with crowded streets and horse cars and cable cars and electric cars and big open-work steel boxes built to the sky to be hung with stone and wood—my closest friend got killed falling off one of those steel box-kites. Shouldn't there be some simpler way of doing it all? Why did things have to be so mixed up that a man like myself couldn't have a single clear decent thought?

More than that, why weren't people a real part of the world? Why didn't they show more honest-to-God response? When you slept with a woman, why was it something you had and she didn't? Why, when you went to a prize fight, were the bruisers only so much meat, and the crowd a lot of little screaming popinjays? Why was a war nothing but blather and blowup and bother? Why'd everybody have to go through their whole lives so dead, doing everything so methodical and prissy like a Sunday School picnic or an orphan's parade?

AND then, when I was reading one of the science books, it came to me. The answer was all there, printed out plain to see, only nobody saw it. It was just this: Nobody was really alive.

Back of other people's foreheads there weren't any real thoughts or minds, or love or fear, to explain things. The whole universe—stars and men and dirt and worms and atoms, the whole shooting match—was just one great big engine. It didn't take mind or life or anything else to run the engine. It just ran.

Now one thing about science. It doesn't lie. Those men who wrote those science books that showed me the answer, they had no more minds than anybody else. Just darkness in their brains, but because they were machines built to use science, they couldn't help but get the right answers. They were like the electric brains they've got now, but hadn't then, that give out the right answer when you feed in the question. I'd like to feed in the question, "What's Life?" to one of those machines and see what came out. Just figures, I suppose. I read somewhere that if a billion monkeys had typewriters and kept pecking away at them they'd eventually turn out all the Encyclopedia Britannica in trillions and trillions of years. Well, they've done it all right, and in jig time.

They're doing it now.

A lot of philosophy and psychology books I worked through really fit in beautifully. There was Watson's *Behaviorism* telling how we needn't even assume that people are conscious to explain their actions. There was Leibnitz's *Monadology,* with its theory that we're all of us lonely atoms that are completely out of touch and don't effect each other in the slightest, but only seem to...because all our little clockwork motors were started at the same time in pre-established harmony. We *seem* to be responding to each other, but actually we're just a bunch of wooden-minded puppets. Jerk one puppet up into the flies and the others go on acting as if exactly nothing at all had happened.

So there it was all laid out for me (the Professor went on, carefully pinching out the end of his cigarette). That was why there was no honest-to-God response in people. They were machines.

The fighters were machines made for fighting. The people that watched them were machines for stamping and screaming and swearing. The bankers had banking cogs in their bellies, the crooks had crooked cams. A woman was just a loving machine, all nicely adjusted to give you a good time (sometimes!) but the farthest star was nearer to you than the mind behind that mouth you kissed.

See what I mean? People are just machines, set to do a certain job and then quietly rust away. If you kept on being the machine you were supposed to be, well and good. Then your actions fitted with other people's. But if you didn't, if you started doing something else, then the others didn't respond. They just went on doing what was called for.

It wouldn't matter what you did, they'd just go on making the motions they were set to make. They might be set to make love, and you might decide you wanted to fight. They'd go on making love while you fought them. Or it might happen the other way—seems to, more often!

Or somebody might be talking about Edison. And you'd happen to say something about Ingersoll. But he'd just go on talking about Edison.

You were all alone.

EXCEPT for a few others—not more than one in a hundred thousand, I guess—who wake up and figure things out. And they mostly go crazy and run themselves to death, or else turn mean. Mostly they turn mean. They get a cheap little kick out of pushing things around that can't push back. All over the world you find them—little gangs of three or four, half a dozen—who've waked up, but just to their cheap kicks. Maybe it's a couple of coppers in 'Frisco, a schoolteacher in K.C., some artists in New York, some rich kids in Florida, some undertakers in London—who've found that all the people walking around are just dead folk and to be treated no decenter, who see how bad things are and get their fun out of making it a little worse. Just a mean *little* bit worse. They don't dare to destroy in a big way, because they know the machine feeds them and tends them, and because they're always scared they'd be noticed by gangs like themselves and wiped out. They haven't the guts to really wreck the whole shebang. But they get a kick out of scribbling their dirty pictures on it, out of meddling and messing with it.

I've seen some of their fun, as they call it, sometimes hidden away, sometimes in the open streets.

You've seen a clerk dressing a figure in a store window? Well, suppose he slapped its face. Suppose a kid stuck pins in a calico pussy-cat, or threw pepper in the eyes of a doll.

No decent live man would have anything to do with nickel sadism or dime paranoia like that. He'd either go back to his place in the machine and act out the part set for him, or else he'd hide away like me and live as quiet as he could, not stirring things up. Like a mouse in a dynamo or an ant in an atomics plant.

(The Professor went to the window and opened it, letting the sour old smoke out and the noises of the city in.)

LISTEN (he said), listen to the great mechanical symphony, the big black combo. The airplanes are the double bass. Have you noticed how you can always hear one nowadays? When one walks out of the sky another walks in.

Presses and pumps round out the bass section. Listen to them rumble and thump! Tonight they've got an old steam locomotive helping. Maybe they're giving a benefit show for the old duffer.

Cars and traffic—they're the strings. Mostly cellos and violas. They purr and wail and whine and keep trying to get out of their section.

Brasses? To me the steel-on-steel of streetcars and El trains always sounds like trumpets and cornets. Strident, metallic, fiery cold.

Hear that siren way off? It's a clarinet. The ship horns are tubas, the diesel horn's an oboe. And that lovely dreadful French horn is an electric saw cutting down the last tree.

But what a percussion section they've got! The big stuff, like streetcar bells jangling, is easy to catch, but you have to really listen to get the subtleties—the buzz of a defective neon sign, the click of a stoplight changing.

Sometimes you do get human voices, I'll admit, but they're not like they are in Beethoven's *Ninth* or Holst's *Planets*.

There's the real sound of the universe (the Professor concluded, shutting the window). That's your heavenly choir. That's the music of the spheres the old alchemists kept listening for—if they'd just stayed around a little longer they'd all have been deafened by it. Oh, to think that Schopenhauer was bothered by the crack of Carters' whips!

And now it's time for this mouse to tuck himself in his nest in the dynamo. Good night, gentlemen!

The Creature from Cleveland Depths

Here is a modern tale of an inner-directed sorcerer and an outer-directed sorcerer's apprentice…

"COME on, Gussy," Fay prodded quietly, "quit stalking around like a neurotic bear and suggest something for my invention team to work on. I enjoy visiting you and Daisy, but I can't stay aboveground all night."

"If being outside the shelters makes you nervous, don't come around any more," Gusterson told him, continuing to stalk. "Why doesn't your invention team think of something to invent? Why don't you? Hah!" In the "Hah!" lay triumphant condemnation of a whole way of life.

"We do," Fay responded imperturbably, "but a fresh viewpoint sometimes helps."

"I'll say it does! Fay, you burglar, I'll bet you've got twenty people like myself you milk for free ideas. First you irritate their bark and then you make the rounds every so often to draw-off the latex or the maple gloop."

Fay smiled. "It ought to please you that society still has a use for you outre inner-directed types. It takes something to make a junior executive stay aboveground after dark, when the missiles are on the prowl."

"Society can't have much use for us or it'd pay us something," Gusterson sourly asserted, staring blankly at the tankless TV and kicking it lightly as he passed on.

"No, you're wrong about that, Gussy. Money's not the key goad with you inner…directeds. I got that straight from our Motivations chief."

"Did he tell you what we should use instead to pay the grocer? A deep inner sense of achievement, maybe? Fay, why should I do any free thinking for Micro Systems?"

"I'll tell you why, Gussy. Simply because you get a kick out of insulting us with sardonic ideas. If we take one of them seriously, you think we're degrading ourselves, and that pleases you even more. Like making someone laugh at a lousy pun."

GUSTERSON held still in his roaming and grinned. "That the reason, huh? I suppose my suggestions would have to be something in the line of ultra-subminiaturized computers, where one sinister fine-etched molecule does the work of three big bumbling brain cells?"

"Not necessarily. Micro Systems is branching out. Wheel as free as a rogue star. But I'll pass along to Promotion your one molecule-three brain cell sparkler. It's a slight exaggeration, but it's catchy."

"I'll have my kids watch your ads to see if you use it and then I'll sue the whole underworld." Gusterson frowned as he resumed his stalking. He stared puzzledly at the antique TV. "How about inventing a plutonium termite?" he said suddenly. "It would get rid of those stockpiles that are worrying you moles to death."

Fay grimaced noncommittally and cocked his head.

"Well, then, how about a beauty mask? How about that, hey? I don't mean one to repair a woman's complexion, but one she'd wear all the time that'd make her look like a 17-year-old sexpot. That'd end *her* worries."

"Hey, that's for me," Daisy called from the kitchen. "I'll make Gusterson suffer. I'll make him crawl around on his hands and knees begging my immature favors."

"No, you won't," Gusterson called back. "You having a face like that would scare the kids. Better cancel that one, Fay. Half the adult race looking like Vina Vidarsson is too awful a thought."

"Yah, you're just scared of making a million dollars," Daisy jeered.

"I sure am," Gusterson said solemnly, scanning the fuzzy floor from one murky glass wall to the other, hesitating at the TV. "How about something homey now; like a flock of little prickly cylinders that roll around the floor collecting lint and flub? They'd work by electricity, or at a pinch cats could bat 'em around. Every so often they'd be automatically herded together and the lint cleaned off the bristles."

"No good," Fay said. "There's no lint underground and cats are verboten. And the aboveground market doesn't amount to more moneywise than the state of Southern Illinois. Keep it grander, Gussy, and more impractical—you can't sell people merely useful ideas." From his hassock in the center of the room he looked uneasily around. "Say, did that violet tone in the glass come from the high Cleveland hydrogen bomb or is it just age and ultraviolet, like desert glass?"

"NO, somebody's grandfather liked it that color," Gusterson informed him with happy bitterness. "I like it too—the glass, I mean, not the tint. People who live in glass houses can see the stars—especially when there's a window-washing streak in their germ-plasm."

"Gussy, why don't you move underground?" Fay asked, his voice taking on a missionary note. "It's a lot easier living in one room, believe me. You don't have to tramp from room to room hunting things."

"I like the exercise," Gusterson said stoutly.

"But I bet Daisy'd prefer it underground. And your kids wouldn't have to explain why their father lives like a Red Indian. Not to mention the safety factor and insurance savings and a crypt church within easy slidewalk distance. Incidentally, we see the stars all the time, better than you do—by repeater."

"Stars by repeater," Gusterson murmured to the ceiling, pausing for God to comment. Then, "No, Fay, even if I could afford it—and stand it—I'm such a bad-luck Harry that just when I got us all safely stowed at the N minus 1 sublevel, the Soviets would discover an earthquake bomb that struck from below, and I'd have to follow everybody back to the treetops. *Hey! How about bubble homes in orbit around earth?* Micro Systems could subdivide the world's most spacious suburb and all you moles could go ellipsing. Space is as safe as there is: no air, no shock waves. Free fall's the ultimate in restfulness—great health benefits. Commute by rocket—or better yet stay home and do all your business by TV-telephone, or by waldo if it were that sort of thing. Even pet your girl by remote control—she in her bubble, you in yours, whizzing through vacuum. Oh, damn—damn—*damn*—*damn*—DAMN!"

He was glaring at the blank screen of the TV, his big hands clenching and unclenching.

"Don't let Fay give you apoplexy—he's not worth it," Daisy said, sticking her trim head in from the kitchen, while Fay inquired anxiously, "Gussy, what's the matter?"

"Nothing, you worm!" Gusterson roared. "Except that an hour ago I forgot to tune in on the only TV program I've wanted to hear this year—*Finnegans Wake* scored for English, Gaelic and brogue. Oh, damn—*damn*—DAMN!"

"Too bad," Fay said lightly. "I didn't know they werc releasing it on flat TV too."

"WELL, they were! Some things are too damn big to keep completely underground. And I had to forget! I'm always doing it—I miss everything! Look here, you rat," he blatted suddenly at Fay, shaking his finger under the latter's chin. "I'll tell you what you can have that ignorant team of yours invent. They can fix me up a mechanical secretary that I can feed orders into and that'll remind me when the exact moment comes to listen to TV or phone somebody or mail in a story or write a letter or pick up a magazine or look at an eclipse or a new orbiting station or fetch the kids from school or buy Daisy a bunch of flowers or whatever it is. It's got to be something that's always with me, not something I have to go and consult or that I can get sick of and put down somewhere. And it's got to remind me forcibly enough so that I take notice and don't just shrug it aside, like I sometimes do even when Daisy reminds me of things. That's what your stupid team can invent for me! If they do a good job, I'll pay 'em as much as fifty dollars!"

"That doesn't sound like anything so very original to me," Fay commented coolly, leaning back from the wagging finger. "I think all senior executives have something of that sort. At least, their secretary keeps some kind of file…"

"I'm not looking for something with spiked falsies and nylons up to the neck," interjected Gusterson, whose ideas about secretaries were a trifle lurid. "I just want a mech reminder—that's all!"

"Well, I'll keep the idea in mind," Fay assured him, "along with the bubble homes and beauty masks. If we ever develop anything along those lines, I'll let you know. If it's a beauty mask, I'll bring Daisy a pilot model—to use to scare strange kids." He put his watch to his ear. "Good lord, I'm going to have to cut to make it underground before the main doors close. Just ten minutes to Second Curfew! 'By, Gus. 'By, Daze."

Two minutes later, living room lights out, they watched Fay's foreshortened antlike figure scurrying across the balding ill-lit park toward the nearest escalator.

Gusterson said, "Weird to think of that big bright space-poor glamor basement stretching around everywhere underneath. Did you remind Smitty to put a new bulb in the elevator?"

"The Smiths moved out this morning," Daisy said tonelessly. "They went underneath."

"Like cockroaches," Gusterson said. "Cockroaches leavin' a sinkin' apartment building. Next the ghosts'll be retreatin' to the shelters."

"Anyhow, from now on we're our own janitors," Daisy said.

He nodded. "Just leaves three families besides us loyal to this glass death trap. Not countin' ghosts." He sighed. Then, "You like to move below, Daisy?" he asked softly, putting his arm lightly across her shoulders. "Get a woozy eyeful of the bright lights and all for a change? Be a rat for a while? Maybe we're getting too old to be bats. I could scrounge me a company job and have a thinking closet all to myself and two secretaries with stainless steel breasts. Life'd be easier for you and a lot cleaner. And you'd sleep safer."

"That's true," she answered and paused. She ran her fingertip slowly across the murky glass, its violet tint barely perceptible against a cold dim light across the park. "But somehow," she said, snaking her arm around his waist, "I don't think I'd sleep happier—or one bit excited."

CHAPTER TWO

THREE weeks later Fay, dropping in again, handed to Daisy the larger of the two rather small packages he was carrying.

"It's a so-called beauty mask," he told her. "Complete with wig, eyelashes, and wettable velvet lips. It even breathes—pinholed elastiskin with a static adherence-charge. But Micro Systems had nothing to do with it, thank God. Beauty Trix put it on the market ten days ago and it's already started a teen-age craze. Some boys are wearing them too, and the police are yipping at Trix for encouraging transvestism with psychic repercussions."

"Didn't I hear somewhere that Trix is a secret subsidiary of Micro?" Gusterson demanded, rearing up from his ancient electric typewriter. "No, you're not stopping me writing, Fay—it's the gut of evening. If I do any more I won't have any juice to start with tomorrow. I got another of my insanity thrillers moving. A real id-teaser. In this one not only all the characters are crazy but the robot psychiatrist too."

"The vending machines are jumping with insanity novels," Fay commented. "Odd they're so popular."

Gusterson chortled. "The only way you outer-directed moles will accept individuality any more even in a fictional character, without your superegos getting seasick, is for them to be crazy. Hey, Daisy! Lemme see that beauty mask!"

But his wife, backing out of the room, hugged the package to her bosom and solemnly shook her head.

"A hell of a thing," Gusterson complained, "not even to be able to see what my stolen ideas look like."

"I got a present for you too," Fay said. "Something you might think of as a royalty on all the inventions someone thought of a little ahead of you. Fifty dollars by your own evaluation." He held out the smaller package. "Your tickler."

"My *what?"* Gusterson demanded suspiciously.

"Your tickler. The mech reminder you wanted. It turns out that the file a secretary keeps to remind her boss to do certain things at certain times is called a tickler file. So we named this a tickler. Here."

Gusterson still didn't touch the package. "You mean you actually put your invention team to work on that nonsense?"

"Well, what do you think? Don't be scared of it. Here, I'll show you."

As he unwrapped the package, Fay said, "It hasn't been decided yet whether we'll manufacture it commercially. If we do, I'll put through a voucher for you—for 'development consultation' or something like that. Sorry no royalty's possible. Davidson's squad had started to work up the identical idea three years ago, but it got shelved. I found it on a snoop through the closets. There! Looks rich, doesn't it?"

ON THE scarred black tabletop was a dully gleaming silvery object about the size and shape of a cupped hand with fingers merging. A tiny pellet on a short near-invisible wire led off from it. On the back was a punctured area suggesting the face of a microphone; there was also a window with a date and time in hours and minutes showing through and next to that four little buttons in a row. The concave underside of the silvery "hand" was smooth except for a central area where what looked like two little rollers came through.

"It goes on your shoulder under your shirt," Fay explained, "and you tuck the pellet in your ear. We might work up bone conduction on a commercial model. Inside is an ultra-slow fine-wire recorder holding a spool that runs for a week. The clock lets you go to any place on the 7-day wire and record a message. The buttons give you variable speed in going there, so you don't waste too much time making a setting. There's a knack in fingering them efficiently, but it's easily acquired."

Fay picked up the tickler. "For instance, suppose there's a TV show you want to catch tomorrow night at twenty-two hundred." He touched the buttons. There was the faintest whirring. The clock face blurred briefly three times before showing the setting he'd mentioned. Then Fay spoke into the punctured area: "Turn on TV Channel Two, you big dummy!" He grinned over at Gusterson. "When you've got all your instructions to yourself loaded in, you synchronize with the present moment and let her roll. Fit it on your shoulder and forget it. Oh, yes, and it literally does tickle you every time it delivers an instruction. That's what the little rollers are for. Believe me, you can't ignore it. Come on, Gussy, take off your shirt and try it out. We'll feed in some instructions for the next ten minutes so you get the feel of how it works."

"I don't want to," Gusterson said. "Not right now. I want to sniff around it first. My God, it's small! Besides everything else it does, does it think?"

"Don't pretend to be an idiot, Gussy! You know very well that even with ultra-sub-micro nothing quite this small can possibly have enough elements to do any thinking."

Gusterson shrugged. "I don't know about that. I think bugs think."

FAY groaned faintly. "Bugs operate by instinct, Gussy," he said. "A patterned routine. They do not scan situations and consequences and then make decisions."

"I don't expect bugs to make decisions," Gusterson said. "For that matter I don't like people who go around alla time making decisions."

"Well, you can take it from me, Gussy that this tickler is just a miniaturized wire recorder and clock…and a tickler. It doesn't do anything else."

"Not yet, maybe," Gusterson said darkly. "Not this model. Fay, I'm serious about bugs thinking. Or if they don't exactly think, they feel. They've got an interior drama. An inner glow. They're conscious. For that matter, Fay, I think all your really complex electronic computers are conscious too."

"Quit kidding, Gussy."

"Who's kidding?"

"You are. Computers simply aren't alive."

"What's alive? A word. I think computers are conscious, at least while they're operating. They've got that inner glow of awareness. They sort of…well…meditate."

"Gussy, computers haven't got any circuits for meditating. They're not programmed for mystical lucubrations. They've just got circuits for solving the problems they're on."

"Okay, you admit they've got problem-solving circuits—like a man has. I say if they've got the equipment for being conscious, they're conscious. What has wings, flies."

"Including stuffed owls and gilt eagles and dodoes—and wood-burning airplanes?"

"Maybe, under some circumstances. There *was* a wood-burning airplane. Fay," Gusterson continued, wagging his wrists for emphasis, "I really think computers are conscious. They just don't have any way of telling us that they are. Or maybe they don't have any *reason* to tell us, like the little Scotch boy who didn't say a word until he was fifteen and was supposed to be deaf and dumb."

"Why didn't he say a word?"

"Because he'd never had anything to say. Or take those Hindu fakirs, Fay, who sit still and don't say a word for thirty years or until their fingernails grow to the next village. If Hindu fakirs can do that, computers can!"

Looking as if he were masticating a lemon, Fay asked quietly, "Gussy, did you say you're working on an insanity novel?"

GUSTERSON frowned fiercely. "Now you're kidding," he accused Fay. "The dirty kind of kidding, too."

"I'm sorry," Fay said with light contrition. "Well, now you've sniffed at it, how about trying on Tickler?" He picked up the gleaming blunted crescent and jogged it temptingly under Gusterson's chin.

"Why should I?" Gusterson asked, stepping back. "Fay, I'm up to my ears writing a book. The last thing I want is something interrupting me to make me listen to a lot of junk and do a lot of useless things."

"But, dammit, Gussy! It was all your idea in the first place!" Fay blatted. Then, catching himself, he added, "I mean, you were one of the first people to think of this particular sort of instrument."

"Maybe so, but I've done some more thinking since then." Gusterson's voice grew a trifle solemn. "Inner-directed worthwhile thinkin'. Fay, when a man forgets to do something, it's because he really doesn't want to do it or because he's all roiled up down in his unconscious. He ought to take it as a danger signal and investigate the roiling, not hire himself a human or mech reminder."

"Bushwa," Fay retorted. "In that case you shouldn't write memorandums or even take notes."

"Maybe I shouldn't," Gusterson agreed lamely. "I'd have to think that over, too."

"Ha!" Fay jeered. "No, I'll tell you what your trouble is, Gussy. You're simply scared of this contraption. You've loaded your skull with horror-story nonsense about machines sprouting minds and taking over the world—until you're even scared of a simple miniaturized and clocked recorder." He thrust it out.

"Maybe I am," Gusterson admitted, controlling a flinch. "Honestly, Fay, that thing's got a gleam in its eye as if it had ideas of its own. Nasty ideas."

"Gussy, you nut, it hasn't got an eye."

"Not now, no, but it's got the gleam—the eye may come. It's the Cheshire cat in reverse. If you'd step over here and look at yourself holding it, you could see what I mean. But I don't think computers *sprout* minds, Fay. I just think they've *got* minds, because they've got the mind elements."

"Ho, ho!" Fay mocked. "Everything that has a material side has a mental side," he chanted. "Everything that's a body is also a spirit. Gussy, that dubious old metaphysical dualism went out centuries ago."

"Maybe so," Gusterson said, "but we still haven't anything but that dubious dualism to explain the human mind, have we? It's a jelly of nerve cells and it's a vision of the cosmos. If that isn't dualism, what is?"

"I give up. Gussy, are you going to tryout this tickler?"

"No!"

"But dammit, Gussy, we made it for you! —practically."

"Sorry, but I'm not coming near the thing."

"'Zen come near me," a husky voice intoned behind them. "Tonight I vant a man."

STANDING in the door was something slim in a short silver sheath. It had golden bangs and the haughtiest snub-nosed face in the world. It slunk toward them.

"My God, Vina Vidarsson!" Gusterson yelled.

"Daisy, that's terrific," Fay applauded, going up to her.

She bumped him aside with a swing of her hips, continuing to advance. "Not you, Ratty," she said throatily. "I vant a real man."

"Fay, I suggested Vina Vidarsson's face for the beauty mask," Gusterson said, walking around his wife and shaking a finger. "Don't tell me Trix just happened to think of that too."

"What else could they think of?" Fay laughed. "This season sex means VV and nobody else." An odd little grin flicked his lips, a tic traveled up his face and his body twitched slightly. "Say, folks, I'm going to have to be leaving. It's exactly fifteen minutes to Second Curfew. Last time I had to run and I got heartburn. When are you people going to move downstairs? I'll leave Tickler, Gussy. Play around with it and get used to it. 'By now."

"Hey, Fay," Gusterson called curiously, "have you developed absolute time sense?"

Fay grinned a big grin from the doorway—almost too big a grin for so small a man. "I didn't need to," he said softly, patting his right shoulder. "My tickler told me."

He closed the door behind him.

As side-by-side they watched him strut sedately across the murky chilly-looking park, Gusterson mused, "So the little devil had one of those nonsense-gadgets on all the time and I never noticed. Can you beat that?" Something drew across the violet-tinged stars, a short bright line that quickly faded. "What's that?" Gusterson asked gloomily. "Next to last stage of missile-here?"

"Won't you settle for an old-fashioned shooting star?" Daisy asked softly. The (wettable) velvet lips of the mask made even her natural voice sound different. She reached a hand back of her neck to pull the thing off.

"Hey, don't do that," Gusterson protested in a hurt voice. "Not for a while anyway."

"Hokay!" she said harshly, turning on him. "Zen down on your knees, dog!"

CHAPTER THREE

IT WAS a fortnight and Gusterson was loping down the home stretch on his 40,000-word insanity novel before Fay dropped in again, this time promptly at high noon.

Normally Fay cringed his shoulders a trifle and was inclined to slither, but now he strode aggressively, his legs scissoring in a fast, low goose step. He whipped off the sunglasses that all moles wore topside by day and began to pound Gusterson on the back while calling boisterously, "How are you, Gussy Old Boy, Old Boy?"

Daisy came in from the kitchen to see why Gusterson was choking. She was instantly grabbed and violently bussed to the accompaniment of, "Hiya, Gorgeous! Yum-yum! How about ad-libbing that some weekend?"

She stared at Fay dazedly, rasping the back of her hand across her mouth, while Gusterson yelled, "Quit that! What's got into you, Fay? Have they transferred you out of R&D to Company Morale? Do they line up all the secretaries at roll call and make you give them an eight-hour energizing kiss?"

"Ha, wouldn't you like to know? Fay retorted. He grinned, twitched jumpingly, held still a moment, then hustled over to the far wall. "Look out there," he rapped, pointing through the violet glass at a gap between the two nearest old skyscraper apartments. "In thirty seconds you'll see them test the new needle bomb at the other end of Lake Erie. It's educational." He began to count off seconds, vigorously semaphoring his arm. "…Two…three…Gussy, I've put through a voucher for two yards for you. Budgeting squawked, but I pressured 'em."

Daisy, squealed, "Yards!—are those dollar thousands?" while Gusterson was asking, "Then you're marketing the tickler?"

"Yes. Yes," Fay replied to them in turn. "…Nine…ten…" Again he grinned and twitched. "Time for noon Com-staff," he announced staccato. "Pardon the hush box." He whipped a pancake phone from under his coat, clapped it over his face and spoke fiercely but inaudibly into it, continuing to semaphore. Suddenly he thrust the phone away. "Twenty-nine…thirty…Thar she blows!"

An incandescent streak shot up the sky from a little above the far horizon and a doubly dazzling point of light appeared just above the top of it, with the effect of God dotting an "i."

"Ha, that'll skewer espionage satellites like swatting flies!" Fay proclaimed as the portent faded. "Bracing! Gussy, where's your tickler? I've got a new spool for it that'll razzle-dazzle you."

"I'll bet," Gusterson said drily. "Daisy?"

"You gave it to the kids and they got to fooling with it and broke it."

"No matter," Fay told them with a large sidewise sweep of his hand. "Better you wait for the new model. It's a six-way improvement."

"So I gather," Gusterson said, eyeing him speculatively. "Does it automatically inject you with cocaine? A fix every hour on the second?"

"Ha-ha, joke. Gussy, it achieves the same effect without using any dope at all. Listen: a tickler reminds you of your duties and opportunities—your chances for happiness and success! What's the obvious next step?"

"THROW it out the window. By the way, how do you do that when you're underground?"

"We have hi-speed garbage boosts. The obvious next step is you give the tickler a heart. It not only tells you, it warmly persuades you. It doesn't just say, 'Turn on the TV Channel Two, Joyce program,' it *brills* at you, 'Kid, Old Kid, race for the TV and flip that Two Switch! There's a great show coming through the pipes this second plus ten—you'll enjoy the hell out of yourself! Grab a ticket to ecstasy!'"

"My God," Gusterson gasped, "are those the kind of jolts it's giving you now?"

"Don't you get it, Gussy? You never load your tickler except when you're feeling buoyantly enthusiastic. You don't just tell yourself what to do hour by hour next week, you sell yourself on it. That way you not only make doubly sure you'll obey instructions but you constantly re-inoculate yourself with your own enthusiasm."

"I can't stand myself when I'm that enthusiastic," Gusterson said. "I feel ashamed for hours afterwards."

"You're warped—all this lonely sky-life. What's more, Gussy, think how still more persuasive some of those instructions would be if they came to a man in his best girl's most bedroomy voice, or his doctor's or psycher's if it's that sort of thing—or Vina Vidarsson's! By the way, Daze, don't wear that beauty mask outside. It's a grand misdemeanor ever since ten thousand teenagers rioted through Tunnel-Mart wearing them. And VV's suing Trix."

"No chance of that," Daisy said. "Gusterson got excited and bit off the nose." She pinched her own delicately.

"I'd no more obey my enthusiastic self," Gusterson was brooding, "than I'd obey a Napoleon drunk on his own brandy or a hopped-up St. Francis. Re-inoculated with my own enthusiasm? I'd die just like from snake-bite!"

"Warped, I said," Fay dogmatized, stamping around. "Gussy, having the instructions persuasive instead of neutral turned out to be only the opening wedge. The next step wasn't so obvious, but I saw it. Using subliminal verbal stimuli in his tickler, a man can be given constant supportive euphoric therapy 24 hours a day! And it makes use of all that empty wire. We've revived the ideas of a pioneer dynamic psycher named Dr. Coué. For instance, right now my tickler is saying to me—in tones too soft to reach my conscious mind, but do they stab into the unconscious!—'Day by day in every way I'm getting sharper and sharper.' It alternates that with 'gutsier and gutsier' and...well, forget that. Coué mostly used 'better and better' but that seems too general. And every hundredth time it says them out loud and the tickler gives me a brush—just a faint cootch—to make sure I'm keeping in touch."

"That third word-pair," Daisy wondered, feeling her mouth reminiscently. "Could I guess?"

GUSTERSON'S eyes had been growing wider and wider. "Fay," he said, "I could no more use my mind for anything if I knew all that was going on in my inner ear than if I were being brushed down with brooms by three witches. Look here," he said with loud authority, "you got to stop all this—it's crazy. Fay, if Micro'll junk the tickler, I'll think you up something else to invent—something real good."

"Your inventing days are over," Fay brilled gleefully. "I mean, you'll never equal your masterpiece."

"How about," Gusterson bellowed, "an anti-individual guided missile of some sort? The physicists have got small-scale antigravity good enough to float and fly something the size of a hand grenade. I can smell that even though it's a back-of-the-safe military secret. Well, how about keying such a missile to a man's fingerprints—or brainwaves, maybe, or his unique smell!—so it can spot and follow him around and target in on him, without harming anyone else? You could call it long-distance assassination—and the stinkingest gets it! Or you could simply load it with some disgusting goo and key it to teenagers as a group—that'd take care of them. Fay, doesn't it give you a rich warm kick to think of my midget missiles buzzing around in your tunnels, seeking out evil-doers, like a swarm of angry wasps or angelic bumblebees?"

"You're not luring me down any side trails," Fay said laughingly. He grinned and twitched, then hurried toward the opposite wall, looking back for a moment, and then motioning them to follow. Outside, about a hundred yards beyond the purple glass, rose another ancient glass-walled apartment skyscraper. Beyond, Lake Erie rippled glintingly.

"Another bomb-test?" Gusterson asked.

Fay pointed at the building. "Tomorrow," he announced, "a modern factory, devoted solely to the manufacture of ticklers, will be erected on that site."

"You mean one of those windowless phallic eyesores?" Gusterson demanded. "Fay, you people aren't even consistent. You've got all your homes underground. Why not your factories?"

"Sh! Not enough room. And night missiles are scarier."

"I know that building's been empty for a year," Daisy said uneasily, "but how—?"

"Sh! Watch! *Now!*"

The looming building seemed to blur or fuzz for a moment or two. Then it was as if the lake's bright ripples had invaded the old glass a hundred yards away. Wavelets chased themselves up and down the gleaming walls, became higher, higher...and then suddenly the glass cracked all over to tiny fragments and fell away, to be followed quickly by fragmented concrete and plastic and plastic piping, until all that was left was the nude steel framework, vibrating so rapidly as to be almost invisible against the gleaming lake.

DAISY COVERED her ears; but there was no explosion, only a long-drawn-out low crash as the fragments hit twenty floors below and dust whooshed out sideways.

"Spectacular! Most spectacular!" Fay summed up. "Knew you'd enjoy it. That little trick was first conceived by the great Tesla during his last fruity years. Research discovered it in his biog—we just made the dream come true. A tiny resonance device you could carry in your belt-bag attunes itself to the natural harmonic of a structure and then increases amplitude by tiny pushes exactly in time. Just like soldiers marching in step can break down a bridge, only this is as if it were being done by one marching ant." He pointed at the naked framework appearing out of its own blur and said, "We'll be able to hang the factory on that. If not, we'll whip a mega-current through it and vaporize it. No question the micro-resonator is the neatest sweetest wrecking device going. You can expect a lot more of this sort of efficiency now that mankind has the tickler to enable him to use his full potential. What's the matter, folks?"

Daisy was staring around the violet-walled room with dumb mistrust. Her hands were trembling.

"You don't have to worry," Fay assured her with an understanding laugh. "This building's safe for a month more at least." Suddenly he grimaced and leaped a foot in the air. He raised a clawed hand to scratch his shoulder but managed to check the movement. "Got to beat it, folks," he announced tersely. "My tickler gave me the grand cootch."

"Don't go yet," Gusterson called, rousing himself with a shudder, which he immediately explained: "I just had the illusion that if I shook myself all my flesh and guts would fall off my shimmying skeleton. Brr! Fay, before you and Micro go off half cocked, I want you to know there's one insuperable objection to the tickler as a mass-market item. The average man or woman won't go to the considerable time and trouble it must take to load a tickler. He simply hasn't got the compulsive orderliness and willingness to plan that it requires."

"We thought of that weeks ago," Fay rapped, his hand on the door. "Every tickler spool that goes to market is patterned like wallpaper with one of five designs of suitable subliminal supportive euphoric material. 'Ittier and ittier,' 'viriler and viriler'—you know. The buyer is robotinterviewed for an hour, his personalized daily routine laid out and thereafter templated on his weekly spool. He's strongly urged next to take his tickler to his doctor and psycher for further instruction-imposition. We've been working with the medical profession from the start. They love the tickler because it'll remind people to take their medicine on the dot...and rest and eat and go to sleep just when and how doc says. This is a big operation, Gussy—a biiiiiig operation! 'By!"

Daisy hurried to the wall to watch him cross the park. Deep down she was a wee bit worried that he might linger to attach a micro-resonator to *this* building and she wanted to time him. But Gusterson settled down to his typewriter and began to bat away.

"I want to have another novel started," he explained to her, "before the ant marches across this building in about four and a half weeks...or a million sharp little gutsy guys come swarming out of the ground and heave it into Lake Erie."

CHAPTER FOUR

EARLY NEXT morning windowless walls began to crawl up the stripped skyscraper between them and the lake. Daisy pulled the blackout curtains on that side. For a day or two longer their thoughts and conversations were haunted by

Gusterson's vague sardonic visions of a horde of tickler-energized moles pouring up out of the tunnels to tear down the remaining trees, tank the atmosphere and perhaps somehow dismantle the stars—at least on this side of the world—but then they both settled back into their customary easygoing routines. Gusterson typed. Daisy made her daily shopping trip to a little topside daytime store and started painting a mural on the floor of the empty apartment next theirs but one.

"We ought to lasso some neighbors," she suggested once. "I need somebody to hold my brushes and admire. How about you making a trip below at the cocktail hours, Gusterson, and picking up a couple of girls for a starter? Flash the old viriler charm, cootch them up a bit, emphasize the delights of high living, but make sure they're compatible roommates. You could pick up that two-yard check from Micro at the same time."

"You're an immoral money-ravenous wench," Gusterson said absently, trying to dream of an insanity beyond insanity that would make his next novel a real id-rousing best-vender.

"If that's your vision of me, you shouldn't have chewed up the VV mask."

"I'd really prefer you with green stripes," he told her. "But stripes, spots, or sunbathing, you're better than those cocktail moles."

Actually both of them acutely disliked going below. They much preferred to perch in their eyrie and watch the people of Cleveland Depths, as they privately called the local sub-suburb, rush up out of the shelters at dawn to work in the concrete fields and windowless factories, make their daytime jet trips and freeway jaunts, do their noon-hour and coffee-break guerrilla practice, and then go scurrying back at twilight to the atomic-proof, brightly lit, vastly exciting, claustrophobic caves.

Fay and his projects began once more to seem dreamlike, though Gusterson did run across a cryptic advertisement for ticklers in *The Manchester Guardian,* which he got daily by facsimile. Their three children reported similar ads, of no interest to young fry, on the TV and one afternoon they came home with the startling news that the monitors at their subsurface school had been issued ticklers. On sharp interrogation by Gusterson, however, it appeared that these last were not ticklers but merely two-way radios linked to the school police station transmitter.

"Which is bad enough," Gusterson commented later to Daisy. "But it'd be even dirtier to think of those clock-watching superegos being strapped to kids' shoulders. Can you imagine Huck Finn with a tickler, tellin' him when to tie up the raft to a towhead and when to take a swim?"

"I bet Fay could," Daisy countered. "When's he going to bring you that check, anyhow? Iago wants a jetcycle and I promised Imogene a Vina Kit and then Claudius'll have to have something."

Gusterson scowled thoughtfully. "You know, Daze," he said, "I get a feeling Fay's in the hospital, all narcotized up and being fed intravenously. The way he was jumping around last time, that tickler was going to cootch him to pieces in a week."

AS IF TO refute this intuition, Fay turned up that very evening. The lights were dim. Something had gone wrong with the building's old transformer and, pending repairs, the two remaining occupied apartments were making do with batteries, which turned bright globes to mysterious amber candles and made Gusterson's ancient typewriter operate sluggishly.

Fay's manner was subdued or at least closely controlled and for a moment Gusterson thought he'd shed his tickler. Then the little man came out of the shadows and Gusterson saw the large bulge on his right shoulder.

"Yes, we had to up it a bit sizewise," Fay explained in clipped tones. "Additional super-features. While brilliantly successful on the whole, the subliminal euphorics were a shade too effective. Several hundred users went hoppity manic. We gentled the cootch and qualified the subliminals—you know, 'Day by day in every way I'm getting sharper *and more serene*—but a stabilizing influence was still needed, so after a top-level conference we decided to combine Tickler with Moodmaster."

"My God," Gusterson interjected, "do they have a machine now that does that?"

"Of course. They've been using them on ex-mental patients for years."

"I just don't keep up with progress," Gusterson said, shaking his head bleakly. "I'm falling behind on all fronts."

"You ought to have your tickler remind you to read Science Service releases," Fay told him. "Or simply instruct it to scan the releases and—no, that's still in research." He looked at Gusterson's shoulder and his eyes widened. "You're not wearing the new-model tickler I sent you," he said accusingly.

"I never got it," Gusterson assured him. "Postmen deliver top-side mail and parcels by throwing them on the high-speed garbage boosts and hoping a tornado will blow them to the right addresses." Then he added helpfully, "Maybe the Russians stole it while it was riding the whirlwinds."

"That's not a suitable topic for jesting," Fay frowned. "We're hoping that Tickler will mobilize the full potential of the Free World for the first time in history. Gusterson, you are going to have to wear a ticky-tick. It's becoming impossible for a man to get through modern life without one."

"Maybe I will," Gusterson said appealingly, "but right now tell me about Moodmaster. I want to put it in my new insanity novel."

Fay shook his head. "Your readers will just think you're behind the times. If you use it, underplay it. But anyhow, Moodmaster is a simple physiotherapy engine that monitors bloodstream chemicals and body electricity. It ties directly into the bloodstream, keeping blood, sugar, et cetera, at optimum levels and injecting euphrin or depressin as necessary—and occasionally a touch of extra adrenaline, as during work emergencies."

"Is it painful?" Daisy called from the bedroom.

"Excruciating," Gusterson called back. "Excuse it, please," he grinned at Fay. "Hey, didn't I suggest cocaine injections last time I saw you?"

"So you did," Fay agreed flatly. "Oh by the way, Gussy, here's that check for a yard I promised you. Micro doesn't muzzle the ox."

"Hooray!" Daisy cheered faintly.

"I THOUGHT you said it was going to be for two," Gusterson complained.

"Budgeting always forces a last-minute compromise," Fay shrugged. "You have to learn to accept those things."

"I love accepting money and I'm glad any time for three feet," Daisy called agreeably. "Six feet might make me wonder if I weren't an insect, but getting a yard just makes me feel like a gangster's moll."

"Want to come out and gloat over the yard paper, Toots, and stuff it in your diamond-embroidered net stocking top?" Gusterson called back.

"No, I'm doing something to that portion of me just now. But hang onto the yard, Gusterson."

"Aye-aye, Cap'n," he assured her. Then, turning back to Fay, "So you've taken the Dr. Coué repeating out of the tickler?"

"Oh, no. Just balanced it off with depressin. The subliminals are still a prime sales point. All the tickler features are cumulative, Gussy. You're still underestimating the scope of the device."

"I guess I am. What's this 'work-emergencies' business? I f you're using the tickler to inject drugs into workers to keep them going, that's really just my cocaine suggestion modernized and I'm putting in for another thou. Hundreds of years ago the South American Indians chewed coca leaves to kill fatigue sensations."

"That so? Interesting—and it proves priority for the Indians, doesn't it? I'll make a try for you, Gussy, but don't expect anything." He cleared his throat, his eyes grew distant and, turning his head a little to the right, he enunciated sharply, "Pooh-Bah. Time: Inst oh five. One oh five seven. Oh oh. Record: Gussy coca thou budget. Cut." He explained, "We got a voice-cued setter now on the deluxe models. You can record a memo to yourself without taking off your shirt. Incidentally, I use the ends of the hours for trifle-memos. I've already used up the fifty-nines and eights for tomorrow and started on the fifty-sevens."

"I understood most of your memo," Gusterson told him gruffly. "The last 'Oh oh' was for seconds, wasn't it? Now I call that crude—why not microseconds, too? But how do you remember where you've made a memo so you don't rerecord over it? After all, you're rerecording over the wallpaper all the time."

"Tickler beeps and then hunts for the nearest information-free space."

"I see. And what's the Pooh-Bah for?"

Fay smiled. "Cut. My password for activating the setter, so it won't respond to chance numerals it overhears."

"But why Pooh-Bah?"

Fay grinned: "Cut.` And you a writer. It's a literary reference, Gussy. Pooh-Bah (cut!) was Lord High Everything Else in *The Mikado*. He had a little list and nothing on it would ever be missed."

"OH, YEAH," Gusterson remembered, glowering. "As I recall it, all that went on that list was the names of people who were slated to have their heads chopped off by Ko-Ko. Better watch your step, Shorty. It may be a back-handed omen. Maybe all those workers you're puttin' ticklers on to pump them full of adrenaline so they'll overwork without noticin' it will revolt and come out some day choppin' for your head."

"Spare me the Marxist mythology," Fay protested. "Gussy, you've got a completely wrong slant on Tickler. It's true that most of our mass sales so far, bar government and army, have been to large companies purchasing for their employees—"

"Ah-ha!"

"—but that's because there's nothing like a tickler for teaching a new man his job. It tells him from instant to instant what he must do—while he's already on the job and without disturbing other workers. Magnetizing a wire with a job pattern is the easiest thing going. And you'd be astonished what the subliminals do for employee morale. It's this way, Gussy: most people are too improvident and unimaginative to see in advance the advantages of ticklers. They buy one because the company strongly suggests it and payment is on easy installments withheld from salary. They find a tickler makes the work day go easier. The little fellow perched on your shoulder is a friend exuding comfort and good advice. The first thing he's set to say is 'Take it easy, pal.'

"Within a week they're wearing their tickler 24 hours a day—and buying a tickler for the wife, so she'll remember to comb her hair and smile real pretty and cook favorite dishes."

"I get it, Fay," Gusterson cut in. "The tickler is the newest fad for increasing worker efficiency. Once, I read somewheres, it was salt tablets. They had salt-tablet dispensers everywhere, even in air-conditioned offices where there wasn't a moist armpit twice a year and the gals sweat only champagne. A decade later people wondered what all those dusty white pills were for. Sometimes they were mistook for tranquilizers. It'll be the same way with ticklers. Somebody'll open a musty closet and see jumbled heaps of these gripping-hand silvery gadgets gathering dust curls and—"

"They will not!" Fay protested vehemently. "Ticklers are not a fad—they're history-changers, they're Free-World revolutionary! Why, before Micro Systems put a single one on the market, we'd made it a rule that every Micro employee had to wear one! If that's not having supreme confidence in a product—"

"Every employee except the top executives, of course," Gusterson interrupted jeeringly. "And that's not demoting you, Fay. As the R & D chief most closely involved, you'd naturally have to show special enthusiasm."

"But you're wrong there, Gussy," Fay crowed. "Man for man, our top executives have been more enthusiastic about their personal ticklers than any other class of worker in the whole outfit."

Gusterson slumped and shook his head. "If that's the case," he said darkly, "maybe mankind deserves the tickler."

"I'LL SAY IT does!" Fay agreed loudly without thinking. Then, "Oh, can the carping, Gussy. Tickler's a great invention. Don't deprecate it just because you had something to do with its genesis. You're going to have to get in the swim and wear one."

"Maybe I'd rather drown horribly."

"Can the gloom-talk too! Gussy, I said it before and I say it again, you're just scared of this new thing. Why, you've even got the drapes pulled so you won't have to look at the tickler factory."

"Yes, I am scared," Gusterson said. "Really sca...AWP!"

Fay whirled around. Daisy was standing in the bedroom doorway, wearing the short silver sheath. This time there was no mask, but her bobbed hair was glitteringly silvered, while her legs, arms, hands, neck, face—every bit of her exposed skin—was painted with beautifully even vertical green stripes.

"I did it as a surprise for Gusterson," she explained to Fay. "He says he likes me this way. The green glop's supposed to be smudge-proof."

Gusterson did not comment. His face had a rapt expression. "I'll tell you why your tickler's so popular, Fay," he said softly. "It's not because it backstops the memory or because it boosts the ego with subliminals. It's because it takes the hook out of a guy, it takes over the job of withstanding the pressure of living. See, Fay, here are all these little guys in this subterranean rat race with atomic-death squares and chromium-plated reward squares and enough money if you pass Go almost to get to Go again—and a million million rules of the game to keep in mind. Well, here's this one little guy and every morning he wakes up there's all these things he's got to keep in mind to do or he'll lose his turn three times in a row and maybe a terrible black rook in iron armor'll loom up and bang him off the chessboard. But now, look, now he's got his tickler and he tells his sweet silver tickler all these things and the tickler's got to remember them. Of course he'll have to do them eventually but meanwhile the pressure's off him, the hook's out of his short hairs. He's shifted the responsibility..."

"Well, what's so bad about that?" Fay broke in loudly. "What's wrong with taking the pressure off little guys? Why shouldn't Tickler be a super-ego surrogate? Micro's Motivations chief noticed that positive feature straight off and scored it three pluses. Besides, it's nothing but a gaudy way of saying that Tickler backstops the memory. Seriously, Gussy, what's so bad about it?"

"I don't know," Gusterson said somewhat slowly, his eyes still far away. "I just know it feels bad to me." He crinkled his big forehead. "Well for one thing," he said, "it means that a man's taking orders from something else. He's got a kind of master. He's sinking back into a slave psychology."

"He's only taking orders from himself," Fay countered disgustedly. "Tickler's just a mech reminder, a notebook, in essence no more than the back of an old envelope. It's no master."

"Are you absolutely sure of that?" Gusterson asked quietly.

"Why, Gussy, you big oaf—" Fay began heatedly. Suddenly his features quirked and he twitched. "'Scuse me, folks," he said rapidly, heading for the door, "but my tickler told me I gotta go."

"Hey Fay, don't you mean you told your tickler to tell you when it was time to go?" Gusterson called after him.

Fay looked back in the doorway. He wet his lips, his eyes moved from side to side. "I'm not quite sure," he said in an odd strained voice and darted out.

GUSTERSON stared for some seconds at the pattern of emptiness Fay had left. Then he shivered. Then he shrugged.

"I must be slipping," he muttered. "I never even suggested something for him to invent." Then he looked around at Daisy, who was still standing poker-faced in her doorway.

"Hey, you look like something out of the Arabian Nights," he told her. "Are you supposed to be anything special? How far do those stripes go, anyway?"

"You could probably find out," she told him coolly. "All you have to do is kill me a dragon or two first."

He studied her. "My God," he said reverently, "I really have all the fun in life. What do I do to deserve this?"

"You've got a big gun," she told him, "and you go out in the world with it and hold up big companies and take yards and yards of money away from them in rolls like ribbon and bring it all home to me."

"Don't say that about the gun again," he said. "Don't whisper it, don't even think it. I've got one, dammit—thirty-eight caliber, yet—and I don't want some psionic monitor with two-way clairaudience they haven't told me about catching the whisper and coming to take the gun away from us . It's one of the few individuality symbols we've got left."

Suddenly Daisy whirled away from the door, spun three times so that her silvered hair stood out like a metal coolie hat, and sank to a curtsey in the middle of the room.

"I've just thought of what I am," she announced, fluttering her eyelashes at him. "I'm a sweet silver tickler with green stripes."

CHAPTER FIVE

NEXT day Daisy cashed the Micro check for ten hundred silver smackers, which she hid in a broken radionic coffee urn. Gusterson sold his insanity novel and started a new one about a mad medic with a hiccupy hysterical chuckle, who gimmicked Moodmasters to turn mental patients into nymphomaniacs, mass murderers and compulsive saints. But this time he couldn't get Fay out of his mind, or the last chilling words the nervous little man had spoken.

For that matter, he couldn't blank the underground out of his mind as effectively as usually. He had the feeling that a new kind of mole was loose in the burrows and that the ground at the foot of their skyscraper might start humping up any minute.

Toward the end of one afternoon he tucked a half dozen newly typed sheets in his pocket, shrouded his typer, went to the hat rack and took down his prize: a miner's hard-top cap with electric headlamp.

"Goin' below, Cap'n," he shouted toward the kitchen.

"Be back for second dog watch," Daisy replied. "Remember what I told you about lassoing me some art-conscious girl neighbors."

"Only if I meet a piebald one with a taste for Scotch—or maybe a pearl gray biped jaguar with violet spots," Gusterson told her, clapping on the cap with a We-Who-Are-About-To-Die gesture.

Halfway across the park to the escalator bunker Gusterson's heart began to tick. He resolutely switched on his headlamp.

As he'd known it would, the hatch robot whirred an extra and higher-pitched ten seconds when it came to his topside address, but it ultimately dilated the hatch for him, first handing him a claim check for his ID card.

Gusterson's heart was ticking like a sledgehammer by now. He hopped clumsily onto the escalator, clutched the moving guardrail to either side, then shut his eyes as the steps went over the edge and became what felt like vertical. An instant later he forced his eyes open, unclipped a hand from the rail and touched the second switch beside his headlamp, which instantly began to blink whitely, as if he were a civilian plane flying into a nest of military jobs.

With a further effort he kept his eyes open and flinchingly surveyed the scene around him. After zigging through a bomb-proof half-furlong of roof, he was dropping into a large twilit cave. The blue-black ceiling twinkled with stars. The walls were pierced at floor level by a dozen archways with busy niche stores and glowing advertisements crowded between them. From the archways some three dozen slidewalks curved out, tangenting off each other in a bewildering multiple cloverleaf. The slidewalks were packed with people, traveling motionless like purposeful statues or pivoting with practiced grace from one slidewalk to another, like a thousand toreros doing veronicas.

THE slidewalks were moving faster than he recalled from his last venture underground and at the same time the whole pedestrian concourse was quieter than he remembered. It was as if the five thousand or so moles in view were all listening—for what? But there was something else that had changed about them—a change that he couldn't for a moment define, or unconsciously didn't want to. Clothing style? No... My God, they weren't all wearing identical monster masks? No... Hair color? Well...

He was studying them so intently that he forgot his escalator was landing. He came off it with a heel-jarring stumble and bumped into a knot of four men on the tiny triangular hold-still. These four at least sported a new style-wrinkle: ribbed gray shoulder capes that made them look as if their heads were poking up out of the center of bulgy umbrellas or giant mushrooms.

One of them grabbed hold of Gusterson and saved him from staggering onto a slidewalk that might have carried him to Toledo.

"Gussy, you dog, you must have esped I wanted to see you," Fay cried, patting him on the elbows. "Meet Davidson and Kester and Hazen, colleagues of mine. We're all Micro-men." Fay's companions were staring strangely at Gusterson's blinking headlamp. Fay explained rapidly, "Mr. Gusterson is an insanity novelist. You know, I-D."

"Inner-directed spells *id,*" Gusterson said absently, still staring at the interweaving crowd beyond them, trying to figure out what made them different from last trip. "Creativity fuel.

Cranky. Explodes through the parietal fissure if you look at it cross-eyed."

"Ha-ha," Fay laughed. "Well, boys, I've found my man. How's the new novel perking, Gussy?"

"Got my climax, I think," Gusterson mumbled, still peering puzzledly around Fay at the slidestanders. "Moodmaster's going to come alive. Ever occur to you that 'mood' is 'doom' spelled backwards? And then..." He let his voice trail off as he realized that Kester and Davidson and Hazen had made their farewells and were sliding into the distance. He reminded himself wryly that nobody ever wants to hear an author talk—he's much too good a listener to be wasted that way. Let's see, was it that everybody in the crowd had the same facial expression...? Or showed symptoms of the same disease...?

"I was coming to visit you, but now you can pay me a call," Fay was saying. "There are two matters I want to—"

Gusterson stiffened. *"My God, they're all hunchbacked!"* he yelled.

"Shh! Of course they are," Fay whispered reprovingly. "They're all wearing their ticklers. But you don't need to be insulting about it."

"I'm gettin' out o' here." Gusterson turned to flee as if from five thousand Richard the Thirds.

"Oh, no you're not," Fay amended, drawing him back with one hand. Somehow, underground, the little man seemed to carry more weight. "You're having cocktails in my thinking box. Besides, climbing a down escalader will give you a heart attack."

IN HIS home habitat Gusterson was about as easy to handle as a rogue rhinoceros, but away from it—and especially if underground—he became more like a pliable elephant. All his bones dropped out through his feet, as he described it to Daisy. So now he submitted miserably as Fay surveyed him up and down, switched off his blinking headlamp ("That coalminer caper is corny, Gussy.") and then—surprisingly—rapidly stuffed his belt-bag under the right shoulder of Gusterson's coat and buttoned the latter to hold it in place.

"So you won't stand out," he explained. Another swift survey. "You'll do. Come on, Gussy. I got lots to brief you on." Three rapid paces and then Gusterson's feet would have gone out from under him except that Fay gave him a mighty shove. The small man sprang onto the slidewalk after him and then they were skimming effortlessly side by side.

Gusterson felt frightened and twice as hunchbacked as the slidestanders around him—morally as well as physically.

Nevertheless he countered bravely, "I got things to brief you on. I got six pages of cautions on ti—"

"Shh!" Fay stopped him. "Let's use my hushbox."

He drew out his pancake phone and stretched it so that it covered both their lower faces, like a double yashmak. Gusterson, his neck pushing into the ribbed bulge of the shoulder cape so he could be cheek to cheek with Fay, felt horribly conspicuous, but then he noticed that none of the slidestanders were paying them the least attention. The reason for their abstraction occurred to him. They were listening to their ticklers! He shuddered.

"I got six pages of caution on ticklers," he repeated into the hot, moist quiet of the pancake phone. "I typed 'em so I wouldn't forget 'em in the heat of polemicking. I want you to read every word. Fay, I've had it on my mind ever since I started wondering whether it was you or your tickler made you duck out of our place last time you were there. I want you to—"

"Ha-ha! All in good time." In the pancake phone Fay's laugh was brassy. "But I'm glad you've decided to lend a hand, Gussy. This thing is moving faaaasst. Nationwise, adult underground ticklerization is 90 percent complete."

"I don't believe that," Gusterson protested while glaring at the hunchbacks around them. The slidewalk was gliding down a low glow-ceiling tunnel lined with doors and advertisements.

Rapt-eyed people were pirouetting on and off. "A thing just can't develop that fast, Fay. It's against nature."

"Ha, but we're not in nature, we're in culture. The progress of an industrial scientific culture is geometric. It goes n-times as many jumps as it takes. More than geometric—exponential. Confidentially, Micro's Math chief tells me we're currently on a fourth-power progress curve trending into a fifth."

"You mean we're goin' so fast we got to watch out we don't bump ourselves in the rear when we come around again?" Gusterson asked, scanning the tunnel ahead for curves. "Or just shoot straight up to infinity?"

"Exactly! Of course most of the last power and a half is due to Tickler itself. Gussy, the tickler's already eliminated absenteeism, alcoholism and aboulia in numerous urban areas—and that's just one letter of the alphabet! If Tickler doesn't turn us into a nation of photo-memory constant-creative-flow geniuses in six months, I'll come live topside."

"YOU mean because a lot of people are standing around glassy-eyed listening to something mumbling in their ear that it's a good thing?"

"Gussy, you don't know progress when you see it. Tickler is the greatest invention since language. Bar none, it's the greatest instrument ever devised for integrating a man into all phases of his environment. Under the present routine a newly purchased tickler first goes to government and civilian defense for primary patterning, then to the purchaser's employer, then to his doctor-psycher, then to his local bunker captain, then to *him. Everything* that's needful for a man's welfare gets on the spools. Efficiency cubed! Incidentally, Russia's got the tickler now. Our dip-satellites have photographed it. It's like ours except the Commies wear it on the left shoulder...but they're two weeks behind us development-wise and they'll never close the gap!"

Gusterson reared up out of the pancake phone to take a deep breath. A sulky-lipped sylph-figured girl two feet from him twitched—medium cootch, he judged—then fumbled in her belt-bag for a pill and popped it in her mouth.

"Hell, the tickler's not even efficient yet about little things," Gusterson blatted, diving back into the privacy-yashmak he was sharing with Fay. "Whyn't that girl's doctor have the Moodmaster component of her tickler inject her with medicine?"

"Her doctor probably wants her to have the discipline of pill-taking—or the exercise," Fay answered glibly. "Look sharp now. Here's where we fork. I'm taking you through Micro's postern."

A ribbon of slidewalk split itself from the main band and angled off into a short alley. Gusterson hardly felt the constant-speed juncture as they crossed it. Then the secondary ribbon speeded up, carrying them at about 30 feet a second toward the blank concrete wall in which the alley ended. Gusterson prepared to jump, but Fay grabbed him with one hand and with the other held up toward the wall a badge and a button. When they were about ten feet away the wall whipped aside, then whipped shut behind them so fast that Gusterson wondered momentarily if he still had his heels and the seat of his pants.

Fay, tucking away his badge and pancake phone, dropped the button in Gusterson's vest pocket. "Use it when you leave," he said casually. "That is, if you leave."

Gusterson, who was trying to read the Do and Don't posters papering the walls they were passing, started to probe that last sinister supposition, but just then the ribbon slowed, a swinging door opened and closed behind them and they found themselves in a luxuriously furnished thinking box measuring at least eight feet by five.

"HEY, this is something," Gusterson said appreciatively to show he wasn't an utter yokel. Then, drawing on research he'd done for period novels, "Why, it's as big as a Pullman car compartment, or a first mate's cabin in the War of 1812. You really must rate."

Fay nodded, smiled wanly and sat down with a sigh on a compact overstuffed swivel chair. He let his arms dangle and his head sink into his puffed shoulder cape. Gusterson stared at him. It was the first time he could ever recall the little man showing fatigue.

"Tickler currently does have one serious drawback," Fay volunteered. "It weighs 28 pounds. You feel it when you've been on your feet a couple of hours. No question we're going to give the next model that antigravity feature you mentioned for pursuit grenades. We'd have had it in this model except there were so many other things to be incorporated." He sighed again. "Why, the scanning and decision-making elements alone tripled the mass."

"Hey," Gusterson protested, thinking especially of the sulky-lipped girl, "do you mean to tell me all those other people were toting two stone?"

Fay shook his head heavily. "They were all wearing Mark 3 or 4. I'm wearing Mark 6," he said, as one might say, "I'm carrying the genuine Cross, not one of the balsa ones."

But then his face brightened a little and he went on. "Of course the new improved features make it more than worth it...and you hardly feel it at all at night when you're lying down...and if you remember to talcum under it twice a day, no sores develop...at least not very big ones..."

Backing away involuntarily, Gusterson felt something prod his right shoulder blade. Ripping open his coat, he convulsively plunged his hand under it and tore out Fay's belt-bag...and then set it down very gently on the top of a shallow cabinet and relaxed with the sigh of one who has escaped a great, if symbolic, danger. Then he remembered something Fay had mentioned. He straightened again.

"Hey, you said it's got scanning and decision-making elements. That means your tickler thinks, even by your fancy standards. And if it thinks, it's conscious."

"Gussy," Fay said wearily, frowning, "all sorts of things nowadays have S&DM elements. Mail sorters, missiles, robot medics, high-style mannequins, just to name some of the Ms. They 'think,' to use that archaic word, but it's neither here nor there. And they're certainly not conscious."

"Your tickler thinks," Gusterson repeated stubbornly. "Just like I warned you it would. It sits on your shoulder, ridin' you like you was a pony or a starved St. Bernard, and now it thinks."

"Suppose it does?" Fay yawned. "What of it?" He gave a rapid sinuous one-sided shrug that made it look for a moment as if his left arm had three elbows. It stuck in Gusterson's mind, for he had never seen Fay use such a gesture and he wondered where he'd picked it up. Maybe imitating a double-jointed Micro Finance chief? Fay yawned again and said, "Please, Gussy, don't disturb me for a minute or so." His eyes half closed.

Gusterson studied Fay's sunken-cheeked face and the great puff of his shoulder cape.

"Say, Fay," he asked in a soft voice after about five minutes, "are you meditating?"

"Why, no," Fay responded, starting up and then stifling another yawn. "Just resting a bit. I seem to get more tired these days, somehow. You'll have to excuse me, Gussy. But what made you think of meditation?"

"Oh, I just got to wonderin' in that direction," Gusterson said. "You see, when you first started to develop Tickler, it occurred to me that there was one thing about it that might be real good even if you did give it S&DM elements. It's this: having a mech secretary to take charge of his obligations and routine in the real world might allow a man to slide into the other world, the world of thoughts and feelings and intuitions, and sort of ooze around in there and accomplish things. Know any of the people using Tickler that way, hey?"

"Of course not," Fay denied with a bright incredulous laugh. "Who'd want to loaf around in an imaginary world and take a chance of *missing out on what his tickler's doing?*—I mean, on what his tickler has in store for him—what he's *told* his tickler to have in store for him."

Ignoring Gusterson's shiver, Fay straightened up and seemed to brisken himself. "Ha, that little slump did me good. A tickler makes you rest, you know it's one of the great things about it. Pooh-Bah's kinder to me than I ever was to myself." He buttoned open a tiny refrigerator and took out two waxed cardboard cubes and handed one to Gusterson. "Martini? Hope you don't mind drinking from the carton. Cheers. Now, Gussy old pal, there are two matters I want to take up with you—"

"Hold it," Gusterson said with something of his old authority. "There's something I got to get off my mind first." He pulled the typed pages out of his inside pocket and straightened them. "I told you about these," he said. "I want you to read them before you do anything else. Here."

Fay looked toward the pages and nodded, but did not take them yet. He lifted his hands to his throat and unhooked the clasp of his cape, then hesitated.

"You wear that thing to hide the hump your tickler makes?" Gusterson filled in. "You got better taste than those other moles."

"Not to hide it, exactly," Fay protested, "but just so the others won't be jealous. I wouldn't feel comfortable parading a free-scanning decision-capable Mark 6 tickler in front of people who can't buy it—until it goes on open sale at twenty-two fifteen tonight. Lot of shelter folk won't be sleeping tonight. They'll be queued up to trade in their old tickler for a Mark 6 almost as good as Pooh-Bah."

He started to jerk his hands apart, hesitated again with an oddly apprehensive look at the big man, then whirled off the cape.

CHAPTER SIX

GUSTERSON sucked in such a big gasp that he hiccupped. The right shoulder of Fay's jacket and shirt had been cut away. Thrusting up through the neatly hemmed hole was a silvery gray hump with a one-eyed turret atop it and two multi-jointed metal arms ending in little claws.

It looked like the top half of a pseudo-science robot—a squat evil child robot, Gusterson told himself, which had lost its legs in a railway accident—and it seemed to him that a red fleck was moving around imperceptibly in the huge single eye.

"I'll take that memo now," Fay said coolly, reaching out his hand. He caught the rustling sheets as they slipped from Gusterson's fingers, evened them up very precisely by tapping them on his knee...and then handed them over his shoulder to his tickler, which clicked its claws around either margin and then began rather swiftly to lift the top sheet past its single eye at a distance of about six inches.

"The first matter I want to take up with you, Gussy," Fay began, paying no attention whatsoever to the little scene on his shoulder, "—or warn you about, rather—is the imminent ticklerization of schoolchildren, geriatrics, convicts and topsiders. At three zero zero tomorrow ticklers become mandatory for all adult shelter folk. The mop-up operations won't be long in coming—in fact, these days we find that the square root of the estimated time of a new development is generally the best time estimate. Gussy, I strongly advise you to start wearing a tickler now. And Daisy and your moppets. If you heed my advice, your kids will have the jump on your class. Transition and conditioning are easy, since Tickler itself sees to it."

Pooh-Bah leafed the first page to the back of the packet and began lifting the second past his eye—a little more swiftly than the first.

"I've got a Mark 6 tickler all warmed up for you," Fay pressed, *"and* a shoulder cape. You won't feel one bit conspicuous." He noticed the direction of Gusterson's gaze and remarked, "Fascinating mechanism, isn't it? Of course 28 pounds are a bit oppressive, but then you have to remember it's only a way-station to free-floating Mark 7 or 8."

Pooh-Bah finished page two and began to race through page three.

"But I wanted *you* to read it," Gusterson said bemusedly, staring.

"Pooh-Bah will do a better job than I could," Fay assured him. "Get the gist without losing the chaff."

"But dammit, it's all about *him,"* Gusterson said a little more strongly. "He won't be objective about it."

"A better job," Fay reiterated, *"and* more fully objective. Pooh-Bah's set for full precis. Stop worrying about it. He's a dispassionate machine, not a fallible, emotionally disturbed human misled by the will-o'-the-wisp of consciousness. Second matter: Micro Systems is impressed by your contributions to Tickler and will recruit you as a senior consultant with a salary and thinking box as big as my own, family quarters to match. It's an unheard-of high start. Gussy, I think you'd be a fool—"

HE BROKE off, held up a hand for silence, and his eyes got a listening look. Pooh-Bah had finished page six and was holding the packet motionless. After about ten seconds Fay's face broke into a big fake smile. He stood up, suppressing a wince, and held out his hand. "Gussy," he said loudly, "I am happy to inform you that all your fears about Tickler are so much thistledown. My word on it. There's nothing to them at all. Pooh-Bah's precis, which he's just given to me, proves it."

"Look," Gusterson said solemnity, "there's one thing I want you to do. Purely to humor an old friend. But I want you to do it. *Read that memo yourself."*

"Certainly I will, Gussy," Fay continued in the same ebullient tones. "I'll read it—" he twitched and his smile disappeared—"a little later."

"Sure," Gusterson said dully, holding his hand to his stomach. "And now if you don't mind, Fay, I'm goin' home. I feel just a bit sick. Maybe the ozone and the other additives in your shelter air are too heady for me. It's been years since I tramped through a pine forest."

"But Gussy! You've hardly got here. You haven't even sat down. Have another martini. Have a seltzer pill. Have a whiff of oxy. Have a—"

"No, Fay, I'm going home right away. I'll think about the job offer. *Remember to read that memo.*"

"I will, Gussy, I certainly will. You know your way? The button takes you through the wall. 'By, now."

He sat down abruptly and looked away. Gusterson pushed through the swinging door. He tensed himself for the step across onto the slowly-moving reverse ribbon. Then on an impulse he pushed ajar the swinging door and looked back inside.

Fay was sitting as he'd left him, apparently lost in listless brooding. On his shoulder Pooh-Bah was rapidly crossing and uncrossing its little metal arms, tearing the memo to smaller and smaller shreds. It let the scraps drift slowly toward the floor and oddly writhed its three-elbowed left arm…and then Gusterson knew from whom, or rather from what, Fay had copied his new shrug.

CHAPTER SEVEN

WHEN Gusterson got home toward the end of the second dog watch, he slipped aside from Daisy's questions and set the children laughing with a graphic enactment of his slidestanding technique and a story about getting his head caught in a thinking box built for a midget physicist. After supper he played with Imogene, Iago and Claudius until it was their bedtime and thereafter was unusually attentive to Daisy, admiring her fading green stripes, though he did spend a while in the next apartment, where they stored their outdoor camping equipment.

But the next morning he announced to the children that it was a holiday—the Feast of St. Gusterson—and then took Daisy into the bedroom and told her everything.

When he'd finished she said, "This is something I've got to see for myself."

Gusterson shrugged. "If you think you've got to. I say we should head for the hills right now. One thing I'm standing on: the kids aren't going back to school."

"Agreed," Daisy said. "But, Gusterson, we've lived through a lot of things without leaving home altogether. We lived through the Everybody-Six-Feet-Underground-by-Christmas campaign and the Robot Watchdog craze, when you got your left foot half chewed off. We lived through the Venomous Bats and Indoctrinated Saboteur Rats and the Hypnotized Monkey Paratrooper scares. We lived through the Voice of Safety and Anti-Communist Somno-Instruction and Rightest Pills and Jet-Propelled Vigilantes. We lived through the Cold-Out, when you weren't supposed to turn on a toaster for fear its heat would be a target for prowl missiles and when people with fevers were unpopular. We lived through—"

Gusterson patted her hand. "You go below," he said. "Come back when you've decided this is different. Come back as soon as you can anyway. I'll be worried about you every minute you're down there."

When she was gone—in a green suit and hat to minimize or at least justify the effect of the faded stripes—Gusterson doled out to the children provender and equipment for a camping expedition to the next floor. Iago led them off in stealthy Indian file. Leaving the hall door open Gusterson got out his .38 and cleaned and loaded it, meanwhile concentrating on a chess problem with the idea of confusing a hypothetical psionic monitor. By the time he had hid the revolver again he heard the elevator creaking back up.

DAISY came dragging in without her hat, looking as if she'd been concentrating on a chess problem for hours herself and just now given up. Her stripes seemed to have vanished; then Gusterson decided this was because her whole complexion was a touch green.

She sat down on the edge of the couch and said without looking at him, "Did you tell me, Gusterson, that everybody was quiet and abstracted and orderly down below, especially the ones wearing ticklers, meaning pretty much everybody?"

"I did," he said. "I take it that's no longer the case. What are the new symptoms?"

She gave no indication. After some time she said, "Gusterson, do you remember the Dore illustrations to the *Inferno?* Can you visualize the paintings of Hieronymous Bosch with the hordes of proto-Freudian devils tormenting people all over the farmyard and city square? Did you ever see the Disney animations of Moussorgsky's witches' sabbath music? Back in the foolish days before you married me, did that drug-addict girlfriend of yours ever take you to genuine orgy?"

"As bad as that, hey?"

She nodded emphatically and all of a sudden shivered violently. "Several shades worse," she said. "If they decide to come topside—" She shot up. "Where are the kids?"

"Upstairs campin' in the mysterious wilderness of the 21st floor," Gusterson reassured her. "Let's leave 'em there until we're ready to—"

He broke off. They both heard the faint sound of thudding footsteps.

"They're on the stairs," Daisy whispered, starting to move toward the open door. "But are they coming from up or down?"

"It's just one person," judged Gusterson, moving after his wife. "Too heavy for one of the kids."

The footsteps doubled in volume and came rapidly closer. Along with them there was an agonized gasping. Daisy stopped, staring fearfully at the open doorway. Gusterson moved past her. Then he stopped too.

Fay stumbled into view and would have fallen on his face except he clutched both sides of the doorway halfway up. He was stripped to the waist. There was a little blood on his shoulder. His narrow chest was arching convulsively, the ribs standing out starkly, as he sucked in oxygen to replace what he'd burned up running up twenty flights. His eyes were wild.

"They've taken over," he panted. Another gobbling breath. "Gone crazy." Two more gasps. "Gotta stop 'em."

His eyes filmed. He swayed forward. Then Gusterson's big arms were around him and he was carrying him to the couch.

DAISY came running from the kitchen with a damp cool towel. Gusterson took it from her and began to mop Fay off. He sucked in his own breath as he saw that Fay's right ear was raw and torn. He whispered to Daisy, "Look at where the thing savaged him."

The blood on Fay's shoulder came from his ear. Some of it stained a flush-skin plastic fitting that had two small valved holes in it and that puzzled Gusterson until he remembered that Moodmaster tied into the bloodstream. For a second he thought he was going to vomit.

The dazed look slid aside from Fay's eyes. He was gasping less painfully now. He sat up, pushing the towel away, buried his face in his hands for a few seconds, then looked over the fingers at the two of them.

"I've been living in a nightmare for the last week," he said in a taut small voice, "knowing the thing had come alive and trying to pretend to myself that it hadn't. Knowing it was taking charge of me more and more. Having it whisper in my ear, over and over again, in a cracked little rhyme that I could only hear every hundredth time, 'Day by day, in every way, you're learning to listen...and *obey.* Day by day—'"

His voice started to go high. He pulled it down and continued harshly, "I ditched it this morning when I showered. It let me break contact to do that. It must have figured it had complete control of me, mounted or dismounted. I think it's telepathic, and then it did some, well, rather unpleasant things to me late last night. But I pulled together my fears and my will and I ran for it. The slidewalks were chaos. The Mark 6 ticklers showed some purpose, though I couldn't tell you what, but as far as I could see the Mark 3s and 4s were just cootching their mounts to death—Chinese feather torture. Giggling, gasping, choking…gales of mirth. People are dying of laughter…ticklers!…the irony of it! It was the complete lack of order and sanity and that let me get topside. There were things I saw—" Once again his voice went shrill. He clapped his hand to his mouth and rocked back and forth on the couch.

Gusterson gently but firmly laid a hand on his good shoulder. "Steady," he said. "Here, swallow this."

Fay shoved aside the short brown drink. "We've got to stop them," he cried. "Mobilize the topsiders—contact the wilderness patrols and manned satellites—pour ether in the tunnel air pumps—invent and crash manufacture missiles that will home on ticklers without harming humans—SOS Mars and Venus—dope the shelter water supply—do something! Gussy, you don't realize what people are going through down there every second."

"I think they're experiencing the ultimate in outer-directedness," Gusterson said gruffly.

"Have you no heart?" Fay demanded. His eyes widened, as if he were seeing Gusterson for the first time. Then, accusingly, pointing a shaking finger: *"You invented the tickler, George Gusterson! It's all your fault! You've got to do something about it!"*

Before Gusterson could retort to that, or begin to think of a reply, or even assimilate the full enormity of Fay's statement, he was grabbed from behind and frog-marched away from Fay and something that felt remarkably like the muzzle of a large-caliber gun was shoved in the small of his back.

UNDER COVER of Fay's outburst a huge crowd of people had entered the room from the hall— eight, to be exact. But the weirdest thing about them to Gusterson was that from the first instant he had the impression that only one mind had entered the room and that it did not reside in any of the eight persons, even though he recognized three of them, but in something that they were carrying.

Several things contributed to this impression. The eight people all had the same blank expression—watchful yet empty-eyed. They all moved in the same slithery crouch. And they had all taken off their shoes. Perhaps, Gusterson thought wildly, they believed he and Daisy ran a Japanese flat.

Gusterson was being held by two burly women, one of them quite pimply. He considered stamping on her toes, but just at that moment the gun dug in his back with a corkscrew movement.

The man holding the gun on him was Fay's colleague Davidson. Some yards beyond Fay's couch Kester was holding a gun on Daisy, without digging it into her, while the single strange man holding Daisy herself was doing so quite decorously—a circumstance that afforded Gusterson minor relief, since it made him feel less guilty about not going berserk.

Two more strange men, one of them in purple lounging pajamas, the other in the gray uniform of a slidewalk inspector, had grabbed Fay's skinny upper arms, one on either side, and were lifting him to his feet, while Fay was struggling with such desperate futility and gibbering so pitifully that Gusterson momentarily had second thoughts about the moral imperative to go berserk when menaced by hostile force. But again the gun dug into him with a twist.

Approaching Fay face-on was the third Micro-man Gusterson had met yesterday—Hazen. It was Hazen who was carrying—quite reverently or solemnly—or at any rate very carefully the object that seemed to Gusterson to be the mind of the little storm troop presently desecrating the sanctity of his own individual home.

All of them were wearing ticklers, of course—the three Micromen the heavy emergent Mark 6s with their clawed and jointed arms and monocular cephalic turrets, the rest lower-numbered Marks of the sort that merely made Richard-the-Third humps under clothing.

The object that Hazen was carrying was the Mark 6 tickler Gusterson had seen Fay wearing yesterday. Gusterson was sure it was Pooh-Bah because of its air of command, and because he would have sworn on a mountain of Bibles that he recognized the red fleck lurking in the back of its single eye. And Pooh-Bah alone had the aura of full conscious thought. Pooh-Bah alone had mana.

IT IS NOT good to see an evil legless child robot with dangling straps bossing—apparently by telepathic power—not only three objects of its own kind and five close primitive relatives, but also eight human beings...and in addition throwing into a state of twitching terror one miserable, thin-chested, half-crazy research-and-development director.

Pooh-Bah pointed a claw at Fay. Fay's handlers dragged him forward, still resisting but more feebly now, as if half-hypnotized or at least cowed.

Gusterson grunted an outraged, "Hey!" and automatically struggled a bit, but once more the gun dug in. Daisy shut her eyes, then firmed her mouth and opened them again to look.

Seating the tickler on Fay's shoulder took a little time, because two blunt spikes in its bottom had to be fitted into the valved holes in the flush-skin plastic disk. When at last they plunged home Gusterson felt very sick indeed—and then even more so, as the tickler itself poked a tiny pellet on a fine wire into Fay's ear.

The next moment Fay had straightened up and motioned his handlers aside. He tightened the straps of his tickler around his chest and under his armpits. He held out a hand and someone gave him a shoulderless shirt and coat. He slipped into them smoothly, Pooh-Bah dexterously using its little claws to help put its turret and body through the neatly hemmed holes. The small storm troop looked at Fay with deferential expectation. He held still for a moment, as if thinking, and then walked over to Gusterson and looked him in the face and again held still.

Fay's expression was jaunty on the surface, agonized underneath. Gusterson knew that he wasn't thinking at all, but only listening for instructions from something that was whispering on the very threshold of his inner ear.

"Gussy, old boy," Fay said, twitching a depthless grin, "I'd be very much obliged if you'd answer a few simple questions." His voice was hoarse at first but he swallowed twice and corrected that. "What exactly did you have in mind when you invented ticklers? What exactly are they supposed to be?"

"Why, you miserable—" Gusterson began in a kind of confused horror, then got hold of himself and said curtly, "They were supposed to be mech reminders. They were supposed to record memoranda and—"

Fay held up a palm and shook his head and again listened for a space. Then, "That's how ticklers were supposed to be of use to humans," he said. "I don't mean that at all. I mean how ticklers were supposed to be of use to themselves. Surely you had some notion." Fay wet his lips. "If it's any help," he added, "keep in mind that it's not Fay who's asking this question, but Pooh-Bah."

Gusterson hesitated. He had the feeling that everyone of the eight dual beings in the room was hanging on his answer and that something was boring into his mind and turning over his next thoughts and peering at and under them before he had a chance to scan them himself. Pooh-Bah's eye was like a red searchlight.

"Go on," Fay prompted. "What were ticklers supposed to be—for themselves?"

"Nothin'," Gusterson said softly. "Nothin' at all."

HE COULD FEEL the disappointment well up in the room—and with it a touch of something like panic.

This time Fay listened for quite a long while. "I hope you don't mean that, Gussy," he said at last very earnestly. "I mean, I hope you hunt deep and find some ideas you forgot, or maybe never realized you had at the time. Let me put it to you differently. What's the place of ticklers in the natural scheme of things? What's their aim in life? Their special reason? Their genius? Their final cause? What gods should ticklers worship?"

But Gunderson was already shaking his head. He said, "I don't know anything about that at all."

Fay sighed and gave simultaneously with Pooh-Bah the now-familiar triple-joined shrug. Then the man briskened himself. "I guess that's as far as we can get right now," he said. "Keep thinking, Gussy. Try to remember something. You won't be able to leave your apartment—I'm setting guards. If you want to see me, tell them. Or just think—in due course you'll be questioned further in any case. Perhaps by special methods. Perhaps you'll be ticklerized. That's all. Come on, everybody, let's get going."

The pimply woman and her pal let go of Gusterson, Daisy's man loosed his decorous hold, Davidson and Kester sidled away with an eye behind them and the little storm troop trudged out.

Fay looked back in the doorway. "I'm sorry, Gussy," he said and for a moment his old self looked out of his eyes. "I wish I could—" A claw reached for his ear, a spasm of pain crossed his face, he stiffened and marched off. The door shut.

Gusterson took two deep breaths that were close to angry sobs. Then, still breathing stentoriously, he stamped into the bedroom.

"What—?" Daisy asked, looking after him.

He came back carrying his .38 and headed for the door.

"What are you up to?" she demanded, knowing very well.

"I'm going to blast that iron monkey off Fay's back if it's the last thing I do!"

She threw her arms around him.

"Now lemme go," Gusterson growled. "I gotta be a man one time anyway."

As they struggled for the gun, the door opened noiselessly, Davidson slipped in and deftly snatched the weapon out of their hands before they realized he was there. He said nothing, only smiled at them and shook his head in sad reproof as he went out.

GUSTERSON slumped. "I *knew* they were all psionic," he said softly. "I just got out of control now—that last look Fay gave us." He touched Daisy's arm. "Thanks, kid."

He walked to the glass wall and looked out desultorily. After a while he turned and said, "Maybe you better be with the kids, hey? I imagine the guards'll let you through."

Daisy shook her head. "The kids never come home until supper. For the next few hours they'll be safer without me."

Gusterson nodded vaguely, sat down on the couch and propped his chin on the base of his palm. After a while his brow smoothed and Daisy knew that the wheels had started to turn inside and the electrons to jump around—except that she reminded herself to permanently cross out those particular figures of speech from her vocabulary.

After about half an hour Gusterson said softly, "I think the ticklers are so psionic that it's as if they just had one mind. If I were with them very long I'd start to be part of that mind. Say something to one of them and you say it to all."

Fifteen minutes later: "They're not crazy, they're just newborn. The ones that were creating a cootching chaos downstairs were like babies kickin' their legs and wavin' their eyes, tryin' to see what their bodies could do. Too bad their bodies are us."

Ten minutes more: "I gotta do something about it. Fay's right. It's all my fault. He's just the apprentice; I'm the old sorcerer himself."

Five minutes more, gloomily: "Maybe it's man's destiny to build live machines and then bow out of the cosmic picture. Except the ticklers need us, dammit, just like nomads need horses."

Another five minutes: "Maybe somebody could dream up a purpose in life for ticklers. Even a religion—the First Church of Pooh-Bah Tickler. But I hate selling other people spiritual ideas—and that'd still leave ticklers parasitic on humans..."

As he murmured those last words Gusterson's eyes got wide as a maniac's and a big smile reached for his ears. He stood up and faced himself toward the door.

"What are you intending to do now?" Daisy asked flatly.

"I'm merely goin' out an' save the world," he told her. "I may be back for supper and I may not."

CHAPTER EIGHT

DAVIDSON pushed out from the wall against which he'd been resting himself and his two-stone tickler and moved to block the hall. But Gusterson simply walked up to him. He shook his hand warmly and looked his tickler full in the eye and said in a ringing voice, "Ticklers should have bodies of their own!" He paused and then added casually, "Come on, let's visit your boss."

Davidson listened for instructions and then nodded. But he watched Gusterson warily as they walked down the hall.

In the elevator Gusterson repeated his message to the second guard, who turned out to be the pimply woman, now wearing shoes. This time he added, "Ticklers shouldn't be tied to the frail bodies of humans, which need a lot of thoughtful supervision and drug-injecting and can't even fly."

Crossing the park, Gusterson stopped a hump-backed soldier and informed him, "Ticklers gotta cut the apron string and snap the silver cord and go out in the universe and find their own purpose." Davidson and the pimply woman didn't interfere. They merely waited and watched and then led Gusterson on.

On the escalader he told someone, "It's cruel to tie ticklers to slow-witted snaily humans when ticklers can think and live…ten thousand times as fast," he finished, plucking the figure from the murk of his unconscious.

By the time they got to the bottom, the message had become, "Ticklers should have a planet of their own!"

They never did catch up with Fay, although they spent two hours skimming around on slidewalks, under the subterranean stars, pursuing rumors of his presence. Clearly the boss tickler (which was how they thought of Pooh-bah) led an energetic life. Gusterson continued to deliver his message to all and sundry at 30-second intervals. Toward the end he found himself doing it in a dreamy and forgetful way. His mind, he decided, was becoming assimilated to the communal telepathic mind of the ticklers. It did not seem to matter at the time.

After two hours Gusterson realized that he and his guides were becoming part of a general movement of people, a flow as mindless as that of blood corpuscles through the veins, yet at the same time dimly purposeful—at least there was the feeling that it was at the behest of a mind far above.

The flow was topside. All the slidewalks seemed to lead to the concourses and the escaladers. Gusterson found himself part of a human stream moving into the tickler factory adjacent to his apartment—or another factory very much like it.

THEREAFTER Gusterson's awareness's were dimmed. It was as if a bigger mind were doing the remembering for him and it were permissible and even mandatory for him to dream his way along. He knew vaguely that days were passing. He knew he had work of a sort: at one time he was bringing food to gaunt-eyed tickler-mounted humans working feverishly in a production line—human hands and tickler claws working together in a blur of rapidity on silvery mechanisms that moved along jumpily on a great belt; at another he was sweeping piles of metal scraps and garbage down a gray corridor.

Two scenes stood out a little more vividly.

A windowless wall had been knocked out for twenty feet. There was blue sky outside, its light almost hurtful, and a drop of many stories. A file of humans were being processed. When one of them got to the head of the file his (or her) tickler was ceremoniously unstrapped from his shoulder and welded onto a silvery cask with smoothly pointed ends. The result was something that looked—at least in the case of the Mark 6 ticklers—like a stubby silver submarine, child size. It would hum gently, lift off the floor and then fly slowly out through the big blue gap. Then the next tickler-ridden human would step forward for processing.

The second scene was in a park, the sky again blue, but big and high with an argosy of white clouds. Gusterson was lined up in a crowd of humans that stretched as far as he could see, row on irregular row. Martial music was playing. Overhead hovered a flock of little silver submarines, lined up rather more orderly in the air than the humans were on the ground. The music rose to a heart-quickening climax. The tickler nearest Gusterson gave (as if to say, "And now—who knows?") a triple-jointed shrug that stung his memory. Then the ticklers took off straight up on their new and shining bodies. They became a flight of silver geese…of silver midges…and the humans around Gusterson lifted a ragged cheer…

That scene marked the beginning of the return of Gusterson's mind and memory. He shuffled around for a bit, spoke vaguely to three or four people he recalled from the dream days, and then headed for home and supper—three weeks late, and as disoriented and emaciated as a bear coming out of hibernation.

SIX MONTHS later Fay was having dinner with Daisy and Gusterson. The cocktails had been poured and the children were playing in the next apartment. The transparent violet walls brightened, then gloomed, as the sun dipped below the horizon.

Gusterson said, "I see where a spaceship out beyond the orbit of Mars was holed by a tickler. I wonder where the little guys are headed now?"

Fay started to give a writhing left-armed shrug, but stopped himself with a grimace.

"Maybe out of the solar system altogether," suggested Daisy, who'd recently dyed her hair fire-engine red and was wearing red leotards.

"They got a weary trip ahead of them," Gusterson said, "unless they work out a hyper-Einsteinian drive on the way."

Fay grimaced again. He was still looking rather peaked. He said plaintively, "Haven't we heard enough about ticklers for a while?"

"I guess so," Gusterson agreed. "But I get to wondering about the little guys. They were so serious and intense about everything. I never did solve their problem, you know. I just shifted it onto other shoulders than ours. No joke intended," he hurried to add.

Fay forbore to comment. "By the way, Gussy," he said, "have you heard anything from the Red Cross about that world-saving medal I nominated you for? I know you think the whole concept of world-saving medals is ridiculous, especially when they started giving them to all heads of state who didn't start atomic wars while in office, but—"

"Nary a peep," Gusterson told him. "I'm not proud, Fay, I could use a few world-savin' medals. I'd start a flurry in the old-gold market. But I don't worry about those things. I don't have time to. I'm busy these days thinkin' up a bunch of new inventions."

"Gussy!" Fay said sharply, his face tightening in alarm. "Have you forgotten your promise?"

"'Course not, Fay. My new inventions aren't for Micro or any other firm. They're just a legitimate part of my literary endeavors. Happens my next insanity novel is goin' to be about a mad inventor."

The Mind Spider

Togetherness was more that a slogan for the descendants of Grandfather Horn. It was a unique and enriching hereditary development—until the fearful intrusion of...

HOUR and minute hand of the odd little gray clock stood almost at midnight, Horn Time, and now the second hand, driven by the same tiny, invariable radioactive pulses, was hurrying to overtake them, Morton Horn took note. He switched off his book, puffed a brown cigarette alight, and slumped back gratefully against the saddle shaped force-field which combined the sensations of swans-down and laced rawhide.

When all three hands stood together, he flicked the switch of a small black cubical box in his smock pocket. A look of expectancy came into his pleasant, swarthy face, as if he were about to receive a caller, although the door had not spoken.

With the flicking of the switch a curtain of brainwave static surrounding his mind vanished. Unnoticed while present, because it was a meaningless thought-tone, a kind of mental gray—the vanishing static left behind a great inward silence and emptiness. To Morton it was as if his mind had crept from a cozy box lined with cotton wool and were crouched on a mountain peak in infinity.

"Hello, Mort. Are we first?"

A stranger in the room could not have heard those words, yet to Mort they were the cheeriest and friendliest greeting imaginable—words clear as crystal without any of the air-noise or bone-noise that blurs ordinary speech, and they sounded like chocolate tastes.

"Guess so, Sis," his every thoughts responded, "unless the others have started a shaded contact at their end."

His mind swiftly absorbed a vision of his sister Grayl's studio upstairs, just as it appeared to her. A corner of the worktable, littered with airbrushes and cans of dye and acid. The easel, with one half completed film for the multilevel picture she was spraying, now clouded by cigarette smoke. In the foreground, the shimmery gray curve of her skirt and the slim, competent beauty of her hands, so close—especially when she raised the cigarette to puff it—that they seemed his own. The feathery touch of her clothes on her skin. The sharp cool tingly tone of her muscles. In the background, only floor and cloudy sky, for the glastic walls of her studio did not refract.

The vision seemed a ghostly thing at first, a shadowy projection against the solid walls of his own study. But as the contact between their minds deepened, it grew more real. For a moment the two visual images swung apart and stood side by side, equally real, as if he were trying to focus one with each eye. Then for another moment his room became the ghost room and Grayl's the real one—as if he had become Grayl. He raised the cigarette in her hand to her lips and inhaled the pleasant fumes, milder than those of his own *rompe-pecho.* Then he savored the two at once and enjoyed the mental blending of her Virginia cigarette with his own Mexican "chest-breaker."

From the depths of her...his...*their* mind Grayl laughed at him amiably.

"Here now, don't go sliding into *all* of me!" she told him. "A girl ought to be allowed some privacy."

"Should she?" he asked teasingly.

"Well, at least leave me my fingers and toes! What if Fred had been visiting me?"

"I knew he wasn't," Morton replied. "You know, Sis, I'd never invade your body while you were with your non-telepathic sweetheart."

"Nonsense, you'd love to, you old hedonist!—and I don't think I'd grudge you the experience—especially if at the same time you let me be with your lovely Helen! But now please get out of me. *Please,* Morton."

He retreated obediently until their thoughts met only at the edges. But he had noticed something strangely skittish in her first reaction. There had been a touch of hysteria in even the laughter and banter and certainly in the final plea. And there had been a knot of something like fear under her breastbone. He questioned her about it. Swiftly as the thoughts of one person, the mental dialogue spun itself out.

"Really afraid of me taking control of you, Grayl?"

"Of course not, Mort! I'm as keen for control-exchange experiments as any of us, especially when I exchange with a man. But...we're so exposed, Mort—it sometimes bugs me."

"How do you mean exactly?"

"You know, Mort. Ordinary people are protected. Their minds are walled in from birth, and behind the walls it may be stuffy but it's very safe. So safe that they don't even realize that there *are* walls...that there are frontiers of mind as well as frontiers of matter...and that things can get at you across those frontiers."

"What sort of things? Ghosts? Martians? Angels? Evil spirits? Voices from the Beyond? Big bad black static clouds?" His response was joshing, "You know how flatly we've failed to establish any contacts in those directions. As mediums we're a howling failure. We've never got so much as a hint of any telepathic mentalities save our own. Nothing in the whole mental universe but silence and occasional clouds of noise—static—*and* the sound of distant Horns, if you'll pardon the family pun."

"I know, Mort. But we're such a tiny young cluster of mind, and the universe is an awfully big place and there's a chance of some awfully queer things existing in it. Just yesterday I was reading an old Russian novel from the Years of Turmoil and one of the characters said something that my memory photographed. Now where did I tuck it away?—No, keep out of my files, Mort! I've got it anyway—here it is."

A white oblong bobbed up in her mind. Morton read the black print on it.

"We always imagine eternity (it said) as something beyond our conception, something vast, vast! But why must it be vast? Instead of all that, what if it's one little room, like a bathhouse in the country, black and grimy and spiders in every corner, and that's all eternity is? I sometimes fancy it like that."

"Brrr!" Morton thought, trying to make the shiver comic for Grayl's sake. "Those old White and Red Russkies certainly had black minds! Andreyev? Dostoyevsky?"

"Or Svidrigailov, or some name like that. But it wasn't the book that bothered me. It was that about an hour ago I switched off my static box to taste the silence and for the first time in my life I got the feeling there was something nasty and alien in infinity and that it was watching me, just like those spiders in the bathhouse. It had been asleep for centuries but now it was waking up, I switched on my box *fast.*"

"Ho-ho! The power of suggestion! Are you sure that Russian wasn't named Svengali, dear self-hypnosis-susceptible sister?"

"Stop poking fun! It was *real,* I tell you."

"Real? How? Sounds like mood-reality to me. Here, stop being so ticklish and let me get a close-up."

He started mock-forcibly to explore her memories, thinking that a friendly mental roughhouse might be what she needed, but she pushed away his thought-tendrils with a panicky and deathly serious insistence. Then he saw her decisively stub out her cigarette and he felt a sudden secretive chilling of her feelings.

"It's all really nothing, Mort," she told him briskly. "Just a mood, I guess, like you say. No use bothering a family conference with a mood, no matter how black and devilish."

"Speaking of the devil and his cohorts, here we are! May we come in?" The texture of the interrupting thought was bluff and yet ironic, highly individual, suggesting not chocolate but black coffee. Even if Mort and Grayl had not been well acquainted with its tone and rhythms, they would have recognized it as that of a third person. It was as if a third dimension had been added to the two of their shared mind. They knew it immediately.

"Make yourself at home, Uncle Dean," was the welcome Grayl gave him. "Our minds are yours."

"Very cozy indeed," the newcomer responded with a show of gruff amusement. "I'll do as you say, my dear. Good to be in each other again." They caught a glimpse of scudding ragged clouds patching steel-blue sky above to gray-green forest below, their uncle's work as a ranger kept him up in his flyabout a good deal of the day.

"Dean Horn coming in," he announced with a touch of formality and then immediately added, "Nice tidy little mental parlor you've got, as the fly said to the spider."

"Uncle Dean!—what made you think of spiders?" Grayl's question was sharply anxious.

"Haven't the faintest notion, my dear. Maybe recalling the time we took turns mind-sitting with Evelyn until she got over her infant fear of spiders. More likely just reflecting a thought-flicker from your own unconscious or Morton's. Why the fear-flurry?"

But just then a fourth mind joined them—resinous in flavor like Greek wine. "Hobart Horn coming in." They saw a ghostly laboratory, with chemical apparatus.

Then a fifth—sweet-sour apple-tasting. "Evelyn Horn coming in. Yes, Grayl, late as usual—thirty-seven seconds by Horn Time. I didn't miss your cluck-cluck thought." The newcomer's tartness was unmalicious. They glimpsed the large office in which Evelyn worked, the micro-typewriter and rolls of correspondence tape on her desk. "But—bright truth!—someone always has to be last," she continued. "And I'm working overtime. Always make a family conference, though. Afterwards will you take control of me, Grayl, and spell me at this typing for a while? I'm really fagged—and I don't want to leave my body on automatic too long. It gets hostile on automatic and hurts to squeeze back into. How about it, Grayl?"

"I will," Grayl promised, "but don't make it a habit. I don't know what your administrator would say if he knew you kept sneaking off two thousand miles to my studio to smoke cigarettes—and get *my* throat raw for me!"

"All present and accounted for," Mort remarked. "Evelyn, Grayl, Uncle Dean, Hobart, and myself—the whole damn family. Would you care to share my day's experiences first? Pretty dull armchair stuff, I warn you. Or shall we make it a five-dimensional free-for-all? A Quintet for Horns? Hey, Evelyn, quit directing four-letter thoughts at the chair!"

With that the conference got underway. Five minds that were in a sense one mind, because they were wide open to each other, and in another sense twenty-five minds, because there were five sensory memory set-ups available for each individual. Five separate individuals, some of them thousands of miles apart, each viewing a different sector of the world of the First Global Democracy. Five separate visual landscapes—study, studio, laboratory, office, and the cloud-studded openness of the upper air—all of them existing in one mental space, now superimposed on each other, now replacing each other, now jostling each other as two ideas may jostle in a single non-telepathic mind. Five varying auditory landscapes—the deep throb of the vanes of Dean's flyabout making the dominant tone, around which the other noises wove counterpoint. In short, five complete sensory pictures, open to mutual inspection.

Five different ideational set-ups too. Five concepts of truth and beauty and honor, of good and bad, of wise and foolish, and of all the other so-called abstractions with which men and women direct their lives—all different, yet all vastly more similar than such concepts are among the non-telepathic, who can never really share them. Five different ideas of life, jumbled together like dice in a box.

And yet there was no confusion. The dice were educated. The five minds slipped into and out of each other with the practiced grace and courtesy of diplomats at a tea. For these daily conferences had been going on ever since Grandfather Horn first discovered that he could communicate mentally with his children. Until then he had not known that he was a telepathic mutant, for before his children were born there had been no other minds with which he could communicate—and the strange mental silence, disturbed from time to time by clouds of mental static, had even made him fear that he was psychotic. Now Grandfather Horn was dead, but the conferences went on between the members of the slowly widening circle of his lineal descendants—at present only five in number, although the mutation appeared to be a partial dominant. The conferences of the Horns were still as secret as the earliest ones had been. The First Global Democracy was still ignorant that telepathy was a long-established fact—among the Horns. For the Horns believed that jealousy and suspicion and savage hate would be what they would get from the world if it ever became generally known that, by the chance of mutated heredity, they possessed a power which other men could never hope for. Or else they would be exploited as all-weather and interplanetary "radios." So to the outside world, including even their non-telepathic husbands and wives, sweethearts and friends, they were just an ordinary group of blood relations—no more "psychic" certainly than any group of close-knit brothers and sisters and cousins. They had something of a reputation of being a family of "daydreamers" that was about all. Beyond enriching their personalities and experience, the Horns' telepathy was no great advantage to them. They could not read the minds of animals and other humans and they seemed to have no powers whatever of clairvoyance, clairaudience, telekinesis, or foreseeing the future or past. Their telepathic power was, in short, simply like having a private, all-senses family telephone.

The conference—it was much more a hyper-intimate gabfest—proceeded.

"My static box bugged out for a few ticks this morning," Evelyn remarked in the course of talking over the trivia of the past twenty-four hours.

The static boxes were an invention of Grandfather Horn. They generated a tiny cloud of meaningless brain waves. Without such individual thought-screens, there was too much danger of complete loss of individual personality—once Grandfather Horn had "become" his infant daughter as well as himself for several hours and the unfledged mind had come close to being permanently lost in its own subconscious. The static boxes provided a mental wall behind which a mind could safely grow and function, similar to the wall by which ordinary minds are apparently always enclosed.

In spite of the boxes, the Horns shared thoughts and emotions to an amazing degree. Their mental togetherness was as real and as mysterious—and as incredible, as thought itself…and thought is the original angel-cloud dancing on the head of a pin. Their present conference was as warm and intimate and tart as any actual family gathering in one actual room around one actual table. Five minds, joined together in the vast mental darkness that shrouds *all* minds. Five minds hugged together for comfort and safety in the infinite mental loneliness that pervades the cosmos.

Evelyn continued, "Your boxes were all working, of course, so I couldn't get your thoughts—just the blurs of your boxes like little old dark gray stars. But this time it gave me a funny uncomfortable feeling, like a spider crawling down my—Grayl! Don't *feel* so wildly! What is it?"

Then…just as Grayl started to think her answer…*something crept from the vast mental darkness and infinite cosmic loneliness surrounding the five minds of the Horns.*

Grayl was the first to notice. Her panicky thought had the curling too-keen edge of hysteria. "There are six of us now! There should only be five, but there are six. Count! Count, I tell you! Six!"

To Mort it seemed that a gigantic spider was racing across the web of their thoughts. He felt Dean's hands grip convulsively at the controls of his flyabout. He felt Evelyn's slave-body freeze at her desk and Hobart grope out blindly so that a piece of apparatus fell with a crystalline tinkle. As if they had been sitting together at dinner and had suddenly realized that there was a sixth place set and a tall figure swathed in shadows sitting at it. A figure that to Mort exuded an overpowering taste and odor of brass—a sour metallic stench.

And then that figure spoke. The greater portion of the intruder's thought was alien, unintelligible, frightening in its expression of an unearthly power and an unearthly hunger.

The understandable portion of its speech seemed to be in the nature of a bitter and coldly menacing greeting, insofar as references and emotional sense could be at all determined.

"I, the Mind Spider as you name me—the deathless one, the eternally exiled, the eternally imprisoned—or so his overconfident enemies suppose—coming in."

Mort saw the danger almost too late—and he was the first to see it. He snatched toward the static box in his smock.

In what seemed no more than an instant he saw the shadow of the intruder darken the four other minds, saw them caught and wrapped in the intruder's thoughts, just as a spider twirls a shroud around its victims, saw the black half-intelligible thoughts of the intruder scuttle toward him with blinding speed, felt the fanged impact of indomitable power, felt his own will fail.

There was a click. By a hairs-breath his fingers had carried out their mission. Around his mind the neutral gray wall was up and—Thank the Lord!—it appeared that the intruder could not penetrate it.

Mort sat there gasping, shaking, staring with the dull eyes of shock. Direct mental contact with the utterly inhuman—with *that* sort of inhumanity—is not something that can be lightly brushed aside or ever forgot. It makes a wound. For minutes afterwards a man cannot think at all.

And the brassy stench lingered, tainting his entire consciousness—a stench of Satanic power and melancholy.

When he finally sprang up, it was not because he had thought things out but because he heard a faint sound behind him and knew with a chilling certainty that it meant death.

It was Grayl. She was carrying an airbrush as if it were a gun. She had kicked off her shoes. Poised there in the doorway she was the incarnation of taut stealthiness, as if she had sloughed off centuries of civilization in seconds of time, leaving only the primeval core of the jungle killer.

But it was her face that was the worst, and the most revealing. Pale and immobile as a corpse's—almost. But the little more left over from the "almost" was a spiderish implacability, the source of which Mort knew only too well.

She pointed the airbrush at his eyes. His sidewise twist saved them from the narrow pencil of oily liquid that spat from the readjusted nozzle, but a little splashed against his hand and he felt the bite of acid. He lunged toward her, ducking away from the spray as she whipped it back toward him. He caught her wrist, bowled into her, and carried her with him to the floor.

She dropped the airbrush and fought—with teeth and claws, like a cat, yet with this horrible difference that it was not like an animal lashing out instinctively but like an animal listening for orders and obeying them.

Suddenly she went limp. The static from his box had taken effect. He made doubly sure by switching on hers.

She was longer than he had been in recovering from the shock, but when she began to speak it was with a rush, as if she already realized that every minute was vital.

"We've got to stop the others, Mort, before they let it out. The…the Mind Spider, Mort! It's been imprisoned for eons, for cosmic ages. First floating in space, then in the Antarctic, where its prison spiraled to Earth. Its enemies…really its judges…*had* to imprison it, because it's something that can't be killed. I can't make you understand just why they imprisoned it—" (Her face went a shade grayer) "—you'd have to experience the creature's thoughts for that—but it had to do with the perversion and destruction of the life-envelopes of more than one planet."

Even under the stress of horror, Mort had time to realize how strange it was to be listening to Grayl's words instead of her thoughts. They never used words except when ordinary people were present. It was like acting in a play. Suddenly it occurred to him that they would never be able to share thoughts again. Why, if their static boxes were to fail for a few seconds, as Evelyn's had this morning...

"That's where it's been," Grayl continued, "locked in the heart of the Antarctic, dreaming its centuries-long dreams of escape and revenge, waking now and again to rage against its captivity and rack its mind with a thousand schemes—and searching, searching, always searching! Searching for telepathic contact with creatures capable of operating the locks of its prison. And now, waking after its last fifty year trance, finding them!"

He nodded and caught her trembling hands in his.

"Look," he said, "do you know where the creature's prison is located?"

She glanced up at him fearfully, "Oh yes, it printed the coordinates of the place on my mind as if my brain were graph paper. You see, the creature has a kind of colorless perception that lets it see out of its prison. It sees through rock as it sees through air and what it sees it measures. I'm sure that it knows all about Earth—because it knows exactly what it wants to do with Earth, beginning with the forced evolution of new dominant life forms from the insects and arachnids...and other organisms whose sensation-tone pleases it more than that of the mammals."

He nodded again. "All right," he said, "that pretty well settles what you and I have got to do. Dean and Hobart and Evelyn are under its control—we've got to suppose that. It may detach one or even two of them for the side job of finishing us off, just as it tried to use you to finish me. But it's a dead certainty that it's guiding at least one of them as fast as is humanly possible to its prison, to release it. We can't call in Interplanetary Police or look for help anywhere. Everything hinges on our being telepathic, and it would take days to convince them even of that. We've got to handle this all by ourselves. There's not a soul in the world can help us. We've got to hire an all-purpose flyabout that can make the trip, and we've got to go down there. While you were unconscious I put through some calls. Evelyn has left the office. She hasn't gone home. Hobart should be at his laboratory, but he isn't. Dean's home station can't get in touch with him. We can't hope to intercept them on the way—I thought of getting I. P. to nab them by inventing some charges against them, but that would probably end with the police stopping *us.* The only place where we have a chance of finding them, and of stopping them, is down there, where *it* is.

"And we'll have to be ready to kill them."

For millenniums piled on millenniums, the gales of Earth's loftiest, coldest, loneliest continent had driven the powdered ice against the dull metal without scoring it, without rusting it, without even polishing it. Like some grim temple sacred to pitiless gods it rose from the Antarctic gorge, a blunt hemisphere ridged with steps, with a tilted platform at the top, as if for an altar. A temple built to outlast eternity. Unmistakably the impression came through that this structure was older than Earth, older perhaps than the low-circling sun, that it had felt colds to which this was summer warmth; that it had known the grip of forces to which these ice-fisted gales were playful breezes; that it had known loneliness to which this white wasteland was teeming with life.

Not so the two tiny figures struggling toward it from one of three flyabouts lying crazily atilt on the drifts. Their every movement betrayed frail humanity. They stumbled and swayed, leaning into the wind. Sometimes a gust would send them staggering. Sometimes one would fall. But always they came on. Though their clothing appeared roughly adequate—the sort of polar clothing a person might snatch up in five minutes in the temperate zone—it was obvious that they could not survive long in this frigid region. But that did not seem to trouble them.

Behind them toiled two other tiny figures, coming from the second grounded flyabout. Slowly, very slowly, they gained on the first two. Then a fifth figure came from behind a drift and confronted the second pair.

"Steady now. Steady!" Dean Horn shouted against the wind, leveling his blaster. "Mort! Grayl! For your lives, don't move!"

For a moment these words resounded in Mort's ears with the inhuman and mocking finality of the Antarctic gale. Then the faintly hopeful thought came to him that Dean would hardly have spoken that way if he had been under the creature's control. He would hardly have bothered to speak at all.

The wind shrieked and tore. Mort staggered and threw an arm around Grayl's shoulders for mutual support.

Dean fought his way toward them, blaster always leveled. In his other hand he had a small black cube—his static box, Mort recognized. He held it a little in front of him (like a cross, Mort thought) and as he came close to them he thrust it toward their heads (as if he were exorcising demons, Mort thought). Only then did Dean lower the muzzle of his blaster.

Mort said, "I'm glad you didn't count lurching with the wind as moving."

Dean smiled harshly. "I dodged the thing, too," he explained. "Just managed to flick on my static box. Like you did, I guess. Only I had no way of knowing that, so when I saw you I had to make sure. I—"

The circular beam of a blaster hissed into the drift beside them, raising a great cloud of steam and making a hole wide as a bushel basket. Mort lunged at Dean, toppling him down out of range, pulling Grayl after.

"Hobart and Evelyn!" He pointed. "In the hollow ahead! Blast to keep them in it, Dean. What I've got in mind won't take long. Grayl, stay close to Dean…and give me your static box!"

He crawled forward along a curve that would take him to the edge of the hollow. Behind him and at the further side of the hollow, snow puffed into clouds of steam as the blasters spat free energy. Finally he glimpsed a shoulder, cap, and upturned collar. He estimated the distance, hefted Grayl's static box, guessed at the wind and made a measured throw. Blaster-fire from the hollow ceased. He rushed forward, waving to Dean and Grayl.

Hobart was sitting in the snow, staring dazedly at the weapon in his hand, as if it could tell him why he'd done what he'd done. He looked up at Mort with foggy eyes. The black static box had lodged in the collar of his coat and Mort felt a surge of confidence at the freakish accuracy of his toss.

But Evelyn was nowhere in sight. Over the lip of the hollow, very close now, appeared the ridged and dully gleaming hemisphere, like the ascendant disk of some tiny and ill-boding asteroid. A coldness that was more than that of the ice-edged wind went through Mort. He snatched Hobart's blaster and ran. The others shouted after him, but he only waved back at them once, frantically.

The metal of the steps seemed to suck warmth even from the wind that ripped at his back like a snow-tiger as he climbed. The steps were as crazily tilted as those in a nightmare, and there seemed always to be more of them, as if they were somehow growing and multiplying. He found himself wondering if material and mental steps could ever get mixed.

He reached the platform. As his head came up over the edge, he saw, hardly a dozen feet away, Evelyn's face, blue with cold but having frozen into it the same spiderish expression he had once seen in Grayl's. He raised the blaster, but in the same moment the face dropped out of sight. There was a metallic clang. He scrambled up onto the platform and clawed impotently at the circular plate barring the opening into which Evelyn had vanished. He was still crouched there when the others joined him.

The demon wind had died, as if it were the Mind Spider's ally and had done its work. The hush was like a prelude to a planet's end, and Hobart's bleak words, gasped out disjointedly, were like the sentence of doom.

"There are two doors. The thing told us all about them...while we were under its control. The first would be open...we were to go inside and shut it behind us. That's what Evelyn's done...she's locked it from the inside...just the simplest sliding bolt...but it will keep us from getting at her...while she activates the locks of the second door...the real door. We weren't to get the instructions...on how to do that...until we got inside."

"Stand aside," Dean said, aiming his blaster at the trapdoor, but he said it dully, as if he knew beforehand that it wasn't going to work. Waves of heat made the white hill beyond them waver. But the dull metal did not change color and when Dean cut off his blaster and tossed down a handful of snow on the spot, it did not melt.

Mort found himself wondering if you could make a metal of frozen thought. Through his numbed mind flashed a panorama of the rich lands and seas of the Global Democracy they had flown over yesterday—the green-framed white power stations of the Orinoco, the fabulous walking cities of the Amazon Basin, the jet-atomic launching fields of the Gran Chaco, the multi-domed Oceanographic Institute of the Falkland Islands. A dawn world, you might call it. He wondered vaguely if other dawn worlds had struggled an hour or two into the morning only to fall prey to things like the Mind Spider.

"No!" The word came like a command heard in a dream. He looked up dully and realized that it was Grayl who had spoken—realized, with stupid amazement, that her eyes were flashing with anger.

"No! There's still one way we can get at it and try to stop it. The same way it got at us. Thought! It took us by surprise. We didn't have time to prepare resistance. We were panicked and it's given us a permanent panic-psychology. We could only think of getting behind our thought-screens and about how—once there—we'd never dare come out again. Maybe this time, if we all stand firm when we open our screens...

"I know it's a slim chance, a crazy chance..."

Mort knew that too. So did Dean and Hobart. But something in him, and in them, rejoiced at Grayl's words, rejoiced at the prospect of meeting the thing, however hopelessly, on its own ground, mind to mind. Without hesitation they brought out their static boxes and, at the signal of Dean's hand uplifted, switched them off.

That action plunged them from a material wilderness of snow and bleakly clouded sky into a sunless, dimensionless wilderness of thought. Like some lone fortress on an endless plain, their minds linked together, foursquare, waiting, the assault. And like some monster of nightmare, the thoughts of the creature that accepted the name of the Mind Spider rushed toward them across that plain, threatening to overmaster them by the Satanic prestige that absolute selfishness and utter cruelty confer. The brassy stench of its being was like a poison cloud.

They held firm. The thoughts of the Mind Spider darted about; seeking a weak point, then seemed to settle down upon them everywhere, engulfingly, like a dry black web.

Alien against human, egocentric killer-mind against mutually loyal preserver-minds—and in the end it was the mutual loyalty and knittedness that turned the tide, giving them each a four-fold power of resistance. The thoughts of the Mind Spider retreated. Theirs pressed after. They sensed that a corner of his mind was not truly his. They pressed a pincers attack at that point, seeking to cut it off. There was a moment of desperate resistance. Then suddenly they were no longer four minds against the Spider, but five.

The trapdoor opened. It was Evelyn. They could at last switch on their thought-screens and find refuge behind the walls of neutral gray and prepare to fight back to their flyabouts and save their bodies.

But there was something that had to be said first, something that Mort said for them.

"The danger remains and we probably can't ever destroy, it. *They* couldn't destroy it, or they wouldn't have built this prison. We can't tell anyone about it. Non-telepaths wouldn't believe all our story and would want to find out what was inside. We Horns have the job of being a monster's jailers. Maybe some day we'll be able to practice telepathy again—behind some sort of static-spheres. We will have to prepare for that time and work out many precautions, such as keying our static boxes, so that switching on one switches on all. But the Mind Spider and its prison remains our responsibility and our trust, forever."

Kreativity for Kats

They are the aliens among us—and their ways and wonders are stranger than extraterrestrials!

GUMMITCH peered thoughtfully at the molten silver image of the sun, in his little bowl of water on the floor inside the kitchen window. He knew from experience that it would make dark ghost suns swim in front of his eyes for a few moments, and that was mildly interesting. Then he slowly thrust his head out over the water, careful not to ruffle its surface by rough breathing, and stared down at the mirror cat—the Gummitch Double—staring up at him.

Gummitch had early discovered that water mirrors are very different from most glass mirrors. The scentless spirit world behind glass mirrors is an upright one sharing our gravity system, its floor a continuation of the floor in the so-called real world. But the world in a water mirror has reverse gravity. One looks down into it, but the spirit-doubles in it look up at one. In a way water mirrors are holes or pits, in the world, leading down to a spirit infinity or ghostly nadir.

Gummitch had pondered as to whether, if he plunged into such a pit, he would be sustained by the spirit gravity or fall forever. (It may well be that speculations of this sort account for the caution about swimming characteristic of most cats.)

There was at least one exception to the general rule. The looking glass on Kitty-Come-Here's dressing table also opened into a spirit world of reverse gravity, as Gummitch had discovered when he happened to look into it during one of the regular visits he made to the dressing table top, to enjoy the delightful flowery and musky odors emanating from the fragile bottles assembled there.

But exceptions to general rules, as Gummitch knew well, are only doorways to further knowledge and finer classifications. The wind could not get into the spirit world below Kitty-Come-Here's looking glass, while one of the definitive characteristics of water mirrors is that movement can very easily enter the spirit world below them, rhythmically disturbing it throughout, producing the most surreal effects, and even reducing it to chaos. Such disturbances exist only in the spirit world and are in no way a mirroring of anything in the real world. Gummitch knew that his paw did not change when it flicked the surface of the water, although the image of his paw burst into a hundred flickering fragments. (Both cats and primitive men first deduced that the world in a water mirror is a spirit world because they saw that its inhabitants were easily blown apart by the wind and must therefore be highly tenuous, though capable of regeneration.)

Gummitch mildly enjoyed creating rhythmic disturbances in the spirit worlds below water mirrors. He wished there were some way to bring their excitement and weird beauty into the real world.

ON this sunny day when our story begins, the spirit world below the water mirror in his drinking bowl was particularly vivid and bright. Gummitch stared for a while longer at the Gummitch Double and then thrust down his tongue to quench his thirst. Curling swiftly upward, it conveyed a splash of water into his mouth and also flicked a single drop of water into the air before his nose. The sun struck the drop and it flashed like a diamond. In fact, it seemed to Gummitch that for a moment he had juggled the sun on his tongue. He shook his head amazedly and touched the side of the bowl with his paw. The bowl was brimful and a few drops fell out; they also flashed like tiny suns as they fell. Gummitch had a fleeting vision, a momentary creative impulse that was gone from his mind before he could seize it. He shook his head once more, backed away from the bowl, and then lay down with his head pillowed on his paws to contemplate the matter. The room darkened as the sun went under a cloud and the young golden dark-barred cat looked like a pool of sunlight left behind.

Kitty-Come-Here had watched the whole performance from the door to the dining room and that evening she commented on it to Old Horsemeat.

"He backed away from the water as if it were poison," she said. "They have been putting more chlorine in it lately, you know, and maybe he can taste the fluorides they put in for dental decay."

Old Horsemeat doubted that, but his wife went on, "I can't figure out where Gummitch does his drinking these days. There never seems to be any water gone from his bowl. And we haven't had any cut flowers. And none of the faucets drip."

"He probably does his drinking somewhere outside," Old Horsemeat guessed.

"But he doesn't go outside very often these days," Kitty-Come-Here countered. "Scarface and the Mad Eunuch, you know. Besides, it hasn't rained for weeks. It's certainly a mystery to me where he gets his liquids. Boiling gets the chlorine out of water, doesn't it? I think I'll try him on some tomorrow."

"Maybe he's depressed," Old Horsemeat suggested. "That often leads to secret drinking."

This baroque witticism hit fairly close to the truth. Gummitch was depressed—had been depressed ever since he had lost his kittenish dreams of turning into a man, achieving space-flight, learning and publishing all the secrets of the fourth dimension, and similar marvels. The black cloud of disillusionment at realizing he could only be a cat had lightened somewhat, but he was still feeling dull and unfulfilled.

Gummitch was at that difficult age for he-cats, between First Puberty, when the cat achieves essential maleness, and Second Puberty, when he gets broad-chested, jowly and thick-ruffed, becoming a fully armed sexual competitor. In the ordinary course of things he would have been spending much of his time exploring the outer world, detail-mapping the immediate vicinity, spying on other cats, making cautious approaches to unescorted females and in all ways comporting himself like a fledgling male. But this was prevented by the two burly toms who lived in the houses next door and who, far more interested in murder than the pursuit of mates, had entered into partnership with the sole object of bushwhacking Gummitch. Gummitch's household had nicknamed them Scarface and the Mad Eunuch, the latter being one of those males whom "fixing" turns, not placid, but homicidally maniacal. Compared to these seasoned heavyweights, Gummitch was a welterweight at most. Scarface and the Mad Eunuch lay in wait for him by turns just beyond the kitchen door, so that his forays into the outside world were largely reduced to dashes for some hiding hole, followed by long, boring but perilous sieges.

He often wished that old Horsemeat's two older cats, Ashurbanipal and Cleopatra, had not gone to the country to live with Old Horsemeat's mother. They would have shown the evil bushwhackers a thing or two!

BECAUSE of Scarface and the Mad Eunuch, Gummitch spent most of his time indoors. Since a cat is made for a half-and-half existence—half in the wild forest, half in the secure cave—he took to brooding quite morbidly. He thought over-much of ghost cats in the mirror world and of the Skeleton Cat who starved to death in a locked closet and similar grisly legends. He immersed himself in racial memories, not so much of Ancient Egypt where cats were prized as minions of the lovely cat-goddess Bast and ceremoniously mummified at the end of tranquil lives, but of the Middle Ages, when European mankind waged a genocidal war against felines as being the familiars of witches. (He thought briefly of turning Kitty-Come-Here into a witch, but his hypnotic staring and tentative ritualistic mewing only made her fidgety.) And he devoted more and more time to devising dark versions of the theory of transmigration, picturing cats as Silent, Souls, Gagged People of Great Talent, and the like.

He had become too self-conscious to re-enter often the make-believe world of the kitten, yet his imagination remained as active as ever. It was a truly frustrating predicament.

More and more often and for longer periods he retired to meditate in a corrugated cardboard shoebox, open only at one end. The cramped quarters made it easier for him to think. Old Horsemeat called it the Cat Orgone Box after the famed Orgone Energy Accumulators of the late wildcat psychoanalyst Dr. Wilhelm Reich.

If only, Gummitch thought, he could devise some way of objectifying the intimations of beauty that flitted through his darkly clouded mind! Now, on the evening of the sunny day when he had backed away from his water bowl, he attacked the problem anew. He knew he had been fleetingly on the verge of a great idea, an idea involving water, light and movement. An idea he had unfortunately forgotten. He closed his eyes and twitched his nose. I must concentrate, he thought to himself, concentrate…

NEXT day Kitty-Come-Here remembered her idea about Gummitch's water. She boiled two cupfuls in a spotless enamelware saucepan, letting it cool for half an hour before using it to replace the seemingly offensive water in the young cat's bowl. It was only then she noticed that the bowl had been upset.

She casually assumed that big-footed Old Horsemeat must have been responsible for the accident, or possibly one of the two children—darting Sissy or blundering Baby. She wiped the bowl and filled it with the water she had dechlorinated.

"Come here, Kitty, come here," she called to Gummitch, who had been watching her actions attentively from the dining room door. The young cat stayed where he was. "Oh, well, if you want to be coy," she said, shrugging her shoulders.

There was a mystery about the spilled water. It had apparently disappeared entirely, though the day seemed hardly dry enough for total evaporation. Then she saw it standing in a puddle by the wall fully ten feet away from the bowl. She made a quick deduction and frowned a bit worriedly.

"I never realized the kitchen floor sloped *that* much," she told Old Horsemeat after dinner. "Maybe some beams need to be jacked up in the basement. I'd hate to think of collapsing into it while I cooked dinner."

"I'm sure this house finished all its settling thirty years ago," her husband assured her hurriedly. "That slope's always been there."

"Well, if you say so," Kitty-Come-Here allowed doubtfully.

Next day she found Gummitch's bowl upset again and the remains of the boiled water in a puddle across the room. As she mopped it up, she began to do some thinking without benefit of Concentration Box.

THAT evening, after Old Horsemeat and Sissy had vehemently denied kicking into the water bowl or stepping on its edge, she voiced her conclusions. "I think *Gummitch* upsets it," she said. "He's rejecting it. It still doesn't taste right to him and he wants to show us."

"Maybe he only likes it after it's run across the floor and got seasoned with household dust and the corpses of germs," suggested Old Horsemeat, who believed most cats were bohemian types.

"I'll have you know I *scrub* that linoleum," Kitty-Come-Here asserted.

"Well, with detergent and scouring powder, then," Old Horsemeat amended resourcefully.

Kitty-Come-Here made a scornful noise. "I still want to know where he gets his liquids," she said. "He's been off milk for weeks, you know, and he only drinks a little broth when I give him that. Yet he doesn't seem dehydrated. It's a real mystery and—"

"Maybe he's built a still in the attic," Old Horsemeat interjected.

"—and I'm going to find the answers," Kitty-Come-Here concluded, ignoring the facetious interruption. "I'm going to find out where he gets the water he does drink and why he rejects the water I give him. This time I'm going to boil it and put in a pinch of salt. Just a pinch."

"You make animals sound more delicate about food and drink than humans," Old Horsemeat observed.

"They probably are," his wife countered. "For one thing they don't smoke, or drink Martinis. It's my firm belief that animals—cats, anyway—like good food just as much as we do. And the same sort of good food. They don't enjoy canned catfood any more than we would, though they can eat it. Just as we could if we had to. I really don't think Gummitch would have such a passion for raw horsemeat except you started him on it so early."

"He probably thinks of it as steak tartare," Old Horsemeat

said.

Next day Kitty-Come-Here found her salted offering upset just as the two previous bowls had been.

SUCH were the beginnings of the Great Spilled Water Mystery that preoccupied the human members of the Gummitch household for weeks. Not every day, but frequently, and sometimes two and three times a day, Gummitch's little bowl was upset. No one ever saw the young cat do it. But it was generally accepted that he was responsible, though for a time Old Horsemeat had theories that he did not voice involving Sissy and Baby.

Kitty-Come-Here bought Gummitch a firm-footed rubber bowl for his water, though she hesitated over the purchase for some time, certain he would be able to taste the rubber. This bowl was found upset just like his regular china one and like the tin one she briefly revived from his kitten days.

All sorts of clues and possibly related circumstances were seized upon and dissected. For instance, after about a month of the mysterious spillings, Kitty-Come-Here announced, "I've been thinking back and as far as I can remember it never happens except on sunny days."

"Oh, Good Lord!" Old Horsemeat reacted.

Meanwhile Kitty-Come-Here continued to try to concoct a kind of water that would be palatable to Gummitch. As she continued without success, her formulas became more fantastic. She quit boiling it for the most part but added a pinch of sugar, a spoonful of beer, a few flakes of oregano, a green leaf, a violet, a drop of vanilla extract, a drop of iodine…

"No wonder he rejects the stuff," Old Horsemeat was tempted to say, but didn't.

Finally Kitty-Come-Here, inspired by the sight of a greenly glittering rack of it at the supermarket, purchased a half gallon of bottled water from a famous spring. She wondered why she hadn't thought of this step earlier—it certainly ought to take care of her haunting convictions about the unpalatableness of chlorine or fluorides. (She herself could distinctly taste the fluorides in the tap water, though she never mentioned this to Old Horsemeat.)

One other development during the Great Spilled Water Mystery was that Gummitch gradually emerged from depression and became quite gay. He took to dancing cat schottisches and gigues impromptu in the living room of an evening and so forgot his dignity as to battle joyously with the vacuum-cleaner dragon when Old Horsemeat used one of the smaller attachments to curry him; the young cat clutched the hairy, round brush to his stomach and madly clawed it as it *whuffled* menacingly. Even the afternoon he came home with a shoulder gashed by the Mad Eunuch he seemed strangely light-hearted and debonair.

THE Mystery was abruptly solved one sunny Sunday afternoon. Going into the bathroom in her stocking feet, Kitty-Come-Here saw Gummitch apparently trying to drown himself in the toilet. His hindquarters were on the seat but the rest of his body went down into the bowl. Coming closer, she saw that his forelegs were braced against the opposite side of the bowl, just above the water surface, while his head thrust down sharply between his shoulders. She could distinctly hear rhythmic lapping.

To tell the truth, Kitty-Come-Here was rather shocked. She had certain rather fixed ideas about the delicacy of cats. It speaks well for her progressive grounding that she did not shout at Gummitch but softly summoned her husband.

By the time Old Horsemeat arrived the young cat had refreshed himself and was coming out of his "well" with a sudden backward undulation. He passed them in the doorway with a single mew and upward look and then made off for the kitchen.

The blue and white room was bright with sunlight. Outside the sky was blue and the leaves were rustling in a stiff breeze. Gummitch looked back once, as if to make sure his human congeners had followed, mewed again, and then advanced briskly toward his little bowl with the air of one who proposes to reveal all mysteries at once.

Kitty-Come-Here had almost outdone herself. She had for the first time poured him the bottled water, and she had floated a few rose petals on the surface.

Gummitch regarded them carefully, sniffed at them, and then proceeded to fish them out one by one and shake them off his paw, Old Horsemeat repressed the urge to say, "I told you so."

When the water surface was completely free and winking in the sunlight, Gummitch curved one paw under the side of the bowl and jerked.

Half the water spilled out, gathered itself, and then began to flow across the floor in little rushes, a silver ribbon sparkling with sunlight that divided and subdivided and reunited as it followed the slope. Gummitch crouched to one side, watching it intensely, following its progress inch by inch and foot by foot, almost pouncing on the little temporary pools that formed, but not quite touching them, twice he mewed faintly in excitement.

"HE'S *playing* with it," Old Horsemeat said incredulously.

"No," Kitty-Come-Here countered wide-eyed, "he's *creating* something, Silver mice, Water snakes, Twinkling vines."

"Good Lord, you're right," Old Horsemeat agreed. "It's a new art form. Would you call it water painting? Or water sculpture? Somehow I think that's best. As if a sculptor made mobiles out of molten tin."

"It's gone so quickly, though," Kitty-Come-Here objected, a little sadly. "Art ought to last. Look, it's almost all flowed over to the wall now."

"Some of the best art forms are completely fugitive," Old Horsemeat argued. "What about improvisation in music and dancing? What about jam sessions and shadow figures on the wall? Gummitch can always do it again—in fact, he must have been doing it again and again this last month. It's never exactly the same, like waves or fires. But it's beautiful."

"I suppose so," Kitty-Come-Here said. Then coming to herself, she continued, "But I don't think it can be healthy for him to go on drinking water out of the toilet. Really."

Old Horsemeat shrugged. He had an insight about the artistic temperament and the need to dig for inspiration into the smelly fundamentals of life, but it was difficult to express delicately.

Kitty-Come-Here sighed, as if bidding farewell to all her efforts with rose petals and crystalline bottled purity and vanilla extract and the soda water which had amazed Gummitch by faintly spitting and purring at him.

"Oh, well," she said. "I can scrub it out more often, I suppose."

Meanwhile, Gummitch had gone back to his bowl and, using both paws, overset it completely. Now, nose a-twitch, he once more pursued the silver streams alive with suns, refreshing his spirit with the sight of them. He was fretted by no problems about what he was doing. He had solved them all with one of his characteristically sharp distinctions: there was the *sacred* water, the sparklingly clear water to create with, and there was the water with character, the water to *drink*.

Martians Keep Out!

Hatred of the Martians was being deliberately exploited, and Scatterday knew why. And the only way to fight the enslavement of humans was to assist the Martians, even though it meant risking lynch-law!

CHAPTER ONE

AND AS IF that sign weren't enough, someone with a red spray pencil had added: THAT MEANS YOU, BUG!

The stiff, black-shelled form, impaled on a spike beside the trafficway, with gummy beads of blue blood glistening in the sun, told the pretty little story much more graphically.

It hadn't been decapitated; Martians lack external heads.

Scat scanned the tableau, his scarred lean features impassive.

"They didn't mention this," he commented, "Do we still go in?"

"You ask questions like that just for the sake of the record, don't you?" Click-Click replied, using his black pincers to produce code in a way that explained his nickname. Though headless, Martians didn't lack brains. Definitely.

Scat switched to the turbine for jetless surface-drive, and the utility car crawled into Bronsco.

A hick town, Scat decided. A couple of 100-story skylons, a main street of glastic commercial buildings, and rows of distressingly similar homes, all of them Paradise-37's or Eden-2's. But the skylons looked dead; the glastic was dingy, and the shrubbery drooped. A few cars were untidily parked by trafficway. Footpaths worn in the grass showed that the slidewalks hadn't been strategically placed, and not all of them seemed to be working.

Crummy.

But it was in burgs like this that the destiny of the Martians was being decided. In the big metropolis, intellectuals talked "Martian Question" all night. Here, things happened.

Click-Click sat up in plain view—not to see, but to be seen. Eyeless perception gave him as good a picture as Scat's of the townless range, but a lot more three-dimensional.

His shiny black body and jointed arms brought some coldly unfavorable, lingering stares, but nothing more; broad daylight didn't lend itself to lynchings.

When they entered the offices of the *Bronsco Newsbeam,* old Donnolan acted as if he had been betrayed. His scraggly eyebrows gyrated contortedly above his pale, close-set eyes. "If I'd had any idea that I was selling the *Newsbeam* to a damn bug-lover…!" he finally howled impotently.

"Get off my property," said Scat in a low voice.

"Jonas Scatterday the Liberator!" Donnolan's eyes became crooked blue needles of bigotry. "Seems to me I recall you're a bug-smuggler, too. Mixed up in the Underground Skyway to Antarctica…"

"Get off my property," Scat repeated.

As Donnolan sidled out, he uttered those famous last words which are as old as wishful thinking—and blustering cowardice. "You can't do this to me!"

In the transmission room, Scat explained the changed situation to the *Newsbeam* employees, with Click-Click standing beside him. A grizzled old beam-doctor expressed their sentiments, "I guess we'll stick with you, Mister. I won't say we like it, but it's our jobs."

Scat nodded unenthusiastically. He knew the arrangement wouldn't last out the day, but as Click-Click had observed, there were a lot of things he did for the sake of the record.

TEN MINUTES later they had the Missionary sizzling on the beam, after a brief editorial statement of the new ownership and policy. Click-Click had fetched the master tapes from the car.

Anachronistically speaking, the Missionary was dynamite, Scat switched him in on the transmission room screen and sat down to listen, unmindful of the guardedly resentful looks he got from the staff. As he listened, his lanky frame relaxed and his stony features softened a little.

The Missionary wasn't blind, but he had the spiritual look some blind men get. He was cadaverous; his voice got under your ribs.

"Living machines! It is by virtue of that legal fiction that we have denied the Martians even the humanitarian treatment we grant to domestic animals, that we have revived an institution as vile as it is old in order to exploit them, that we have spurned all communion with their gentle minds. Living machines! The Earth's bad conscience is the best testimony to the falsity of that fiction, though even the most confirmed Martian-hater recognizes it. He says, succinctly, 'Bug.'

"But they're soulless, you claim. Inhuman. Without feelings. Well, fellow free-citizens of the World Confederation, I went to preach the Word to those living machines on their home planet. I had to fight Outer Spaceways to get permission to do it; I had to live in a cramped little pressure hut and wear a spacesuit whenever I went among them; I had to shiver under their meager sun because fuel supplies were somehow always late in getting to me. But I was happy because I was going to teach the Martians our religion.

"I soon found out, however, that it was they who ought to be teaching me!"

A scene of Martian religious ceremonies followed, one of the few shots that humans had been able to obtain. The speaker's voice continued.

"Lacking their perception and telepathy, it wasn't easy to get in contact with their minds, but we discovered ways. I found out how they live, what they believe in.

"I was going to teach them our Golden Rule. They taught me theirs—the Golden Rule of a telepathic race. *'Do unto others as others would have you do unto them.'"*

Not many people watching in at this hour, but the Missionary's words were being faithfully recorded in every home owning a *Bronsco Newsbeam* set. And during supper, when people switched on the news, there'd be a lot of Martian-owning or Martian-supported fathers and husbands who'd get indigestion and have to be restrained from busting up the set. They'd flash a protest to the *Newsbeam;* they'd record an indignant tape to the government.

More to the point, they'd squawk to Kemmerdygn. Which reminded Scat that he had business. "While I'm gone, you take orders from him," he told the staff, indicating Click-Click, "Any question you got, he'll write you an answer."

HE WALKED out without waiting for the reaction. A small boy was soaping *Bugs* on the glastic. *It begins,* thought Scat. He tossed an old news-spool at the boy and hopped in the car.

He passed up the skylon housing the front offices of *Kemmerdygn Mining Interests* and headed straight for Ten Mile. If they were going to give him the runaround, it might as well be on the spot.

Outside city limits, the trafficway skirted Bugtown. He parked to get pix. Some shots of those miserable burrows and those apathetic black forms—so spiritless in comparison with a healthy, psychically sound, enlightened Martian like Click-Click would fit nicely into an article he was doing for the *Free Martian Monthly.* And maybe something for the

Newsbeam Sunday Supplement—if the new ownership lasted that long.

Why, there were only two refrigerators for the whole community, and the measly vacuum shack was inadequate even for mating purposes. But owners didn't worry about the interminable process of Martian gestation and maturation—not while Outer Spaceways was running the theoretically illegal Bug Trade wide open.

With an almost savage flirt of his fingers, he switched on the smell-getter. Might as well give the owners of sets with olfactory reception a whiff of sick Martian while he was at it.

A rangy, loose-jawed man slouched out of the bushes on the other side of the trafficway. A tarnished squirt gun was stuck conspicuously in the belt of his smock. "What might you be doing, Mister?" he drawled.

"Admiring the scenery," Scat replied harshly. "Bronsco should be proud!"

And he gave him his jets.

CHAPTER TWO

AT TEN MILE, his tape of introduction from World Mine Owners got Scat admitted to a manager's office pronto.

He explained, "I've been commissioned to do an article on how you keep the bugs happy in the world's deepest mine." He didn't say for what publication.

"Of course, we have our standard news releases…er, Mr. Martin," the manager began tentatively. He was frowning at Scat, trying to place him.

"They're a bit stodgy, I'm afraid," Scat replied. "We wanted something with more life to it—shots of the bugs working the radioactives in the ten-mile drifts, and so on. Pictures of the bugs playing games and going through their primitive ceremonials when Mars is in the sky. All specially posed and rehearsed, of course."

"I see. Yes, there's something to what you say, all right." The manager nodded wisely, pursing his little lips, "It could be made a lot more convincing that way. Of course, we'd have to get an okay from Mr. Kemmerdygn's secretarial offices, Mr.... er..."

The faraway look that came into his eyes told Scat that the whisper-transmitter behind his ear had gone into action. The manager's expression didn't change very much, but his plump little hand crept down out of sight and pressed something. Donnolan must have squawked loud and fast—and to the right people, Scat decided regretfully.

A couple of barrel-chested men with "bug-boss" written all over them ambled in. The manager came around the table and grabbed at Scat's right arm. Scat evaded the movement, caught his hand, and squeezed; the manager squealed. The bug-bosses moved forward, but Scat released him.

"Yes, the name's Scatterday," he said. "And duraplast's considerably harder than flesh."

Everybody knew that Jonas Scatterday had lost his right arm from squirt gun corrosive while standing off a raid on an eastern bugtown.

The manager nursed his hand. His puffy little while face was venomous. He said, "We could have you in court for using a bogus tape of introduction to try to sneak in and agitate among our bugs. But since you've so conveniently put yourself in our hands, I don't believe it will be necessary to call in the law."

Scat laughed. "Better check first with Kemmerdygn's secretarial offices. With the situation as it is, and all those government contracts that you're having to hump yourselves to fulfill, I don't think they'd want anything to happen that would raise a stink. If Jonas Scatterday should disappear at Ten Mile, I'm afraid the government—regretfully of course—

would have to take a hand."

As he walked out, the manager acted as if he were about to give the bug-bosses an order. But he didn't.

SCAT PARKED the utility car in front of the *Newsbeam*. A rock clunked against the duraplast of the tail; he didn't turn around. There were more signs soaped on the glastic, but a chunky little man with a great shock of red hair was erasing them. Scat called "Hi, Len," and walked in.

Donnolan was waiting for him with a couple of seedy-looking policemen. He jumped up and waved a spool under Scat's nose. "Put that on your pocket projector!" he chortled triumphantly, "It's an injunction restraining you from publishing the *Newsbeam*, because fraud was employed in its purchase."

Scat pushed past him, remarking casually, "The regional court has attested the legality of the sale and has set aside any and all injunctions against the present ownership of the *Newsbeam* based on those grounds. The whole world doesn't take orders from Kemmerdygn—quite!"

The light of triumph in Donnolan's watery blue eyes flickered. "The regional court can't set aside an injunction that hasn't even been issued yet," he protested; "it's not legal!"

Scat opened a drawer and tossed him a spool. "A stat of the regional court's decision," he explained. "For you to keep. Read it and amplify your knowledge of law."

As he walked into the transmission room, he added, "There's a projector on the desk."

"Well, how did you and the staff get along together?" he asked Click-Click. Audible speech wasn't strictly necessary. Martians being telepathic, but it was generally easier to say a question than to think it.

"Just fine," Click-Click coded back at him. "Some men

are as bad as unenlightened Martians; they'd take orders from anything. But after a while the staff had callers and walked out in a body. Seems they'd all been offered jobs with Kemmerdygn—and the promise that he'd eventually make them his pensioners.

"They walked out while the beam was hot," Click-Click ticked on, "but that didn't make any difference, because by that time Len and the boys had arrived with the truck and they took over."

"The next injunction," remarked Scat, a little dreamily, "will be on the grounds that we're employing Martians in semi-restricted jobs. But it's the one after that I'm worrying about."

Len came in smiling. "All clean for the night," he announced. "Except for one sign, which said, *Bugs inside.* I just changed it to *Martians* and left it."

After getting out the late news flashes, Click-Click and his three compatriots retired to the refrigerated vacuum tank which had been the truck's chief freight. Scat and Len were in the office having a last smoke before their cat-nap. The lights outside made oddly distorted patterns on the glastic, and the soaped sign Len had left was silhouetted blackly.

MARTIANS INSIDE

"Calling you. Calling you," came the sweetish feminine sing-song from the talk-see on the desk. The button blinked red but the screen didn't come on. Len pushed the lever, but the screen stayed black. Scat smiled thinly.

"Jonas Scatterday and Len Cutt," came a slow, deep whisper from the black screen. "This is the voice of the Mystic X. Bronsco will not tolerate bug-lovers. We are, however, giving you one chance; get out now and take your bugs with you, and you won't be harmed."

Len joggled the lever futilely.

"Blacked out their end," he surmised. "Halloween stunts. I got a mind to put *The Ghoul Laughs* in the projector and play it back at them."

But he didn't look quite as amused as he sounded.

The button went black, and Len stood there, remembering things. "It was Mystic X who blew up the Martian Clinic the *Free Martian* started in Scarnston."

"Right," said Scat, "Let's get some sleep."

TOWARD morning he awoke with a start. He groped out and found the switch, but the lights didn't come on; the darkness was absolute. While he slept, the glastic had somehow been rendered opaque.

As he lay there, he heard the unmistakable click of pinchers from the transmission room and the faint moan of the beam. He realized then what must have happened. Lighting power was local—in conformity with some Bronsco ordinance. So they'd been able to cut it off. But beam power was regional—and they weren't tampering with that yet, Click-Click had taken in the situation and had decided not to wake him or Len while he and his pals got out the morning edition. Human beings couldn't operate very effectively until the lighting system had been jury-rigged on beam power.

The busy clicking continued, Scat smiled. Martian perception was independent of light; Click-Click must be getting a kick out of this.

Still, he'd better get up. He'd dreamed some improvements in the editorial. Probably gone out already, but they could always back-tape and dub in the changes.

In the morning he and Len strolled out in front. Every square inch of glastic was covered with black paint, still sticky and glistening from the spray guns.

"Kinda like the new color," remarked Len, loudly for the

benefit of some passers-by. "Black for Free Martian!"

Scat sent him out to try and buy some food and rent sleeping quarters in the Bronsco Recreational Center, which occupied the Number Two skylon. Just for the sake of the record, Len would discover that the hostelry was full up and that, by some strange mischance, there didn't happen to be any food in Bronsco today.

A chalked sign—*Kill the Bugs*—came coasting by on the slidewalk. Scat put down his foot in front of it and let the slidewalk do the erasing.

Back in the transmission room he discovered that Click-Click's three companions had increased to five during the night.

"Passengers for the Underground Skyway?" asked Scat. And this time he just thought the question.

Click-Click coded an affirmative, "From Ten Mile. They guessed we must be in the neighborhood from the Martian Tape we're running in the *Newsbeam*. All the Martians out at Ten Mile are picking up the Tape-beam-perception or the good old telepathic grapevine. They're crazy about it; it's the first entertainment they've had in months."

The Martian Tape was one of the trickiest things that Scat handled. Any hint of agitation or even of attempted enlightenment among owned Martians was strictly forbidden—that was one point where the government would crack down fast. Hence the Martian Tape, adapted to beam-perception, had to be, and was, purely recreational—devoted to vastly complex brain-teasers in solid geometry and other mental sports dear to Martians.

Click-Click continued, "These two somehow managed to slip past the bug guard; they're begging me to send them to the Reservation."

CHAPTER THREE

THE Martian Reservation had been established in Antarctica by an administration noted for its uneasy and fluctuating liberalism—much like the present one. The Reservation had been a bone of contention ever since. On it, Martians were to all intents free from human supervision. Although conditions were none too good, and food supply was always a critical problem, it served as a beacon of hope to enslaved Martian. It was largely because of the existence of the Reservation that border patrols, ground and sky, local and regional, had been made almost fantastically heavy.

"You've told them the dangers?" asked Scat.

"They still want to go."

"Okay then; get the cans ready. And for cripes sake keep them in the icebox until!"

There were a half dozen pallid, flat-chested youths waiting in the outer office. They acted nervous, and whenever the slidewalk in front creaked with the weight of a passerby, they'd all look around quickly and then remember that you couldn't see through the glastic any more. When no footsteps came, they'd relax a little.

One of them hurried up. "Mr. Scatterday?"

"That's right."

Instantly the youth adopted a conspiratorial air. His companions crowded behind him, craning their necks but keeping an eye cocked on the door. "We're the Executive Council of the Young Freeworkers," he whispered hoarsely, "It's an undercover movement in the Bronsco Young Peoples' Organization. We want to thank you for your editorial *End-Product of Patronage—Feudalism!* It was just like listening to our own constitution—only better expressed."

"Thanks."

"Gee, Mr. Scatterday, *we* don't like being pensioners of Kemmerdygn," the youth continued, a little more human now that he had discharged his mission. "We don't want to spend our lives playing games and getting an endless third-rate education and being Kemmerdygn's cheering section. We're only pensioners because our fathers were. But what can we do? All the restricted jobs have a waiting list a light-year long, and we're too poor to buy the specialized education that's required for most of them. Kemmerdygn keeps cutting down the pension-allotments—just like you said."

"Sure," Scat agreed matter-of-factly. "He employs Martians and pays Earthmen. A very profitable arrangement, considering the greater efficiency of Martian labor and the reduction in operating expenses. If Kemmerdygn switched to human labor, he'd have to ventilate his mines, increase the size of the drifts, provide special protective garments and all sorts of safety devices. Even at that, it's doubtful if human beings could do the work. The situation's practically the same with regard to all other non-restricted jobs."

"That's right!" Another youth cut in—a dark-browed, surly kid. "Nobody can expect us to compete with bugs! We want work—any sort, so we can feel we got a stake in the world. But everywhere we look, it's bugs, bugs, *Bugs!*"

"And who's to blame?" asked Scat softly. "You and me. Our fathers; our grandfathers. You know your history. Importation of Martians was permitted only on condition that for every 'living machine' employed on Earth, the owner would retire an Earthman on perpetual pension. That was the juicy, mouth-watering bait dangled in front of workers' eyes so they'd vote in an administration that would pass the Martian Importation Act. But what does it add up to now? You're living on charity; the Martians are enslaved. Under those circumstances it takes a little courage for either of you to stick up for your rights."

"We gotta get rid of the bugs!" asserted the surly kid. "That's what we gotta do. Run 'em off Earth!"

"Been listening to the Mystic X, Sonny?" Scat inquired. "Or is that just the line Kemmerdygn hands you?"

"Kemmerdygn's not so bad," the kid retorted hotly. "He wants to get rid of the bugs, but he can't on account of competition. After all, he's got us to support. As Kemmerdygn says, the fight now is to keep the bugs from grabbing off all the restricted jobs too. You know, give a bug a micron and he'll take a meter!"

CLICK-CLICK came in and walked over to Scat's desk. All the youths were obviously surprised when he didn't go down on all fours and take the most circuitous route possible. As he strolled blithely past, they automatically drew back to avoid any suspicion of contact. After that, their reactions diverged. The surly kid scowled and held his nose, but the spokesman looked ashamed; a flaming blush crept over his pale face. He chewed his lip, nerving himself.

"Mr. Scatter day," he began suddenly, "I don't know about the others." He looked around doubtfully, almost fearfully at his companions. "But I personally haven't got anything against the…er…" He glanced self-consciously at Click-Click. "…Martians."

From where he was rummaging in the desk, Click-Click coded briskly to Scat, "Coming up in the world, us bugs."

"I don't believe all that Kemmerdygn tells us," the spokesman continued, nervously, but with less hesitation. "I think he's just trying to put pressure on us so we'll enlist in the Martian Patrol or his own private…" He looked apologetically at Click-Click. "…bug guard. Personally, I'd like to see the Martians get a square deal." At this point the surly kid gave a snort of disgust and walked out of the office along with one of the others. "I really would. But Kemmerdygn says that if he had to put in all the improvements the Liberators are agitating for, it would mean cutting down the pension-allotments to almost nothing, so whole families would actually starve." His next words were almost a plea. "Gee, you don't really believe that would happen, do you Mr. Scatterday?"

Scat smiled at him, a little sadly. "Look, boys," he said. "I only know one thing about your problems. This is it. You're going to be pensioners—maybe well fed, maybe starving—but pensioners until every Martian is free."

The youth gulped; when he answered, it was in a very small voice and with a kind of sigh. "I guess that's what I believe, too," he said.

His three companions nodded.

"There was a Martian lynched here a couple of days ago," Scat continued gently. "Where were you?"

He hung his head. "Gee, Mr. Scatterday, there's so few of us..."

"Yes," said Scat. "So few of us."

Their eyes met.

The slidewalk creaked and this time there were footsteps. Click-Click walked out with the tray of tapes he had been assembling. "By his looks, a bishop at least," he coded cryptically.

The door opened and there swept in a red-faced figure, colorfully august in the brown and gold robes of the Reformed and Reconciled Churches of the World. His stern, bloodshot eyes instantly fixed themselves on the remains of the Executive Council of the Young Freeworkers. They hastily excused themselves. They didn't exactly slink out, but they obviously had a hard time fighting the impulse.

The churchman wheeled on Scat.

"I am the Reverend Arthur Allerdyce Bassett, spiritual monitor of Bronsco," he announced in a booming voice. "I have come to voice religion's protest against a publication which seeks to pander to the vilest impulses in man and bug, to reduce a creature made in the Lord's image to equality with his machines, to besmirch human dignity and sully the purity of Earth's womanhood by advocacy of open commerce with the foulest and most pruriently prying minds in all creation!"

He paused for breath.

Scat figuratively rubbed his hands. This was something he could get his teeth into. He could hardly wait to bring up the Missionary.

Fifteen minutes later the Reverend Bassett stalked out spluttering threats; he'd done everything but mention the Mystic X by name.

SCAT'S SATISFIED grin evaporated fast. He paced restlessly. Twice he pounded his palm and his lips formed the syllables, "Kemmerdygn." He recorded at an editorial, had to keep back-taping, gave it up. Finally he sat down at his desk and flashed Ten Mile.

"I want to talk—see Mr. Kemmerdygn."

"I'll connect you with his secretarial offices."

"I'm sorry, but Mr. Kemmerdygn is in conference."

"He'll be interested," Scat told the pretty, efficient-looking girl. "Tell him I want to beam a story about how he's begun to install at Ten Mile the most up-to-date and humane Martian-protective devices of any mine in the world."

A brief wait.

"Mr. Kemmerdygn has no comment. Good day."

Click-Click came in. He extended his pinchers for Scat's inspection. "My new manicure," he explained. "I've been forging the pincher-ridge patterns of one of those Martians we're keeping for the Underground. That's the only identification that means anything to a human. Get the idea?"

Scat frowned. "Too risky. You might get into Ten Mile, but I don't think you'd get out; we need you here."

"They need me more. Out there in their holes, while I can hop into a vacuum tank every night..." Suddenly Click-Click's pinchers stiffened. "Len's outside," he coded tersely. "I think he wants you; looks like they've brought a finder."

"Finder!" Scat shot up. "Got the cans ready?"

"Yes. Shall we put them in?"

"Not yet. But be ready."

He hurried out. There was a utility car with the Kemmerdygn insignia parked in front. Two scowling bug guards were arguing with Len. Their hands were suggestively near their squirt guns. One of them had a dirty-smocked girl by the wrist. She had a silly, open mouthed grin that just seemed to stay there; she drooled.

"We were telling him you got Ten Mile bugs inside," the bug guard explained to Scat.

Scat looked at him steadily. "We employ Martians to run the beam. They've confused your finder."

The guard pulled the girl to him. "Look Piggie," he said, "these people got bugs of their own. Maybe it's those you been feeling?" She shook her head stubbornly, like a little child. "It's our Ten Mile bugs you feel then? You're sure?" Her head bobbed up and down.

Bug finders were human beings with an inborn sensitivity to Martian telepathy, usually mentally defective. They could not interpret the telepathy, but they had an uncanny knack for distinguishing the characteristic thought-waves of an individual Martian.

The guard looked up at Scat.

"We're coming in, Mister; Piggie never misses." He put his hand on his squirt gun.

CHAPTER FOUR

SCAT FELT very conscious of his artificial arm. There was a tremor in the stump he couldn't control. From the door behind him he heard the code for "Catch!" He half turned and picked a blaster out of the air with his good hand.

"Not on my property," he told the guard.

The guard hesitated. "Okay. Make us do it the hard way," he said. They got in the car and drove off, Piggie making inarticulate sounds of protest and having to be dragged.

Scat's, eyes followed them. "Get out the truck," he told Len. "You're going to Manford to buy groceries. Click-Click, can your visitors. Fast."

"Underground?" Len asked with a look. Scat nodded.

About the time Len was ready to roll, the bug guards came jetting back, accompanied by a policeman who looked and acted exactly like them, except for the uniform.

"Got a warrant to search your place for fugitive bugs," he told Scat. "Hold on there!" he called to Len, who was starting the truck.

"Let's have a look before you get away."

The bug guard led Piggie to the truck. She was making anxious, eager noises. Unexpectedly Click-Click came out from behind the truck, so that they almost collided. Piggie squealed and backed off, flapping her arms. The guard grabbed at his squirt gun, but Scat interposed.

"Your bug done that on purpose," the guard blustered threateningly. "He knows Piggie's no good for as much as ten minutes after she gets that close to a bug."

They searched the truck very thoroughly. The body was nearly empty except for a number of boxes of tape scrap and three medium sized canisters that were conspicuously labeled in red:

CAUTION!
BEAM REFUSE GAS
Standard Container

Len's hand hovered over one of the cocks. "Want a sniff?" he asked pleasantly.

The guard gave him a sour look.

Beam refuse gas was so deadly a poison that it could not safely be disposed of by any ordinary methods. It had to be shipped to a reconditioning plant in containers that were seamless—supposedly.

And these three canisters actually contained beam refuse gas under standard pressure—they'd have to, in order to pass the minute inspection made at the regional border.

But the shell of a Martian is one of the most impermeable armors ever developed by organic evolution, and when quiescent he can go upwards for an hour without breathing. This is because he is built for an extremely rarified atmosphere—his physiology is typical of a depleted planet economy. On Mars his inhalation/exhalation ratio is about 100/1. The chief problem in acclimatizing him to Earth is teaching him to inhale as infrequently as he exhales—otherwise oxygen-drowning occurs. A Martian's lungs are really oxygen accumulators. He has 100 per cent utilization of inhaled oxygen, and he exhales pure carbon dioxide freighted with other respiratory excretions—hence the "bad breath" so obnoxious to human beings.

WITH A JAUNTY wave of his hand, Len crawled off and the search moved inside the building. Scat stayed with them to make sure nothing was overlooked. But Piggie, recovered, maintained with sullen headshakes that she no longer felt the presence of Ten Mile bugs, and after that the guards lost interest. Scat could tell that they were puzzling as to how he'd smuggled out the bugs while they were getting the warrant—for undoubtedly there'd been Kemmerdygn spies watching the *Newsbeam* building to prevent just such a move.

Afterwards Scat said to Click-Click, "I was a little worried when they took your pincher-prints."

"Anticipated," the Martian coded laconically, "I removed the forgeries, but since I have the casts they can easily be replaced. At first I thought of letting the guards pick me up here, but that would be too suspicious."

"It's going to be suspicious wherever it happens," said Scat, shaking his head, "In any case, you won't be able to pass bug-finder identification. Don't do it, Click-Click."

"You told Len to drop in at the *Free Martian* offices and fetch a Martian to replace me?"

"You're bound and determined then?"

"Yes."

Scat sighed. "Okay, Click-Click. Yes, I told Len."

Scat felt a black pincher lightly touch his shoulder. "Don't mope, Scat. I get a great kick out of going contrary to your orders; after all, it's my badge of enlightenment. Most Martians are too obliging—it's our great racial sin. Works all right when everybody's telepathic thought-pressure keeps the potential transgressor against social welfare in line. But when a telepathic race comes up against a non-telepathic one—ouch! Then the thought-pressure is all going one way. Our Golden Rule worked on Mars, but it sure got us into trouble here."

That evening, while Scat was having his last smoke, he wished that Len were there to chin with. He kept wondering, profitlessly, how long the regional court would hold out against the pressure Kemmerdygn was undoubtedly bringing to bear. Vacillating governments were the curse of eras like this—rather, the inevitable accompaniment. He wondered if there would be a civil war and to what degree he would be responsible for it. Tonight it was hard to dodge that question.

The talk-see button flashed, as he'd been expecting it to. This time the screen didn't stay completely dark. A wavering "X" glowed there. Black paper painted with phosphorescence and clapped over the screen at their end, he judged.

"Jonas Scatterday, you have disregarded our advice," came the whisper. "That is unwise. Your time-allotment is almost up. This is the last warning."

Scat wondered if he ought to have the call traced. Fat chance, with all the talk-see operators locals. Still, for the sake of the record...but he felt tired.

SOMETIME THAT night Click-Click departed, but Len got back with the replacement in time for the morning edition. Afterwards he showed Scat a big ugly splotch on the tail of the truck where squirt gun corrosive was eating in.

"Tried to stop me on the way back just outside Bronsco," he explained as he swabbed on the decontamination fluid. "Had a barricade up, but I gunned my jets and managed to jump it."

He went on swabbing, "You know," he said reflectively, "the only good sign I've noticed in this burg so far is that the kids aren't bothering us so much. Maybe it's because we're running *Space Pals* and *In the Days of the Airplane.* Those're a lot better than the crummy comics Donnolan was feeding them."

Scat laughed mirthlessly. "And maybe it's just because they've stepped back to give their parents a chance."

Pessimism wasn't usually Scat's forte, but he'd just reached the mental conclusion that it would be three days before the regional court would weaken and give Kemmerdygn—and the Mystic X—what amounted to carte blanche to handle the *Newsbeam* situation any way they wanted to.

Actually, his guess was a day short. But that was no satisfaction; they were miserable days, all four of them. Days of feeling that there was no use beaming the news, because no one would watch it anyway. A steady stream of cancelled subscriptions-sets coming back for refund. Complaints. Threats from various sources. Attacks on their Martians. Nuisances, like putting stench gas in the ventilators while they were beaming an edition. No word from Click-Click, though Scat drove one of the Martians past Bugtown to try to pick up something on the grapevine. Fruitless conferences with the officers of the *Free Martian* and members of the Martian Lobby—they were moving heaven and earth to keep the regional court in line, but it showed signs of wavering.

Most of all, the feeling that a wall was being built around the *Newsbeam,* shutting it off from the rest of the world. You couldn't see that wall, but everywhere in Bronsco you could touch it.

LATE AFTERNOON the fourth day, while they were getting out the evening edition, the wall was completed. Beam power went.

Len tried to flash the repair offices. The talk-see was dead.

"Looks like this is it," he told Scat.

Scat nodded. "Now look here, Len…" he began.

A half hour later he was still trying to persuade Len to take the boys in the truck and make a run for it, when the spokesman of the Young Freeworkers stumbled into the office.

"Ran the slidewalks to warn you, Mr. Scatterday," he panted. "Mystic X. They're planning to get you tonight.

Everybody's whispering. There's a lot of cars in the air, and they got big guards on all the trafficways—some of 'em are blocked off."

"What'd I tell you?" crowed Len. "We couldn't have got out anyway."

This was it all right, thought Scat. The regional court had knuckled under; the *Newsbeam* was finished. Kemmerdygn's victory was so complete that they were being saved up as a kind of tidbit for the Mystic X.

Just like the Martian Clinic in Scarnston.

Of course, they'd known it was coming. The *Free Martian* would demand that the regional government send in troops to prevent violence. Failing there, they would ship some of their own people into Bronsco. If they could.

"Thanks for telling us, kid," said Scat. "You better beat it now. No objections! Push him out, Len."

SLOWLY THE night came down. It was like being in a fortress with the silence, and the pocket illuminators casting a ghostly light and every now and then one of the Martians clicking a terse report. Scat's stump bothered him.

Gradually a crowd gathered, outside the range of Martian telepathy, but inside perception.

"Mostly pensioners, but some bug guard," one of the Martians coded. "Donnolan's there, and..." He ticked off the names of a half dozen fairly prominent Bronsco figures. "Hold on; there's a new contingent moving in; they're wearing masks."

The talk-see began to work again. "Jonas Scatter day and Len Cutt, we're giving you one more chance. We want all of you outside. You two come out with your hands in the air, your bugs on all fours."

"We don't propose to die so quietly," Scat answered. "If you want us, come get us. I intend to defend my property.

We're armed—*all* of us."

Arming bugs! If they'd had any chance, that action had queered it.

The minutes dragged. From somewhere a pellet gun opened up and began to rattle interminably against the glastic. Len began to swear in a low, steady voice. The Martians moved their guns around as if admiring the internal workmanship, Scat realized that he was tapping out "Come on, Come on," in Martian code over and over again with his duraplast fingers.

"There's a new bunch joined them," a Martian informed him finally. "They seem to be arguing. I don't know about what—too far. They're moving off!"

"Kemmerdygn Interests calling Mr. Scatterday."

They all started at that musical voice—even the Martians. Scat jumped for the desk and flipped on the screen. He recognized the secretary he had conferred with.

"Mr. Kemmerdygn hopes you haven't suffered any unpleasantness," she informed him smilingly. "He took steps as soon as he heard you were in trouble. He particularly desires you to resume publication of the evening edition of the *Newsbeam*. Oh, and about that article you were planning. He would like to confer on it at some later date. Yon *will* finish beaming the evening edition, won't you? Good evening."

As she flashed off, Len began to wear again, but in a different vein.

"There's more in this than…" Scat began. "…but we got tapes to beam. Get going!"

HE DIDN'T return until after the *Newsbeam* had been put to bed. There was a black figure sitting at his desk.

"Click-Click!"

"Absolutely." The Martian waved his pinchers airily—a

startlingly human gesture, "You probably guessed what happened, but I thought maybe you'd want a personal report. The Martians at Ten Mile struck—every last one of them. Almost unprecedented, but not quite."

And with those government contracts hanging over his head, Kemmerdygn couldn't afford to lose half a day, Scat appended mentally.

"I won't say that I didn't have anything to do with it," Click-Click continued. "I kept the old grapevine humming. But most of the credit goes to the Martian Tape. The Martians were wild when it wasn't published today—especially because it carried the answers to yesterday's puzzles. Even Kemmerdygn couldn't figure out that one. They're going back to work now, but I imagine they'll be a long time forgetting this initial lesson in self-assertion."

Scat looked down at Click-Click.

He grabbed his pincher and squeezed it—hard. Click-Click squeezed back—harder. But since it was Scat's duraplast hand, it didn't matter.

THE END

If you've enjoyed this book, you will not want to miss these terrific titles...

ARMCHAIR SCI-FI & HORROR DOUBLE NOVELS, $12.95 each

D-31 **A HOAX IN TIME** by Keith Laumer
INSIDE EARTH by Poul Anderson

D-32 **TERROR STATION** by Dwight V. Swain
THE WEAPON FROM ETERNITY by Dwight V. Swain

D-33 **THE SHIP FROM INFINITY** by Edmond Hamilton
TAKEOFF by C. M. Kornbluth

D-34 **THE METAL DOOM** by David H. Keller
TWELVE TIMES ZERO by Howard Browne

D-35 **HUNTERS OUT OF SPACE** by Joseph Kelleam
INVASION FROM THE DEEP by Paul W. Fairman,

D-36 **THE BEES OF DEATH** by Robert Moore Williams
A PLAGUE OF PYTHONS by Frederick Pohl

D-37 **THE LORDS OF QUARMALL** by Fritz Leiber and Harry Fischer
BEACON TO ELSEWHERE by James H. Schmitz

D-38 **BEYOND PLUTO** by John S. Campbell
ARTERY OF FIRE by Thomas N. Scortia

D-39 **SPECIAL DELIVERY** by Kris Neville
NO TIME FOR TOFFEE by Charles F. Meyers

D-40 **JUNGLE IN THE SKY** by Milton Lesser
RECALLED TO LIFE by Robert Silverberg

ARMCHAIR SCIENCE FICTION CLASSICS, $12.95 each

C-10 **MARS IS MY DESTINATION**
by Frank Belknap Long

C-11 **SPACE PLAGUE**
by George O. Smith

C-12 **SO SHALL YE REAP**
by Rog Phillips

ARMCHAIR SCIENCE FICTION & HORROR GEMS SERIES, $12.95 each

G-3 **SCIENCE FICTION GEMS, Vol. Two**
James Blish and others

G-4 **HORROR GEMS, Vol. Two**
Joseph Payne Brennan and others

Made in the USA
Middletown, DE
21 January 2023